D0592116

CLARA AND
MR. TIFFANY

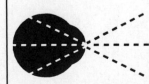

This Large Print Book carries the
Seal of Approval of N.A.V.H.

CLARA AND MR. TIFFANY

SUSAN VREELAND

THORNDIKE PRESS
A part of Gale, Cengage Learning

GALE
CENGAGE Learning

Detroit • New York • San Francisco • New Haven, Conn • Waterville, Maine • London

GALE
CENGAGE Learning™

Copyright © 2011 by Susan Vreeland.
Thorndike Press, a part of Gale, Cengage Learning.

Thorndike Press® Large Print Basic.
The text of this Large Print edition is unabridged.
Other aspects of the book may vary from the original edition.
Set in 16 pt. Plantin.

LIBRARY OF CONGRESS CATALOGING-IN-PUBLICATION DATA

Vreeland, Susan.
  Clara and Mr. Tiffany / by Susan Vreeland.
    p. cm. — (Thorndike Press large print basic)
  ISBN-13: 978-1-4104-3423-4
  ISBN-10: 1-4104-3423-0
  1. Driscoll, Clara, 1861–1944—Fiction. 2. Women glass artists—Fiction. 3. Tiffany, Louis Comfort, 1848–1933—Fiction. 4. Tiffany and Company—History—Fiction. 5. Large type books. I. Title.
  PS3572.R34C63 2011
  813'.54—dc22   2010044612

Published in 2011 by arrangement with Random House, Inc.

Printed in the United States of America
1 2 3 4 5 6 7 15 14 13 12 11

FOR
Barbara Braun
and John Baker,
who led me to
Clara and Tiffany

Beauty is what Nature has lavished upon us as a Supreme Gift.
— LOUIS COMFORT TIFFANY

CONTENTS

BOOK ONE
1892–1893

CHAPTER 1
PEACOCK

I opened the beveled-glass door under the sign announcing Tiffany Glass and Decorating Company in ornate bronze. A new sign with a new name. Fine. I felt new too.

In the ground-floor showroom of the five-story building, stained-glass windows hung from the high ceiling, and large mosaic panels leaned against the walls. Despite the urgency of my business, I couldn't resist taking a quick look at the free-form vases, bronze desk sets, pendulum clocks, and Art Nouveau candelabras. It was the oil lamps that bothered me. Their blown-glass shades sat above squat, bulbous bases too earthbound to be elegant. Mr. Tiffany was capable of more grace than that.

A new young floor manager tried to stop me at the marble stairway. I gave him a look that implied, *I was here before you were born,* and pushed his arm away as though it were a Coney Island turnstile.

On the second floor, I peered into Mr.

15

Tiffany's large office-studio. With a gardenia pinned to his lapel, he sat at his desk behind a row of potted orchids. In February, no less! Such were the extravagances of wealth. His formerly trim bottle brush of a mustache had sprouted into robust ram's horns.

His own paintings hung on the walls — *Citadel Mosque of Old Cairo,* with tall, slender minarets, and *Market Day at Tangier,* with a high tower on a distant hill. A new one depicted a lily on a tall stalk lording over a much shorter one. Amusing. Little Napoléon's self-conscious preoccupation with height was alive and well.

New tall pedestals draped with bedouin shawls flanked the fireplace. On them Oriental vases held peacock feathers. In this his design sense went awry, sacrificed to his flamboyancy. If he wanted to appear taller, the pedestals should have been shorter. Someday I would tell him.

"Excuse me."

"Why, Miss Wolcott!"

"Mrs. Driscoll. I got married, you remember."

"Oh, yes. You can't be wanting employment, then. My policy hasn't —"

I pulled back my shoulders. "As of two weeks ago, I'm a single woman again."

He was too much the gentleman to ask questions, but he couldn't hide the gleam in his eyes.

16

"I've come to inquire if you have work for me. That is, if my performance pleased you before." A deliberate prompt. I didn't want to be hired because of my need or his kindness. I wanted my talent to be the reason he wanted me back.

"Indeed" was all he offered.

What now to fill the suspended moment? His new projects. I asked. His eyebrows leapt up in symmetrical curves.

"A Byzantine chapel for the World's Columbian Exposition in Chicago next year. Four times bigger than the Paris Exposition Universelle. It will be the greatest assembly of artists since the fifteenth century." He counted on his fingers and then drummed them on the desk. "Only fifteen months away. In 1893 the name of Louis Comfort Tiffany will be on the lips of millions!" He stood up and swung open his arms wide enough to embrace the whole world.

I sensed his open palm somewhere in the air behind the small of my back, ushering me to his massive, carved mahogany exhibit table to see his sketches and watercolors. "Two round windows, *The Infancy of Christ* and Botticelli's *Madonna and Child,* will be set off by a dozen scenic side windows."

A huge undertaking. How richly fortunate. Surely there would be opportunity for me to shine.

Practically hopping from side to side, he

17

made a show of slinging down one large watercolor after another onto the Persian carpet, each one a precise, fine-edged rendering of what he wanted the window to be.

"Gracious! You've been on fire. Go slower! Give me a chance to admire each one."

He unrolled the largest watercolor. "An eight-foot mosaic behind the altar depicting a pair of peacocks surrounded by grapevines."

My breath whistled between my open lips. Above the peacocks facing each other, he had transformed the standard Christian icon of a crown of thorns into a shimmering regal headdress for God the King, the thorns replaced by large glass jewels in true Tiffany style.

Astonishing how he could get mere watercolors so deep and saturated, so like lacquer that they vibrated together as surely as chords of a great church pipe organ. Even the names of the hues bore an exotic richness. The peacocks' necks in emerald green and sapphire blue. The tail feathers in vermilion, Spanish ocher, Florida gold. The jewels in the crown mandarin yellow and peridot. The background in turquoise and cobalt. Oh, to get my hands on those gorgeous hues. To feel the coolness of the blue glass, like solid pieces of the sea. To chip the gigantic jewels for the crown so they would sparkle and send out shafts of light. To forget everything but the glass before me and make of it something resplendent.

When I could trust my voice not to show too much eagerness, I said, "I see your originality is in good health. Only you would put peacocks in a chapel."

"Don't you know?" he said in a spoof of incredulity. "They symbolized eternal life in Byzantine art. Their flesh was thought to be incorruptible."

"What a lucky find for you, that convenient tidbit of information."

He chuckled, so I was on safe ground.

He tossed down more drawings. "A marble-and-mosaic altar surrounded by mosaic columns, and a baptismal font of opaque leaded glass and mosaic."

"This dome is the lid of the basin? In opaque leaded glass?"

He looked at it with nothing short of love, and showed me its size with outstretched arms as though he were hugging the thing.

I was struck by a tantalizing idea. "Imagine it reduced in size and made of translucent glass instead. Once you figure how to secure the pieces in a dome, that could be the method and the shape of a lampshade. A wraparound window of, say" — I looked around the room — "peacock feathers."

He jerked his head up with a startled expression, the idea dawning on him as if it were his own.

"Lampshades in leaded glass," he said in

19

wonder, his blue eyes sparking.

"Just think where that could go," I whispered.

"I am. I am!" He tugged at his beard. "It's brilliant! An entirely new product. We'll be the first on the market. And not just peacock featherth. Flowerth too!"

Excitement overtook his struggle to control his lisp, which surfaced only when he spoke with passion.

"But the chapel first. This will be our secret for now."

Men harboring secrets — I seemed attracted to them unwittingly.

"Besides the window department and the mosaic department, I have six women working on the chapel windows. I've always thought that women have greater sensitivity to nuances of color than men do. You've proved that yourself, so I want more women. You'll be in charge of them."

"That will suit me just fine."

CHAPTER 2
FLAMINGO

"You have to love it enough to forgo and forget all other loves," I told her. "Including men, Wilhelmina."

Women around us cutting glass or drawing or painting in the women's studio on the fifth floor lifted their heads at this truth, sizing her up.

"If you're not willing to, go right out the door you came in, and look for other work."

"I'm willing." Her tone carried impatience as surely as mine carried brusqueness.

"All right, then." I gave her a steel cutting wheel and a four-inch scrap of glass, and showed her how to score it.

"Don't be afraid. Press firmly," I said. "You have to be in command of the glass, telling it where to release its hold on itself. Just like life. Otherwise it will splinter."

"It's none too easy the first time, Mrs. Driscoll," said Wilhelmina.

"You can call me Clara."

I had found this flaxen-haired, broad-

21

shouldered, bosomy Swede at the YWCA, where she was taking the free art classes. Despite her arms like a stevedore's and her imposing six-foot stature, she was only seventeen years old.

Wilhelmina scored the glass against a straight edge.

"Now tap it gently."

She tapped it over the edge of the table, and the released piece fell to the floor and broke. "Cripes!"

"Make sure your hand is under it to grab it. This is only practice, but once you start, broken pieces will be charged against your wage."

"Too many broke ones, and I'd be paying you. What kind of a job is that?"

Agnes Northrop cleared her ticklish throat at that and aimed a judgmental look not at Wilhelmina but at me.

The two other girls I had just hired came through the door together — maybe they would please her more — Mary McVickar, eighteen, red-haired, freckle-faced, and full of bright anticipation, and Cornelia Arnoth, a few years older, quieter, more serious, as though she were carrying a burden. Cornelia had asked if the job would be permanent, and I had replied that it would be, though I wasn't at all sure of what would happen after the fair. Both had been recommended by my

22

former teacher at the Metropolitan Museum School.

I'd already interrogated them the same way I had done with Wilhelmina, warning them that Mr. Tiffany had a policy against having married women working for him. When they pledged their commitment to work over love, I walked them around the workroom among sawhorse tables and high stools, tall wooden easels for the enlarged drawings, and clear glass easels for glass selection, introducing the new girls along the way to the six original women in the department and the three I had hired a week earlier. I showed them where the tools were kept — watercolor sets, brushes, india ink, pens, drawing pencils, grease pencils, copper pattern shears, paper shears, three-bladed shears, scoring wheels, glass nippers, files, needle-nose pliers, small hammers, and chisels.

I introduced Agnes as Miss Northrop and explained that she was expanding a small painting of birds on a branch to a full-size watercolor of the window, called a cartoon.

"Cartoon? Like the funny picture of your Uncle Samuel in the red striped trousers and high hat?" Wilhelmina asked.

"No. The term is much older than that. When Michelangelo enlarged a drawing for a fresco to the size it would eventually be, that was called a cartoon."

I told them that Agnes would decide where

to draw in lead lines to indicate the separate pieces of glass, and that Mr. Tiffany's own style was to have the lead lines follow the shapes in the design wherever possible.

"The birds are good," Wilhelmina said. "They're parakeets."

I was amused that she thought of herself as qualified to critique it. Agnes sent me another loaded look, this one insinuating *Who does she think she is?*

"Over here, Edith Mitchill is working on a finished cartoon, which has two sheets of paper under it with carbon paper in between each. She is going over all the lead lines with a pointed stylus to transfer the design to the two sheets beneath it, which will only show the outline of each individual shape, not the shadings. Mary, this outlining will be your first task."

I lifted the corner of the cartoon to reveal the carbon copies.

"It's a bloomin' jigsaw puzzle," said Mary.

I walked them over to another cartoon on an easel, which would be their first assignment. "It's called *Feeding the Flamingoes.*"

Wilhelmina snickered. "Who painted it?"

"Mr. Tiffany. It's for the World's Columbian Exposition in Chicago, so it's very important to him."

"It's silly," Wilhelmina blurted. "Flamingoes don't eat out of a person's hand."

"How do you know?" asked Mary.

"Just look at their beaks. Anyone can see that they're made to scoop up food upside down in the water. We painted birds from a book at the YWCA. Holding out her hand like that, this lady doesn't know the first thing about feeding a flamingo. You expect me to work on something that's wrong?"

Agnes pressed her lips together in a tight line like a disapproving schoolmarm. It threatened to dampen my joy in teaching the new girls, which was exactly what she intended.

I liked Wilhelmina for speaking her mind, if she didn't do it too often or too loud.

"I suppose artists call this a caprice," I said. "It's something Mr. Tiffany imagined. The fountain and the columns suggest a Roman villa."

"What's that circle?" Wilhelmina asked.

"A fishbowl. Two pieces of glass were made specially for it. The front layer is turquoise and green ripple glass, and the back layer has a swish of orange for the goldfish. We call that plating. Sometimes we use as many as four or five layers to get the depth and color we want. Just wait. It will be gorgeous."

Curiously, I felt I had to defend Mr. Tiffany despite having teased him in private about this window. "Peacocks aren't enough for you?" I had said. "You need flamingoes in the chapel too? Are you collecting a Noah's Ark? How about a pair of ostriches? Kangaroos?" It was good for him to be teased once in a while. In his domain, where his word was law, nobody else dared to.

Now I told Mary to number the individual sections, left to right.

"If a body can count that high," she said.

"This one only has several hundred pieces because they're large, but some windows have thousands of smaller ones. When she's finished, Cornelia, you will cut up the first copy into its sections using these special scissors with three blades."

I showed the girls how the lower blade fit between the two upper parallel blades to remove a one-sixteenth-inch strip, which would create space for the lead strips that hold the pieces of glass together.

"It looks hard with those big scissors," Cornelia said.

"You'll get used to them."

I told her to leave the cutting of the woman's profile, her hand, and the birds' necks to me, and to practice drawing some curves on stiff paper and cutting them, keeping the drawn lines evenly visible in the channel between the two upper blades.

"While she's doing that, Wilhelmina, since you're tall, you'll paste the other copy of the cartoon to the back side of this big sheet of clear glass in a frame, which we call an easel. You'll paint those lines on the glass using a fine-tipped brush and black paint. Then you'll remove the paper backing.

"Cornelia, you will put a dot of this wax on the back of each of the numbered sections, which we call pattern pieces, and Wilhelmina, you attach them to the clear glass in their exact positions that you painted. Then your jobs are finished and the window will be ready for the glass selector, who will choose glass in the colors and shadings and textures needed to convey the subject. The colors could be transparent, opaque, or in between. We call glass that transmits light but is not clear opalescent."

"How will we ever do the lady's face?" Worry wormed its way across Cornelia's forehead. Oh, she was so deadly serious.

"Mr. Tiffany will do that with enamel paint. The figure's hand too. It's his only concession to medieval stained-glass craftsmanship of painting on glass with powdered enamels and then firing the pieces." I explained that we avoid enameling whenever possible because it cuts out some of the light.

They were sweet girls, excited but anxious, especially Cornelia. I would have to guard against her overly intense desire to please. It would limit her originality.

"Soon these steps will be second nature to you."

I heard the Tiffany tap, his malachite-tipped cane striking the wooden floor with authority. It was a blatant affectation. He was only

27

in his early forties. The reddish brown hair in his beard struggling to hold its own against the onslaught of premature gray still had some years left. He didn't need a cane any more than I did. He just used it to create a mystique about himself. Right behind him was Mr. Henry Belknap, slick and tidy.

Mr. Tiffany set a vase of hothouse irises on a worktable and tapped his cane lightly, three times. All except Agnes Northrop looked up in unison, like birds alerted to some potential danger, poised to fly. With her customary mien of a prima donna, Agnes remained seated on her stool as though exempt, barely turning toward Mr. Tiffany. Since she was his first female glass artist, she fancied herself a favorite.

"Good afternoon, ladies. You're doing beautiful work." He turned one iris to face Agnes. "Have I ever told you how important it is to have beauty in our lives?"

"Not less than a hundred times," Agnes said, studying the painting she was enlarging.

"Why, I don't believe you, Miss Northrop." His tone of mock disbelief revealed his playful side, which I loved. Addressing the new girls, he said, "I want to welcome you to Tiffany Glass and Decorating Company and introduce you to Mr. Belknap, the artistic director who will consult with Mrs. Driscoll in my absence. She has chosen you with great care because you will be involved in a stupen-

28

dous undertaking."

Here it comes. One of his declamations. The peacock spreading his tail feathers.

"The World's Columbian Exposition in Chicago commemorates Christopher Columbus's discovery of the New World in 1492, four hundred years ago, though it won't actually open until next year. This fair will be the greatest event in the history of our country since the Civil War, and you will be my contributing partners."

Pure bluster. He didn't need this to set the girls at awe. His art itself would do that. His comparison of the fair, an event likely to be wonderful, with an event so devastating and tragic was insensitive to the gravity of the war. Sometimes his inflated style tripped him up.

"The American exhibits will show that the New World has taken its rightful place among older nations, so we want to demonstrate to the Old World what we've accomplished here in terms of the arts and culture and industry."

I clamped shut my jaw. Cornelia was Prussian, Mary was Irish, and Wilhelmina was Swedish. Others were just one generation removed from the Old World. They certainly didn't grasp the significance of our Civil War.

Wilhelmina raised her hand to her shoulder and wiggled her fingers. She towered over Mr. Tiffany by a foot.

"Excuse me, sir, but flamingoes eat with

their beaks upside down. Even girls from the Old World know that if they've ever opened a book."

Mary jabbed an elbow into her ribs. "Mind your mouth," she whispered. "It's Himself that's speakin'."

Now Agnes stood up, her stiff posture elegantly commanding despite her small stature. I felt as if the politeness of the whole studio rested with me, and judgment might be leveled against me for hiring such a brazen girl. Mr. Belknap cast an amused glance at Mr. Tiffany, waiting for his response. I held my breath, but was amused along with him. It must have been a new experience for Mr. Tiffany to have to justify himself to a seventeen-year-old immigrant, but he stood unflinching before this formidable Amazon.

"What is your name?"

"Wilhelmina A. Wilhelmson, sir."

"Granted, Miss Wilhelmson, flamingoes don't eat this way. You're smart to see that. But they are tamed this way. The woman is offering the bird a rock, not food."

"It looks like a bun."

"If the bird tries to peck at the woman's hand, he hurts his beak on the rock, so he stops."

"Then you should call it *Taming the Flamingoes*," Wilhelmina declared.

Mr. Tiffany lifted his shoulders. "Maybe I will," he said, a gentleman from sole to crown. "Take it as a fantasy of a happy land where things that please the eye do not have to make sense. Just being beautiful is enough. Art for art's sake, we say, because beauty blesses humanity with a better life."

He couldn't get the s's right in *art's sake,* which made me think Wilhelmina had upset him, but he went right on. How bravely he struggled against his lisp. I prayed that Wilhelmina wouldn't snicker.

"The window is a display of shape and color," he said, "with shadows, not in gray but in blues and greens, as they are in the revolutionary work of Mr. Édouard Manet, who was a fine painter of your Old World. We stand on the shoulders of those before us, but we also stretch.

"Train yourselves by seeking and acknowledging beauty moment by moment every day of your lives," he told them. "Exercise your eyes. Take pleasure in the grace of shape and the excitement of color."

I was glad he said this. It was what made even the simplest day a thrill. On the street or in a park or a room, I often felt I was seeing small glories that the rest of the world didn't notice.

"What if we see something ugly?" Wilhelmina asked, her voice tinged with challenge.

"Don't look at it."

She pulled back her chin and made a face.

I gave her a stern look so she wouldn't say more.

"Be courageous with color. Let it pour out of you." He touched his chest and then opened his palms toward the girls. "That's the way to bring out the drama in nature. There's a feeling these days that color is a danger. People are timid because they can't distinguish between deep, strong coloration and gaudiness, so they choose pale, anemic colors to be safe. That just makes art bland. They have to be educated, and our new windows can do that. Thousands will see them. Even hundreds of thousands. So be brave." He ended with his habitually evoked maxim, "Infinite, meticulous labor makes a masterpiece."

He was in his own world, oblivious of whom I had hired, girls taken away from their own languages. How could he expect them to know words like *gaudiness* and *anemic* and *bland?* I would have to show them examples of these words as part of their training. He made the rounds of the new girls, starting with Wilhelmina, which was a touch of grace on his part. She blushed, looking down at him. Cornelia's slight Old World curtsy brought a pinch of benevolence to Agnes's face.

Soon after the two men left, Agnes followed me into my office-studio, which was partitioned off from the department but with wide double doors so I could see the whole room. She said under her breath, " 'Infinite, meticulous labor.' As if we don't do that already. If I hear that one more time I'm going to cut his tongue out."

She shook her cutting wheel at the place where he had stood. It was my good diamond-edged wheel with the red handle that fit my hand perfectly, the only diamond wheel in the department. The others were steel. She must have appropriated it after I left, and wanted me to know it. Tool envy. I let it be. As department head, I could order another.

"I've been meaning to ask you," she said in a near whisper. "How did you get him to take you back, you being a married woman?"

Stiffness shot up my backbone. "My husband died a month ago," I answered, equally softly.

There was a general intake of breath throughout the big studio. Amazing the aural capacities of female glass workers.

"Oh! I'm sorry." Hardly finishing her obligatory condolence, she returned to her worktable, having gotten what she wanted.

Some time later, Mr. Belknap came into my studio and set a pot of cyclamen on the sill of my tall window.

"I bought this yesterday for my office, but I want you to have it. You might need some

33

encouragement."

"Why, Mr. Belknap, that's sweet of you. It's beautiful. The petals look like wings of fuchsia butterflies about to fly out the window."

He was a slim, small-boned man half a head shorter than I but I was perched on my stool so we were eye to eye. His blond hair was slicked down with Brilliantine from a center part. Following the design principle of harmony in repetition, his waxed mustache carried the same center division of hair neatly below his nose.

He leaned toward me. "You'll have your hands full with that saucy blonde."

"The bird expert. We might come to need one sometime. Don't worry. When I taught school in Ohio I learned that the most impertinent ones are often the most lovable."

At this close range, I was startled to see that he had drawn his eyebrows on with a sepia-colored grease pencil — artistically.

"If at any time I could offer you some diversion, I would be honored," he said, scraping the pad of his thumb with the nail of his index finger, a quick, nervous mannerism.

"That's very kind of you."

In the hierarchy of the firm, he was the intermediary between Mr. Tiffany and me. I might come to need him to champion my requests.

"There are two more operas this season,"

34

he said. "Verdi's *Otello* and Mozart's *Marriage of Figaro*."

"I adore opera. That is, operas from the *Old World*."

A long, loud, unladylike sigh came from the studio. We both looked out the double doors. At that moment, Wilhelmina stood up and stretched, her big arms high in the air, her fingers wiggling, her bosoms thrust forward.

"The cheeky one." Mr. Belknap tipped his head toward her. "She'll keep you on your toes."

I agreed, knowing that bumpy times lay ahead.

"Oh, Louis wants to see you in his office right away," he mentioned on his way out.

"Then why didn't you tell me right away?" Exasperated, I grabbed my notepad and pencil and flew out the door.

CHAPTER 3
OPAL

A white-haired man with a cottony beard was crouching close to the floor when I entered Mr. Tiffany's office-studio.

"What happened? Can I help?"

"Have a seat," Mr. Tiffany said, dabbing a paintbrush on his palette, his opal ring shooting out the colors of the wet paint. "I've wanted you to meet my father, Charles Tiffany, and he came today to pose. This is Mrs. Driscoll, head of the Women's Department."

"Oh, hello," I said. "Nice to meet you." An inane thing to say to a man draped in a classical red robe and wearing sandals. I ought to have exclaimed, "Hail, Caesar," or implored, "Lead us to the Promised Land."

"A pleasure." The father kept his pose, his craggy face tipped down.

On the unfinished canvas I recognized Joseph of Arimathea having just lowered Christ from the cross. Barely sketched in with charcoal, Mary Magdalene knelt at Jesus's

36

feet, and the Virgin Mother looked heavenward. The scene had the look of a Dutch Renaissance pietà, and the father's face could have been painted by Hans Holbein the Elder.

"The window is called *The Entombment.* It's for the chapel. Your department will make it."

Mr. Mitchell, the stout business manager, burst in waving a page from a newspaper. "Do you know about this? The city Lead Glaziers and Glass Cutters' Union is demanding higher wages."

"Well, satisfy them." Mr. Tiffany went right on mixing a touch of yellow ocher into white for the winding cloth draped over his father's arm.

"They also want shorter hours, only fifty a week, and a beer break at three o'clock."

Tiffany the Elder broke his pose. "Now, that's a problem. Shorter hours."

The splotch on Mr. Mitchell's cheek in the shape of Africa was redder than usual. "If the union strikes," he said, "our men will be forced to strike too, for solidarity, no matter what agreement you have with them, wages or hours."

"When might that happen?"

"Only after several rounds of discussion."

"The union has to whip up the spirit of strike," the elder Tiffany said. "That will take a while."

My mind did a flip, seeing this man looking as though he stepped straight out of the Bible talking about a labor strike.

"We can move slowly in negotiation to forestall it," Mr. Mitchell said. "It's the worst possible time. Any other year, we could sail through it with our stock on hand."

"It doesn't matter. The experiments in iridescent blown glass can go on regardless. I want them in Chicago."

"Don't be stubborn, son. Let that lie. Your iridescent glass will be in the mosaics. Devote all the furnaces to that."

"Does the article mention us?" asked Tiffany the Younger.

"Yes. And Maitland, Armstrong, Colgate, Lathrop, and Lamb."

"Ha! Then La Farge will be held back too."

I could smell competition brewing in him like molten glass.

"You can still top me if you're canny about how you handle things," Charles Tiffany said. "I expect nothing less from you."

"Not with all your diamonds and silver masterpieces."

"You have one advantage," said the father.

"Over you?"

"Over other stained-glass houses." He tipped his head toward me. "Women aren't allowed in the union, so they won't be called upon to strike."

He stepped behind an Oriental lacquered

screen to dress.

"How many girls did you hire?" Mr. Tiffany asked me.

"Six, just as you said. There are twelve now, and me."

"Double the department, as soon as you can. You'll need to take over some of the men's projects."

"If I might say so, doubling the department all at once would mean some of the experts and I would be drawn off our projects to train so many new girls. It wouldn't result in accomplishing twice as much work."

"She's right, son. Don't go off half-cocked."

"Well, then, take on teams of three as you see fit, but quickly."

"There's another issue," I said, thinking of Cornelia. "I don't want to hire them as temporaries. They would be viewed as scabs. It's not fair to hire them without a commitment that they'll have permanent work after the exposition."

"They'll have work. Once the world sees what we do here, there'll be plenty of work."

"*If* you use the fair to your marketing advantage," remarked the elder Tiffany as he came out from behind the screen, dressed properly now for the nineteenth century.

"Hire them as permanents," Tiffany the Younger said.

Was that bluster or well-founded confidence? I knew risk was inevitable in New

York, but I hadn't counted on being the person forcing others to take risks on an egotist's say-so.

"We'll talk tonight." His father delivered that last directive with an ominous air, and beckoned to Mr. Mitchell to leave with him.

"Don't get too cozy, now." Mr. Tiffany scowled as the two men left together.

He was quiet and distant as he cleaned his brushes, so I made a move to leave.

"The director of the fair sent out a memo," he said, detaining me by pointing to a letter on his desk. " 'Make no little plans,' it says. 'They have no magic to stir men's blood.' "

"I would never doubt the size of your plans."

"I have twenty embroiderers doing piecework with gold thread on altar cloths, miters, and vestments."

"Ah, nuns of the cloth, Order of Tiffany. How fortunate for you that Catholics haven't outgrown their taste for pomp. Now poor Protestants can catch envious glimpses of the trappings of sacred royalty."

He gave me a playful, shame-on-you look.

"You can't help but think extravagantly," I said more seriously.

"I'm thinking *innovatively*. This chapel will announce an entirely new direction — the ecclesiastic *landscape* window to help people worship God's creation. Narrow-minded clergymen can resist all they want. Nature is

40

God's work, so I say nature motifs are just as spiritual, just as inspirational, as biblical images. The mind of the Creator is unlimited in devising the forms of nature. Do you see what that means? There are infinitely more ways for us to express spiritual truth than just the tired old figures crammed into every medieval church across Europe."

"Therefore the peacocks."

"The goodly wings of the peacocks, the Bible says, and therefore the trees and the flowers and the streams. There are birds and mountains and hills all through the Bible. So for the first time the general public, not just my wealthy clients who buy landscape windows for their homes, will see the art of Louis Comfort Tiffany convey the beauties of nature. No temporary strike is going to stop me."

He sounded like P. T. Barnum bragging about his circus.

"But I made a mistake."

He sat at his desk and plunked down his elbows with a thud. "John La Farge slipped into that Paris Exposition three years ago with one measly window, and was decorated as Chevalier of the Legion of Honor of France, and I didn't exhibit."

He flung out his arm, and the opal glinted in envious green.

"The Paris papers hailed him as the inventor of opalescent glass. Puh! I made it before he ever did. Several window makers used it here before La Farge took it to Paris."

He looked at me with steely eyes. "This World's Columbian Exposition is going to turn the tables."

After his braggadocio was spent, he said, "From now on, it's a race against time. We barely have fourteen months. How much do you have left to do on *The Infancy of Christ?*"

"Ten thousand pieces of glass to select and cut is slow going. I've finished the central medallion. Now I'm working on the left cross panel of *Mary Presenting Christ to the Wise Men.* Miss Egbert will help me with the three other pictorial panels as soon as she finishes her window. She can train my best new girl on the decorative spaces between the pictures."

"Good." He drummed his fingers on his desk. "I saw the way you devoured the double-peacock watercolor the first day you came back. As soon as you finish the Christ window, you can start on it."

Splendor! All I could think of between the quick beats of my heart was splendor and joy.

"Thank you."

"Hire from Art Students League and the Metropolitan."

"The tuition there is costly. The Cooper Union art program is free. I'm likely to find girls who really need the money there. They might be more committed."

"Fine. Ask Miss Mitchill too. She founded the National Association of Women Painters. She'll know of someone capable of doing the enlargements. We need more than her and Miss Northrop and you for that."

"All right. One thing you ought to know. Miss Northrop hasn't seemed very pleased at my being department head."

"I need her doing exactly what she's doing. She's the best glass selector and a fine watercolorist, but she's not as sensible as you are. You'll win her over eventually."

I wasn't so sure. Once when I complimented her on her selection of glass, she acted as though she was above needing any comment from me.

"Don't be hurt, Agnes," I had said. "He needs your artistry more than mine."

She'd held a piece of glass against the light, turned it, discarded it, and picked another, all without a glance at me.

"He gave you the Christ window," she'd remarked. "I designed it."

"I didn't know. He didn't mention that."

"No, he wouldn't. At the fair, it will be assumed to be his design."

"Does that bother you?"

Raising one eyebrow to a perfect arch, she finally turned to me. "It's the way it is."

Her temperament was delicate. I had to tread lightly. The same with Mr. Tiffany. At the moment, he was intent on studying his *Entombment* painting.

"May I ask, who will pose for Mary?"

"I would like Louise to. My wife. If it's not too hard on her."

"The pose?"

"The idea. A mother grieving over her dead child." He took a slow, energy-gathering breath. "We just lost our daughter." He closed his paint box slowly. The click of the latch made a hollow, final sound. "Our little Annie. Three years old."

Grief pressed down on him like a giant paw. I offered him the condolence of my eyes, knowing that words would do nothing to lessen his suffering.

In a faraway voice he added, "My first wife, Mary, and I lost our baby boy too, after three weeks. Mary never recovered, and I lost her as well. Now this child of Lou."

A slight lisp escaped on the word *lost.* What an enormous, constant effort it must take for him to keep it under control.

"She died with a gardenia in her hand."

I knew it was he who had put it there, the last loving thing he could do for her. His eyes revealed the fear that he would never get over it.

"Your work, is it compensation enough?" I ventured.

The skin between his eyebrows wrinkled.

"Flamingoes and peacocks don't make up for a child."

CHAPTER 4
FEATHERS

I had already interviewed landladies in the East Side vicinity of the Tiffany Glass and Decorating Company, had rejected the suspicious, the severe, and the skeletal, and had gone home to soak my discouraged feet. I set out again this Saturday to circle the Tiffany building in ever-widening routes, determined to find exactly the right place.

I couldn't bear to stay at the boardinghouse in Brooklyn where Francis and I had occupied a suite of rooms. Ever since he died, the boarders spoke to me in hushed and awkward tones as they slithered past me in the corridor like nuns and monks. It was as if they had drawn a black circle around my name in their roster of friends and labeled it: *New widow. Treat with kid gloves.* They meant well, but their averted eyes told me that they held the notion that a widow must creep through life as though she no longer belonged, taking one tedious, lonely breath after another during the long wait to be reunited with her other half in the hereafter.

Was it wrong for me to want more than constrained existence? Wrong to hunger for change, new faces, a full life? Surprises to please my eyes and ears? Was it improper to seek healing in the roaring crush of Manhattan, city of brilliance and possibility?

I walked on, erect, not creeping, and discovered a little run of quiet blocks called Irving Place between Union Square and Gramercy Park, which promised to be leafy come spring. Greek Revival, Italianate, and Renaissance Revival townhouses lined the street. I saw a ROOM TO LET sign in a window and bounded up the stoop. A gaunt woman answered the buzzer, portending skimpy portions at the dinner table and plates that were whisked away before a second helping could enter the boarders' minds. The cramped, cheerless parlor had only itchy horsehair settees constraining sitters to maintain Egyptian posture at all times. Apparently she considered the ten-inch-wide ribbon of gauze an adequate runner for the passageway to the bathroom.

"Thank you, no," I said, and escaped.

Down the block at number 44 I found another sign, this one with a caricature of laughing people at a dining table with the warning SOUR-PUSSES AND CIGAR SMOKERS NEED NOT APPLY. A wide-hipped woman decorated with a fluff of dyed red-orange hair

47

piled on top of her head welcomed me. Hmm. Colorful.

"Come in and have a look, dearie. We won't bite. I'm Miss Merry Owens."

She tucked her feather duster into her waistband above her ample hindquarters like a tail. That and her tuft of orange hair made her look like no spring chicken, rather like a mother hen.

"There's right sweet folks here, artists and such, women on the second floor, men on the third, the help on the fourth. Seventeen paying souls, and all of them respectable, mind you, but not particular fashionable. Of the men, there's not a good-for-naught or a tippler in the bunch, though there be a couple of mollies, if you don't mind that. We even have a bona fide doctor, Griggs is his name, and an actor, Mr. Bainbridge. In the evenings we have musicales or read-alouds or charades or drawing lessons and such."

"Drawing lessons?" Drawing was my embarrassing weakness, which I tried to hide from Mr. Tiffany.

"Oh, 'tis a grand arrangement we have. Mr. Dudley Carpenter is teaching Miss Hettie to draw, and Miss Hettie is teaching piano to Mr. Hackley, and Mr. Hackley is teaching singing to Miss Lefevre, and Miss Lefevre is teaching French to Mr. McBride, and Mr. McBride is teaching art history to Mr. Booth, and Mr. Booth is teaching accounting to Miss

Merry Owens, that's me, and I'm teaching Irish tatting to Mrs. Hackley, and she is teaching the zither to Dudley, so it all comes 'round, ye see, in a happy circle." She made a circle with fingers plump as sausages and laughed her big bosoms into action.

"And what can you do?" she demanded, knuckles on the shelves of her hips, her head cocked to the side as though the hen's neck were broken.

"I can recite poetry. I particularly like Emily Dickinson."

"A lady poet, eh? There's somes here would like that. Give us a wee morsel."

" 'Each that we lose takes part of us.' Oh, no. That's too dreary. How about this?

" 'Hope' is the thing with feathers
That perches in the soul,
And sings the tune without the words
And never stops at all."

"Ah, sweeter than wine."
Apparently I passed muster, because she brought me into an airy parlor with comfortable easy chairs and freshly starched antimacassars. Two landscape prints of the Hudson River School hung on the walls, and a bowl of lemon drops sat on a crocheted doily. The Twelve Apostle spoons hanging in their wooden rack on the wall were all bright. Not one, not even the betrayer, was tarnished.

Clearly this was a better sort of boarding-house, probably with a price to match.

Up carpeted stairs that did not creak she showed me to a bedroom all done up in pink and spring green with a window onto Irving Place. Above the iron bedstead a landscape mural had been painted of a pond with floating lilies.

"Charming."

"George, a former boarder, painted it when he lived here, but Dudley chose the colors for the curtains and spread."

Decent bed, small desk with an oil lamp and a bookshelf above it, one easy chair, clean, bathroom down the hall. "How much?"

"Fifty dollars a month, and that includes three hearties a day, full Irish breakfast, dessert on Sundays and holidays, hot water all hours. T'would be forty-five but for the window."

That was higher than I had anticipated, but I earned twenty a week with a promise of a moderate raise every two years.

"I'll take it. May I move in tomorrow?"

"To be sure you can."

I returned to Brooklyn elated, and late into the night I packed the last things — my alcohol lamp for heating my curling iron, and my grandmother's porcelain washbowl and pitcher — but the things on Francis's desk and dresser, I didn't even touch.

With a trace of sadness I had sold my two evening gowns at the Second Time Around and bought three shirtwaists, ready-mades with narrow skirts, for work, and a new pair of lace-ups so I wouldn't come back to Tiffany's looking down-at-the-heels. I took Francis's silk black-on-black bow tie that I particularly liked. I could wear it hanging down loosely in the modern style. I packed my wedding dress, not out of sentiment but out of longing for spring. It was sky-blue poplin. I packed my opera cloak too, even if I had to wear it over a muslin shirtwaist in the standing-room-only section.

And then I carefully wrapped in a hand towel the one thing I had that no one could wrench from me — the kaleidoscope, his engagement gift to me. Bits of richly colored glass in a chamber served as his sweet acknowledgment that I'd had to give up my joyous work with just such glass in order to marry him. At the slightest turn of the maplewood tube, the design collapsed with a tiny rattle of falling objects, and in a burst of an instant, nothing was the same.

It was our books that remained. I was careful to pick out my own, leaving his. Into my carpetbag first went my mother's Shakespeare, the plays and the sonnets. I couldn't help but think of the first line of Sonnet Twenty-nine, which seemed to be aimed at me this last month as it never had before.

When in disgrace with fortune and men's eyes.

In went my mother's etiquette book, *The Habits of Good Society: A Handbook for Ladies and Gentlemen,* which I read with some levity, and my stepfather's Bible and his Minister's Bible Concordance, which bristled when I put Whitman's *Leaves of Grass* next to it. My leather-bound Keats and Wordsworth came next, reminding me that it wasn't a bad thing to brighten one's days with snips of poetry, like my mother did. Then Ibsen's plays, Vasari's *Lives of the Artists,* and Henry James's *Daisy Miller* and *The Portrait of a Lady.* There stood Emily Dickinson. The 1890 collection, her first, Francis had given me. The 1891 collection I had given him. I took them both, wondering what follows *The Sweeping up the Heart, / And putting Love away.*

On Sunday evening in Miss Owens's dining room, a tall, smartly dressed man pulled out my chair for me, motioned for me to sit, and scooted it in with utter grace but without a word, an easy gesture for him, though one that carried a sense of the momentous for me. A serving girl set down a platter of corned beef and cabbage, and Merry Owens brought in bowls of boiled potatoes and creamed lima beans, then sat at the head of the table.

"Why so glum tonight, you two?" she said

to two men just entering.

"Walt Whitman died yesterday." One of them choked getting out the words. His eyes glistened, and his curly hair grew like a wild garden.

"Walt Whitman, a cosmos, of Manhattan the son," said the other, a studious type wearing horn-rimmed spectacles with expensive gold hinges.

"Song of Myself," I was quick to say. I had always liked that title.

"Well, then, we'll have a read-aloud after supper. It'll make you feel a mite better," Miss Owens said. "Start the praties and beans around, Maggie. We have a new boarder. Mrs. Clara Driscoll. She's in George's old room. Dudley redecorated it."

"Good thing, unless she likes little Egyptian alligators painted on the walls," replied a matronly woman with long earlobes, whose cheeks were etched with a fretwork of finely penned wrinkles.

"Much to my dismay, Mrs. Hackley, Merry made me paint over them gators when I told her they were aphrodisiacal."

Ah, the sad, curly-haired one must be Dudley. Definitely a Southern twang, unless it was put on to be funny. Prolonged vowels. *Pa-int* said as two slow syllables. I liked it.

"It's a lovely room. I'm sure I'll be happy in it."

Miss Owens asked those seated at my table

to introduce the person to their right. There were four men, three women, and an empty chair next to Dudley Carpenter, who kept looking behind him through the arch to the parlor.

"He'll be along, Dudley," Miss Owens assured him.

"Will Mr. Driscoll be joining you soon?" Mrs. Hackley asked.

"No." She wasn't wasting any time in zeroing in on the suspicion attached to any woman my age living alone. "There is no Mr. Driscoll."

"Then you're a working woman?" Mr. Hackley asked.

"Yes. I work at Tiffany's studio."

"Polishing silver, I should guess," Mrs. Hackley declared authoritatively.

"As a matter of fact, no."

"It can't be selling jewelry. The sales clerks are all men," she said.

"That's Tiffany and Company, owned by Charles Tiffany. I work for his son, Louis Tiffany, in his glass workshop, making leaded-glass windows and mosaics."

"Workshop! Then you consider yourself a New Woman, do you?" Mrs. Hackley looked down her nose at her plate. "It's my opinion, and that of many social commentators, that when a woman joins the ranks of men in workshops, her morals sink, so mind your step."

"She's employed in the arts, Mrs. Hackley, not in a carriage factory, and the arts are a moral force."

"Thank you, Mr. —"

"McBride. Henry McBride."

Him, the scholarly Whitman quoter, I wanted to remember. Longish hair, cleft chin, Cupid's-bow mouth redder than was common, pearl stud in his flowing maroon four-in-hand necktie, positioned off center. Was that intentional, a rejection of convention?

"Call him Hank," drawled Dudley. "It takes him down a peg from his high falutin self-appointment as headmaster of Forty-four Irving Place."

Hank folded his hands in a professorial way. "I know a good deal about the elder Tiffany, if you care to ask me sometime."

"I will!"

"Plato wrote that men and women would eventually respond much in the same way to the same conditions." This interjected by Francie, an older woman delicate as a wren, with a complexion the pale pink of her blouse. "I take that to mean that if a man can have integrity and morality in factories and workshops, then so can women."

"Oh, you and your books," Mrs. Hackley grumbled. "Will you never stop prattling on about those philosophers? They're all dead, Francie." Frumpish Mrs. Hackley forked an overlarge morsel of corned beef and chewed vigorously, her mouth making all sorts of exaggerated shapes. "I have never been able to understand how a true lady could accept money from anyone but a father, a husband, an uncle, or a brother."

"Enough, Maggie. I'll shut off your radiator if you go on against my new boarder. She's right proper, and I won't have you laying damage to her person."

"In this tippy world, Mrs. Hackley, a single woman does what she has to," I said, "and if she enjoys it, as I do, so much the finer her life."

"Brava, Mrs. Driscoll," ventured the gentleman who had pushed in my chair.

I saw now his clean-shaven skin taut over elegant, defined cheekbones.

"Ah, I'd begun to think you were mute," I said. "Handsome, but mute." Francie snickered daintily. "Remind me of your name, please."

"Bernard Booth."

Not even a full sentence and I could tell he was English. I always melted at an English accent.

The front door opened and slammed shut. A beardless man with ruddy complexion and black hair entered through the arch from the parlor. Whistling "Yankee Doodle," he swept off his black fedora with its small red feather, flung it onto the hat rack along with his long red silk scarf, and did a little dance step.

"Great news, comrades." He held out both arms. "You are, at this moment, looking at the recipient of the honor of having my portrait of Helena Modjeska hung in the Players Club."

Applause burst forth from both tables.

He was a bit of a Yankee Doodle dandy himself, with his red handkerchief pointing up out of the pocket in his frock coat. He bent to lay a humorously loud kiss on Miss Owens's cheek.

"Sorry I'm late, Merry. The discussion of where it would hang went on and on. In the end it was decided that because of Modjeska's role as Ophelia, it should hang next to John's of Edwin Booth as Hamlet."

"Mind letting us in on who you mean, or are we supposed to know?" asked Merry.

"Why, John Singer Sargent, of course."

That was impressive enough to me, but Dudley scowled. "You're on a first-name basis now? Georgie and Johnny?"

"Not just yet."

"Don't be filling yourself up with grand ideas like some lawdy-daw or you won't want to keep taking your meals with the likes of us. I need your tuppence." Miss Owens turned to me. "Moved out, he did, into his studio. It's only a good spit from here to next door, so he's always fiddle-faddling around here as if he owns the place."

"So this is the artist who painted the lovely

pond in my room."

"A mere caprice done on a rainy day." He dismissed it with a flip of his slender hand.

"All it needs is the ruins of a temple in the background," I said.

George made a circle of his lips. "Great idea, Miss —"

"Driscoll. But please call me Clara."

"Clara."

"Claire," said Bernard Booth. "Light. Brilliant. Clear-sighted." He held up his water glass. "To Clara, our brilliant new friend."

"Flattery in the Queen's English sends me to the moon," I murmured, and our eyes met for an instant.

"And to George." Dudley raised his glass. "Our brilliant old friend."

"And to Walt, our forever friend," Hank McBride added.

"All right," Merry said. "You can have your read-aloud now."

"I know one line by heart," I said. " 'A morning-glory at my window satisfies me more than the metaphysics of books.' "

Hank nodded as if in appreciation for my offering. We adjourned to the parlor, and Dudley produced *Leaves of Grass* and read,

"I believe a leaf of grass is no less than the
    journey-work of the stars,
And the pismire is equally perfect, and a
    grain of sand, and the egg of the wren,

58

And the tree-toad is a chef-d'oeuvre for the
    highest."

"*Pismire.* That's an offensive word in a
poem," scoffed Mrs. Hackley, making a big
puff of air on the *p,* which shook her earlobes. *"Pismire."*
If it was so offensive, why did she take such
pleasure in saying it twice?
"Madam, your pious offense weighs no
more than a straw against the great tide of
humanity that celebrates this magnanimous
mind," said Hank.
Madam made a face and wagged her head
at him.
"I want a Manhattan poem," said George,
the latecomer with the red handkerchief. He
thumbed through the book and read.

"Manhattan crowds, with their turbulent
    musical chorus!
Manhattan faces and eyes forever for
    me . . ."

Oh, what promise in that, I thought.

"Be not disshearten'd, affection shall solve
    the problems of freedom yet.
Those who love each other shall become
    invincible."

He balled his hand into a fist and gave it a

59

little shake.

Not a peep out of Mrs. Hackley, but Mr. Hackley humphed. "It will take more than affection to solve the problems of freedom. Affection can't solve bank and brokerage failures or railroad bankruptcies or the recession that's sure to follow. Labor unions strike at the drop of a hat," Mr. Hackley continued. "That's not affection. Affection can't bring rain to the drought in the West. It's a poet's pipe dream. Affection can't stop the rich from getting richer, and the immigrant populations poorer."

"Yes, perhaps it *can* do that," said Bernard Booth. "What you need is another Lincoln to demonstrate that."

"We need the idealism and values of a Lincoln, certainly," Hank said. "And the foundation of his values was love for humanity." He reached for the book, adjusted his spectacles, found a particular page, and read in his deep voice.

"For You O Democracy

Come, I will make the continent
    indissoluble,
I will make the most splendid race the sun
    ever shone upon,
I will make divine magnetic lands,
    With the love of comrades,
    With the life-long love of comrades.

I will plant companionship thick as trees
　along all the rivers of America,
　and along the shores of the great lakes,
　and all over the prairies,
I will make inseparable cities with their
　arms about each other's necks,
　By the love of comrades,
　By the manly love of comrades."

I was impressed by the quiet attentiveness of everyone, even the Hackleys, when Hank read so reverently a passage full of fair prospects and broad affection.

"May our comrade go onward peacefully," George said.

"Amen," murmured Dudley, his head lowered.

CHAPTER 5
FIRE AND THE
KING OF DIAMONDS

Mr. Tiffany laid seven huge garnets and a handful of copper beads on my sample table for me to work into the peacock mosaic.

"Put metallic foil beneath the plainer pieces," he said, "even those you've already placed, to intensify their brilliance. Choose carefully, though, because the eye will naturally go there. In other areas, I want you to use my new iridescent glass."

He untied a drawstring bag and let half a dozen gorgeous pieces of glass tumble out. Seen from one direction, they were deep turquoise and cobalt blue. From another direction, shimmery silver.

"I've never seen any glass like this." Another piece was golden or emerald green, depending on how I held it. "They're like pigeons' necks."

"Like peacock feathers," he said, correcting my analogy to be more apropos. "With my own glassmaking factory in Queens now, nobody can snatch this secret. The formulas,

I mean."

"You *made* these?"

"No. These are ancient, dug up in the Middle East, but at my glasshouse we've learned to duplicate what nature took centuries to do."

"Amazing."

At that moment, he became the Creator of Marvels, the Artificer of Beauty, second only to God.

"Come with me now to see it."

"Now?"

"Why not?"

Why not? Because of the work ahead of me. Yet I gladly threw out all thought of it in favor of time alone with him. I felt proud, sure of myself, elevated. He had not asked Agnes, or the oldest member of our department, Miss Stoney of the hard, serious face, to see what he had made. Only me. Privileged, happy me.

At the Corona end of the rail line, Tiffany Furnaces took up a whole walled block. Fumes and smoke and spurts of flame spewed out of its looming brick smokestack, and nine smaller metal chimneys sent up waves of heat.

Just inside the factory, Mr. Tiffany struck his cane against the floor to announce his presence. Through the open door to an office, a man with a grizzled mustache looked up and hastened to stand and extend his hand.

"Good timing, Louis. They're just about to pour."

Mr. Tiffany introduced me to Arthur Nash, the glasshouse manager. We walked past the chemist's laboratory and into the heat of a vast factory and stopped at the first furnace.

"Don't get too close," Mr. Nash warned. He pointed to a round opening that glowed and sent out waves of heat. "That glory hole is twenty-three hundred degrees."

A squat, thick-armed man in a leather protection vest but no shirt hefted a giant ladle out of the glory hole and poured molten glass thick and incandescent into a rectangular oiled pan two feet long. It sent up smoke. Pot metal, Mr. Nash called it, and he called the man a gatherer.

"Beautiful!" Mr. Tiffany said over the roar of the furnace. He turned to me. "We've devised a new method of annealing so we can pour more than one color onto a single sheet, and stir a bit so the different glass bodies will adhere and marbleize. Do you see what that allows us to do?"

"Cut pieces from a single multihued sheet so they'll be in harmony?"

"Exactly."

"More than that," Mr. Nash said. "We can now control clarity, color, and surface to create nuances in an infinite variety of glass. We're approaching five thousand types now."

"That's staggering," I said, knowing I had

64

to keep all of them in mind when I placed my glass orders for each window and mosaic that my department would create.

"Watch closely." Mr. Tiffany held up his index finger. "This is when the artistry happens."

The gatherer drew a different mix out of a smaller glory hole, and another man whom Mr. Nash called a gaffer directed its pour over the first layer in a thin stream that widened slowly.

"This sheet will cool into cream-colored glass with shadings of amber," Mr. Nash said. "It will be used for a woman's robe."

The gaffer and his assistant on opposite sides set metal bars inside the pan, and pushed them toward each other. The glass yielded and buckled like hanging drapery.

"More." Mr. Tiffany couldn't just watch. With the air of a boy at play, he put on padded leather gloves and pushed the bar again, which raised the folds higher and made more of them.

"Give them a slight curve," he said.

The gaffer jostled the pan in a quick movement. Instantly, the folds curved. In my mind's eye, I could see the woman's robe drape gracefully.

Mr. Tiffany looked at me. "This was how mountain ranges were created, eh?" he said, as if he suspected I had thought of him as God's assistant.

We moved on to another shop, which meant another glory hole and its team of men, some in overalls, some in leather aprons, one wearing an undershirt and another oddly wearing a necktie. Mr. Nash introduced Tom Manderson as the gaffer, the chief craftsman of this blowing team in charge of every piece his shop creates. Tom was bare to the waist, broad-shouldered, and muscular.

Mr. Tiffany stood back and said to me, "I'm hoping for some good news today. We've succeeded in making iridescent flat glass, but that's made with lime. Blown glass is made with lead, and it's been giving us problems."

I distinctly remembered his father telling him to postpone these experiments until after the fair.

Mr. Tiffany explained that the process exposed the blown piece to various metallic vapors. "We're trying a new formula on this batch."

Mr. Nash stopped him with a scowl. Apparently he didn't want to reveal his formulas out in the shop for fear they might leak to competing glass factories.

Mr. Tiffany tugged at his beard. "What happened to the last batch?"

"It didn't adhere." Mr. Nash's voice was flat with disappointment. "I saved samples in the take-out room."

On a standing blackboard, Mr. Tiffany sketched an irregular bulb shape with a long, curved neck and a lip taller on one side than the other, stretched outward like a tongue. "Try this," he said to Tom. "Like a Persian flask, only more spontaneous. Let yourself go." He flung out his hand. "Forget those classical shapes. They're too much like the conventional English shapes coming out of Stourbridge. We want natural shapes."

"You want that crooked neck?" Tom asked, his voice rising in pitch, his eyes squinting at the blackboard.

"Yes, I want that crooked neck!" he fired back. "Nature is always right, and always beautiful."

I was anxious to see if this Tom fellow could please the perfectionist.

"Think of an asymmetrical gourd hanging on a vine. Let the neck relax. Tolerate its lopsidedness."

Tom looked skeptical, and gestured to the gatherer to prepare a fresh pipe for him.

The gatherer turned the long blowpipe in the glory hole, drew out a red-hot gob of glass, like honey in consistency, and handed it off to Tom. In one swift movement, Tom rolled the gather of glass on a wet steel slab until it held its roundness, took it to his bench, sat, and rested the pipe on the supports on each side of him. Another man blew on the mouthpiece of the pipe to create a bulb at the other end, and Tom spun it and began shaping it with a wooden paddle as it

67

changed from glowing red to orange, then amber. When it started to harden, his server rushed it back into the glory hole to reheat it for more shaping. All that in less than three minutes. It was like an ancient fire dance.

I wanted to watch him finish, but Mr. Tiffany stepped away and murmured, "Maybe this batch."

In the take-out room large rectangles of the new iridescent flat glass in blues and greens and golds were propped against one wall.

"You'll use this for the double-peacock mosaic," said Mr. Tiffany. "By God, this will make the world take notice. La Farge will seethe with envy. Eighteen ninety-three will be a big year for us."

"If we finish in time," Mr. Nash said.

And if they didn't, what kind of angry boss would we have?

"How many sheets do we have now for the columns and altar?"

"Forty or fifty," Mr. Nash said.

"Set two more shops on this. Take them off the commissioned windows. Clients can wait. We'll never have enough for sixteen columns at this rate."

Mr. Tiffany turned his attention to the two dozen blown vases on the sample table. On one batch, the slight iridescence had begun to flake off. On another, there was only dullness. No sheen at all. He let out a roar and swept them off the table with his cane, two-handed, in a powerful, shocking swing. I scooted back as they flew off the table and shattered on the floor.

"Mr. Tiffany!"

"I'll be its master yet," he bellowed, shaking his cane, fire in his eyes, shoving the pieces to the edge of the floor with the side of his foot.

I'd never seen such explosive, dangerous rage, and could hardly believe what had happened. In my shock and embarrassment for him, for my presence witnessing this, my throat was instantly parched, and it was impossible to swallow.

He glanced at me, looked abashed, and lowered his voice. "Too much Stourbridge, anyway. We want original shapes derived from nature, not these tired old classics." He waved his arm derisively at the rubble on the floor.

I felt protective of my girls if he would ever unleash his dissatisfaction with our work with a swing of his cane.

"You still want us to keep experimenting with iridescence?" Mr. Nash asked in a surprisingly calm tone.

"Perfection, Arthur! Nothing less! We work until we attain it."

"But the time. The fair is only ten months away now."

"Don't tell me what I already know!"

"And the expense. We've already spent —"

"Don't tell me that either!"

That evening at the dinner table I described Mr. Tiffany's outburst and glass smashing.

"What is he? A maniac?" Mrs. Hackley asked.

"I never thought so before this," I said.

Hank patted his mouth with his napkin. "There are a few things I know that might explain his behavior. I've been researching his family history for an article to come out during the Chicago Fair."

"Please, tell me everything."

"You sure you want the whole deal?" Dudley asked. "Nobody's windier than Hank when he gets rolling."

"The lady asked, Dudley, so I have to start with Theophania, a Greek merchant named after a festival honoring Apollo, where he sold silk. His descendants inched northward across Europe, selling what came to be known as tiffin silk."

"How did you find that out?" I asked.

"The New York Genealogical and Biographical Society and early company brochures in the Astor Library. One leap took the family from England to New England, and a few more generations followed as cotton merchants in Connecticut, each one shrewdly outdoing the preceding one. Comfort Tiffany rose above his father by hiring

Indians to build a mill, and then selling them molasses and rum to recoup the wages he had paid."

"A canny business move," said Bernard Booth, the Englishman, an import businessman himself.

"Comfort's son Charles, Louis's father, had ambitions that stretched beyond backwater towns."

"He's the one who established Tiffany and Company," I said.

"By buying crates of goods abandoned on the docks during a depression, and selling the contents to the carriage trade, since the upper class wasn't affected. When working-class people could buy again, he opened a gimcracks emporium selling glass 'diamond' necklaces, Japanese fans, Chinese parasols. For the middle class, he imported Bohemian glass and French porcelain."

"Smart to offer a range of products to entice people to buy *up*," said Bernard.

"Everything had a price tag, an innovation that put a stop to undignified haggling over every sale," Hank said.

"I believe his company was one of the first to send out mail-order catalogs," Bernard remarked.

"They still do. I have one," boasted Mrs. Hackley.

"Save it. It will be a collector's item someday," Bernard said.

"How did Charles Tiffany elevate the company into fine jewelry?" I asked.

"That happened through blind luck."

Hank explained that Charles's partner was in Paris on a buying mission in 1848 when Louis Philippe's regime collapsed and the aristocracy was on the run and sold their jewels for half their value. The partner bought up as much as he could. Charles had the gems reset in new styles, and the Goulds, Morgans, Vanderbilts, and Astors all came running. Even Queen Victoria. So he became known as the King of Diamonds."

"From gilt to gold, from glass to gems," said Bernard, piling mashed potatoes and peas on the back of his fork. "Ingenuity bred wealth, and now wealth is breeding art. We could call it the Tiffany Imperative for each son to exceed his father."

"And that was behind his fiery temper in the take-out room," I said, understanding more now.

"You near 'bout done?" Dudley asked.

"No! Charles capitalized on the notoriety by selling silver officers' swords in Central Park during the Civil War."

"An opportunist!" said Mrs. Hackley. "Who can respect an opportunist?"

"I can," Bernard said. "Who was hurt by this? No one."

"Tell that to the Tennessee boy soldier who had one of those fancy swords planted in his

72

gut," said Dudley. Such a sensitive one, he was.

Hank told us that through Charles's friendship with P. T. Barnum he learned the benefits of linking his name with fame by giving magnificent silver loving cups to Jenny Lind, the midget Tom Thumb, and the sculptor of the Statue of Liberty. Newspapers picked up the stories. Free publicity for Tiffany & Company.

"A conniver," Mrs. Hackley muttered.

"One of Barnum's circus elephants ran amok once," Hank said.

"I remember that," said Merry, brightening. "It trampled a few chaps, so it had to be killed."

"Charles bought the carcass, had it stuffed, and put it in his store window with a sign: 'Killer elephant to be made into commemorative belts, fine wallets, ivory cuff links. Order yours while the finest parts last.' It was a huge success."

"Bully for him!" Bernard said. "The King of Diamonds tops the Prince of Humbug."

"But there's one more generation." Hank peered at me. "I don't know if you're aware, Clara, that your employer has never finished a year in the black. It's Charles and his Tiffany and Company, not Louis, that keeps your Tiffany Glass and Decorating Company afloat."

Then everyone, even Mrs. Hackley, looked

at me. I swallowed the morsel of fish in my mouth without chewing. I was not working in a carefree land of fantasy flamingoes and jeweled peacocks. Now I understood the tension that made him smash vases.

"I suppose the stakes for him in Chicago rest in part on your shoulders." Bernard patted my arm. "No need to worry. Diamonds are made under pressure, and you're our brilliant *Claire.*"

CHAPTER 6
DAFFODIL

Spring, and Gramercy Park was dressed this Sunday in yellow daffodils, frilly-edged goblets on six-pointed saucers. They reminded me of Wordsworth's poem about wild ones. How did it begin? Oh, yes. "I wandered lonely as a cloud." And later, "What wealth the show to me had brought." Fine for him. Only a poet or a woman in love could measure wealth by flowers. I wasn't either one.

Wandering too, and in a similar mood, I came to Madison Square Park. An organ-grinder had stationed himself and his monkey beneath a magnolia tree radiant with enormous creamy blossoms, each petal a cup of sunlight. He was surrounded by children, nannies, and white-veiled prams looking like mobile wedding cakes. Everyone in the park was with someone. Even the organ-grinder had a furry friend. Loneliness crept over me despite his cheerful tune.

A bent woman was selling violets and daffodils. Francis had brought me daffodils every week when they were in season. Two springs' worth of daffodils.

"May I buy just two daffodils?" I asked.

"They're three for a dime." Her voice was a rasp against metal.

I put a dime in her deeply creased palm, thanked her, and walked away, watching the blooms bounce and flutter.

A top-heavy omnibus pulled by two lathered Clydesdales stopped at the corner, headed uptown. I got on. The clop-clop of the heavy hooves sent up a languid rhythm as we passed the shops of Ladies' Mile and then the mansions of Fifth Avenue. I descended at Fifty-seventh Street and walked to Alice Gouvy's West Side flat close to the Art Students League, where she was studying. I hadn't seen her since the service for Francis.

As young girls in Tallmadge, Ohio, we had spent delicious days along a clear stream that emptied into the filthy Cuyahoga River. In one place on the bank, a spot we called "the theater," we acted out *Hiawatha,* trading off reading it aloud and doing hand gestures. In summer, feeling daring and giddy, we lifted our skirts and stepped in. The sensuality of the cool water moving against our bare legs thrilled us. We liked best those places where the water rippled and light danced on the surface. In quiet moments we shared our curiosity about men and wondered whether we would be housewives like our mothers

76

when we grew up, or something daring, modern, and mysterious — women of the professions.

Alice answered my knock in her terry-cloth robe and slippers as she was towel-drying her hair.

"Clara!" She wrapped me in her arms and pulled me inside. "I've been wanting to get over to Brooklyn to see you."

"That's good of you, but I'm not there anymore. I live just south of Gramercy Park now."

I sank into the cushions of her wicker armchair. The familiar worn pink chenille bedspread, the potbellied oil lamp with parchment shade on the drop-leaf table that served for writing, eating, and drawing, and the woven rag rug like mine that we'd bought at a women's craft center in Cleveland made me feel instant warmth, instant comfort.

"I've gone back to work for Tiffany."

"Oh?"

"Francis left me no money."

Her jaw dropped open.

"Well, just enough to cover the burial and two months of living expenses. The rest, a substantial amount, went to a daughter I hadn't known about. Apparently there was an earlier woman."

"No! I can't believe it."

I hadn't been able to either. Shocked, I had grabbed the will out of the attorney's hands, and the edge of the paper, sharp as the realization of my worth in his eyes, had cut my skin — as if the contents of the will hadn't cut enough.

"The alleged daughter was one Sister Maria Theresa, so the inheritance went to a convent. And I, the stepdaughter of a Protestant minister, was out on the street." The sarcasm gave me a moment's release. I'd had no one I could tell it to.

Alice slammed down her hairbrush onto the bare table. "That's horrible. You've been wronged. I feel awful for you."

"Don't feel too sorry for me, Alice. I wouldn't want to stay married one more day to a man so deceptive."

"Aren't you the least bit angry?"

"In my low moments, of course I am."

She thrust forward her chin. "Could you sue?"

"Who? The convent? The Holy Roman Church? And with what? When I moved out of the boardinghouse in Brooklyn I left all of his things for the daughter to collect, even his spare change. Maybe some poor, plain soul in black habit could use his mustache cup. What tickled me most was to imagine what use the nuns would have for his copy of Darwin."

Alice slapped her hand over her mouth. "Locked it up, I should guess, instead of burning it, so the Mother Superior could feed her curiosity on it between Compline and Matins. And when she was occupied during Mass, some wayward sister would be madly trying to filch the key."

I let out a smirky kind of chuckle.

"I'm sorry, Clara. I shouldn't make a joke of it. Do you have any idea why he did that?"

"Yes, I do. His incapacity in bed. He didn't look it, but he was sixty-two."

"Twice your age. I didn't realize."

"He, we, tried and tried, but he couldn't produce anything harder than a stern look. He ate oysters, hated the rubbery slipperiness of them but still downed them one after another with eyes squeezed shut like stitched wounds. He offered suggestions, whispered so the boardinghouse walls wouldn't hear. Time after time in bed, after trying everything we knew, I saw hope go out of his eyes, and they filled with accusation."

Alice let out a low, wordless murmur. I picked up her hairbrush, lifted her damp hair, and began to brush.

"He was unwilling to talk about it, though I could tell it was on his mind as we went walking, or as he methodically washed his face, came to bed, and then absently went back to the bathroom to wash it again."

Sentences came out slowly, with pauses in between for long, slow strokes of the hairbrush. I told her how Francis took out his frustration against me in subtle ways, for

79

example, saying that a new hat made me look foolish when it was really his sense of failure that was speaking.

"Whether he failed me or I failed him, I don't know, but he may have had glorious memories of his earlier woman."

"Had he been married to her?"

"I'll never know, but that's immaterial. His money went to commemorate his success, not his failure."

"Maybe it was remorse money for something."

I shrugged. "Leaving me without money isn't what grieves me most. I would have gone back to work for Tiffany anyway. I don't want to be a kept woman to a dead man. It's that he left me without any sign of regard."

"Did you love him?"

Instantly I saw the adorable creases around his lips, the way he stretched his face to shave, and heard his sweet murmured apologies in his sleep when I nudged him to stop snoring. Maybe it was just the intimacy of those things that I loved, and I would love them pasted on another man. Did all men stretch their faces to shave and murmur apologies for snoring?

Alice's hair got caught in the prongs of my wedding ring, and I had to work to free it. Ridiculous to keep wearing it. I should sell it and buy opera tickets. Francis and I did enjoy opera together, and our quiet walks in bucolic

Fort Greene Park, and our thrilling ones on the Brooklyn Bridge. I had always held the notion that if two people love the same thing, they must love each other as well, but now the memories of that love had been tarnished by betrayal.

"I miss him. Does one spiteful action kill love? If it can, then what sort of flimsy love was it?"

I wound her hair in a figure eight and let it tumble down.

"Yes, I did come to love him, though I wasn't sure I did when I married him. You might call it a marriage of sacrifice. I still love him for many things he did, but now I wonder if he did those things for the first woman.

"Listen, Clara, I might be all wrong, but maybe he did it to force you to go back to work for Tiffany. Maybe he knew that was the best way to provide a life for you."

That startled me. Could he have been that calculating?

"You still like it there, don't you?"

"I love it. When I left to get married, I intended to work for another glass company that didn't have a policy against hiring married women, but I found that no other company wanted a woman in a man's job, married or not."

"It's not a man's job."

"I suppose some people would call it mannish work because of the tools we use. I've always loved hand tools — chisels, rasps, pliers, calipers. I got that from my own father, and was forever following him around as a child when he was making something."

"I remember the birdhouses he built."

"Once he was on his knees working on one, and I was handing him tools. I was playing at swinging a hammer like an ax, enjoying the lopsided weight of it, and it flew out of my hands and hit him in the forehead. I was horrified. I'll never forget the bloody gash. Soon after that, his health started to fail, and in two years, he was dead. I blamed myself, but was too ashamed to tell you."

"It wasn't your fault."

"I can see that now, but nightmares of flying hammers tortured me for years afterward. Burdens of responsibility have hounded me ever since."

"That has nothing to do with Francis."

"Yes, it does. Put the pieces together, Alice. Girl feels responsible for father's death. Uses family money to go to art school. Later, younger sister wants to go too. Crisis: Stepfather earns little as village minister. Family funds dwindle. Older gentleman comes along offering to pay younger sister's tuition. A fatherly gesture. Complication: Proper mother thinks it unseemly to accept money unless he's part of the family. Gentleman proposes marriage to elder daughter. Out of guilt for loss of father's income, elder daughter gives up job in the arts to marry him. Younger sister goes to art school. Climax: Younger sister quits art school. Dénouement: Older sister becomes disenfranchised widow. I could have sold the plot to Ibsen."

My momentary glibness was a mask. The scars ran deeper than I let on. "Too much irony tastes bitter," I murmured.

I squeezed Alice's hand. "Come to work for Tiffany. We need you. At the worst possible time, Edith Mitchill left to marry an artist and go with him to paint the West. You could take her place. We could be together every day."

"I have another year here."

"We need talented women *now,* to finish our projects for the Chicago World's Fair on time."

"I'm sorry, but I want to complete my certificate. You'll find others."

"Then come live at my boardinghouse. It's full of interesting, creative people. In the evenings we have sing-alongs around the piano, or we read poetry aloud, or plays that are in the theaters, each of us taking parts. We're a literary society, a theater critics circle, an artists' group, a philosophical society. I've stumbled upon the perfect place to live."

"Sounds nice, but this room is so convenient to my classes."

"Then think about it for the future, and

come to the park with me now. We'll wrap ourselves in green grass and see what's blooming and be part of the grand mix of people and the babble of languages."

"I'd like to, but I can't." Her cheeks became pink like the delicate petals of sweet peas. She was as pretty as a china doll. "A man from the league asked me to go to a concert with him."

The lightness I'd felt at the thought of a stroll in Central Park with Alice was snuffed out like a candle in a draft.

"Well, some other time."

I kissed her cheek and took my walk alone and tried not to brood. Central Park was still Central Park, bathing New Yorkers with spring, each person adding joy to others. I gave myself over to its refreshment.

When I went home to my second-floor room, my door was ajar, and I heard whistling. I nudged it open cautiously.

"George!"

He was standing on my bed in his stockinged feet, paintbrush in one hand, palette in the other, an elfish grin on his face.

"I took your comment as an invitation. A caprice must be" — he flicked his brush in the air — "capricious."

"Is it customary here to enter other people's rooms, capriciously?"

I kept the door open so anyone passing in

the corridor could see what was, and wasn't, going on. Mother's handbook would have advised me so.

"Customary for me and Dudley and Hank, but not the Hackleys. They're premature fuddy-duddies. And not Mr. York, too quiet, or Dr. Griggs, too busy, or Bernard Booth, too English. Very proper — cheerio, jolly good, and all that." George used his palette to doff an imaginary hat.

"I'm not accustomed to it."

"Face it, Clara. You've moved into bohemia. Just down West Twenty-third is where the painters, artist models, poetry scribblers, actors, playwrights, set designers, costumers, wig makers, feather merchants, bird stuffers, wooden-toy painters, tarot card designers, fortune-tellers, accordion players, and tambourine makers live."

I had to laugh. It was impossible not to like him. What I needed was a friend.

"Continue, then."

"And the patron saint of Irving Place, Washington Irving, lived across the street once, so goes the legend, in a house now occupied by Elsie de Wolfe, actress, stage designer, and interior decorator, and her lover, Bessie Marbury, literary agent to Oscar Wilde and George Bernard Shaw, my heroes. Wags call the women 'the bachelors,' but what do they care? Elsie's silk parlor cushions are embroidered with her motto, 'Never

85

complain. Never explain.' Macy's sells copies. I call that high bohemia. Oh, you're on the slippery edge of it here."

He was a hopeless name-dropper, but I didn't mind. It was fascinating, and for the present, I wasn't alone.

"As opposed to low bohemia?"

"The Jewish immigrant quarter south of us. Dingy pockets of progressive politics, serious theater, social art, and violin virtuosos, the nursery for great contributions someday."

"If all that culture is going on there, how can you call it 'low'?"

"Only because it's in the Lower East Side. My brother's in the thick of it there. So is our comrade, Hank McBride. The horn-rims, remember? He teaches drawing from classical sculpture at the East Side Artist and Educational Alliance. His favorite is the *Apollo Belvedere,* a Greek god coveted by a pope and swiped by Napoléon. He calls it the epitome of male beauty."

"Interesting, but what I meant was to continue with your painting."

He had blocked in a meadow and a distant hill in a lavender haze, and on it, the ruins of a Greek temple. He set to work again, painting swiftly.

"Are you sure you wouldn't like an Apollo just visible between the columns of this temple, my lady?" He waved his brush as though it were a magic wand. "Just a few touches and he would sweeten your fancies."

"You remind me of Puck from *A Midsummer Night's Dream.*"

" 'Thou speak'st aright. I am that merry wanderer of the night.' "

"In your fairy palette, do you have any chrome yellow?"

"Indeed, my lady. Puck splashes it about through all the kingdom."

"Do you think he has the magic to put a few daffodils in the meadow?"

CHAPTER 7
WHITE

Late one afternoon I was sewing a band of lace onto a collar to disguise its worn condition when George came in, pulled my curtains aside, and peered out into the early twilight.

"It's beginning to snow," he said. "Tomorrow everything will be covered in white. White buildings. White streets. White omnibuses. White lampposts. An alabaster city."

"I get the idea, George. You don't have to catalog every snowflake."

Snow meant three months left until the fair would open in May. With so much still left to do, I felt as nervous as a sparrow pecking at the frayed edge of resolve.

George was bursting to tell me something, but he kept it in, nosing around, picking up my powder puff, rearranging the things on my dresser scarf, making it seem as though he was only going to reveal it if I asked. To tease him, I refused to, which sooner or later would force him to reveal it on his own. Over the last several months it had become our mutual cat-and-mouse game.

He adjusted the curtain, he twirled the tassel on the curtain tieback, he played with my kaleidoscope, and he asked me what I did at work today.

"The same things I did yesterday and the day before that. Chipped chunks of lime green, orange, and gold glass into jewels for the crown in the double-peacock mosaic. It's still not finished because we've had to take over some of the windows from the men's department so they could stay home, sleep late, talk, talk, talk, and create a work stoppage. You can't choose a million unique pieces of glass in a week, you know. And none of these are tesserae — simple rectangles. They're sectiliae, cut to conform to the shapes outlined on the cartoon. Much more work because they're irregular. It's going to be gorgeous, but it's nerve-racking because I hear the clock ticking every time I lay down a piece."

That made him cock his head from side to side and cluck like a metronome. "I'm going to see it."

"I don't have a spare minute to show you."

He stuck his nose in the air. "You can't stop me." He straightened the rug beside my bed. "What did your girls do today?"

"Three glass selectors, three cutters, and three assistants finished the big *Angel of the*

89

Resurrection window. The angel's face and hands and feet have just been enameled and fired. You should have seen the girls, so giddy to see all the pieces assembled but sad to part with what they created. It took four men to carry each of the four easels to the metal shop to have the leads soldered. The girls were beside themselves with worry. They surrounded the men and held up their aprons along the edges of the easels in case any pieces fell off. The angel's foot did fall, but a big Swede named Wilhelmina dove for it and saved it."

"Ah, a fallen angel with feet of glass. I adore fallen angels. Was she wearing white lace? Were her white wings moving like this when she lost her toes?"

He flapped his arms crazily.

"All right, tell me. Why are you being so silly?"

"I'll give you a hint. White."

"I don't want a hint. I want the reason."

"I'll tell you at dinner. Hank and I will tell you." He flapped his wings out the door.

George grinned in his impish way as he passed me a serving bowl. "Here, Clara, have some white potatoes. To go with your white-fish and cauliflower."

I turned to Merry. "Did George have anything to do with this menu?"

She held up her hands. "None atallatall.

The praties is me own favorite, you know."

"I don't believe you. George has to orchestrate everything. All right, Puck, now that you have an audience, tell us what's sizzling inside of you."

He chewed; he took a drink of water; he flipped his white napkin and wiped his mouth with it. "Hank and I are going to the White City."

I was puzzled.

"He means the Columbian Exposition," Hank explained.

"No! Truly?"

"It's called the White City because the buildings are being painted to look like alabaster," Hank said. "A swamp outside Chicago is being transformed into canals, promenades, towers, and classical arches and façades. I just received a press release. I'll be writing about it."

"Then it's true, what Mr. Tiffany says. The greatest meeting of artists —"

"Since the fifteenth century," said Hank. "Some sixty-five thousand exhibits."

"Among which will be your chapel, peacocks and all," George said.

"And my Christ window! And the flamingo window. And you're going to see it all assembled. I'm green with envy."

"Don't forget Tiffany and Company's extravaganza," said Hank. "Father and son competing with each other on the world stage. Definitely worth my writing about for *The Century Magazine*."

"*If* we finish on time."

That doubt plagued me, so I worked extra hours almost every day. One evening in early June when I came home from work too late for dinner, Dudley and George were playing the popular new tune "Oh My Darling Clementine" on their zithers. George followed me up to my room, singing,

> "How I missed her! how I missed her,
> How I missed my Clementine,
> Till I kissed her little sister
> And forgot my Clementine."

"Brilliant. When is your debut at Carnegie Hall?"

"Dudley will be in Paris while Hank and I are in Chicago, so I've asked my brother Edwin to check in on you from time to time."

"I don't need someone to oversee my activities, thank you very much."

"Woo-whoo. Why so cranky?"

"I'll do just fine without your zither duets too, you and Dudley serenading each other across the parlor."

George screwed up his face in a pout so tight that it made me laugh. He could always make me laugh, no matter how tired I was. I sat at my dressing table, noticed mauve-colored cups under my eyes, and undid the pins in my chignon. They'd given me a headache. George came up behind me and unwound the twist, picked up my hairbrush and brushed from my forehead out to the ends, holding up my hair in his other hand.

"That's one thing you know how to do. Brush hair."

"You've been overworking yourself."

"So has everyone else. It's practically summer. What do you expect me to do?"

"Just what you've been doing, dear heart."

"Mr. Tiffany set too big a task for us. He designed too much, and now he's driven to complete it all."

The Lead Glaziers and Glass Cutters' Union had gone on strike, and the mosaics on the chapel arches and columns, as well as the leaded-glass dome on the baptismal font, weren't finished. Some of the glaziers would have wanted to be loyal to Tiffany, but union solidarity prevailed. For one, Joe Briggs, a fine mosaicist, would have worked all night if he could have found a way in, and Frank, the deaf-and-dumb janitor and errand boy, would have stayed with him to help. I had shown Mr. Belknap how to apply the tesserae, but what could one man do for a task that required twenty?

As a result, the remaining five chapel windows originally assigned to the men's department had fallen to my department. I hired more girls to do the mechanical work and elevated Mary and Wilhelmina to be junior selectors. I even gave Frank some simple tasks. Now everyone was putting in extra hours. We had to work by those wretched electric lightbulbs hanging from the ceiling, which bled out the colors. There was no time to savor our feelings about what we were making.

May Day had come and gone without notice. Any other year I would have been ecstatic about spring, but the entire Tiffany Glass and Decorating Company exhibit had not been ready when the exposition opened mid-May. The fair would last six months, but it was still a devastating disappointment to Mr. Tiffany. News reports said that tens of thousands of people visited the fair each day, and he was exasperated to be missing out. His dream of introducing landscape windows for churches and showcasing his iridescent glass was threatened.

He was short-tempered. Everyone in the studios was walking on eggshells. We were all excited about what we were making but also irritable under the pressure, sometimes both in the same breath. Expletives in German and Swedish erupted when nervous fingers fumbled and a piece of glass fell to the floor.

Just this morning Mr. Tiffany had yanked off half a dozen pieces of glass that I had selected to show the pathos of the crucified

Christ in the *Entombment* window.

"Can't you see that the winding cloth in the cartoon has more white across his groin and below his hip?" he had snapped, all gentility gone.

"We'll be happy to take them off ourselves, sir. You don't have to yank," Wilhelmina retorted, even though it wasn't her window.

"You ought to have known that Jesus must be the brightest figure in the window," he said angrily as he pried off Jesus's kneecap.

I winced. His impetuous desecration struck me as sacrilegious. Cornelia crumpled in shame. It wasn't her fault. She had only cut what I'd given her. After he left, she sobbed out her humiliation.

"It wasn't aimed at you," I said.

I had selected for that area using electric lights and should have caught my errors before he saw them this morning.

In a few minutes, Agnes came over to my easel. I felt the muscles around my eyes tighten. She laid a paper cone of gingersnaps on my sample table.

"Don't take it to heart. He's a raging lion some days, a lamb other days. He's not fault-less, you know."

She joined me in my work on *The Entombment* while her own window was left waiting. Working side by side in quiet harmony, we finished Jesus's torso, legs, and feet, the winding cloth, and part of Mary Magdalene's robe

95

before quitting time.

I had walked home in a whirlpool of anger, embarrassment, and gratitude. Now, upstairs in my bedroom with George brushing my hair, I was sorry I'd been cranky to him.

"Haven't you liked doing the work?" he asked as he took long, firm strokes with the hairbrush.

"Of course I have. I just wish I could go slower in order to enjoy selecting the glass more, to feed myself with each beautiful swirl, to linger over the nuances building up. If I don't love the feelings I have while creating those windows, I'm only working for coin and not from soul."

"A little bit of pain always rides in the pocket of pleasure," George said.

I didn't want to agree. "It's not just that."

"Then what?"

I took the hairbrush from his hand. "It's that I want to go with you."

A puff of air exploded from between his lips.

"Imagine what it would feel like to work on something six days a week and to care about it so intently that you spend the seventh day worrying about it — did I choose the right spot on that sheet of glass for the ultramarine shadow on the Virgin Mary's white head scarf? Will Mr. Tiffany be pleased with the striated glass I used for the sky at dawn over the figures? Why won't this chunk of glass

96

chip sharply where I want it to? Imagine living it, breathing it, pouring into each piece of glass my grief at the Crucifixion, or my excitement at a dazzling bird of splendor, dreaming of it week after week for a year, loving it with every ounce of my being, and then not being able to see it all assembled. You're an independent artist, George. You can paint what you want, take commissions or not, work at whatever speed you want, go wherever you want, whenever you want. You're entirely free."

"You're free too. No one's stopping you."

"No, George. I'm not free. I have twenty-eight girls that I have to keep busy immediately after our fair projects are finished or the business manager will force me to choose which ones to fire. The wheel's in motion. We'll have to design on speculation to tide us over until some orders come from the fair. If they come."

"They'll come."

"Your saying so doesn't stop me wanting to watch people in the chapel as they look, to see what they take away from it — joy or awakening or upliftment or peace or reverence — and to say to someone, anyone, 'That's *my* work you're looking at,' and at least one person in a million will say to my face, 'That's beautiful,' or 'That's an extraordinary achievement,' or 'That *helped* me.' "

In my dressing-table mirror, I saw my face

taut with yearning, eyes squinting into slits, lips pulled in. "I want to be in the pressing crowds so I can feel I'm part of this great world event, even if I'm not acknowledged."

I swung around to face George and grasped his arm.

"You'll tell me everything, won't you? You'll listen to what people say in front of my peacock wall, and watch to see if anyone is moved by *The Entombment?* You'll remember and tell me, won't you?"

He patted my cheek. "I'll memorize every word, and I'll take photographs for Hank's articles."

"I'll see them here, won't I? And I can borrow some to show the girls?"

"Of course."

Two simple words but uttered with such kindness and understanding. I closed my eyes a moment to reconcile myself.

I had begged Hank and George to postpone their trip until all parts of Mr. Tiffany's exhibit were in place — not just the chapel but the secular windows in the Dark and Light Rooms as well. Although postponement wasn't in Hank's best interest for his articles, George had prevailed on him, and that obliged me to be courteous to his brother.

"All right. Tell me about this Edwin fellow."

"You'll like him. He's much smarter than I am. He reads constantly. He's idealistic. He

98

works for the University Settlement."

"Whatever that is."

"He'll tell you. And he's different than I am."

"No one could be like you. Not even a brother."

"I mean, he's not a nellie."

CHAPTER 8
LADY LIBERTY

When we gathered in the parlor the Sunday morning that George and Hank were to leave, Edwin turned out to be taller than George, handsomer than George, and, thank goodness, quieter than George. Although they both had the same black hair and dark eyes, and the same clean-shaven, well-defined jaw, George was slender as a willow wand and as easily bendable, whereas Edwin was sturdier, more solid. Merry shooed the four of us out the door, saying to me, "You be sure that our George gets on the right train."

A torrent of words poured out of George's mouth in the horsecab on the way to Grand Central Depot. There was much hoopla on the platform because this was a special Columbian Exposition train. A four-piece band played beneath a banner, and boys wore sandwich boards advertising various exhibits, guesthouses, and restaurants. Hank stood quietly, jotting them down, while George trotted up and down the platform like a terrier on a leash until the conductor opened the doors.

"I hope you have many adventures," I said quietly to Hank.

"A person has adventures only when he's traveling alone. Traveling with another, he has comfort."

George performed a few dance steps — loose body, arms akimbo, head waggling — just before he stepped on board.

Edwin looked on indulgently. "My brother, the antic."

"Has he always been like that?"

"Always. Our mother used to call him Georgie the Jester. That only made him sillier."

"And what did she call you?"

With an expression of embarrassment, he murmured, "Edwin the Educator."

Once inside the passenger car, George opened the window to shout and wave his hat as the train pulled out.

"See everything. Learn all you can," Edwin shouted back.

"Aha. The Educator indeed," I said, and his tawny cheeks reddened.

I watched George's head and flailing arm shrink and blur in the distance. The gleaming rails coming together behind the train pointed toward beauties and advancements beyond my imagination, including our finished windows, shipped a month late. The only word that could describe how I felt was bereft.

Yet there beside me, stately as a statue, was Edwin. Around our awkward silence moved a fluid, noisy crowd. I would have preferred to nurse my sullen mood alone, but Edwin's gesture invited me to walk back into the terminal with him.

"And what art do you do?" I asked, facing forward, making an assumption, intending brusqueness.

"The art of making people happy, or at least happier."

"That's what all artists do, or aim to do."

"I work for the University Settlement in the Lower East Side, helping immigrants get their bearings."

"Oh." It came out feebly, flat, and final.

He invited me to an English tearoom nearby, and since I had promised George, I said yes. There wasn't much conversation on the way, only that George had told him all about me. At the tearoom, he insisted that I have a scone.

Feeling obligated to be friendly, I asked, "So what do you actually do at this settlement place?"

"I help new immigrants learn English and find jobs, enroll their children in school, find doctors and dentists who will take impoverished patients for fifty cents a visit, intervene in cases of tenement disputes, instruct them on the importance of labor unions."

Labor unions. Just what caused me to work like a fiend while the men paraded up and down Fourth Avenue for a month.

"Sometimes I give speeches to society clubs to persuade them to donate, and to political organizations to support changes in labor laws. Other times, I ladle soup."

"Soup?"

"That's right. Soup. The Fourth Ward of the Lower East Side beneath the Brooklyn Bridge is flooded with immigrants living in poverty, sometimes ten to a room. New arrivals live in hall rooms."

"What, pray tell, is a hall room?"

He adjusted his gold-rimmed spectacles. "Imagine a large old house turned into a boardinghouse with a hundred people living in the bedrooms and only one indoor bathroom and an outdoor privy. The poorest immigrants rent space in the corridors, priced per foot, barely wide enough for a cot, one family's space partitioned off from another's by a shredded curtain if they're lucky."

"No privacy?"

"None. Other families have to walk through the hall to get to their space." A musing grunt came from deep in his throat. "Shared experience makes the Fourth Ward a tightly knit community."

My girls — my Tiffany Girls, as they liked to call themselves — had any of them lived in a hall room when they arrived? Maybe that's what made Cornelia so serious.

"It's all pretty bleak, then?"

"Not entirely. I've met wonderful, hard-working people who want to give back to the country that took them in. Poverty isn't something deserved because of lack of character. There's nobility in the Lower East Side, just in their perseverance. At the settlement house where I live we're proud that we are now offering the first public bath in the city, soap included. We want to provide services free of the paybacks that Boss Tweed required whenever he did an ounce of charity."

His eyes, dark as jet, flared with specks of light when he said that. He was radiant, happy about making a difference, pleased to tell me about this world so far removed from jeweled peacocks.

"You actually live there?"

"Yes, I do. So I can be more available in crises."

How could a handsome, clean, immaculately dressed, intelligent man be content to be surrounded by poverty?

"You might say I live in the teeming cradle of the promise of this country. The immigrants of the Fourth Ward have troubles, almost insurmountable troubles, but they have dreams too, and ambitions and loves and sorrows. Each person may have left parents and grandparents behind, sisters behind. They gave up their languages and their countries, but each one brings with him a story. Some bring a skill, furniture making or saddlery or ironwork or baking."

"Or glassmaking."

Edwin nodded. "Some bring memories of injustice. Some, only hope. They're going to give us more than they'll get."

I lathered my scone with clotted cream, a twinge of shame at its excess.

He asked, "Do you know this poem?

"Give me your tired, your poor,
Your huddled masses yearning to breathe
    free,
The wretched refuse of your teeming
    shore.
Send these, the homeless, tempest-tost to
    me.

"To *me,* Mrs. Driscoll."

"Clara, please."

"Clara, then. 'To me. I lift my lamp beside the golden door!' "

"No. I haven't heard it before. It's very moving."

"Imperative, you might say. A woman named Emma Lazarus wrote that poem as a donation to an auction to help fund the pedestal of the Statue of Liberty. It's not well known, but I believe someday it will be." He finished his tea in one gulp. "Have you ever been on an excursion boat that circles the statue?"

"Never."

He gripped the edge of the table and leaned toward me. "Let's."

"Now?"

His intensity was magnetic, irresistible.

"Yes. Now."

The new open-air electric streetcar clanged and rattled as it sped us down Fourth Avenue and along Bowery Street, jammed with people and lined with tenements, flophouses, tawdry saloons, and smoldering ash barrels. Pushcarts piled with pots and pans, potatoes and carrots, shoes and used clothing clogged the street. Boys hurried in all directions carrying bundles as if they had immigrated too late and were racing to catch up. For want of a clothespin, some woman's washing that had been draped over a line between two buildings blew off into the running gutter.

"Don't ever come down here by yourself," Edwin said. "The Bowery Boys are more or less gone, but other gangs have taken their place."

As if I would want to. I put my handkerchief to my nose against the foul odor of unwashed bodies. The ceiling strap held by countless grimy hands before me swung like a noose. Apprehensiveness kept my arm tight to my side, but at a lurch of the streetcar, I quickly

106

grabbed it.

Why did he take me this way rather than straight down Broadway to the Battery? Was he in love with misery?

"Where is it you live?"

"A few blocks from here."

Standing on a street corner, a thickset woman in a babushka raised her hand in a timid wave, and Edwin waved back. I was immediately aware of my stylish rose-colored tie at my throat lifting in the breeze in the open car as though it were greeting her too. I took her glance at me not as accusatory of my well-being, only curious.

When the streetcar slowed for a stop, Edwin leapt off and ran to her. He spoke quickly, urgently, leaning down and holding both her hands in his upraised palms. Her head bobbed in happy acknowledgment. He made a move to jump back onto the running board, but then she said something more and he turned back to her and scribbled something on a scrap of paper. The streetcar started to roll and gain speed.

"Stop! Stop!" I shouted in a panic.

The conductor sounded an alarm and the driver slammed on the brakes, which jostled everyone. A little boy was thrown off his mother's lap, and when I stepped off, the conductor yelled at me. I was rattled and miffed as I hurried back to Edwin, who was running toward me.

"What were you thinking?" I cried. "The conductor, the driver, all those people were angry with me. I had to step over a child."

"I'm sorry. I'm sorry, Clara. Are you all right?"

"What was I supposed to do, riding off to God knows where without you?"

"I'm sorry. I had to tell that woman that I found a job for her son. She doesn't speak much English, so I didn't think she got the name of the factory right. I needed to write it for her. I thought I could get back on in time."

I calmed down as we waited for the next streetcar. We sat inside this time, quiet for a few minutes. I could not begrudge Edwin his impulse to help. He had given the woman kindness and a moment of extraordinary humanity, and that was of inestimable value. Could a mosaic or a leaded-glass window do that?

"What's remarkable," he murmured, intent on his thought, as though he had not done anything impulsive or reckless or disregardful of me, "is that most newcomers get out of here in one generation, working day and night to honor the parents who brought them here."

"The same ethic as the Tiffanys," I said, "but I'm sure Mr. Tiffany has never set foot here — he of the opal ring who preaches that beauty is within the reach of everybody."

"There are other kinds of beauty."

108

And he had just shown me one kind. I forgave him at once.

The Iron Steamboat Company's excursion sternwheeler eased out into the harbor among clipper ships, freighters, coal barges, and ferries. Edwin put his frock coat over my shoulders and stood close to block the wind that plastered his white shirtsleeves to his muscular arms. What a shift between rash disregard and thoughtful caring. We chugged near Ellis Island's new immigration station, a two-story wooden structure with low towers at the corners. Nearly half a million people came through last year, Edwin said.

"That's only the beginning. The floodgates are open, Europe is pouring itself out, and we are witnessing the great drama of human migration."

He asked me to imagine the steerage immigrants wearing numbers pinned to their clothing and crowding through turnstiles to have their eyelids pulled up with buttonhooks during the brusque medical checks and health interrogation, New York's version of Judgment Day. The rejected had to go back.

My stomach revolted. What bewilderment had my girls felt as little tots? What humiliation and physical suffering had their parents endured first to get here, and then to be admitted? If the daughters were any indication, Wilhelmina's parents would have stood

109

up to it with square shoulders, but I wasn't so sure about Cornelia's.

Up, out of murky water, the Statue of Liberty proclaimed with upraised arm thirty stories in the air the principles of friendship and welcome and hope, the possibilities of contribution and achievement. Edwin called it by its official name, *Liberty Enlightening the World*. The copper robes of this mighty woman fluttered in the same wind as my muslin skirt did, stirring me to shine.

In the other direction, high above the East River, a roadway had been flung over the tops of masts, suspended on wire threads between two lordly towers with double Gothic arches, six times taller than the five-story skyline. The colossus of the Brooklyn Bridge spoke of courage and daring, genius and human effort on a grand scale. Its effect was inspirational, declaring that sustained effort will bring about brilliant accomplishment. The wind blew away my morose self-pity at not being able to go to the fair as I recognized what a glorious city and time I lived in.

Wilhelmina came to work one morning with a black eye. Shock sliced through me.

"What happened?"

"Nothing."

"Did some man do that to you?" I was outraged at an imagined assailant.

"Oh, no, Mrs. Driscoll. My sweetheart isn't

that kind. He's a gentleman and a butcher."

I would have laughed at what she said if I didn't have to get to the bottom of this. I studied her skeptically. "Then tell me."

"You know how Mr. Tiffany told me not to look at anything ugly but to look for beauty? I was practicing. I walked home through Union Square and saw a handsome young man selling flowers, but when I got to my own street, I only saw ugly things like garbage piles and broken houses and ragged people, so I closed my eyes to walk past them. I bumped into a gaslight."

The story was delivered in fits and starts, and I began to think that it was just that, a preposterous story to cover up what she was too ashamed to tell me. There probably wasn't a single gaslight in her neighborhood in the first place.

"Does it hurt?"

"It hurts you to look at it, so don't. It's ugly."

"Can you see?"

"Oh, I can see all right, but I won't try that again."

Wilhelmina had possibilities here. She was doing fine as a junior selector. If I could get her some outside instruction, I could foresee her as a design assistant someday. Cooper Union had free evening art classes.

"You're right that Mr. Tiffany told us to exercise our eyes. I take that to include looking at good art. Have you ever been to the Metropolitan Museum?"

"No. I don't go uptown."

"Well, then, there's an art exhibit by the night-school art students of Cooper Union, and that's not too far from where you live. I want you to see it. Let's go together on Sunday."

Edwin's descriptions of immigrant life still haunted me, and I needed to see if Wilhelmina lived in a hall room, or just what her living situation was like. I looked at my list of the girls' addresses. Hers wasn't in the worst part of the slums I had seen from the Bowery streetcar.

"I'll come by to pick you up."

"No, no, no," she said with wild eyes. "I'll meet you there."

We finally agreed to meet on her street corner at one o'clock.

I arrived on time and waited, feeling conspicuous just standing there. At one-fifteen there was no sign of her but plenty of lewd looks. This was what Wilhelmina dealt with every day. I kept looking at my watch, though I didn't want to reveal I had one when men or boys passed by. Waiting here was ridiculous. At one-thirty I walked to her address.

The building wasn't a block-long tenement, only a shabby wooden apartment house, a fire trap if there ever was one. As I walked up bare stairs, through a corridor with odd little twists and turns, up a step, down two, the deafening hum and rattle of treadle sewing machines assailed me. I could see half a dozen machines going at once through doors open for a breath of air, whole families bending over them. So this was what Edwin meant by tenement sweatshops organized by middlemen, each driving a closer bargain than his rival tyrant across the hall. Trade unions had no jurisdiction over such enterprises, he had said.

A mere girl at one machine, her arms to the elbows smeared black with the color of the cloth, looked up as I passed, her feet at that instant riding the momentum of the treadle passively. I carried the stark image of her with me down the hall.

Steam came out of Wilhelmina's open door, and irons for pressing clothes were heating on a stove. She held one in her hand, wearing only her shift. Apparently proprieties didn't matter here. Piles of garments lay on the floor.

"I'm not finished," she wailed.

A large woman I took to be her mother was working next to her on another pressing board.

"Who's this?" the woman snapped. Her hair was tangled into greasy hanks, and I saw at once what a mammoth, complicated effort it was for Wilhelmina to come to work looking groomed and respectable.

"This is Mrs. Driscoll, Mama. She's the lady I work for."

The woman's crazed eyes darted uncontrollably, as though looking for something familiar from the Old World that would give her respectability. Finding nothing, she snarled, "Who told you she could come here?" Her thick arm was in the air in a flash, and she landed a stinging slap on Wilhelmina's cheek underneath the black eye.

Wilhelmina didn't flinch, just turned her mother's rage on me. "I didn't say you could come here. I told you to meet me at the corner."

"I'm sorry. I should have waited. We'll do it another time."

I escaped quickly, feeling awful about abandoning her to her life.

On the way home, I wondered when the brutality had begun. Wilhelmina had taken the slap without so much as a blink. How strong she was, able to put the rawness of her life behind her the moment she stepped into the studio.

The trip over must have started the mother on this road — being crammed into pens and processed like cattle, not at all what she had imagined — and seeing now that she would never live comfortably in the new country, she struck out at any provocation. If only her mother were working at Tiffany's too. I felt sure the beauty of the work and the kindness of the girls would soften her. A woman can't stay hard when all around her is loveliness.

When I walked in the front door of 44 Irving Place, the parlor was crowded and noisy with shouts and clapping. George was dancing on a table in stockinged feet, swiveling his narrow hips suggestively, pushing out his flat chest, gyrating his shoulders, twirling his red handkerchief above his head.

"What in the world?"

"It's the hootchy-kootchy!" he shouted.

"Little Egypt performed it in the Cairo section of the Midway Plaisance," Hank explained, "wearing only fringe and a veil. She scandalized and delighted thousands."

"All along I thought the fair was about art and industry," said Mr. Hackley.

"It was! The belly dance is an art form." George gave a quick thrust of his hip sideways as he flung his handkerchief at Mrs. Hackley. "And it takes industry to perform it."

Mrs. Hackley swatted the handkerchief away from her as though it were his unmentionables.

"Begging the gentleman's pardon," Merry said. "Get down off my table, George Waldo, or I'll take a shillelagh to your backside and send you flying clear to Dublin!"

George wagged his behind in her direction, tempting her, then jumped down and held out his palm for tips.

"Which one of you gave him permission to be so corky?" Merry demanded.

"No one. Our George doesn't suffer from requiring permission," I said. "Tell us about the fair."

"The Midway leading to the entrance was a mile long," George said.

"Decidedly lowbrow," Hank scoffed. "Barnum's circus, William Cody's Wild West Show, and Blarney Castle." He gave a nod to Merry who huffed at his insinuation.

"There was a giant wheel more than twenty-five stories high." George swung his arm up in a big arc. "Our answer to the Eiffel Tower, only you could ride it, sixty people in a cabin."

"You could see the whole White City laid out between canals with hundreds of gondolas and gondoliers, lovely boys they were, imported from Venice," Hank said.

"Six hundred acres of bridges, arches, temples, palaces, monuments, hanging gardens." George was flailing his arms. "At night it was a fairyland."

"Blazing with three times the electricity used by all of Chicago," Hank the Fact-finder added. "People came from all over the world. It's expected that by the end of the fair, twenty-seven million people will have attended. That's roughly half the population of the country!"

"Hard to believe," said Mr. Hackley.

"A guide told me that he answered a hundred questions an hour, and three-quarters of them repeated the same thing." Hank looked at me. " 'Where's Tiffany's exhibit?' "

"Truly?"

"To be honest, they probably meant Tiffany and Company, to see the one-hundred-twenty-five-carat diamond revolving and shooting off sparks. There was also a smaller one, a mere seventy-seven carats, along with the most costly array of jewelry, gems, tiaras —"

"What about *my* Tiffany?"

"Clocks, crystal, and silver ever made. Even engraved silver spurs."

"Oh, wonder of wonders. I'm sure the horse gallops faster spurred on by a work of art," I said.

"Smith and Wesson revolvers made of silver and inset with turquoise and lapis lazuli."

"I'd much prefer being killed by a gun with turquoise rather than lapis."

"And gold and silver vases, bowls, and platters studded with enormous pearls, jade, cut gems —" Hank said.

"Tell me about the chapel!" I demanded.

"And a magnificent silver ice bowl decorated with enameled holly leaves and mother-of-pearl berries. Two silver polar bears supported it, surrounded by large rock-crystal chunks that represented icebergs protruding from pine needles and pinecones worked in silver. So gorgeous it made me shiver."

"Quit teasing me. What about *my* Tiffany?"

"Fifty-four medals to his father's fifty-six," Hank said. "Their joint pavilion was well positioned in the center of the behemoth Manufacturing and Liberal Arts Building, the largest building in the world."

With an air of importance, George declared, "No doubt about it, your chapel is the most original contribution to the fair."

I slapped my hand over my mouth.

"People were astonished at being surrounded by the exhibit, freely walking around *inside* a work of art rather than looking at something untouchable beyond a silk museum cord," George said. "You could stand under an enormous electrolier shaped like a cross no matter from what direction you looked at it. Green fire gleamed behind emerald glass."

He pulled out a small notebook from his breast pocket. "The altar was white marble with a mosaic front of iridescent glass, mother-of-pearl, onyx, and alabaster. Risers faced with mosaic led up to it, and it displayed a jeweled filigree tabernacle of brass, amber, abalone shell, and jade. Behind it, a series of wide concentric arches were supported by mosaic columns in rose and green."

"What about my peacock panel?"

"Stunning. The arches framed it, and it was set into a wall of black marble, which made it all the more brilliant. Light from the electro-lier created highlights on the chipped chunks of glass you talked about. A triumph, Clara."

"People crowded in day and night," Hank said, "because your windows were lit with electric lights behind them and diffused by a plate of milky glass so it looked like daylight."

"How did people respond?"

George gave me a loving look. "Oh, Clara." He sighed. "They were entranced. They took off their hats and spoke in low voices as if they were in a holy place."

BOOK TWO
1895–1897

CHAPTER 9
EMERALD

"I'm proposing marriage to you." George dropped to the floor on one knee. "On behalf of my brother."

I laughed. "Get up, Puck. He's had more than two years to do it for himself if he had wanted to."

I laid out my mended silk stockings on the bed next to my new emerald-green skirt, way beyond my means. George had picked it out on a shopping trip for me to wear this evening with his brother. My sly black satin sash and the deceptive leg-of-mutton sleeves on my white organdy blouse would magically make my waist look smaller.

"Magic in love plots only works in Shakespeare's comedies and Italian opera," I said. "One has a happy ending, and the other . . . Well, you know how most operas end."

"With a swan song." He let his head fall.

"Marriage is risky business under the best of circumstances, let alone when orchestrated by a sprite."

"Edwin yearns for you. His admiration makes him tongue-tied. He's afraid you'll turn him down." He got up and walked in a circle, exhilarated by an idea. "It would be a delicious kind of union — plucky New Woman and idealistic New Man."

I gazed at George, slightly younger than Edwin, more spirited, more creative, more intoxicated with life.

"I'd much rather it were you," I said softly.

"No, you wouldn't. Two artists in a marriage make for a slippery fish of an existence."

"I'd be willing to be the steady breadwinner, though it wouldn't be for conservative Mr. Tiffany, and you could continue to carry on with Hank and Dudley."

He patted my cheek. "Generous of you, but that wouldn't satisfy you, and you know it, nor would it do your reputation any good."

"It was just a wild thought."

"Besides, I'm irresponsible. He's responsible. I'm capricious. He's merely precious." He made it rhyme, and then giggled at his own cleverness.

"True. You are capricious."

George and Edwin were brothers in blood but not in temperament. Where Edwin read about great artists of the past, George himself was a painter and a designer. While Edwin became sullen in temperatures below forty degrees, George was wild about ice skating. While Edwin scrupulously saved half of every paycheck, George scrupulously spent all — on paint and canvas, opera and concert tickets, dinners at the Waldorf Hotel — and sometimes had to appeal to Edwin to tide him over. To George, "the humanities" meant the enjoyment of art and theater. To Edwin, it meant the struggling immigrants on the Lower East Side. I gave serious, depressing novels to Edwin, like Stephen Crane's new *Maggie: A Girl of the Streets.* With George I gave myself over to frivolity and singing popular tunes.

Edwin's thoughtful aspects had revealed themselves modestly during the last two years. He had deep compassion for people, an understanding of social forces, and an appreciation for history as a record of the triumphs and tragedies of the common man — all of which I admired.

While I was putting on my one pair of earrings, George peered through my kaleidoscope. "Oh! Ah! I see a bright future for you."

"You have to leave. I have to get dressed."

"You have to think about it."

"You have to be quiet about it." I shooed him out with a wave of both hands.

It was hard to imagine that they were brothers. Edwin was economical with his emotions, spending them on ideas and near strangers, whereas George was a spendthrift of sentiment in all directions. Edwin demonstrated his emotional range by a tipping of his head, a raised eyebrow, a slow smile I cherished all the more for its rarity when it was directed at me. George demonstrated his by a flapping of arms, a loud whistle, a few dance steps. Edwin stated, whereas George cooed.

As I came downstairs, I heard Edwin talking to Mr. Hackley about Utah becoming a state. Mr. Hackley objected because of the polygamy practiced there. Edwin was more tolerant, reasoning that, like the other love that cannot be named, it fell under Thomas Jefferson's category of the pursuit of happiness. He cut off the conversation and stood up when he heard my taffeta skirt rustle on the stairs.

"You look beautiful tonight," he said, and he did smile, broadly, genuinely, handsomely. There was something more in it than usual, something barely contained about to burst out.

He traced a circle in the air, and I spun around. "A regular Gibson girl, you are," he said. "I'm enchanted."

I glanced at George, whose expression was like a boy having just won a game of marbles. I put on my hat at the front entry mirror. It was my old black velvet, but I had taken it to a milliner who spruced it up with curled black feathers and a black satin ribbon.

George pursed his lips and shook his head. "No." He tugged it to one side a bit. "There. Divine."

I had the feeling he wanted to be a mouse in my pocket, peering out into this evening.

Edwin helped me on with my opera cloak and donned his top hat, which seemed to signal that great things would happen tonight. We were off in a hired carriage to the Tiffany Ball at the Majestic Hotel, uptown on Central Park West and Seventy-second Street, where new luxury apartments overlooking the park were creeping northward. A yearly winter event, the ball was a magnanimous thing for Mr. Tiffany to provide for his employees and friends.

A bevy of footmen in livery met us at the hotel entrance. Inside, butlers in tuxedos ushered us into the upstairs ballroom, where mirrors multiplied the massive flower arrangements. Beneath hanging crystal electroliers, guests were announced as they approached the receiving line. I caught the names of people Mr. Tiffany had mentioned to me — the notoriously wild, redheaded architect Stanford White; the textile designer and Mr. Tiffany's onetime partner, Candace Wheeler; the painters Samuel Colman and William Merritt Chase; and the designer Lockwood de Forest. I was surprised to hear Mr. Tiffany's rival, John La Farge, announced. Apparently their competition had a veneer of gentility.

Mr. Nash, manager of the glass factory; Mr. McIlhenny, the chemist; Mr. Platt, treasurer;

Mr. Mitchell, business manager; and Mr. Belknap, artistic director, all wearing black swallowtail coats, stood in the receiving line like a quintet of starched penguins. Mr. Belknap was the only one with a red rather than white carnation. I felt proud of Edwin in his paisley silk waistcoat under his black frock coat. Mr. Tiffany was charming everyone at the end of the line. With a flutter inside, I anticipated my turn to be greeted.

"How canny you are, Mrs. Driscoll. You knew that emerald green is my favorite color."

"I don't believe you have a favorite color, Mr. Tiffany. It would cause you pain to leave a single color out of your affections."

He introduced his wife informally as Lou. A socialite at ease, bedecked in orchids, she wore a silk gown in heliotrope to match the flowers, designed, no doubt, by Worth or Paquin. She was gracious, sensuous, and over-jeweled — a hothouse bloom. When I introduced Edwin as assistant to the director of University Settlement, she became animated rather than polished, and spoke of her own charitable work for the New York Infirmary for Women and Children, particularly its tenement outpatient and hygiene service. Later they had a lengthy conversation that left me free to dance with Mr. Belknap, whose feet, I noticed, were definitely shorter than mine.

I couldn't look him in the face at that close

range. The eyebrows. At a distance of eight feet, they looked natural enough, but four feet was dicey and one foot impossible. For our opera and philharmonic evenings, I'd had to train myself to look at his meticulously clipped and waxed mustache.

As we spun around in a waltz, I could see over his shoulder, and spotted Frank, the deaf-and-dumb janitor, for once not in his dungarees, radiant. With his eyes riveted to my every move, he bobbed his head in time to my steps.

When the orchestra took a break, Mr. Belknap introduced me to Candace Wheeler, and I asked her how she became interested in the decorative arts. She explained that at the Philadelphia World's Fair almost twenty years earlier, she had seen a needlework exhibit of the Kensington School in London, which provided training and commercial outlets in needlework to what the English called "decayed gentlewomen." Seeing a similar need in America, she established the Society of Decorative Art.

"You make it sound like it happened easily."

"Oh, no. It was a challenge to convince women that their handwork was worthy of monetary remuneration, and wasn't just something they did to decorate their own linens."

She informed me that Mr. Tiffany was on

the advisory board, and that led to their eventual partnership in the early interior decorating firm of Associated Artists.

"He's a reckless genius, more in love with ways than means. He was haunted by the windows of Notre Dame and Chartres in those early days." She reflected a moment, and then added, "I owe to him my change of perspective from running a philanthropic organization and amateur educational scheme to running a business. I'll never forget the day he declared, in that boastful way he has, 'We're going after the money that there is in art.' "

I wondered if she knew that he hadn't "gone after" it with the success he had claimed he would have. Instead, he had "gone after" beauty, whatever the cost.

I told her that there were thirty-five girls in the Women's Department now, and she commended me enthusiastically, which made me feel wonderful. Almost all of them were here. The younger ones were chatty and nervous in their best muslin frocks. A few clung to me and ogled Edwin. I was sure he would be the subject of whispers in the studio next week.

Wilhelmina had her butcher boy in tow, the Romeo she prattled on about to anyone who would listen, proclaiming how much he loved her. Fortunately he cleaned up pretty well and didn't appear to have a film of beef blood on his knuckles. The free champagne, which her constitution wasn't accustomed to, had gone to her head, and she promenaded around the room, swaying like a tree in a windstorm, talking to anyone who gave her a glance, and after each circumnavigation, with flushed face and chest heaving, she gave me a report.

Leaning toward me, she said, "Take a look at Mrs. Tiffany's fingers. That isn't no chipped glass in those rings. Those are genuine rubies and emeralds."

"Oh, so you're not only an expert on birds. You're a gemologist now. What's next? Archeology?"

She was having the time of her life, and I was glad for her.

"How much of this night are you going to tell your mother?"

"Not one stinking word. I don't live with her now."

"Then where do you live?"

"I stayed with my aunt for a while, but she got to tattling to my mother, so I moved in with some girls who work at the big Triangle Shirtwaist Factory. They're not allowed to talk at work. You'll never find me working in a jail like that."

Off she went blithely on another circuit of the room while Candace Wheeler told me about the success of her Women's Exchange in finding markets for women's crafts. Wil-

131

helmina came back to report that Mr. Belknap smelled like a flower and wore a paper collar. After peering at Edwin out of the corner of her eye, she whispered, "I oughta tell you that Mr. Tall-enough gives you the glad-eye every time you're not looking his way. Has he asked you to marry him yet? He looks rich enough."

"Don't talk nonsense, Wilhelmina."

God love her, she had become a favorite.

I was proud of Edwin's ability to mingle as comfortably with Wilhelmina's gentleman butcher as with Mr. and Mrs. Tiffany. I found Edwin more than adequate in the waltz but a little less comfortable with the new two-step. It didn't matter. What did matter were the little signs of affection he gave me. Still, I didn't want to fall prey to a man just because I wanted to have that weightless gladness of being in love.

In the carriage coming home, he said, "Mrs. Tiffany is a marvel of the double standard. She can give attention to a tenement mother's hygienic needs in the morning, and spend enough at Delmonico's that evening to feed that mother's family for a year."

It was true. We straddled a double world.

"Better that than her not doing anything at all, Edwin."

Although he was restless on the way back to Irving Place, he did not get out of the carriage in front of the boardinghouse. Instead,

132

he took both my hands in his, and with a deep breath that raised his chest, he said without preamble, "I'm in love with you, Clara. You must know that."

An instant of perilous pleasure flared in me and then subsided just as quickly.

"What's more, I want you to love me. There's a kind of love that makes you feel like you can do anything. That's what I feel for you. Have I only imagined that you could give that love to me?"

I wasn't going to answer that. I certainly didn't know.

"I have a plan for us. A business opportunity has been offered to me, which I'm keen to pursue. It's to assist in managing a coffee plantation owned by a stock company in Mexico near Veracruz. I want you to come with me, Clara. As my wife."

My throat and face burned as though I had gulped hot coffee. Yearning and skepticism and the incipient love I had kept at a distance tumbled chaotically, each holding an instant's sway.

"We would have a plantation house built to suit us."

Mexico. I had always been fascinated by Mexico. Artists needed travel to deepen their well of creative sources. Was I to limit myself to Tiffany as my sole source of inspiration?

"If I accept for two years, I would earn enough to set us up in a fine apartment like we saw tonight overlooking Central Park — I know how you love it. I've thought of little else for half a year. It has taken me that long to muster the courage to ask. If I had let this chance slip by, I was afraid I'd never ask. Please, Clara, tell me you will."

"I . . . This is too much to grasp all at once. I'm so fully involved at the studio. Mr. Tiffany has a policy not to keep on any married women."

I felt him back away on the carriage seat. "You never told me that."

"I never had occasion to."

He rallied enough to say, "You do care for me, don't you? Tell me that."

I touched his smooth cheek in the darkness. "Yes, I do care for you." And I felt myself caring more and more.

"You know that I'm reliable. My parents in Connecticut are in favor of the plan and will provide for our needs in the transition."

"How can you leave your work at the settlement house?"

He was quiet a moment. "It's draining, sometimes overwhelming. It will still be there when I, when we, come back, and I'll be in a better position then to help in larger ways. In politics, I mean."

I felt his hands tight around mine.

"And George? He knows about this?"

"Yes. He will come twice a year to paint. You could paint with him. Will you at least consider it?"

I gave him the slightest of nods, and instantly felt the turn of the kaleidoscope, a faint clatter of glass in colors of emerald and ruby and sapphire.

CHAPTER 10
ROSE

"The real art, after the preliminary design of a window, is in the hands of the glass selector," I said to the three I was promoting to glass selection, among them my friend Alice Gouvy, who had finished at Art Students League and had come to work here.

"Mr. Tiffany says the first thing a person sees in a window isn't the subject. It's the color," I continued.

It was a perfect day to be teaching glass selection because light was pouring in through the big windows. I demonstrated by choosing an outlined shape from a cartoon, peeling off the corresponding pattern piece stuck on the clear-glass easel, and holding a large, uncut panel of multihued glass up to the cartoon and then to the easel to see what that glass would look like with light shining through it. I moved it around, turned it over, rotated it, and found an area on it that suited that section of the cartoon.

"One wrong piece, wrong in color or in

texture or in degree of opacity or transparency, can ruin a window. By its disharmony, it will attract the eye." I showed them pieces that would be mistakes.

"What if we can't carry on because there isn't a piece of glass that suits us?" asked Minnie Henderson, an English girl, very refined. She lived uptown with her parents and always wore a narrow black silk tie over her starched, high-necked white waist, a different one for each day of the week. Then she would start over with the Monday one the next week. Alice had found her for me at Art Students League.

"Then go to Miss Stoney, or come to me. We can combine two or three layers, even four or five, to get the exact color or depth that you need. Or I can go down to the basement and have a look."

"Ask me," Wilhelmina said from her worktable. "I like mucking around down there. We got thousands of types and colors of glass all stacked on their edges in wooden slots, thirty or forty shades of green, enough to make a body dizzy."

"Since when have you been down there?"

"Since the first week I came to work, truth to tell. I went during lunch, and nobody stopped me. I've been all over this building. The furniture department, the fabrics and wallpapers room, the metal shop, the men's glass studio. There's a nice view of Madison

Square Garden tower from the roof. Mr. Tiffany said always to look for beauty."

Why was I surprised? It was Wilhelmina, after all. Brazen Wilhelmina, toughened by a crazed mother.

She had their attention, so I let her continue. "We got glass that's ridged, rippled, bumpy with big and little bumps, rough, and wavy. Some bubbly like with blisters, and some like you scraped it with a comb."

"How are they made that way?" Minnie asked.

I explained that texture makers, like bakers' rolling pins, are rolled across molten glass poured into a pan at a precise temperature. "Sometimes glass shards or flakes of a different color are scattered before the glass is poured. That's called fractured glass, or confetti glass."

I showed them a piece that had lighter spots in it called mottles, which were good for showing light coming through petals and leaves.

"Don't forget twig glass," Wilhelmina said.

She had named glass with threads or striations of other hues twig glass because we used it for trees.

"Take advantage of irregularities and happy accidents of coloring. When you find an area that satisfies you, use a narrow grease pencil to trace the paper pattern onto the glass, and give it to your cutter."

"What if it's in the middle of a sheet of glass?" Alice asked.

"That's all right. Nothing will be wasted."

I showed them the traditional method of securing the pieces together with flexible lead strips called cames. "Look straight at the end of this came. See how it's shaped like the capital letter *I* with a groove on both sides? That's so it surrounds the edges of two pieces of glass at once. When all the pieces are stuck to the glass easel with wax and the cames are in place, the window will go to the Glazing Department, where the cames will be soldered and patinated."

"We're not permitted to see it when it's finished?" Minnie asked.

"Not usually."

"But you can sneak into the men's department when they're having their beer break at three o'clock and take a look, and no one's the wiser," Wilhelmina said.

I pretended exasperation, and went on to explain Mr. Tiffany's new method for smaller pieces or complicated patterns. In those cases, narrow strips of thin copper foil were wrapped around the edges of each piece of glass. In order to make it stick, the side of the foil that would touch the glass was coated with beeswax. The outer side of the foil was treated with muriatic acid, which allowed the solder to bond the foiled edges of two pieces of glass.

"After each piece of glass is cut and foiled, the assistants apply a spot of beeswax on the back of it and stick it onto the clear easel. That helps the selector see what she's building up."

Mr. Belknap came into the studio, so I gave the girls their assignments and had them begin. He showed me a small brochure titled *Louis Comfort Tiffany's Glass Mosaics, 1895,* and told me to look on the second page. There it was in black and white: "Many of the firm's great mosaic projects have been executed by women."

"Wonder of wonders! It's the first time he's publicly acknowledged that the fifth floor exists. He didn't waste much ink, though. Just a little more and he could have put in my name."

"Then what would you do with it?"

Show it to Edwin. I wanted him to understand what I would be giving up if I married him. If. If. The big If.

I lifted my shoulders. "It just hurts to be anonymous."

He offered a consoling look. "The Philharmonic is presenting a Mozart program. Are you at liberty to accompany me the Saturday after next?"

After only a moment's hesitation I replied, "Yes. I love Mozart."

"Then let's meet at Sherry's, Fifth Avenue at Thirty-seventh, at five o'clock for dinner first. Oh, and Mr. Tiffany wants you to come to his office."

"Is something wrong?"

His precisely drawn eyebrows lifted in unison. "Something is very right!"

Humming mysteriously, he accompanied me downstairs, but he wouldn't tell me what it was. When I peeked in the open door little Napoléon was hopping, actually hopping from side to side, next to Mr. Nash.

"Look, Clara! A breakthrough! Iridescence on blown glass! We've done it!"

The second breakthrough: my first name. He used my first name.

A dozen vases stood on the display table. Iridescence bathed the full bodies of some, and only glinted in decorative gesture strokes on others. He pranced around the table, and we looked at them together from all angles.

"They're gorgeous. I knew you would succeed."

He was breathing the heady ether that lingers after high moments of life, and I was inhaling his exhale. Though my department had nothing to do with blown glass, he had called me downstairs to see what was so vital to him, knowing I would rejoice with him. That had to mean *something.*

"We've been calling it Favrile glass to make the Italian term, *fabrile,* for 'handmade,' sound more French," Mr. Tiffany explained.

141

"When do you think you'll begin selling them?"

"Not yet. This first year's production will go to museums — the Smithsonian, the Art Institute of Chicago, the Victoria and Albert, the Musée des Arts Décoratifs du Louvre, and the Imperial Museum of Tokyo."

"What about the Metropolitan? You're leaving out your own hometown!"

He lifted his chin, as though that would make him taller to match this success. "Henry Havemeyer has promised to purchase at least fifty to present to them. I'm setting aside the finest for him."

With a pang, I thought, How could I ever think of leaving this melting pot of creativity? Or leaving him? He had mentioned my department in the brochure, a sure sign of broader recognition to come. And he had wanted to share his triumph with me — no other woman. Now, with connections to the world's greatest museums, what might the future of my own work be? Would it ever be in a museum? What about our secret of leaded-glass lampshades?

On my bed that evening lay a letter under a single creamy white rose.

My dear Clara,
May I call you that? I have done so in my own mind for months.

142

I can see you are the archetype of an independent woman who lives singly, experiences broadly, and has a fine and satisfying vocation. I respect you for that, but I promise that you will have more adventures with me than by yourself.

I've been extremely busy, which is the only thing that has kept me from your doorstep day and night. Wednesday evening I met with a group beginning to organize a Citizens Union to support governmental reform in the interests of the common citizen. J. P. Morgan was there. I made my last speech at eleven-thirty. Then last night was the meeting of the Allied Political Clubs and I was at work all afternoon and until midnight with them. The striking garment workers are having a starving time. I am doing all I can to help them, and am confident they will win. I'm scheduled to speak at another mass meeting at the Great Hall of the Cooper Union on Monday evening. There will be plenty of left-wing progressives there to hear me. They have asked me to run for the State Assembly, but it's the wrong time if we go to Mexico. (I am using "we" even though you haven't said yes, so you will get used to the idea. I hope I will hear it from your lips soon.) If they want me now, they'll want me in a year or two, and then I'll have seed money to mount a campaign. So, as I promised you, life with me will be adventurous.

I am studying Spanish.

Con amor,
Tu apasianado Edwin

Oh, sweet Edwin! How fast his thinking flew. Feverishly fast. It bedazzled me.

Despite my admiration for his commitment to social concerns, he would have done just as well sending only the rose. One rose alone. I appreciated his restraint from Gilded Age excess, but more than that, I appreciated the reflectiveness a single bloom offers. This one, not fully open, had no blemish visible to signal a premature demise, unless one lurked unseen in the whorl of its petals. From what I could see now, the curled petals promised the joy of a full life in which, yes, there might be extraordinary adventures. Yet I longed to render roses in glass. My double-lobed heart split with a thunderous crack, Mr. Tiffany and Edwin each claiming half.

I sat on my bed in a haze, twirling the rose between my thumb and finger until a solution presented itself. I would have to convince Mr. Tiffany to change his policy — if not for all, then just for me, if I could get him to consider me indispensable. If I couldn't, and if I did marry Edwin, I might come to resent it as my second marriage of sacrifice. In the months ahead, I would have to be brilliant enough that Mr. Tiffany would grant me anything.

Chapter 11
Chrysanthemum

I arrived at work the next day to find Wilhelmina sitting on my desk.

"I will be married soon," she said, "so I guess that means I have to leave."

"I won't hear of it. You're too young." I gave her a backhand wave, and she hopped off.

"I'm eighteen. Old enough. My mother married younger than that in Sweden."

"You told me you were seventeen when I hired you, and that was three years ago!"

She looked me dead in the eye. "I lied."

Momentary shock turned to anger that I'd been duped. "You're a liar, then? You lied about that black eye too. Your mother did that, didn't she?"

"Doesn't matter. I want what's due me so I can set up a room for us."

"For you and this butcher boy? You're serious, then."

"He has a name, Mrs. Driscoll. It's Ned Steffens, and he loves me."

"This studio means nothing to you? The

146

joy in the work? This is a good life, Wilhelmina, infinitely better than what you would have . . . otherwise. You're a fine selector, one of the best."

"I'll be a fine wife. It's decided."

She picked up a chipped chunk of amber glass and held it to her ring finger. "May I have this? Mr. Tiffany told me to look for beauty."

"Take it. Take it. Maybe it will remind you of what you've left."

I was stricken by her shortsighted decision. I imagined the narrow steps to the cramped room she would share with Ned, a mere crevice between dingy, windowless walls without so much as room enough to swing her arms, the stairway leading only to the blind alleys of her life. I insisted on having her address even if it was temporary, and her aunt's as well, so that I could keep track of her and send her something, which I did, two sets of towels, with a note wishing her well.

She responded a few weeks later to thank me and tell me that her butcher had a chance as a foreman at a Chicago slaughterhouse, so the wedding was put off for a while. I wrote her a note saying I would take her on again at the studio, even for a short time. I never heard back from her.

Glum Mr. Bainbridge, the portly actor with an expensive toupee well worn, I mean worn

147

well, had written a play, and most of the boarders plus Edwin and George were going to see him perform in it.

"What kind of a role do you play?" asked Edwin, whom I had invited to dinner.

Mr. Bainbridge stared solemnly at his meat pie. "A rollicking young man of twenty-three who is very funny."

Him? I had to control a snicker.

The buzzer sounded, and Merry excused herself to answer it. She came back ashen-faced.

"Clara, there's an Officer O'Malley wants to speak with you."

Edwin, George, and Bernard all raised their heads.

Mrs. Hackley poked the air with her fork. "See? I told you, Mr. Hackley. The morals of women who work in factories eventually decline."

"Shush, Maggie," Mr. Hackley snapped.

I felt all eyes following me through the arch into the parlor. Not a single teacup clattered in a saucer. The stocky, sandy-haired policeman stood with his hands behind his back, looking tired and bored.

"Evenin' to you. Might you be Clara?"

"I am. Clara Driscoll."

He pulled a letter from his pocket. "This be your hand?"

"Yes, I wrote this. How did you get it, if I may ask?"

148

"Her complete name."

"Wilhelmina Agnes Wilhelmson. She used to work at Tiffany Glass and Decorating Company. I was her immediate superior." Queasiness washed over me. "What happened?"

"Recognize this?" He pulled from his pocket the amber chunk of chipped glass. It was encased in rusty wire, which had been formed into a ring.

"Yes. I gave it to her. Tell me what happened."

"Worth anything?"

"No. It's only glass."

"A girl was found in Blind Man's Alley in the Fourth Ward just before six this morning, writhing and groaning but unable to speak. An empty bottle labeled CARBOLIC ACID was found next to her. Your letter and this piece of glass were in her pocket. She died in hospital an hour after they got her there."

A small, shrill sound came out of my mouth as I sank onto the settee. Edwin and George rushed into the parlor and surrounded me, holding me from both sides, and Bernard and Merry stood by helplessly.

"Will you kindly come with me to identify the body?"

I agreed, numb at the thought.

"I'm going with you," Edwin said.

"There was no envelope," the officer said, "only this address written on your letter. Do

149

you know where she lived?"

"I can't be sure. I have three addresses for her."

"Bring them."

Climbing into the police wagon, I glanced back at George and Bernard and Merry watching from the stoop, and I missed the running board. Edwin caught me. Inside, he drew my head to his shoulder and held it there.

"I'm sorry. I know she meant a lot to you," he said.

It was all too much like a seduced-and-abandoned tale in a cheap novel.

"Why didn't she come to me? I could have told her that she would live through it, whatever it was. We could have had her back working in the studio. Her love for the work would have saved her."

"Don't take it on yourself."

The foyer of the morgue in the Fourth Ward was a New World Bedlam, packed with weeping immigrants. Languages didn't divide people here. Crying was universal. Officer O'Malley pushed his way through to the coroner's desk, and I followed, my legs untrustworthy. I held on to Edwin.

The coroner led us through a cold hallway where small bodies lay shoulder to shoulder under a filthy cloth. In the women's hall, he found number 2487 and peeled back the gray covering down to her shoulders. Her face was grotesquely contorted. I nodded yes and buried my face in Edwin's chest.

Back in the corridor, the policeman spoke to two reporters, and then asked me, "Do you know of anyone who had reason to kill her?"

"No one."

He flattened a crumpled piece of paper for me to read.

Wilhelmina,

I'm staying at Chicago. The slotterhouse work is stedy. Don't try to find me. The place will make you sick. I never ment to marry you any how. That was all your fansy idea. Stay with your pretty peeple and pretty little glass things and forgit I ever lived.

Ned

Fury exploded in my chest.
When in disgrace with fortune and men's eyes leapt to mind.

"Those addresses, ma'am. I have to notify next of kin."

I pictured the crazed mother raving at the news in that steamy room, flinging out her heavy arm, shame making her unhinged, afraid of me, of the police, the landlord, the sweatshop boss. Dread threatened to sink me.

"May I come with you?" I blurted.

Edwin grabbed my shoulders. "You don't have to do that."

"I loved her, Edwin."

The officer put the letter into his coat pocket. "Suit yourself."

No one answered the knock at her parents' apartment, where the sewing machines were still going even in the evening. We checked in the rooms next door to no avail, so we went to the aunt's address. Wretched smells assaulted us at each dark landing. Wilhelmina's mother and aunt and three small children huddled together, terrified at the sight of the policeman. I identified myself to try to make them less fearful.

"What happened?" Her mother's face was drawn tight to steel herself.

The officer's explanation brought wails and sobbing from the aunt but stony silence from the mother. It was her eyes that wrenched me — dark bubbles floating in watery milk, defeated eyes that saw the new country the way it would always be for her — unjust and barren.

"She lied to us." The aunt turned to me as though it were my fault. "She told us she was working as a laundress in Connecticut."

The officer showed Ned's letter to Wilhelmina's mother.

"She was a fool!" the mother said.

"Whatever else you might think of her, Mrs.

152

Wilhelmson, she was a good girl and a fine worker, well liked by the other girls. I looked forward to seeing her every day. Please try not to harden your heart against her."

First thing the next morning I went to Mr. Tiffany's office and told him, holding myself together while I spoke.

"Oh, no, no, no," he murmured, shaking his head slowly. "Was she the big girl who told me flamingoes don't eat out of a person's hand?"

"Yes." The memory gave us a moment's respite. "She had cheek."

"I'm so sorry. I know how you care for all your girls." The lines in his forehead deepened. "Did she have a father?"

"Yes, and a mother."

The thought of Wilhelmina's hardened mother brought on embarrassing tears. I should never have gone to their house when Wilhelmina told me not to. Instantly Mr. Tiffany offered me his crisp white handkerchief, and I sobbed into its embroidered LCT.

After I got control of myself, he asked softly, "Would you like me to tell the girls?"

"No. Thank you. I will, but it would be nice if you came upstairs later and said something to them."

At that moment, I didn't know what to do with his handkerchief.

"You keep it, Clara."

■ ■ ■ ■

In the big studio, the morning started the same as any other morning, and I realized that the younger girls did not read newspapers. It would be the hardest thing I would ever have to do in this room, I hoped. I could tell by Alice's face that she already knew and was waiting for me to tell the others. Agnes came out of her separate studio at the opposite end of the workroom from mine, given to her recently because of her privileged position as a window designer. I could see that the three older women — Miss Stoney, Miss Byrne, and Miss Judd — also knew. All five must have read it in the *Times*. It had to be now.

"I regret that I have something very sad to tell you." I paused for their attention, squeezing his handkerchief. "Our friend and coworker, Wilhelmina, has taken her life."

Stunned silence, and then a barrage of questions and a flood of tears. Alice, Agnes, the three older misses, and I tried to comfort the younger girls, making the rounds, holding those who needed it, lending handkerchiefs.

Mr. Tiffany appeared in the doorway with a bouquet of white chrysanthemums. His mere presence made the girls draw away from one another, blow their noses, and turn toward

154

him. He set the vase on a worktable in the center of the studio.

"I come on a sad occasion today."

Oh, Lord, please don't let him give one of his inflated speeches.

"The loss of any one of you is a loss to all of us. We must remember her for the happiness and humor she brought to us. I hope you'll be comforted in knowing that Wilhelmina will have a spread of chrysanthemums, gladioli, and lilies, and that her parents will be likewise remembered. If any of you wish to go to her services, you may have the time off with no loss of wage."

He almost got through it without a lisp. *Chrysanthemums* tripped him up, but he struck just the right fatherly tone. In that moment, for me, he had grown into his inherited middle name. Comfort.

God taking from us and loving us at the same time by providing comforters was a kind of spiritual equanimity. It seemed a phenomenon of life how a death insinuates us into the debt of those who stand by us in trouble and console us. This morning, I felt utterly bound to Mr. Tiffany and utterly bound to Edwin, contraries though they were. I loved both of them for trying to make it easier on me.

By mid-morning, after the girls had cried themselves out, a dull silence had settled, and one by one, starting with the conscientious

Miss Judd, they took up their work, the soft sounds of glass snippers and double-bladed shears familiar and soothing.

CHAPTER 12
SIDEWALKS

We waited in the parlor for everyone to come in order to go together to see the Tiffany gas tower in Madison Square Garden. Hank entertained us by drawing caricatures. None of them were complimentary. Mrs. Hackley's earlobes rested on her shoulders. Mr. York's eyes bulged like doorknobs. Dudley's hair sprouted daisies, and Merry's frizzed as if shocked with electricity. Francie's head was in profile, and a fish was caught in her crocheted snood. His of me pricked me like a needle. A center part as wide as if a path had been mowed; octagonal rimmed spectacles framing drooping, squinting eyes; a high-arched nose so long I could have passed for Cyrano's sister. There was too much truth in it, but since everyone else was able to laugh at their own worst features exaggerated, I had to too.

Just then Edwin arrived carrying a paper bag, which he handed to Merry.

"They're *vatrushki,* sweet cheese pastries, a

very special gift to me," he announced. "A Russian mother wrapped in a babushka brought her boy to the settlement house to learn English, but she was too ashamed to register herself. I suppose she feared she would utter some strange sound wrongly so that it meant something ugly or impolite. She makes three cents each hemming handkerchiefs as piecework in her tenement. At that rate, it must have taken her several months to save her pennies for the ingredients, so eat slowly."

That touched all of us, so we nibbled quietly.

Edwin must have extended himself to this woman who the world would never know existed. His compassion for others had a strange effect on me. Every time I learned of some help he gave to someone, I felt he was giving the kindness to me. It made no logical sense, but when he found a job on a construction crew for an Italian father of four, established a Polish church in a waterfront warehouse, and helped a bewildered Sicilian mother just out of Ellis Island find her husband and son working on the docks — I thought of these acts as love offerings to me. Despite the time and intensity he gave to others, he made me feel that I was the vessel into which he was pouring his best self. I realized I had come to love him for his hunger to bless.

The times I felt I was pouring out my best self were at the studio, working to become indispensable. I hadn't felt confident yet to ask Mr. Tiffany to make a policy exception for me, and it had been more than a year since Edwin's proposal. Edwin's patience was in itself an act of love.

Into this reverie drifted the soft sound of Merry humming a slow, dreamy tune as she took up the plates. Edwin slid onto the piano bench and picked out the notes.

"Sing it," he said. "It's a waltz, I think."

"Yur tootin', it is. An Irish waltz." Slowly, she began to sing.

"East Side, West Side, all around the town
The tots sang 'ring-a-rosie,' 'London Bridge
    is falling down.'
Boys and girls together, me and Mamie
    O'Rourke
Tripped the light fantastic on the sidewalks
    of New York."

"Keep going," he said. He was playing the simple melody along with her.

"That's where Johnny Casey, little Jimmy
    Crowe,
Jakey Krause, the baker, who always had
    the dough,
Pretty Nellie Shannon with a dude as light
    as cork

159

First picked up the waltz step on the
   sidewalks of New York."

Amazingly, he was playing fully now, chords
and the delicate melody and frippery of his
own invention. I was entranced.

"Things have changed since those times,
   some are up in 'G.'
Others they are wand'rers but they all feel
   just like me.
They'd part with all they've got, could they
   once more walk
With their best girl and have a twirl on the
   sidewalks of New York."

It was so evocative — the measured pace,
the nostalgia, the sweetness of it, the wonder
of his playing — that I felt as though I had
drunk wine. I closed my eyes to give myself
over to the magic of his playing, and lost all
bodily sensation in the consummate joy of
listening. Anyone who could bring that about
had to have a capacious soul. When the last
lovely chord faded into silence, my eyes
opened with deeper love.

"What does 'up in G' mean?" Francie
asked.

"Why, 'tis gaol. The cooler," Merry said.
"Irish lads gone wrong in some desperate
neighborhood like Five Points. You learned
this song, then, in the Bowery where 'twas

born, Edwin?"

"No. I haven't heard it before."

"You never told me you could play the piano like that," I said softly.

"Adventures *and* surprises," he said, sporting with me.

I had been loving him for his goodness, but now my heart was brimming with something new — not only the thrill that he could surprise me so, but that he had this beautiful gift to enrich our lives. He was an artist too!

George peeked his head in the door. "Tally-ho, *allons-y, y vamos.*"

Madison Square Garden, at Twenty-sixth Street, was close enough to walk, so we all donned mufflers, hats, and coats. Edwin looked dashing in a belted Irish ulster with a fur collar turned up. Dudley wrapped his knitted scarf around Hank's neck just so, and we set off. We could see the tower of the palazzo from a block away, designed by Mr. Tiffany's friend Stanford White.

"Can't you just imagine the wild man White cavorting up there with his chorus girls in his tower apartment right now?"

"Careful, Hank. You'll go to hell for gossiping just as fast as for stealing chickens," deadpan Dudley warned.

"White keeps his Gramercy Park house for his wife. Propriety's sake."

"How do you know that for sure?" I asked.

"By being chummy in the right circles. You

161

want to know who else lived around Gramercy Park?"

"We know you're fixin' to tell us," Dudley muttered.

"Herman Melville, Henry James, Stephen Crane. The actor Edwin Booth, who founded the Players Club there, brother of Lincoln's assassin. And Peter Cooper, the inventor and philanthropist who founded Cooper Union."

"*And* founded the all-female School of Design there," I said, "as well as the very building where Edwin gives union-rallying speeches. Edwin is magnificent in front of a crowd. I know that for a fact. I went to one."

"You did?" Edwin's voice rose.

I loved turning the tables and giving him a surprise. "He makes a person see great possibilities. He's charismatic."

When he gave that speech, I saw that humanity was his canvas. To him the immigrant population wasn't a single nondescript body. He saw each one individually, an infinitude of voices, passions, griefs, fears, yearnings.

The crowd got noisier as we approached the palazzo, and we couldn't carry on a conversation, so Edwin just squeezed my hand and kissed it. The Tiffany gas tower was the showpiece of the whole Gas Exhibition. Gothic arches, one above the other, culminated in an immense glowing torch of blue gas flame at the top. Finials and crockets on

162

the lower spires spewed out turquoise steam that created a vaporous rainbow. Thousands of gaslights illuminated the steam, while jets sent water sliding down stained-glass windows lit from within the building and tumbling over huge rock crystals.

Many of the Tiffany employees were there congratulating one another. Impressed with Mr. Tiffany's extravaganza, Edwin shook their hands. A light snow began to fall, and flakes sparkled in the gaslights, adding a magical effect. We were all feeling lighthearted.

On the way back, Merry started singing low, "East Side, West Side, all around the town," and we hummed along, taking slow waltz steps on the sidewalks of New York. The jolly laughter of the crowd, the honey-gold flicker of gas lamps, the fairyland we had just seen, the piano notes in my head, the memory of Edwin's long fingers dancing on the keys, the revelation of this new side to him, all cast a blissful spell on me.

I snuggled up to him and whispered, "Can we have a plantation in our piano house? I mean, a piano in our plantation house?"

He stopped on the sidewalk, and Merry and Mr. York bumped into us from behind, and George and Dudley bumped into them.

" 'We'? 'Our'?" Edwin questioned.

"We. Our."

The euphoria lasted as long as the song.

Then panic at my impulsiveness rose like a steamy specter. How could I tell Mr. Tiffany? How could I leave the girls? How could I give up the work I love? I *had* to become indispensable.

Mercifully, it would be awhile before the plantation was ready to receive Edwin, and so I told no one at work, not even Alice. Instead, I threw myself into our latest window assignment, *Young Woman at a Fountain,* desperate to make it so exquisite that Mr. Tiffany would gladly say he couldn't do without me. In the painting, a red-haired maiden clad in a sheer golden gown with streaks of honey and pale olive stood by an oval stone basin, with water pouring over its edge into a pool. One shapely leg up to her thigh, as well as her hip, waist, and the under portion of one upraised arm, were all subtly visible through the diaphanous fabric.

I propped up several panes against the window ledge to see the light through them, loving what I could suggest with them. Mr. Tiffany would be dazzled if viewers could see through multiple layers of his glass to her flesh. For the shoulder-to-floor gossamer falling in folds, I could use transparent drapery glass with a second layer behind of shimmery gold and amber shadows, and the rear layer cut to reveal the shape of her body within the flowing chiffon. I would have to ask Mr. Nash to make a piece of gold glass with a spot of

164

amber for her navel, shading to darker amber to give the lower curvature of her belly.

Sensuousness was the genius of the original painting, and I wanted Mr. Tiffany to recognize it in my rendition too. I wanted to see his eyes spark at its brilliance, and at me. Maybe that would be the right moment to ask him to make an exception for me as a married woman.

Were the woman's arms raised to her shoulder to fasten or unfasten her robe? A man had commissioned the window. Unfasten, I decided. That would be more erotic. If left to me, I would give it the title *Trembling Maiden Preparing for Her Wedding Night.*

I was an eager devotee of the Wagner craze that swept New York operagoers off their patent-leather feet, so I accepted Mr. Belknap's invitation to see *Tristan und Isolde* despite knowing that I was in for a good cry. The week before the performance, we went to a lecture about it at Cooper Union. In immaculate evening dress, Mr. Belknap sat next to a heavy workman in overalls who wore his cap during the entire evening. That was Peter Cooper's ideal — culture, free and available for all.

The next week Mr. Belknap insisted on getting to the opera house early, part of the ritual of the dress circle life he frequented, to see and to be seen among the plummiest of New

York's high society. We made our way slowly through the foyer among three thousand princes and princesses of fashion pouring into the opera house. Mr. Belknap greeted many whom he knew. Ears dripped diamonds. Necks emerged from jeweled collars. Elegantly coiffed heads supported tiaras. Sequined and beaded dresses sparkled as works of art. Exotic birds they were, with extravagant plumage, enough ostentation and glitter to make my head spin. The richness of their decoration made them beautiful. How rare it was to find a beautiful face in a babushka.

"I wonder how many of these jewels passed from French aristocracy through Tiffany and Company," I whispered to Mr. Belknap.

He rubbed his freshly shaven chin in thought. "All of them, my dear."

Surrounded by the enormous five-tiered horseshoe of crimson velvet seats and walls, I quickly read the program notes to learn the main lyrics in English. From the first strains of the cellos, my whole body tingled with excitement. The aria, "His eyes in mine were gazing," swept me away. The swell of sound made me yearn to yearn like Isolde did.

Realizing the impossibility of their love, Tristan and Isolde drank a death potion in order to be together in the only place they could be, the afterlife, and found out later that it was a love potion, which heightened their passion to the sublime in the duet, "Oh, sink upon us, Night of Love."

They sang of the "sweet little word," *und,* binding Tristan and Isolde together in love's union, and I rolled over in my mind the sound of Edwin and Clara. Not bad. Two syllables each.

In the last act, Tristan and Isolde sang the prophetic lyric "All too brief lasts earthly joy," and I succumbed to the mournfulness of their deaths. I stepped out of the opera house on Mr. Belknap's arm seduced by the beauty and devastated by the sadness.

"Why so serious? It's only a story."

"Regardless, it's very moving," I said as we walked, still choked up by the image and music of Isolde's death.

"Of course it is, but it's not trying to be realistic. No matter how much we love it, opera can't do justice to the depth and complexity of human love, or human nature, for that matter. It theatricalizes experience."

It wasn't until our midnight supper at Sherry's that I was able to formulate my thoughts enough to respond.

"Isolde dying without poison in order to be with Tristan made me think of Wilhelmina. The horror of continuing to live with a pain so overpowering could, in fact, make death —"

"The only peace."

"Yes."

167

"In Wilhelmina's case, the acid only helped her arrive where she wanted to be," he said.

"Then she's a casualty of too much hunger for love."

"Probably so."

"Her dying was like a cheap opera," I said. "I can't see Wilhelmina drinking her death potion as something tragically fine or beautiful. If she were wearing a white silk gown like that diva in an idyllic landscape, with the violins inducing her to drink her death, I might be able to accept it, but not in a fetid alley surrounded by squalor. There, it was only self-pity, a foolish reaction to cheated womanhood and false romance."

"Are you saying that beauty ennobles even foolish actions?"

"Impulsive ones, yes, I suppose I am," I answered, feeling a twinge.

"You're tenderhearted, Clara, but you're missing the point. You're looking for truth in the beauty onstage, but an opera just presents beauty, not truth."

"It could suggest truth."

"It's artifice. If Wilhelmina had taken her life in beautiful surroundings and a lovely gown, her death wouldn't be any more tragic or authentic than it already was. Opera, and ballet too, don't convey the truly tragic. Wilhelmina's death may have been tragic, but Isolde's death is not. It wasn't real love that you saw on the stage tonight. It was style."

I thought that over while we ate our lobster Newburg.

"Consider Tiffany's windows," he said after some time. "A window picturing a garden, for example. Should you take it as a window or as a real garden?"

"A window."

"Right. If you take it as a garden and try to smell or pick a flower, you'll be disappointed because you will not have surrendered to the theatricality. You'd be investing it with undue seriousness. That's what you're doing with this opera, because it touches on someone you know. Instead, an opera, like a pictorial window, is purely aesthetic. Style above truth."

"Art for art's sake?"

"Exactly."

"I'm not so sure. If it gets me to have an emotional response, it's more than merely a beautiful thing made for the sake of being beautiful. It's made for the sake of activating and enriching my affections."

I wanted to see if music alone, without the trappings of character, setting, and story, could have that effect, so when George invited Edwin and me to come to his country studio in Nutley, New Jersey, for a chamber music concert at the nearby community hall, I was eager to go.

The afternoon was blustery, with sleet and

dropping temperatures even this late in March. Edwin was quieter than usual on the train.

"Are you thinking about the people that come to you?" I asked.

"Come to me?"

"The tempest-tossed. On a stormy night like this, do you think of them shivering in their tenements?"

"Yes, I do. They burn coal on Bowery Street on nights like this. Crowds gather. Sometimes fights erupt to get close."

"What was the line in the poem?"

" 'Send these, the homeless, tempest-tost to me. I lift my lamp beside the golden door!' "

"That was it. Do you think there's a moment when God holds our souls in His hand before we're born and decides whether we're going to be one of those troubled ones? Does He give those souls something more, like hope or grace, in order to endure?"

"Clara, how you're talking. It's a matter of social needs, not religion."

I assumed that was meant as a defense of his activities. He began to brood, preoccupied with Bowery Street, I suppose. The starkness of his vacancy unsettled me. I didn't challenge it with words, though I did try to engage him with my eyes. It took the blast of cold air and the snow coming down thick and fast as we stepped out of the train to bring him back to the here and now.

We took a horsecab in the gathering darkness, and he insisted on carrying me from the road to George's studio despite my protests that I had on my rubber overshoes. Nevertheless, his gallantry made me feel cherished. Inside, George gave us a merry welcome, declaring that I looked angelic with snow on my hat and eyelashes, and drew us close to a crackling fire. He showed us the paintings and sketches he had completed, and the cartoon of his mosaic entry for the prize of a three-year residency at the American Academy in Rome.

"We were to have depicted the theme of *The Triumph of Commerce,*" he said. "Dudley entered too."

"Ominous title for a piece of art when art and commerce are often at odds," I remarked.

He served us ham sandwiches, coleslaw, pickles, and hot tea. After half a sandwich, Edwin said he wasn't feeling well. Wind blew snow pellets against the window in a chilling spray.

"You do what you want," Edwin said. "I'm taking the next train back." He held his handkerchief up to his mouth and ducked out the door.

"Edwin!" George called, and went after him. "Edwin, come back!"

In a few minutes George returned. "He's gone. He must have run."

We stared at each other, dumbfounded.

"If he was afraid we would get snowed in, why didn't he insist that we both come with him?" I asked.

George raised his shoulders. "He should have. Maybe he really was sick."

Edwin's bizarre behavior bothered me, but George offered no more explanation beyond that, and we went to the concert anyway. I was distracted, so the music did not have the transporting effect I had hoped it would have. Afterward, George found a room for me in the inn nearby.

It was absolutely frigid. Still wearing my sealskin coat, I tossed between numbing sheets, hearing the ping of ice crystals pelting the window. I wrenched from the night a restless sleep amid a phantasmagoria of images barely discernible in fog and clouds of turquoise steam — Mr. Tiffany walking me down the aisle following my bridesmaid, a big, broad-shouldered blonde with swaying gait — no Mendelssohn — only the slow measures of an organ-grinder wearing an Irish ulster and cranking out "East Side, West Side, all around the town," and his monkey handing out pennies to woebegone immigrants in the pews, and Francis in ghostly gray handing a fistful of hundred-dollar bills to a nun. Waiting at the altar — black hair, narrow hips, with a scarlet handkerchief in his breast pocket — George.

I jerked awake in a sweat, shaken and

ashamed.

The storm had passed, but in the morning on the train back to Manhattan, I was still distressed. Beside the shock of the wrong brother at the altar, the eerie appearance of Francis rewarding the daughter of his successful lover sent a chill I could not ignore.

It was an overcast day, which would limit any success in glass selection. I set some girls on tasks that did not require natural light, and took the ferry and train to the Corona glasshouse, ostensibly to consult with Mr. Nash about glass I would need for upcoming commissions.

In the dim cavernous factory, shafts of fiery light and whooshing sound poured out of the mouths of furnaces. Partially clad men moved in a ritual choreography, swinging red-hot pokers. It was an elemental netherworld charged with maleness — potent, half repulsive, half alluring.

I went right to Tom Manderson's shop. His chest gleamed with a patina of sweat. The gatherer handed off the blowpipe to him, and some dollops fell to the floor from the incandescent gob. The blower blew on the mouthpiece of the pipe to create a bulb, and Tom shaped it with a paddle. This much I'd seen before, but now I saw something new.

Before the gob was fully blown and shaped, a second gatherer brought Tom a ladle of

173

glass from the smaller glory hole, which I presumed was a contrasting color, perhaps in an iridescent formula. With a long metal pincer, Tom directed a trickle of the second glass onto his gob, rotated it by quarter turns, and applied more dabs. I stepped closer and saw him connect those dabs with a thread of dripped glass laid on in arabesques. In that adroit action he planted the seed of the decoration he had in mind.

As the blower gave it more air, the decoration Tom applied when the ball was only an egg spread broadly over the enlarged belly, and Tom caressed it with an asbestos pad. Each time it hardened and cooled, Tom sent it back to be thrust into the glory hole. It was almost too much to take in all at once — the beauty of molten glass on the blowpipe, its slipperiness, its translucence, its expansion, the repeated thrusts into the fiery hole, the mounting rhythm, the speed, Tom's glistening skin, the curly black hair on his chest, the expressiveness of his well-formed muscles working in his arms and chest. Without warning, Tom swung the pipe and vase toward me so I could take a look, and a tremor overtook me.

He handed it off to an assistant, raised his shoulders and pulled them back in a big stretch. He picked up a dollop of glass that had fallen to the floor and stepped out of the workshop area to give it to me. Curling my hand into a fist, I hesitated to receive what I thought would burn me.

"Trust me."

I gasped as he touched the dollop of glass to his lips. Now I took it willingly. It was still warm but not too hot to handle. I kept it in my palm all the way back on the train, exultant at the arousal I'd felt.

And what of Edwin? Would his muscles excite me like Tom's did? Did his black hair grow on his chest too? Would he enjoy having it stroked? Would there be any preamble in bed, or would he be direct and urgent? Rough or gentle? I couldn't imagine him to be oafish. Would there be a sound at his highest moment? A grimace? Any expression of euphoria? Would it be so consuming, so alive, that love of mere inert glass would fade in comparison to what we had done?

What if it wasn't consuming? What if my touch meant nothing, generated nothing in him? What if I would be repeating the painful nights I'd had with Francis? Cold fear froze my nerves. What if Francis had been right, that his inability *had* been my fault? I couldn't go through that humiliation again. Surely there would be more excitement than I had with Francis, whose gray chest hair was patchy and whose belly hung over his belt. I had to be rational about this. *Before* the marriage, while there was still time to back out if I needed to, regardless of my mother's eti-

175

quette handbook and my stepfather's preaching, I had to prove to myself that I wasn't the failure, and that Edwin wouldn't be either.

The next time I saw him we were going to see a short French film of Loïe Fuller performing her Serpentine Dance, swinging yards and yards of silk in a frenzy of moving shapes. I was quite excited because she had not only become a modern dance sensation but the living symbol of Art Nouveau as well.

Walking with Edwin to Madison Square Garden I was still miffed about being left in Nutley, and I let him know it.

"I was going to be sick. I didn't want you to see me that way," he said.

"A little explanation would have gone a long way."

"I had to get out fast. I knew George would take care of you."

"That didn't stop us from worrying about you walking out in the dark with drifts above your ankles. It was inconsiderate."

"I'm sorry."

He took my hand and kissed it as we walked, then cleared his throat and said, "I have something to tell you. In a few months I have to leave you for a while. The University Settlement in Chicago has asked me to give the keynote address at its annual fund-raiser in August." He paused long enough for me to see my opportunity. "And I have accepted."

I stopped abruptly on the sidewalk. I could surprise him just as well as he had surprised me. With no hesitation to receive what might burn me, I said, "Let me go with you. A pre-nuptial honeymoon. I'll quit Tiffany Studios."

CHAPTER 13
LAKE GENEVA

"You were stupendous, Edwin. You had the audience riveted to your words."

My admiration had swelled overnight, and when we left Chicago on the train the morning after his big speech, we both felt exuberant because of his success there, and at least for me, because of the anticipation of making love that night. We were headed north on the Great Northern along Lake Michigan, with no one else in our compartment, and would take a spur line to Lake Geneva, Wisconsin, which had been a favorite place for him since boyhood.

"Have you ever had a standing ovation before?"

He opened the window of the train and held his face to the breeze before he said yes. A modest yes, whisked away on the wind. He ducked back inside.

I winked. "Maybe you'll have another one tonight."

"I think the audience understood that we

need to acknowledge the interdependence between the classes in order to transform settlement houses from charities to a self-propelled force for socialist policy and labor reform."

Dear preoccupied Edwin, so earnest that he missed my little joke.

"After I build up some seed money in Mexico, and after another year working in the Lower East Side, I'll be ready to run for State Assembly."

"I'd like to work on *your* lower east side. Do you think we would both feel tingly? We might both find cause for applause."

His head jerked from the window to me. "Clara! I never knew you could be so . . . saucy."

I gave him a teasing look. "Adventures and surprises."

A one-horse shay took us from the depot at Lake Geneva to Kaye's Park Hotel and Cottages on the south shore. Lovely maples, oaks, and lindens reminded me of my Ohio home. Small excursion steamers and rowboats plied the water, and a windmill at water's edge turned slowly. A row of lounge chairs facing the water, an octagonal pagoda on the lawn, wooden steps down to the water, and a rustic dock made the place charming.

"The ideal Midwestern honeymoon spot,"

I said. "Innocent and unadulterated. Until now."

"Shall I tell the proprietor we're on our honeymoon?"

"No. Don't say that. He'll tell the chef, and the chef will prepare a special breakfast and come out to ask us how it was, and he'll wink at you and he won't mean the breakfast. There's something cruel about that, guessing how the performance was. It's all too Old World, like those villages where the bride's mother had to hang the bloody sheet out the window to prove that her daughter had been a virgin. Just tell him we're married."

"Delighted to, darling."

We were greeted by the proprietor, Arthur Kaye, whom Edwin knew.

"A cottage or two hotel rooms?" Mr. Kaye asked.

"One room. This is Mrs. Clara Waldo."

It gave me a start, the name spoken.

"Congratulations, then."

"Thank you," Edwin said.

In our room on the third floor, I busied myself hanging up my dresses until Edwin began to take off his coat and vest. I stopped and watched his every move. There he stood in his shirtsleeves — the modern style, soft cotton with only the cuffs and collar starched for the world to see. I was seeing what the world didn't — his broad shoulders filling out the shirt, the shape of his arm muscles beneath the cloth, the fringe of hair at his cuffs. We'd had separate rooms in Chicago, so I felt a little jittery now, but I didn't want to be on edge. I wanted to be just like the lake, calm as glass, and step into intimacy unencumbered and enjoy with abandon. After all, I'd given up a lot for this.

Edwin opened the window to a jubilant chorus of birds in a tall butternut tree and I caught a glimpse of an iridescent green dragonfly.

"Look at the geese," he said, diverting my gaze.

Dozens of wild geese dotted the lawns sloping down to the lake. They had brown wings and creamy breasts, and their long, graceful necks were jet-black. A dramatic flash of white shone under their beaks and on their cheeks.

"They're beautiful, don't you think?" I asked.

Edwin came close behind me, reached his arms around me, and placed a single soft kiss on my neck. "If your taste prefers feathers to skin."

"They travel thousands of miles, don't they?"

"They mate for life."

"Truly? They all look alike, so how can they be sure, out of so many, that they've chosen the right one?"

"Instinct." The warm breath of that word

181

fell on my ear.

"Our own snug harbor," Edwin said as he unlocked the door to our room after dinner and a lakeshore stroll. "Our first home," he said softly. "Welcome to our first adventure, Mrs. Waldo."

"I'm not Mrs. Waldo yet, Mr. Waldo. I'm only acting the role in this stage set."

We were talkative for a while, until he turned down the gas lamp. Moonlight gentled itself across the floor and over the bed, and a momentous quiet overtook us. In my mind I heard Tristan and Isolde's sweeping duet, "Oh, sink upon us, Night of Love."

Silhouetted by the pale luminescence behind him, Edwin's shirt glowed blue-white in the moonlight. He pulled it out of his trousers, and the soft whooshing sound gave me a thrill.

I started to unbutton my shirtwaist, and his hand drew mine away. "My pleasure," he whispered, and took up where I'd left off, exploring between each button with warm, sure hands, each exquisite stroke a sweet adventure, as he had promised. He laid me down, and the muscles of my back and arms tightened instantly at my own deliberate licentiousness. I was soon soothed by kisses, mere touches, silent, slow, artfully placed, here, there, there too — quickening, rushing one upon another — abandoning methodical tenderness for jubilant haste — answering urge with urge — his thrust to my push — mine to his — his importunate, important — quaking together joyfully — settling, moment by long moment, into a delicate swoon of slow breathing and peace and rest.

We had not failed each other.

CHAPTER 14
WILD GEESE

A jostling of the bed awakened me, but I didn't turn to him, giving him privacy, since soft daylight had entered the room. I heard him thrust one leg, then the other, into his trousers. The key clicked in the lock. Instantly, I rose on my elbow.

"Edwin?"

"I'll be right back. I'm going to get you something. A surprise."

The place where he had lain was still warm. I moved into it to enjoy the memory — from his kisses, each one a benediction, to his exploratory touch of my thigh, to his startled, wide-eyed look at the moment of effusion. My wild Edwin. Passion and Risk had smiled on me, and I could throw off my worries.

In his plaintive sigh that had signaled his coming back to earth, I sensed that he had been vulnerable to a moment too strong for him. The shadows cast by moonlight had made his face appear troubled. Even so, my happiness had merged into peaceful sleep.

I closed my eyes now to make it night again, and there stretched before me a millennium of Nights of Love. Soon he would give me the surprise, whatever it was, perhaps a breakfast pastry from the dining room, and I would give him this vision of night after night of loving through eternity, like two mirrors facing each other, reflecting smaller and smaller images until they became two pinpoints of color.

The piercingly sharp, two-note song of a wren repeated itself relentlessly, as if saying, "Get up! Get up!" I obeyed it, bathed, dressed, and put up my hair.

Perhaps I had misunderstood. Perhaps I was to meet him in the dining hall for breakfast. I was suddenly overtaken with a ravishing hunger. I crept downstairs feeling like a fugitive. He was not in the parlor reading the Chicago paper, which would have been natural since it probably contained an account of the Settlement House event. He was not in the dining room. He was not on the porch or in a lounge chair on the lawn or in the pagoda. I felt I shouldn't venture far, so I returned to the dining room for breakfast. The waiter who had served us the night before gave me a quizzical look at the doorway.

"One, please," I said. "May I sit by a window?"

I ate looking out and hurried back to the

room, thinking that he had returned and was distressed to find me gone. The room was just as I had left it. I went down to the front desk, and Mr. Kaye greeted me as Mrs. Waldo.

"Have you seen Edwin this morning?"

He thought a moment. "No. Can't say that I have. He probably went to the general store for a newspaper. It's not far."

"If you happen to see him, tell him I went for a walk." I pointed in one direction on the lakeshore path.

"I certainly will, Mrs. Waldo."

Outside, I stepped onto the dock and peered down into the water, ashamed of my gruesome thought. There were only grasses on the sandy bottom. I looked over the other side of the dock, was relieved to see nothing, and headed in the direction I had pointed, making an effort to acknowledge appropriately the promenading guests. I walked the length of Kaye's Park and several mansions beyond, looking between them into the woods, and into the water alongside the pathway. I did the same in the other direction. All I found was an abandoned bird's nest fallen from a tree, once entwined by instinct, now a disheveled bed after a hasty flight, sticks and leaves awry.

Mr. Kaye was working on board his boat when I returned. "Would there be any reason he would go into the woods?" I asked from the dock.

"Only to gather wood violets for you."

"Are there bears?"

"Not often."

"Wolves?"

"Yes." He raised up from his work and looked at me. "Go inside and have a nice lunch. I'll look in the stables and outbuildings, and then you and I will go out in the small launch to have a look."

We spent the afternoon navigating the lake, asking everyone, looking in covered boathouses and boatyards, checking at other hotels. We came back without a shred of information.

"What was the last thing he said to you?"

"That he was going to get something for me, a surprise, and that he would be right back."

Mr. Kaye's puzzlement was written in a scowl. "We should go into town."

We took his trap and mare. No one had seen him at the general store, the post office, the land office, the bank, the barbershop. We even went into the icehouse. Huge iron hooks hung from the rafters. I shuddered.

I spotted a small jewelry and handicraft store, hardly Tiffany & Company. Of course! The surprise! I inquired, and was crestfallen.

At the train depot the stationmaster asked me for a description. I was mortified at how little I could say. "Black hair. Tall."

Mr. Kaye added, "Gold-rimmed glasses."

"But he left without them." I shrank from their concerned expressions as they surmised that he had left hastily.

"How old, Mrs. Waldo?"

Another embarrassment. I didn't know for certain. I knew he was a couple years younger than I. "Thirty-three?"

"What was he wearing?"

"A white shirt. Brown trousers. No vest. No coat. Brown shoes."

"Carrying anything?"

"I don't believe so."

The stationmaster consulted the baggage handler. "Nope. Nobody by that description."

"I didn't think he would take a train. He gets sick on trains."

At the newspaper office, Mr. Kaye put in a missing-person notice. To me, doing that spelled a change of heart, abandonment, escape.

Back in the trap, Mr. Kaye studied the rump of the horse. "I think it's time we notify the authorities."

I acquiesced, numb.

The county seat was in Elkhorn. I would have enjoyed passing through stands of sugar maples, elms, and cottonwoods, seeing sunlight dance through the latticework of leaves, and hearing the hollow rat-a-tat of woodpeckers hammering, if I weren't so plagued by anxiety.

Sheriff Seth Hollister was a broad-chested, capable-looking man wearing boots over his pant legs. We went through the same questions, and he agreed to send out search parties in the woods.

"Do you know any of his relatives and how to reach them?" he asked.

"His younger brother, George, in New York."

"You'd best be thinking of sending a telegram," said Mr. Hollister.

"Can we wait another day? I don't want to alarm him unnecessarily."

"He might know something that would help us."

I nibbled at my thumbnail. "I'll think about it."

I ate dinner in a stupor, went up to our room on shaky legs, and opened the window so that I might hear anything. Sitting up in bed, I smoothed the sheet neatly, the sheet he had crumpled in his fist at the moment of his passion. Does a man lose something of himself at that moment, and does he gain it back after time? Had I lost him forever?

I turned over in my mind every hour of our recent days together, searching for a clue as to what had propelled him out that door. There were so many possible readings of his disappearance: he fell into the lake, encountered a wild animal in the woods, was robbed

189

and beaten, maybe murdered. Or he was afraid of entanglement, leery of marriage, doubtful about his Mexico plan. Or he remembered an earlier woman. Shades of Francis Driscoll! He didn't love me as he had loved her. He found me less beautiful than he had imagined.

What tormented me most was that this might have been caused by my own desire to prove something to myself. Had he thought less of me for my willingness to have intimacies before we were married? He was just as eager. Was I less worthy of respect? Was that what his troubled look meant? It didn't seem possible that he was disappointed in our lovemaking. He was my wild Edwin. But maybe he had come to his senses, and I had not.

Or maybe he had lost his senses.

At the time, I had thought that his leaping from the streetcar was impulsive, thoughtless, and overly zealous but not irrational. Now I wasn't so sure. And the other time, at Nutley, in his mind he had good reason to flee George's studio if he were sick. Fine if he wanted to throw up outside so I wouldn't see, but it made no sense to escape into a snowstorm at night and on foot in that condition. That was worse than unwise. It was unbalanced.

George. I had to tell George. He had a right to know.

■ ■ ■ ■

The first thing in the morning I went to the hotel desk and asked Mr. Kaye to send a telegram to George, at 46 Irving Place, New York.

"Just say, 'Edwin has disappeared from Lake Geneva. Come quickly. Clara.' "

Mr. Kaye set off in the trap at a fast clip.

Impersonating Edwin's wife, not quite Mrs. Waldo but certainly not Mrs. Driscoll anymore, I sat in a lounge chair unable to do anything but watch two steamers drag the lake. From time to time they pulled up something on a gruesome iron hook, and a spasm rattled my chest. I strained to see what it might be, but always, thank God, they let it sink back down.

Still, I kept my eyes on the lake. Its streaks of cool green where there was underwater vegetation contrasted with its range of blues fluctuating in response to passing clouds, as though someone were stirring the lake with a giant spoon, like a gaffer marbling a fresh pour of still-viscous glass.

I felt a flash of shame for letting my thoughts drift to the studio instead of thinking continually of Edwin. What was I to do? Close my eyes to the world around me?

The geese kept up their nibbling in the grass, and mallards with their ducklings

191

paddled back and forth near the shore, puttering hour after hour, looking for something too. An emerald dragonfly with double gauze wings worried its skimming way just above the water and dashed off impulsively, but it came back. It came back.

How beautiful it would be to render that dragonfly in glass. I longed to do it, but how and where? When I had told Mr. Tiffany I was leaving to get married, he shook his head and scowled down at his hands. Rarely was there anything in his domain that was beyond his power to control, so for a moment he didn't know how to react. His credo of being a gentleman prevented him from trying to convince me otherwise, though he did say, "Are you sure, Clara?"

I only nodded, prepared myself, and asked, "Do you think you might make an exception and keep me on?"

"Justifying it by the importance of your work?"

"By my indispensability. And to develop our secret — the lampshade idea. Remember?"

"A crack in the policy and the whole thing will come tumbling down. I wish I could."

I froze and could not take another breath. My breezy plan to be both artist and wife collapsed like a house of glass built on shifting sands. Rising to leave, I heard him say in an uncle's cautionary tone, "Take good care of yourself, Clara." Although my spine had stayed rigid, my step firm, as I left his office, inside I was seared with embarrassment for having asked, devastated for being denied, stung that our mutual love for what we were creating wasn't strong enough to maintain the bond of admiration as two artists that I felt we had. I was cast adrift in an uncertain future with no way back. Now, I had thought, I would have to depend upon love alone to fill my cup of life.

A vagary flitted across my mind with the capriciousness of that dragonfly. Could someone have put Edwin up to it? Someone who would offer him something irresistible if he abandoned me? Someone who knew I would return to Tiffany's studios? Mr. Tiffany himself who offered to reward Edwin extravagantly for giving me back to him? The money might have been too strong a temptation if it were enough to mount a campaign for State Assembly without having to work in Mexico. A freakish thought. I discarded it, but it came back unbidden. How much would my return have been worth to Mr. Tiffany?

Beneath my dark speculation, I felt Edwin's health and safety weighing heavily on my shoulders, and I flailed in a quagmire of doubts and self-recrimination, not knowing whether to feel angry or jilted or guilty. Would he have come here after Chicago if I hadn't come with him? Probably not. Responsibility gouged deep, as it always did. All right, then.

From now on I would stick to my Midwestern values, abide by my mother's etiquette book, and be the honorable stepdaughter of a minister in every proper, humdrum regard.

Two days later, Mr. Kaye pulled up in his trap alongside the hotel, George leapt out, ran across the lawn to me in the pagoda, scattering the geese, and flung himself into my arms. I wasn't sure whether I was comforting him or he was comforting me.

"Tell me everything that led up to this." Mercifully, his tone wasn't accusatory, only panicked.

"He gave a rousing speech in Chicago, and shook a hundred hands at the reception afterward. The next day, on the train, he felt quite buoyed up about it and spoke of running for State Assembly."

"Was he sick on the train?"

"No, but he did open the window. Maybe he was queasy. He was happy to show me the lake. In Chicago we'd given the appearance of brother and sister, and had separate hotel rooms. Here, we registered as husband and wife."

George was expecting more. I blushed to say, "We made love."

"And?"

"It was beautiful, George. We were both very happy. There wasn't anything that would lead to this."

George paced like a caged tiger in the pagoda, muttering, "You don't seem hurt by this at all. You haven't cried. You're not the least bit hysterical."

"Some women have more contained ways of handling despair."

The ache in my jaw from grinding my teeth provided no visible proof, so I showed him my nails bitten down to the quick and my handkerchief balled up in a wrinkled wad.

"Did he ask you to come with him?"

"On this trip? No. It was my idea. He was happy about it, though." I pulled my shawl around me as a way to hold myself together. "After marriage, people make discoveries about each other. I didn't want to assume anything, so I invited myself in order to find out if I could satisfy his body's need, if we were, I might say, compatible."

"And?"

"Oh, we are, George. We are."

Such a serious look on George's face, almost akin to his brother's troubled look after we had made love. I fiddled with my sleeve. "Do you condemn me?"

"No."

"Do you think he changed his mind about marrying me?"

"No. He's wild about you."

"I'm not so sure now. Maybe he thinks poorly of me on moral grounds, he being so high-minded."

"He's a *man,* Clara!"

"A man doesn't just walk off and leave his fiancée in a hotel room. He had to intend to escape."

"But he didn't take his coat."

George pounded the railing once with his fist. "What we don't know is whether he would have come here if you weren't with him."

I felt an unintentional stab of incrimination.

"Has anything like this ever happened before?"

It was the wrong time to ask. Sheriff Hollister was approaching the pagoda.

"Excuse me for interrupting. You the brother?"

"Yes. George Waldo." He held out his hand.

"They're going to drag the west part of the lake tomorrow. If they don't find him, I'm afraid they'll call off the search. The longer you wait, the less likely —"

"I know," George was quick to say.

"It's time to get a detective."

"Let's go."

We waited ten days at Kaye's Park while two detectives tried to track him. Time hung heavy on us. As the reality descended, we were careful not to say anything that might upset each other. We drifted aimlessly in a rowboat some days, and George sketched in a desultory manner other days, until temperatures dropped dramatically and a storm blew in and stayed. Edwin was only in his shirtsleeves! I thought of the bard's sonnet defining love: True love "looks on tempests and is never shaken." I was shaken.

The detectives had traced Edwin passing through Clinton and Beloit, Wisconsin, where he inquired at a bus station how to get to Savannah, Illinois, but there they lost him. A week later they picked up traces of him in Dubuque and Davenport, and lost him again. George's hope was fading. He cabled his parents in Connecticut.

An early frost had turned the maple leaves a deep, blood red vibrating in the wind, and the oaks a sallow yellow. Before breakfast one morning, I came to the parlor window and saw George hurling stones into the lake, one right after another, angrily flailing about, pitching them wildly until he exhausted himself and came in, shivering and embarrassed when he saw that I'd been watching.

During breakfast, a din of honking started the geese moving in agitated fashion on the lawns, stretching their wings. We left our plates and hurried outside. At a distance, one goose flapped its wings and lifted, no longer earthbound, honking wildly. Others near him followed, forming a *V,* their beautiful white underwings tipped in black, their necks stretched forward into the ether. Then the gaggle on the lawn where we stood lifted off the ground with a great thrumming of wings, and another flock became airborne off the water, and formed their *V*'s, each with the lead bird gaining height quickly. All over the lake and shore, the sky became full, the honking a deafening jubilation of flight, of freedom of movement, of instinct.

"A great drama of avian migration, Edwin would have called it," I said.

We watched standing close together but separate in our sorrowful thoughts until the sky was full of mere specks. And then the vastness took them in.

Goose, oh, my wild goose, no longer earthbound, no longer mine. Do not fold your wings.

Still fixed on the sky, I abandoned caution and asked, "You never did answer me. Has he ever flown before?"

During an excruciating silence, George seemed to be at war with himself.

"Once. But that was ten years ago."

"Tell me."

George turned away to speak. "He was studying at Andover Seminary in Massachusetts. During the break between terms, he went south with another student, heading toward Charleston. Coming back north alone, he wound up here at Lake Geneva instead of returning directly to Andover. He had no recollection of how he got here. He didn't remember anything after being on the train heading south. My parents didn't miss him because they assumed he had returned to Andover after his trip with his friend, and he arrived there the day the new term started. Apparently he came to his senses on his own, here at the lake, and then went back to the seminary. It was years before he confessed it to me."

"You knew that and you didn't tell me? You just let me go ahead? Why didn't you say something when he left Nutley like a madman?"

He cringed at my shrieking accusation.

"Why didn't you tell me?"

A long moment passed before he spoke to the empty sky. "Because *I* couldn't have you as my wife. But *he* could." His voice rose in pitch. "The prospect of having you in the family was irresistible. *And* I wanted so badly for him to have you, for him to be happy. He would have been a broken man if you had said no."

■ ■ ■ ■

Book Three
1897–1900

■ ■ ■ ■

CHAPTER 15
NASTURTIUM

At Irving Place again after a month away careening from happiness to anger, wrung by injury and sorrow, I unpacked, stopping often to stare at nothing and wonder what Edwin was doing right at that moment, whether he was suffering, hurt, lucid — or bewildered, like I was. The number of possibilities made my temples throb, my jaw ache. I nestled in my bed in this private crevice of the day to look for comfort from Emily Dickinson, and found not comfort so much as wisdom, with a bookmark at the page. One innocent day I must have thought the verse clever before I knew its truth.

> For each ecstatic instant
> We must an anguish pay
> In keen and quivering ratio
> To the ecstasy.

Discerning and wry, yes, but not comforting. I doubted if she had ever sunk into a night of love like Isolde's, or like mine. If she had, she would have been too controlled to lose her equilibrium, and I didn't want to lose mine either. The words blurred, and that stinging feeling that comes just before tears swelled up around my eyes. I reached for Mr. Tiffany's handkerchief, but not soon enough. Loss overwhelmed me. I had the handkerchief from Mr. Tiffany, the kaleidoscope from Francis, but what from Edwin? Nothing. He had given me nothing but promises. I was bereft of even a memento to clutch in private, desperate moments, like a soul-sick nun clutching a crucifix. What was wrong with me to lose one man after another?

A knock at my door rescued me from at least this bout of self-pity.

"It's me. Alice!"

I flung open the door.

"I live here now," she said. "I took your advice. West Fifty-seventh was too far from Tiffany's."

We fell into each other's arms. "You couldn't have picked a better time. Your face is sunshine after rain."

"You don't have to tell me anything you don't want to."

"Then you know?"

"In a general way. No details. Chatty Miss Owens is cautioning everyone not to be too inquisitive, then leaves them with innuendos, which only makes them more curious."

By now the Lesser Furies at the other dining table had probably discussed it thoroughly, making speculations, leveling judgments. At my table, the only one I had to brace myself for was Mrs. Hackley.

I sat back against the iron headboard and patted the quilt next to me, an invitation to get comfortable.

"He just disappeared. Bolted. One night of love, a glimpse of him out the door the next morning, and then he was gone. Poof. A master of irony."

"What irony?"

"He had promised me adventure and surprise. Who would have thought that by this bizarre surprise he would throw me over? If he had come back the next day or the next week and I had married him, he would have done me the honor of keeping me in perpetual anxiety over another disappearance, or other aberration on his otherwise solid veneer."

"Don't be sharp, Clara. I expected you to be upset and sad."

"I *am* upset. I've been racked with worry for him. It's that responsibility issue torturing me again. What did I do or say that made him run off?"

"Maybe nothing."

"Sad? Of course I'm sad. Deeper than that. Heartsick. That I may have caused him some catastrophe."

"Do you have any idea where he might be?"

"No. Nor how he is living. If I only knew that he was all right." My throat constricted, and my voice was pinched and high. "I'm afraid, Alice."

She wrapped her arms around me. "Oh, no, sweet. He's a man. He'll be all right."

"I'm afraid for me too. I'm afraid I'll never know what happened. I may have to live the rest of my life not knowing."

"Shh," she crooned, rocking me.

"I still have so much to sort out. My feelings, I mean."

I could not hold with the idea of his willfulness in hurting me. I could not believe in deceit. Instead, I could believe in mystery. Even in tragedy.

"He may be dead, for all we know. His brother has diminishing hopes."

I had been furious at George for not warning me before I threw my life at someone who had the stability of a child's top. I had screamed at him, which only made him clam up and pout in remorse. During those silent hours on the train with him I began to realize that for him to take that risk to ensure my presence in his life had not been an act of flippant mischief, like Puck's, only reckless love. But what love doesn't have something of the reckless in it? Both of us were guilty of that. My anger began to melt, and probably his too, in the new knowledge that in some crippled way, we did have each other in our lives. But that was too complicated to get into now with Alice.

"Is his brother named George?" she asked. "The George that everyone talks about here?"

"The same. He takes his meals here and lives in his studio next door. You'll see him at dinner tonight."

"I knew him at Art Students League. A funny fellow."

"On the surface."

His funniness and frivolity had dissolved in those days at Lake Geneva. As we waited in the parlor during the storm that had made our worry excruciating, the man I saw allowed a depth of feeling to emerge. Before this, George was an innocent. The simplicity of his nature prevented him from knowing that people hurt even their loved ones by orchestrating their lives.

"He's a little . . . The men here, don't you find them . . . ?"

"Alice, don't be naïve. This building isn't Greek Revival style by accident. Not all of them. Not Mr. Booth, the Englishman; and not Mr. Bainbridge, the actor; or Dr. Griggs; or Mr. York, an industrial designer, a quiet sort but a good fellow. He smokes sunflower leaves so as to keep the air fresh for the rest of us. And Dr. Griggs has helped everyone here with potions and pills and bandages at one time or another."

"Do I need to be concerned about the others?"

"No. It's safer here than in any other mixed boardinghouse that I know of. Dudley's a cream puff, and Hank would do anything for me. Once when I was sick, I had to get a drawing to Mr. Tiffany right away. Hank delivered it himself. Of course, that got him into Tiffany's studio, which he loved."

"I haven't met any Englishman here, but the others are nice enough."

"Don't try to figure out who's matched with whom. It will drive you crazy trying to pick up on clues. Just think of it as fluid, interchangeable, communal, and let it be."

"Are you coming back to work?"

"Of course, at whatever toll my embarrassment takes. I have struggled out of widow's weeds to gather a wedding trousseau, and now I've packed it in some attic of my mind in order to wear again the garb of the working woman — shirtwaist, tie, and lace-up shoes."

Alice patted my hand.

With the absorption of work and the love of a few good friends, I felt I could solder the brittle pieces together and take up my old life again.

After brief, embarrassed condolences all around, dinner that night was awkward and tense. With dark circles under his eyes, George sat between Dudley and Hank, and I think he drew strength, if not peace, from being in their presence. It was sweet to see the way they made sure he ate. Dudley cut out the choicest morsel of his lamb chop and laid it on George's plate. George and I stole mutual glances to check how the other one was bearing up, and I caught glimpses of Alice checking on us both.

As George was preparing to go back to his studio, I followed him to the door.

"What was that embroidery on your friend's parlor cushions?"

" 'Never complain. Never explain.' "

"Never explain. It's good advice. I'm going back to Tiffany's tomorrow. What will you do?"

"I have to tell them at the University Settlement. Then I'll go to Connecticut to be with my parents for a while. The detectives know how to reach me there."

"Good." Good for his parents, and good for me not to be with him for a while. I had myself to put together again.

"Once I had three brothers," he said. "One died as a baby, another as a schoolboy."

"How do you think your parents will take it?"

"My mother will be tearful. She will have begun a regimen of prayers. My father will be distraught. He had pinned his hopes on Edwin. It was me he thought he would lose next."

That startled me. As he stepped out the door, I felt the thread that had connected us at Lake Geneva snap in two. I was awash with loss.

I managed to get Dr. Griggs in a private moment on the stairs, and I spilled out everything that happened at the lake. "Do you think he could be alive, but just . . ." The only word that came to mind was *lost.*

With his eyebrows pinched together, he said, "If there was some illness or disorder that made him lose his bearings, it's not likely. In that state, similar to sleepwalking and caused by stress or anxiety or psychological factors, he might not have sense enough to nourish himself. And with cold, wet weather, if he has been sleeping out, chances are that he would succumb."

I choked on a gulp of air. "And if he left intentionally?"

"In that case, he might have had a plan, so he's probably all right. I'm sorry I can't be more encouraging."

That left me to hope that his escape was intentional. What kind of wrong-hearted hope was that? A thought wormed its ugly way into my mind: Maybe I was the one who had escaped. I went into my bedroom shocked for having thought that, and lay down with my own betrayal.

With trepidation, I dressed for work the next

morning, knowing I had to confront the man who could do without me, and reveal to him that another man could also do without me. Were it not that I loved Mr. Tiffany's creative fire, and the warm praise he gave me when my work pleased him, I might have sought some other work, but hope that we might pick up where we left off made me take Alice's arm and head up Irving Place. As we stepped around the perimeter of Gramercy Park, dry leaves crunched under our feet, the crackle of autumn's sadness that summer had flown away. Bustling Fourth Avenue was oddly no different than when I had left, with its web of wires overhead pulsing with energy, moving people, making connections. Fervently I hoped for some connection.

How good to feel Alice's support for four blocks, three, two, one. She squeezed my arm and steered me into the showroom, not the usual workers' entrance on Twenty-fifth Street but straight through the grander public entrance and up the Art Nouveau staircase as though we owned it, up to the second floor, where she patted my cheek, waited for the gilded doors of the elevator to open, stepped in, and left me there.

Mr. Tiffany stood up the instant he saw me at his office doorway. His forehead lines contracted with confusion. I told him straight off, and he sat back down at his desk. "Oh, no, no, no," he murmured, the same croon-

211

ing sympathy I had heard from him twice before, the same points of light dancing in his opal ring as he drummed his fingernails on his desk.

"I thought I had decided carefully," I said. "He is, or was, a respectable man of high ideals but apparently low stability, possibly with a hidden streak of a mental disorder, or just plain cowardice. I may never know which."

Hunched forward, his agitated gaze moving among the fabric samples on his desk, he seemed to be processing all I'd said.

"Have you married him?"

Heat rose up my throat to my cheeks. The truth would forfeit my respectability. A lie would forfeit my integrity. Being married to a missing person would put a strain on his policy against hiring married women.

"No."

"Then you are single," he said.

I said yes, realizing that Edwin had given me back my art.

"You are mine again?"

I blushed to think he thought of me as his.

"Yes. I am yours."

He raised both stubby arms in a hallelujah.

"If my work has pleased you," I added, a genial attempt to tease out of him a scrap of praise.

"Shame on you for doubting."

"Who took my place while I was gone?"

"No one. I hadn't decided yet. Henry

Belknap and Miss Stoney and Miss Northrop all filled in."

He smacked both palms down on his ebony desk and trotted over to his display table to show me four watercolors for a large conservatory bay window in two wide panels plus two narrow side windows. Vine leaves and gourds and nasturtiums cascaded down over clear glass.

"A happy profusion of color and growth, eh?"

All the cadmiums — yellow, orange, and red — together with yellow ocher against the fresh greens — emerald, Hooker's green, and sap green — I drank them all in.

"They're cheerful colors," I said.

"Nature always heals. It's proven that the light vibrations of color have a subjective power, and affect the mind and soul. Yellow lifts up, orange rouses, green comforts. You're receptive to that, I know. So soak up what they're offering you."

"I will. Thank you. You know, we would get better color harmonies if we worked on all the windows at once."

"That's true."

"Then I'll need Agnes and Alice and Miss Judd to do the cartoons side by side. I'll be the fourth. We'll have to rearrange the saw-horse tables to have all the glass selected against the same exposure."

"Joe and Frank can move everything when

213

the time comes. How long do you think you would need?"

"If I can free up a dozen cutters, selectors, and assistants to work on it, three to four weeks. May I take the watercolors to the studio? It will help divert the discussion about why I'm back."

"Certainly." He began rolling them up. "I'll go up with you."

In the privacy of the elevator, he murmured, "He was a fool to let you go."

You should have never let me go either, I thought, but that didn't matter now. We would be back together, taking exquisite pleasure in each other's work.

That bolstered me for the reunion with the girls. I knew how it would look to them — that I was jilted three steps from the altar. It wasn't anyone's business, anyway, though it would be a juicy topic for a while. If I could follow the cushion's advice never to explain, it would be easier to keep my dignity.

Mr. Tiffany tapped his cane just inside the women's studio, the girls looked up, and he said blithely, "Look who we have back among us, with a big new project." Immediately he began laying out the watercolors on the sawhorse worktables, doing his best to discourage questions and engaging them in discussion of the windows. Alice must have prepared the girls because just after he cast a supportive look at me and left, Minnie Henderson, the paragon of English reserve, burst out, "We're ever so glad you're back," and in a giddy mob, thirty-three lambs all rushed to hug me, some whispering words of condolence. Agnes looked on from the rear with at least a pleasant expression.

As the news got around, people from other departments stopped by to have a few words with me. Mr. Mitchell, the business manager, offered a casual, "Hello again." Mr. Tiffany must have colored the story as merely "a change of plans" rather than "abandoned by a lunatic." Bless him for that. Joe Briggs extended a halting expression of happiness that we could take up our mosaic work together again. Frank clung on to my second sleeve until I found something for him to do. Such a sweet boy. Despite the transparency of his emotions, I wished I could communicate with him in words instead of pantomime.

Albert, the Irish sheet glass stockman, came up from the basement to welcome me back, sniffling through his red nose that hung down like a trumpet flower. He gave me a long harangue about the difficulty he'd been having of "gitten the coolers loike they're wanting." He digressed to speak of the virtues of Mr. Tiffany and Mr. Mitchell, hoping, no doubt, that I would repeat his obsequious opinion to them. From this he went smoothly and naturally into a graphic account of having had the "dyspeptic." It was about the fiftieth time I'd heard his tale of woe, but I gave him my sympathy once again, knowing I would get special service in hunting glass as a consequence.

Mr. Belknap offered a sincere condolence, hesitated, and added in his thin, reedy voice, "I hope, if and when you're ready, we might resume our musical evenings. They gave me much pleasure."

"I would like that."

"I've become a member of the Egyptology Society, which permits me to bring a guest to their lectures, if that might interest you."

"It would. Thank you."

I realized I could look him in the face now, disregard his made-up eyebrows, his overly Brilliantined hair, and see beyond his fastidious appearance to his sincerity — not because of any change in him but in me.

The rest of the day I found myself peacefully absorbed in making a list of what "coolers" and textures of glass I would need for the nasturtium windows and selecting the sheets in the basement. The real comfort came when I returned after lunch and found my red-handled diamond cutting wheel in my toolbox. I greeted it as I would an old friend.

CHAPTER 16
DAISY

I spread out my accounting papers and chits for each girl on the dining-room table after dinner one evening and slumped in a chair. It had been a hard day, and it was all due to Mr. Mitchell's new scheme to squeeze more work out of us under the guise of rewarding fast workers. He had arbitrarily decreed that his brainchild of a contract system would be started next week, the first week of the new year. Time was running out for me to design a way to do the complicated bookkeeping. Every time I'd begun to draw an accounting chart that afternoon, I had been interrupted — rather, my thoughts of Edwin interrupted me, and now I couldn't hear myself think.

At the other table, Mr. Hackley and Mrs. Slater, who hears through an ear horn, were playing whist with Francie and Mr. Bainbridge, who snapped down a card and said, "Trump!" as loud as if he were onstage so Mrs. Slater could hear it. In the adjoining parlor Miss Lefevre was correcting Hank's

French pronunciation of a passage of dialog from his textbook, Miss Hettie and Alice were reading *Cyrano de Bergerac* aloud, Mrs. Hackley was teaching Dudley a new piece on the zither, and Merry was singing her Irish ballads in the kitchen.

The only quiet one was Bernard Booth, whom I had privately dubbed Mr. Book Booth. He had been away several months and was catching up on reading his accumulated issues of *The Century Magazine.* When he had returned, I could tell he'd been glad to see me, though he did seem disconcerted or troubled by something. Being a gentleman, he didn't ask about my situation. With Mother Hen Owens and the Lesser Furies, he probably didn't have to, so what I had seen on his face might have been compassion.

I didn't see how he was able to keep a thought from one line to the next in this bedlam. I slapped my hands over my ears, but I still couldn't concentrate. Apparently I let out a little wail because Bernard came through the wide arch into the dining room.

"Is there anything I can do to help?" he asked.

"I'm at my wit's end with this. His Lieutenantship, the business manager, is expecting me to come up with a bookkeeping system that allots pay bonuses to those glass selectors who finish their projects before deadline."

"Sounds fair enough."

"Hear the whole thing before you judge. In the new plan, I'm supposed to determine a production cost — time and materials — and an estimated production time for each window before we begin. It's an enticement to work faster because if the head selector on that project finishes sooner, she will receive the difference between my cost estimate and the actual cost accrued, which would be less.

"But here's the rub. Meeting a deadline isn't solely dependent on the glass selector. To make it fair, I think any earned bonus ought to be divided among her helpers — the cartoonist, pattern maker, and cutter — but not necessarily equally. It should be commensurate to the amount of work they do on it as well as their base wages, which differ depending on their classification and longevity."

"That complicates things," he murmured. "You'll need to devise a formula, and will probably need two types of accounting records."

"It's even more complicated, because the amount of time it takes isn't just dependent on the speed of the one who selects the glass but on the speed of the cartoonist and cutter as well. There are going to be hard feelings."

"Maybe the cartoonists and cutters could be rotated," Bernard suggested.

"I have to assign the cartoonists by their

skills and the nature of the project, but maybe the cutters could rotate."

"Just like Mr. Hackley," Mrs. Hackley said. "You tell him your troubles and all he can do is solve them." She let loose a salvo of strumming. "They're both these manager types."

"And what is it that you manage, Mr. Booth, besides managing to read with all this going on?"

"I manage the New York office of a London export firm."

"Fine qualifications, I'm sure. But do you manage thirty-some girls who are used to their partners and won't take lightly to rotation?"

"Excuse me, Clara," Miss Hettie said from the parlor. "This would be so much more enjoyable if we had a man to play Cyrano. Mr. Booth, would you oblige us?"

"Fame calls," he said softly.

"It's poor casting, Hettie," I said. Unlike Cyrano, Bernard had a perfectly formed nose in an appropriate size on his handsome, clean-shaven face. I gave myself time to enjoy him bending over me solicitously before I responded.

"Go to! Thy poor players await."

I was left with my scratched-out charts, seething with resentment toward Mr. Mitchell and wishing I were brighter so I could do this different kind of thinking easily. I planted my elbows on the table and stared down at my vague attempts to diagram my idea, aborted that afternoon when Mr. Tiffany had come in to see our progress on the four big conservatory windows.

He was none too complimentary. Alice; the twins, Lillian and Marion Palmié; Miss Judd, who was so careful about everything; and Miss Stoney, who was one of the original six, had all stood back to let Mr. Tiffany study what we had done so far. He never gave an assessment after only a first impression, so we had to wait in suspense as he scrutinized every aspect — coloring, textures, degree of transparency, grace of the lead lines. I had thought the windows looked gorgeous.

"Very good," he had said.

Not gorgeous. Not splendid. Just very good.

"Colors are good. These three gourds" — he pointed to them — "are too thin. We want them plump so the whole effect is luxuriant, healthy growth at the peak of the season."

I thought we had followed the cartoon, but perhaps the cartoon was in error when his painting was expanded. Or maybe the cutters had skimped.

"Easy enough to cut rounder ones and shave off the contiguous leaves and background so they'll fit," I said. "We'll make sure the ones still to be cut will have big bellies."

"Let in more light in the upper areas between the leaves. In the visual world, the mind naturally seeks light. It's a spiritual hunger. George Inness tells us that. Don't have solid foliage."

"I'm sure we followed the painting," I said.

He gave me an indulgent look. "An artist has the prerogative to change his mind." He tapped his cane once against the floor, always the preamble to his stock saying, "Infinite, meticulous labor makes a masterpiece, ladies."

Remembering him spouting that tired old saying of his was enough to sour my work on the charts that evening, charts that demanded mathematical methods I couldn't clearly conceive of, and then tedious, meticulous labor to get it all down. I puffed out a big breath onto my papers, piled them up, and went upstairs to my room, thinking how pleasant the morning had been, how much I had loved the creative work on the nasturtiums before Mr. Tiffany had come into the studio.

How curious work is. We say that we work on something, but the work is working on us too. Breaking up glass into small shapes, harmonizing colors, choosing textures, and setting them right to make something beautiful was healing. It was more than the pleasure of assembly that made it so. It was letting the colors sing, being open to their song. It was the stray thoughts that came when quietly occupied. Doing something I loved with color and light tended to make those thoughts positive ones.

Even in the throes of despair, I'd thought this morning, before Mr. Tiffany had come in, that if Edwin was walking somewhere, he might see something in cheerful yellow or orange, and it would lift his spirit for a moment. I could only hope.

If he were still in the area around Lake Geneva and heard the honking of geese and looked up, he might think of me. They mate for life, he had said. I wanted him to think of me, but I wasn't so sure that I wanted to pick up where we had left off.

The next morning I stopped at Horton's on my way to work and ordered three quarts of ice cream and a two-pound box of chocolate daisies to be delivered to the fifth floor at one o'clock. I posted a notice saying that there would be a meeting to discuss the new system. By one-fifteen they all sat in a circle, happily eating. Since Agnes was a designer now, and not officially part of the department, she stood outside the circle, but she couldn't resist the ice cream.

"The Powers That Be — I don't mean Mr. Tiffany, and I don't mean Mr. Belknap — have decided, without consulting us, that there will be no raises in wages this year. Instead, a bonus will be paid to the selector on every project if it is completed before the production deadline. However, I want to give each of you the same chance, whether or not you're a selector. We have to decide on a plan to accomplish that. You can ask all the questions and raise all the objections you want today, you can even suggest a better way, but when we come to vote, and the majority favors one plan, we all have to agree to it."

"We get to tell you whether we like it or not?" Mary McVickar asked, her voice rising.

"Today. I'll adopt whatever plan we decide on, whether it's suggested by one of you or by me, and because you decided it, you'll be honor bound to uphold it without complaint."

They looked at one another in astonishment and murmured, not used to having their opinions asked for. I doubt if they had ever heard of any factory or workshop in the city where employees, particularly women, had a say in deciding anything.

I proposed that the bonus awarded to the selector be divided among members of her team, not equally but in ratio to their base wage and the number of hours they put in on the project.

"But those selectors working with slower cutters won't be as likely to finish before deadline," said Agnes.

"True. Therefore, I suggest that the cutters be rotated. Each selector will take a turn with slower and faster cutters. What she would lose with a slower cutter she would gain back with

a faster cutter."

The floodgates opened, and in came the rushing waters.

"What's to prevent a selector from always getting a slow cutter and other selectors getting faster ones?"

"Or a cutter who can cut faster than the selector can select?"

"What will happen when there are two or three selectors working on the same window?"

"Or two or three cutters?"

"Sometimes you have to cut slower on smaller pieces."

"And on pieces with concave curves that have to be snipped round."

"Ripple glass is harder to cut."

"So is drapery glass. Some windows have a lot of it, so you have to go slower."

What seemed a simple solution at the dinner table last night became infinitely more complicated, and I felt my spirit sink. I let them have their say, and then the room fell silent, the mood heavy, all of us realizing the dilemma we shared. They ate their ice cream in slow spoonfuls.

Little by little we came up with a plan, one element of which was to rank the cutters based on the number of pieces of average difficulty they could cut in an hour. I would have to time them. In the end, everyone except the cartoonists seemed content with

what we decided, but since they often served as selectors as well, they acquiesced. I went home that night feeling rather puffed up about it. Bernard was the first to ask, and I explained what we had agreed upon.

"You're a stateswoman of the first order," he said, and I wished that Edwin, wherever he was, could hear that.

"That still leaves me to figure out an accounting system. The amount of detail this requires is appalling."

"Let me help."

Hearing his simple offer relaxed the tension I'd held in my back during the meeting. I took a moment to appreciate his hazel eyes alive with specks of contrasting colors, so sincere in his willingness to help. I felt the lifting of a burden.

After dinner I passed around the remaining chocolate daisies, and together Bernard and I designed a way to record estimates of the cost of materials, as well as enter deadlines and actual finishing dates. Then we set to work on another account book to manage the rotations. Bernard devised formulas to divide the bonuses to establish each girl's share on windows requiring one, two, and three teams, and partial teams.

After three hours, which would have been dreadful if it weren't for Bernard, I slammed closed the second account book.

"Ugh! I've never had anything to do with

this before. I'm being turned into an accountant when I want to be an artist!"

Bernard bit off a petal of the last chocolate. "She loves numbers." He bit off another petal and shook his head slowly. "She loves them not." Another bite. "She loves colors." And then he nodded.

CHAPTER 17
DIAMOND AND EGRET

George was back!

We hugged long and hard right there in the parlor. He followed me upstairs to my room, and I asked him how he was getting along. I was half afraid to hear the answer.

"I think about him constantly." His voice was flat.

I couldn't say that I did. Not constantly, a little less each week, though he regularly occupied my thoughts on weekend evenings at home, and on Sunday afternoons, when we would have gone on outings together.

"Do your parents think it was my fault?"

"They don't know what to think. My mother is still hoping he'll turn up."

I knew it would be indelicate to ask, but I needed to know. And I needed him not to blame me.

"And you?"

He drew in a long nasal breath and straightened my rag rug with his foot.

"I cleared out his things at the settlement

house today." He reached into his pocket and laid a small velvet drawstring bag into my palm. "Open it." Out rolled a narrow gold band with one small diamond. "It must have been meant for you."

Edwin's intention lay in my hand, a raised six-pronged solitaire, pure Charles Tiffany. Unanticipated sorrow threatened to overcome me. I felt ashamed of needing a memento to add to a collection that was maudlin at best, cursed at worst.

"Not exactly the Tiffany diamond, is it?" George said.

"More meaningful." It meant I had not been purposely misled.

Some days I felt the mystery of his disappearance would never reveal itself, never seem natural, never right. Seeing the ring in my palm made this one of those days. Accepting it would bind me to him as a sea captain's wife is bound, pledged to wait for the return of her beloved. I looked at it a moment longer, in case I needed to remember it some troubled night, slipped it into the bag, and folded George's fingers around it.

"Give it to your mother," I said softly.

I had no longing for diamond wedding rings. I had sold the last one. I had no longing for a wedding either. I would proceed solo in the performance of my life, and call it good.

"What will you do now?" I asked.

"Go to Nutley. Try to paint."

"You're not going to be here for New Year's Eve? The big celebration of the consolidation of the boroughs at City Hall Park?"

He hesitated on the brink of agreeing, so I went on.

"Manhattan, Brooklyn, Queens, Staten Island, and the Bronx all one city, the second largest in the world. It fulfills Whitman's prophecy of inseparable cities with their arms about each other's necks. Fireworks, cannons, ferry whistles, bands. It will be just the kind of wild, happy event you love."

"I don't feel much like celebrating anything."

On New Year's Day, Madison Square Park was splendid with every twig of the magnolia tree edged with lofty snow and illuminated by bright winter sunshine. The glory would melt within an hour. What good fortune to experience it.

"Look up! Look at that tree!" I said to an elderly lady picking her way carefully along the already slushy sidewalk.

She stopped and raised her head. Her etched wrinkles lifted in a brief bittersweet smile before she tipped her head down again to continue with the business of walking. I wondered why her smile was so brief. What had her year been like? A year passes like a revolving wheel, and when the spoke of January comes round again, it finds itself in a different place. And so with pain. It does not leave us where it found us.

I walked past a demolition project on the triangle of land created by Broadway's diagonal path, and in a few minutes, I was at the door of Hank and Dudley's studio overlooking the park.

"You bring your diamond cutting wheel?" Dudley asked.

"Of course. I have to earn my lunch."

I had agreed to trim eight large sheets of milk glass to fit into a wooden framework to separate their two working areas.

In a modest way, their studio echoed Tiffany's as a showplace of the artists' sensibilities as well as being a work space. There were the typical patterned and solid drapes for portrait backgrounds, Chinese urns, a red lacquered Japanese screen, a vase of silk irises, a Dutch blue-and-white figured bowl of wax fruit, a model's platform, and various styles of chairs to be used for portrait sittings of tycoons and their bejeweled wives pouring into New York for the high life.

"Window curtains too!" I observed.

"That's Dudley's touch," Hank said.

It was on the walls that their proclivity was evident: unframed prints of Caravaggio's *Musicians,* four feminine boys with creamy skin and full lips positioned at close range, their bodies comfortably touching one another;

231

Saint Sebastian bare to the waist and all stuck through with arrows; and Donatello's girlish *David* with flowers on his hat, standing just the way George often stood, with the back of his hand resting against his hip in a scampish way.

Hank unrolled a large mosaic cartoon to show me Dudley's entry for the American Academy in Rome prize.

"Was this for the *Triumph of Commerce* contest?"

"Yes. It amounted to no great triumph for us, though. George and I tied for third place, but that means our cartoons will be on exhibit at the Fine Arts Society. Maybe that'll bring us some attention."

"So that commerce might follow," I said with what I hoped was an encouraging look. Dudley was a sensitive fellow. I didn't want him to be disheartened.

The cutting of the large glass panels went well, without a wayward crack. It was amusing to do this mannish work while two tall men bustled around making a Waldorf salad and cucumber-and-cream-cheese sandwiches and setting the table for lunch. They were so proud to offer me a meal of their own making. It was topped off with steamed prune pudding served in mismatched teacups.

"Now this *is* a surprise," I said.

"I learned how to make it from a Quaker woman who ran the house where I boarded as a boy," Hank said.

Without a prior hint of what was on his mind, Dudley blurted, "We're worried about George. He's not himself. He's looking mighty sickly."

"We've been out to Nutley. He's had the grippe." Hank stabbed his spoon into his pudding. "He isn't painting."

"Why avoid the subject?" I said. "He thinks his brother is dead."

They both stopped eating.

"You want him to bounce back and be his impish self, like Donatello's *David*," I said. "He's not going to heal until he's working. Get him involved in something."

Dudley ran his hands through his curls. "Tried that already now."

I shared their anxiety. If Edwin's disappearance was permanent, and if George never got over it, I was afraid for our friendship, and I would feel responsible for that loss as well as Edwin's. I needed to see signs of his former frivolity in order to feel our relationship wouldn't be harmed.

George hadn't been the only one who wanted my marriage to Edwin to link us. My dream in Nutley nearly a year ago was indisputable. Only now, and only to myself, could I admit it. That didn't keep my heart from breaking over losing Edwin. It was all too complicated for quick-and-easy peace.

"Don't expect too much of him right now.

It's barely been four months. It will take time."

I put on a good show for them, but Dudley's quick glance at Hank told me they recognized it for what it was — show.

A few weeks later I convinced George to come with me to see the Havemeyer bequest of Tiffany's blown glass at the Metropolitan. I asked Alice to come too. Better to have two of us talking if he was sullen.

On the streetcar he perked up, hearing Alice talk about her favorite paintings. We went right to the gallery of decorative arts. I spotted Tiffany's work from across the room. Five glass cases were filled with blown forms, some with iridescent detailing in the motifs of feathers, flames, and arabesques. In the glass, streams meandered, clouds drifted, blossoms opened.

George stood transfixed in front of an array of free-form goblets twelve inches tall with slender stems. No two bowl portions were the same shape. One spread wide like a champagne glass. Others cupped in like tulips. Some unfurled in wavy lips like Iceland poppies. One had variegated swirls like graceful sea grass. Some coiled stems were like tendrils of a vine wrapped around nothing but air.

"How do they stand with those impossible stems?" George said. "They're so brave they

234

chill my spine."

The expertise of the glassblower to coil the stem to resemble a corkscrew, to stretch it out and set the cup on it and know it would be balanced, was beyond belief.

Of those having iridescent decoration, Alice liked best the matte pastels with pearly arabesques. George was captivated by those suggesting velvety peacock feathers, the fronds delicate and supple, the eyes of the feathers multicolored iridescent highlights.

"The fronds give rhythm to the vase," he said.

I thought of Tom Manderson, who had given me that dollop of glass. No doubt many of these were made by him, but there were no names other than Louis Comfort Tiffany's. That didn't surprise me, but I wondered how that made Tom feel.

"Where can I get peacock feathers?" George asked. "I want to paint them."

A knot of worry began to loosen. For the hour we spent marveling at Tiffany's glass, I felt sure that he didn't think of Edwin once.

"I want to see the mummies," he said.

"No. I refuse. We can't get separated. We'll never find each other."

"Mummies. Please, Mummy," he whined.

He folded his arms across his chest, flattened his hands, turned his head sharply to the left, and walked in mincing steps with both feet pointed to the left. Alice and I laughed. People looked askance at us. I didn't care. It was wonderful to see a glimmer of his former boyish self. Alice and I checked for each other's reaction, tempted to indulge him but knowing it would be dangerous.

"No," she said. "I want to show you my favorite paintings."

A good ploy. Bless her. On the way to the European galleries he stopped for a long time in front of a Chinese scroll from the Ming Dynasty called *Marsh Scene with Egrets.* The pure white birds were feeding, bathing, grooming their feathers. One was airborne, preparing for a gentle landing among the reeds. Trancelike, George didn't move, as if stillness were necessary to hear the birds speak, or the artist, reaching through centuries for the sole purpose of offering him a vision of harmony. Knowing something soulful was happening, we waited until he finally stepped away, his eyes slick as wet pond stones.

With Alice pulling on one arm and I on the other, we dragged him through corridors of Greek vases, Roman sculpture, medieval tapestries and altarpieces. Passing an Italian altar with a wooden triptych of angels in flight hanging above it, George asked, "If God died, what would happen to the angels?"

I braced myself against where he might take this, but I answered, "They'd have no deeds to carry out. No messages to deliver."

"Quite right. They'd be unemployed."

"They'd become bored," Alice offered. "They would wither away."

"No. They would turn into artists," George said, enormously pleased with himself.

Relief! Joy! He was the Jester again.

CHAPTER 18
BUTTERFLY

A wheel! A wheel! My kingdom for a wheel. At the first buds of spring I had enough left from the sale of the wedding ring Francis had given me to lay down the enormous sum of forty-five dollars for this mobile contraption and five dollars and twenty cents more at Wanamaker's for my ready-made linen bicycling costume of a fitted jacket and gored skirt, daringly six inches above my ankles. Nobody said I couldn't.

Encouraged by Bernard shouting "Tally-ho!" I wiggled up Irving Place one Saturday while he trotted alongside me, steadying me, the front wheel wagging like a metronome needle gone crazy. I didn't trust myself to turn the thing while in the saddle, so I had to get off my mechanical stallion, wheel it around, and start again. Mounting the thing was treacherous, but propelling it forward was easier. Bernard let go little by little until I was truly riding by myself.

Dudley and Hank came outdoors to be

entertained, and I felt like a little urchin who makes a couple of feeble hops on one leg without falling down, and is filled with admiration at his dexterity, doubly so because there are onlookers. Wouldn't I ever grow up?

Suddenly, a fat man appeared out of nowhere. Instead of proceeding across the street, he froze in mortal fear, taking up the whole sidewalk like an idiot and waiting for me to pass between him and the mailbox, a space of a mere yard. Such a dainty maneuver demanded more agility than I could command. It was either the squishy fat man or the hard metal U.S. mailbox. Although the former would have been more comfortable for me, I heroically crashed into the federal government, landing on hip and elbow, the back wheel spinning on top of my leg.

"Clara!" Bernard called, rushing to me along with Dudley and Hank.

"Christ a-mighty, she's down!" Dudley yelled.

Bernard lifted off the bicycle. "Are you all right?"

Dudley helped me up and steadied me. My left leg throbbed in several places, but Mother's etiquette handbook surely admonished, "Do not lift your skirt to check for injuries after a fall." My new skirt was torn near the hemline.

The fat man whose life I had saved and who had no business taking up all that space muttered, "A lady's place is in the home."

"And a gentleman's place is to give way to a lady careening toward catastrophe!" I retorted.

If I failed, it would be due to a wobbling wheel, not a wobbling will. To everyone's astonishment, when my legs had stopped trembling I mounted my wheel again and rode the length of Irving Place once more before retiring my steed to the stable.

My vanity forced me to wait for an opportune time that week when the men were gone in order to practice turning around. Not until I was proficient would they see me ride again. I donned my cycling skirt only to find the tear miraculously mended, hardly visible at all. Puzzled, I set out to practice lighting the wick on my oil lamp and found that it had been neatly trimmed. That I knew to be the work of Bernard, but could Dudley sew?

I rode up to Gramercy Park, and with wavering forward movement, I executed successfully one right turn and four lefts around the little park. I dismounted, turned the bicycle in the opposite direction, and remounted to do four semi-elegant right turns. I worked on that for half an hour, until I had the courage to attempt tight, full turns on Irving Place.

Lillian Palmié, one of the Prussian twins, had a wheel too, the Safety Model, like mine, with the two wheels the same size and a chain

balance," I said. "It's a matter of faith. You can keep upright only by moving forward. You have to have your eyes on the goal, not the ground. I'm going to call that the Bicyclist's Philosophy of Life."

"You find marvelous significance in everything, don't you?"

Bernard's brother Alistair, very blond, very British, very athletic, an amateur naturalist visiting from England, was sharing Bernard's room for the summer. One evening, he said with elocution that would please Queen Victoria, "Since we both appear to be free this evening, and Bernard is with his fiancée, would you care for a bit of company on a spin up Riverside Drive?"

A jolt went up my spine. Fiancée? *Fiancée?* I felt disoriented, as one feels the moment after a cataclysm, but it was devoid of any foundation. A couple of cycling outings did not signify any claim.

I recovered my composure enough to say, "That would be lovely," although what my baser nature wanted to say was, "How dare he keep that little tidbit of information a secret!"

We rode uptown all the way to Grant's Tomb, where thousands of New Yorkers on wheels were rolling along gaily, and the only thing that wobbled was my mind, jarred by the collapse of the illusion I had naïvely

243

believed. The shimmering lights on the other shore reflected in the river like shards of golden glass tumbling in the minute turn of a kaleidoscope to reveal an entirely different picture.

While we rested by the river, Alistair asked me if I would like to go with him on a specimen-gathering expedition in the country by bicycle. He collected moths and butterflies and wildflowers, he said.

"Where would we go?"

"Bronxville. A beautiful place near Yonkers. We can put our bicycles on the train, and ride once we get there."

A timid Victorian would say no, politely. I said yes, blithely.

On Sunday morning, Alistair Booth, decked out in a sportsman's brown shirt, knicker-bockers, felt hat, and boots, oiled both of our bicycles and checked the tires. Bernard had not been at breakfast and was nowhere in sight. Two butterfly nets stuck out of Alistair's knapsack, and collecting apparatus was strapped to his bicycle. We were off to Grand Central Depot, and forty minutes on the train brought us to the Bronxville station.

Alistair knew every rock and rut in the track. Excruciating hills alternated with thrilling, breezy descents. The narrow path was a challenge for me, with high grass and daisies on both sides. Branches sprang back at me when Alistair passed them, the names of which he reeled off, inspired.

Sunlight dappled the wild grapevine and laurel. Birds piped to each other in friendly jubilation. The woods and the frequent glimpses of the valley of the Hudson with the blue hills beyond lifted me to a state of grace, at least with nature.

Across a high meadow, goldenrod grew in a beautiful yellow swath. At our approach, the blossoms took flight.

"Butterflies!" I cried. "I thought they were flowers."

"This is what we came for. They're taxiles skippers."

He leapt off his wheel, took out his collecting jars, and tossed me a butterfly net. "See what you can catch."

Never had I seen so many yellow butterflies all in one place. They flew in a dazzling yellow cloud, and I danced in its center. They circled around one another, touched in brief midair flirtations, and darted their separate ways only to repeat the happy ritual a few seconds later. We bounded this way and that, and I swung the net with abandon, not caring whether I caught one or not. If I did by chance, I flung the net upward to send it soaring.

"Don't do that. When you get one, bring it to me."

He captured dozens of them and released

them into a large jar with airholes. One got away in the process, and I was glad. The rest flapped in a frenzy, beating themselves against the glass. I mourned their imminent death, singing to myself, "All too brief lasts earthly joy." Stunned, they lay still a moment, and I could see their beauty — variegated yellow and gold with darker gold on the edges of their wings. Among them was a solitary powder-blue one with black speckles, miraculous and fragile.

"That's a summer azure," he said.

How did they know the right moment to emerge from their cocoons? I imagined the imperceptible din of the cracked cocoon, like a clap of thunder to them, the first threadlike leg feeling its way into a vast, airy world, a faceted eye bewildered by brightness, color, and incomprehensible shapes.

"What will you do with them?"

"Pin them onto a board and seal them with glass to preserve them."

"Impale them? You murder them to study them?"

"How else?"

It was criminal to catch these beauties aloft in their prime of life and suffocate them, and I hated him for it.

He crept, he hunched, he pounced, and shouted, "I've got one! At last! A rare red admiral. *Vanessa atalanta.* I've lusted after one of these for years. This one alone would

246

have been worth the trip!"

"The trip today?"

"From England."

Trapped in a jar by itself, it flaunted its exquisite beauty — dark brown to black velvet wings decorated with a bright vermilion band on each of the four wing sections, and dazzling white patches like dollops of paint, the left wing exactly matching the right. Such care God took to design so dramatic a creature, and yet so restrained He was, not to let humans see it often. Maybe He was offering a lesson about the value of the uncommon. In that moment, I glimpsed how the sheer power of loveliness and rarity could drive the craving to possess. I thought Mr. Tiffany would understand that too. Beauty lust.

At my desk the next day, the cloud of yellow butterflies rose off the goldenrod in my mind's eye. How translucent they had looked with the light passing through their wings like it does through opalescent glass. I relegated Alistair, the killer, to the recesses of my mind, and began to draw the butterflies from memory, guessing their shapes. It was aimless, so I went about my other work, but the image of them persisted. I added more, thinking that butterflies might just be my first original motif.

That evening, I asked Alistair if I could see them. They had all died in a heap in the bottom of the jar. Some were already pinned to a corkboard. Gently, he took one out of a humidifying box, where its wings had softened enough for him to get it to relax and stay open, but when he plunged a pin into its tiny head and I heard a soft pop, I couldn't stand it and had to leave.

In bed that night, an idea flew across my hazy consciousness. Once it landed, I pounced on it as surely as Mr. Butterfly Booth had captured the red admiral. It was the secret that Mr. Tiffany and I had agreed to keep until the right time.

The lampshades of Tiffany Glass and Decorating Company were single pieces of blown or molded glass, but the dome covering the baptismal font for the chapel at the Chicago Fair had been made of hundreds of opaque glass pieces set with lead cames. A small dome constructed in that manner but using transparent and opalescent glass and placed over a light source would transmit a soft light. A lampshade could be a three-dimensional, wraparound leaded-glass window. A hundred yellow butterflies cut and placed as if in joyous flight over a sky-blue dome would revolutionize Tiffany lamp making. I could hardly wait for morning. The right moment for the emergence of our secret idea had come.

No. Not quite. I had to work out the concept first so he could envision what I had in mind. When I had confronted him before I left with Edwin, Mr. Tiffany hadn't thought I was indispensable because I only executed his or someone else's paintings. Any good selector could do that. I needed to contribute something unique and expressive of me, of what excited me, in order to become invaluable. That meant designing from the very inception of a project something he would love as much as he loved his own work.

I had to have a domelike form, wooden or plaster, to support the glass pieces. After some struggle behind my closed studio doors the next day, I fashioned a rough, shallow dome, wider than its height, in muslin stretched over wire.

I looked up, and Frank was peeking in my studio, bucket and rag in hand, to clean my window even though he had already done it once this week. He pointed to the muslin-and-wire form and cocked his head in puzzlement. A longing to tell him came over me, knowing my secret would be safe with him. He raised his hands over his head as though he was putting on a wide hat. I shook my head no, pointed to the hanging lightbulb, and made motions of bringing it down onto the table. I raised the muslin form over it. He opened his mouth wide, and I thought a sound would come out, but he just nodded vigorously, grabbed a pencil from my desk, and wrote "lamp hat." I nodded back at him, and he raised his shoulders in quick little jerks. I put my finger to my lips in a gesture indicating a secret, and he did the same. Delight spread all over his face that he knew something others didn't.

That evening I entered the room that Alistair, Mr. Butterfly Booth, shared with Bernard, Mr. Book Booth, and asked Alistair if he could mount some yellow butterflies with wings closed and some in attitudes of flight, with wings at various angles.

"It's not the scientific way. The scientific way is fully open."

"I'm not asking you to be scientific. I'm asking you to be artistic."

"It will ruin some of the butterflies."

"Then go and get more! Please?"

Alistair gave Bernard a quick, irritated look.

"Do it for her," Bernard said.

"Can't you use a book?"

He showed me a beautiful book with color plates.

"I'll use the book *and* the butterflies. It's best to work directly from nature. This is important. It just might open up a whole new art form. You wouldn't want to be the one who halted the development of art, would you?"

"Do it," Bernard commanded.

Grumbling, Alistair set to work.

Back in the studio with Alistair's collection before me, I wrapped stiff paper around the muslin-and-wire form, cut gussets, and stapled it to fit over the muslin shape. On the paper, I sectioned off what would be one-third of the shade, cut it away from the rest, and laid it flat. A fan shape resulted, much wider at the bottom than the top. Stretching out one threadlike appendage into the bigger world of designing, I drew thirty butterflies on the fan, soaring up and to the left as though a breeze were carrying them aloft. I drew lead lines around them and in the sky, which would be light blue at the bottom rim, becoming darker at the top, with a few blushes of pinkish white for clouds.

I showed Alistair's butterfly case to Lillian Palmié and Miss Stoney, and asked them to look in our bins for some beautiful yellow glass with markings suggestive of the subtle variation of color on the wings.

"What are you going to do for a base?" Miss Stoney asked, skepticism sharpening her voice.

A simple blown vase for the oil wouldn't add much. I needed this to be so spectacular that Mr. Tiffany would shout to have it made.

"A base could be made in mosaics," I said on impulse. "It could depict the meadow." Mr. Tiffany had used mosaics vertically on columns in the chapel. Joe Briggs could tell me how to get mosaics to adhere to an urn shape tapering to a bullet point at the bottom to hold the oil. Its height and slenderness would make it more elegant than the bulbous oil canisters of blown lamps. I sketched it as I imagined.

On our outing, the butterflies had risen above a field of goldenrod, but those blossoms were too spiky to be made in mosaic. The perfect flower would be the evening primrose, the creamy yellow variety, like those edging the neighbor's field on our road in Tallmadge, Ohio. Their flat petals would be easy to cut and would echo the shapes and colors of the butterflies. I went to the reference library on the second floor and found a shelf full of books of flower drawings but no primroses. And the season had passed.

What to do? Just describe it? This was beyond any minimal designing I had done on windows, so it was a risk. I wasn't considered a designer like Agnes was, but nobody told me I couldn't become one. Even a dandelion has aspirations of being a peony in full purple storm. On my desk I caught sight of the dollop of glass Tom Manderson had given me. Trust, he had said. I put it in my pocket for good luck.

With excitement pulsing in my temples, I loaded onto a cart the wire-and-muslin shade form, my fan-shaped drawing watercolored by Alice, Alistair's glass-covered specimen tray, and several pieces of opalescent yellow and amber glass. It was important that Mr. Tiffany see everything at once. I checked my appearance in a mirror and tucked a stray lock of hair behind my ear.

Passing the business office on the way, I found Mr. Tiffany sitting at Mr. Mitchell's desk with an electric fan blowing on him, making his hair move like tall grass in the wind.

"Do you have a few minutes?" I asked.

"Yes. Come in. I can't work in this humidity."

I spread everything out. "Do you remember years ago when you were working on the drawings for the chapel? I looked at the cover of the baptismal font and imagined a smaller version in translucent glass as a lampshade. It was to be our secret until the right time."

He nodded and wiped his forehead with his handkerchief.

"Isn't it inevitable that you should make leaded-glass lampshades, since you are as much in love with light as you are with color?"

"I am."

I took that as encouragement to go on. "I've been thinking how lovely it would be to wrap a window of yellow butterflies around a sun — I mean a light source."

He studied Alistair's butterflies and my drawing. "It just might be possible. Go ahead and work on it a little farther."

"I can't do much more without having a clay mold to work on."

"You have no experience in clay. I'll send Giuseppe Baratta in the plaster room to make a cast to your specifications."

Mr. Mitchell came in.

"Look here, Mitch. A leaded-glass lampshade. Not a wall sconce. This one with butterflies, but it could just as well be flowers or foliage."

"An interesting notion," Mr. Mitchell said, "but riddled with construction problems."

"I realize the shape of the shade is clumsy," I said.

"Don't be embarrassed," Mr. Tiffany said. "Most new ideas start with something clumsy."

"I'd like it to suggest a cloud. If it's possible, I'd like to pull in the bottom rim so it's not so much like the dome of the baptismal font. More like a dollop." I laid Tom's dollop in front of him. "Like this."

Mr. Mitchell rubbed his chin. "If you make a watercolor on a transparency, I'll hang it on that gas globe and think about it for a while."

"Think! I've already thought!" Mr. Tiffany said. "An entirely new line! Affordable for those who can't afford a window. A new market, Mitch. You ought to like that. What about a base?"

"I would like to complement the butterflies by suggesting that they are flying over a meadow. Instead of a blown base, it could be mosaic, couldn't it? So that I could use the

254

motif of primroses? They're yellow, and the petal shapes echo the wing shapes."

"Brilliant. Brilliant! Mosaics freed from historical or religious context. Nature is a newer, less limited, context." He shifted his gaze to me, placed his hands on his knees, and leaned toward me. "Do you realize what a huge step forward this is?"

The intensity of his blue eyes sent me his fervor, and I felt hot with the knowledge that this was a moment of great importance for him, for me, for the company. For us. We were two artists connected by an idea, and he knew it as well as I.

"I do now."

He began to draw quickly all over Mr. Mitchell's clean blotter.

"The base ought to be tall and thin." He lengthened the word *tall* while he drew long vertical lines.

"I was thinking about an urn shape narrowing to a point at the bottom." He started over and drew an urn. "But I don't know how to make it stand."

"A bronze armature with three legs could allow it to be suspended within it." And he drew that too.

How intoxicating it was to play off each other's ideas.

"Could the lines of the armature extend upward to support and enclose the shade as well?"

"Yes! All of a piece. The flowers resembling butterflies!" He stumbled on *flowers* and *butterflies.* "But not anatomically or botanically precise."

When he came to drawing a primrose, he wavered off into vague lines.

"Well, work out your own idea and show me."

My first design assignment! My own concept! This was what I had come back for!

The next morning when I arrived at the studio, a pot of hothouse primroses stood on my desk. Agnes passed by and glanced at them.

"An admirer?" she asked coolly.

"Mr. Tiffany," I said, floating in his new regard for me.

She lowered her spectacles and looked over the top of them at me, blinked once, and walked away. What was that supposed to mean?

Shrugging it off, I rotated the pot of primroses to see them all. They consisted of rosettes of leaves and sprays of blossoms, one, two, or three on tall, slender stalks. Each blossom had five cream-to-yellow flattish petals. I drew them as best I could, but I didn't have Alice's natural skill of shading to render shape. I called her over to help. We drew them botanically first, getting to know them as single flowers with narrow, pointed leaves before designing how they would be placed in relation to one another.

Agnes passed by once more and cast a look at our drawings on the way. The third time, curiosity got the better of her and she asked what we were doing.

"It's the base for a lamp," I said. "Leaded glass for the shade, mosaics for the base."

She pursed her thin lips. "Does Mr. Tiffany know?" Her tone was laced with reprimand, which brought a minute scowl from Alice.

"Oh, yes. He liked the idea," I said.

"How will you ever apply pieces of glass to a surface that isn't flat and horizontal?"

"Against a plaster mold. He's having his mold maker create one. I'll watercolor the shapes and draw the lead lines right on it."

"Freehand?"

"No. Using patterns from this fan-shaped cartoon of one-third of the round." I showed it to her.

"It's impossible to select glass against something solid." A statement delivered with brusque certainty.

I chose to take it as a challenge rather than a wish that I would fail or give up.

"I suppose I'll have to select on a glass easel against the light, just like we do for windows, foil the edges, and then transfer the pieces to the mold before it goes to the metal shop."

"How will they stick?"

"Wax? Like we do for windows?" I wasn't

at all sure wax would adhere to plaster.

"I still don't know how you're going to make flat glass fit a round mold."

"I don't know either, yet. I'll have to work by trial and error to know how small the pieces will have to be to create a smooth curve."

Alice straightened up from her drawing. "Don't worry, Agnes. She'll figure it out."

Agnes shrugged and went back to her studio. She was keeping her distance from this. She must have had reasons. I ought not to pry directly, but maybe someday I could pry open her crust.

Mr. Tiffany came in for his Monday critique of windows under production. He looked at my fan-shaped design of butterflies that would lie against the plaster form, our drawings of primroses and of the tall urn shape of the base. I had drawn a supporting ring that would be bronze, encircling the urn just below its wider shoulder, which connected a delicate trio of legs below to a cage of ribs above that would secure the shade in place.

"Good that you have the direction of the ribs following the direction the butterflies are flying. Try a slight reverse curve where they attach to the ring."

"All right. How are the flowers?"

"Too tight. You're trying too hard. Take a good look at the actual primroses and butterflies, draw them if you like, but don't copy

258

nature. We are not botanists. We are artists. Suggest nature, but conventionalize it. Stylize it. Simplify it to its contour lines to convey structure. It's artifice, after all."

"I see. Only the primness of primroses, without an unnecessary petal or flounce anywhere."

"There you go."

With that, he hadn't just given me project approval. He had given me a joyful future.

Little by little, I drew Agnes into the project. If she made some contribution, she would naturally be more supportive. In a few days, I asked her to critique my first attempt at designing where the flowers, stems, and leaves would be positioned on the base. Together we decided which blossoms would be open flat, which would still be buds, which would face backward or sideways, and where one might be missing a petal.

"Do you think a primrose is conscious of things, in a primitive way?" I asked.

"What things?" Agnes asked.

"The sense of the earth warming up, the feeling of expansion and reaching."

"Like we feel when we stretch our arms?"

"Yes. And when we stretch our minds. Does a primrose feel a new airiness and liberty as it pokes through the darkness of soil? Does it appreciate the warmth of the sun, its source? Is it aware of the cramped tightness in its buds, and the release of the strain when something wants to come out?"

"I suppose it can't stop itself from growing and opening."

CHAPTER 19
XANADU

Not fifteen minutes after I sent down the week's accounting sheets to Mr. Mitchell, he appeared at the doorway to the studio.

"Do you realize what the total is for that lamp of yours?"

"Yes. I —"

"Counting the costs of the glass, the urn, the metal, the fittings, the foundry work —"

"And the hours I put in designing it, and selecting and cutting the glass. And Miss Northrop's time and Miss Gouvy's. And Giuseppe Baratta's time and materials. I included everything. Mr. Tiffany is very pleased with it. He wants more of them."

"Why this wood-shop charge?"

"Plaster molds are good for creating painted prototypes, but they won't hold up with multiple uses. We need to score the pattern pieces onto a mold with a stylus. Soft wood is good for that."

"Well, the total comes to two hundred forty-eight dollars and thirty cents."

"I know. I did the addition."

"What that means is that we'll have to price it at five hundred dollars."

"Whooh! Twice the cost? I didn't realize."

That was ten months' room and board for me. To think that someone might be wealthy enough to buy it. To think that it was my first design.

"Once it goes into production, my design time doesn't need to be factored in," I said.

"We have to be reasonable, Mrs. Driscoll. We do want more, true, but not such extravagant ones that require so much time. Couldn't it be possible that the others you make from this model have an enamel base rather than mosaic?"

"It would lose some of the handmade quality of glass sectiliae cut to the shapes outlined on the cartoon, and perhaps some of the luminosity too."

"I'd like you to try it. It could be priced less, and we could have more on the market. Who do you have who knows enameling?"

"Alice Gouvy."

"Good. Get her started on it."

"All right. *After* we finish the eight mosaic ones that Mr. Tiffany wants."

And after I start a second design. After Mr. Tiffany *and* Mr. Mitchell see me as a regular, prolific designer.

Coming back from lunch at the boarding-

262

house, where I often lie in my darkened room to rest my eyes for twenty minutes, I saw Joe Briggs pinning something to the notice board in the corridor. Joe's talents had developed, and he served as Mr. Tiffany's assistant at times, and as mine when we did mosaic work, and was practically running the Men's Mosaic Department even though he was younger than the others.

"What's that?" I asked, not wanting to put on my glasses until I needed to at my desk.

"The Tiffany Ball. It's at his house this year. December fifteenth."

My birthday. Amid the grand celebration, only I would know I was thirty-seven on that evening.

"He wants all his employees to see his house as an example of the Aesthetic Movement," Joe said. "A synthesis of all the arts, so that we'll create in accord with his taste."

"As if we don't already."

" 'There may be a division of labor but no division of mind,' it says here. Don't you want to see his mansion? It's like nothing you've ever seen before. I've made deliveries there."

"Of course. I've been dying to. This will cause quite a stir."

It was amusing to see the ripple of news spread through the studio, the speculations of what it might be like, and the animated discussions of what to wear and who would escort them.

I knew immediately whom I would ask. I put on my glasses and made a quick sketch of the line drawing of the five-story house that was on the posted notice, complete with peaked roof, three gables, oversized arched entrance, and daring suspended turret at the corner. Under it I wrote, "If you would like to explore this fabled residence on December 15, designed by Stanford White and decorated by Louis Tiffany himself, come to dinner at 44 Irving Place and bring a new *completed* painting." It was manipulation but justified.

A week later I came home from work to find a painting covered with a cloth propped against a table in the parlor. George sat cross-legged on the floor next to it like some East Indian yogi.

"Om," he intoned. "Don't just stand there. Take a look."

I lifted the cloth and saw a lake in muted blue-gray, an empty gray rowboat beached, the oars left haphazardly, vaporous trees in the russet distance, and one lone goose aloft, pure white chest and underwings, black wing tips, neck stretched forward into the unknown. Even the oars akimbo wrenched my heart. Haste. Absentmindedness. Flight. The painting was subtle, sincere, and serious, not at all like his usual playful style.

George sat motionless with his lips pulled

in, pained and waiting.

"It's exquisite, George. You've painted his soul."

The night of the ball, George arrived in top form, wearing a loose jacket of burgundy velvet and a flowing black silk tie. He flipped it about so I would notice it. "In case this is a black-tie affair." He spun around to show off the flaring unfitted jacket with one high button and satin binding on the sleeves.

"It's rather like a bed jacket, isn't it?" I said. "An androgynous one."

He pouted for a second and then rallied. "It's the Aesthetic Dress Movement, the very synonym of style, loose garments like the Pre-Raphaelites, introduced into society by Oscar Wilde. Out with corsets and strangling paper collars. Down with restrictions. One should either be a work of art or wear a work of art. I thought Mr. Tiffany would appreciate it."

"If not him, then his wife," Alice said. She had invited Mr. York, because he's a product designer, she had said, as though she needed to declare a reason.

The four of us arrived at a mansion indeed, on the corner of East Seventy-second and Madison. Taking up four large lots, it dwarfed the mansions of Fifth Avenue. Mr. York called it Romanesque Revival. The arched entrance, wide enough for two carriages to go abreast, had a medieval-looking iron portcullis that

265

could descend and skewer any marauders who dared to lay siege.

"Don't worry. It isn't serious," George said. "It's just . . . style. Someday, there will be a name for things like this."

"Such as bed jackets as evening dress, and operas, and pictorial windows?" I said.

A courtyard beyond the portcullis was surrounded by loggias, balconies, and a grand staircase. We entered a wrought-iron elevator tended by an elevator boy in traditional evening dress who took us to the fourth floor. A ballroom of immense proportions was surrounded by tiers of carved balustrades. Favrile blown vases and flowering plants were everywhere. Walking on Oriental carpets and animal pelts, I felt as though I were entering an exotic Eastern country. No surface was left unadorned. The walls were stenciled with intricate designs, the ceiling ribbed without any square corners, alcoves between pillars canopied by carved cornices, the chimney breast faced with iridescent sea-green glass, cabinets and walls encrusted with round Japanese sword guards, wine casks of teak fretwork inlaid with ivory.

"Moorish," George said.

"Indian," I replied.

"Pakistani," Alice said.

"Turkish," declared Mr. York.

And we went round again.

"Syrian."

"Persian."

"Hindustani."

"A veritable Aesthetic Movement warehouse," Mr. York concluded.

"It's a good thing that he didn't create woman," George said. "Instead of giving her two breasts, she would have ten, and each one would be decorated with a dozen nipples."

Mr. York chortled, but Alice blushed and quickly diverted our attention to a window of iridescent and opalescent glass in orange and russet combined with abalone shell fragments in a dense pattern.

"Butterflies! No wonder he approved my butterfly lamp."

Vines and blossoms and butterflies swirled around a disk made of curved strips of orange ripple glass. The girls gathered around me to study it, with Frank in their midst, scratching his head.

"Is it a window or a mosaic?" Lillian asked.

I was puzzled. "It's hard to tell in this light."

Joe Briggs saw us clustered around it and explained. "It's both. Some of the pieces are backed with copper and gold leaf so the reflected light picks that up, like a mosaic, but the metal is so thin that daylight transmitted through the glass changes the colors completely. In the daytime, light from the room behind makes that orange disk white, and then you can see that it represents a

267

Japanese paper lantern. The butterflies are yellow and gold then."

The younger girls marveled in whispers, craned their necks, darted off to examine everything.

"Except for that magical window," said Mary, "his house is a far sight different from what we do. It's so old-looking."

"Isn't it just," Minnie said in her clipped English accent. "Rather like the *Arabian Nights*."

"Himself wants it a certain way, I suppose," said Mary.

Joe pointed out other things, as though by rights of earlier visits, he could serve as guide. Frank followed him, looking curiously at everything.

Even George was wide-eyed and quiet, taking it all in. Discreetly, he directed my attention to a woman standing with imperial grace at the far end of the room. Her flowing, waistless gown of antique gold was accented by a long peacock-blue sash descending from the back of her neck nearly to the floor like the tail of an exotic bird.

"Absolutely waistless! I've never seen —"

"Aesthetic Dress," he said.

"That's Mrs. Tiffany."

Mr. Tiffany was deep in conversation, so George and I ventured to greet Mrs. Tiffany and their twin daughters without him. I got through by uttering a few commonplaces until she brought us over to him, pronouncing *Louis* the French way, as in Louis Quatorze. I introduced George to the Sun King as an artist and decorator, but I couldn't bring myself to say "Lou-ey."

"George Waldo," Mr. Tiffany said, thinking. "Isn't it you who painted the portrait of the actress Modjeska in the Players Club?"

"Yes."

"Extraordinary. A beautiful Pre-Raphaelite fantasy."

"It's your home that's extraordinary," George said. "A many-cultured fantasy."

"Would you like to see more of it? My studio, for example?"

At that he took us up a curious little winding stair and into a vestibule where tall carved wooden doors that he said came from Ahmadabad announced the studio as if it were the palace of an Indian rajah. It seemed miles long. We peered up to find the room dissolving into night sky.

"There's no ceiling," I said.

"Yes, there is. Forty-five feet up," Mr. Tiffany said.

From that darkness a dizzying array of mouth-blown globes and heavy glass lanterns in Near Eastern shapes hung on ornate chains of different lengths. Not ordinary chains. Of course not. These had cast-iron elephants, bells, peacocks, and female figures between the elongated links. The lanterns cast colored light over Persian carpets, tiger pelts on ottomans, and velvet divans in dark, rich hues to create a luxurious but heavy atmosphere.

In the center of the room, a colossus of a tapered chimney soared into the gloom. At its flared base, four cave-like fireplace openings, one facing in each direction, looked as though they were sculpted from granite. They gave off flickering light, subtle warmth, wisps of smoke, and an aromatic fragrance.

"Is it a chimney or the trunk of a great cedar?" said George, a style assessment, not a question. "It's both, and that long Art Nouveau bracket for hanging plants attached to it is a branch."

"I wanted to bring the forest inside my house so that I might live in nature."

Along one wall a cushioned bench hung under a shimmering canopy of beaded cloth. I immediately nestled in among its pillows and let it swing. My gaze fell upon two stuffed flamingoes and the actual stone basin he had painted in *Feeding the Flamingoes*. Above it hung the round goldfish bowl. I uttered a little cry, and he pointed out his original painting on a wall nearby.

"I've officially changed the name from *Feeding the Flamingoes* to *Taming the Flamingoes*." He gave me a sympathetic look.

There was another doubling of the room in a tall, narrow oil painting depicting a slice of the chimney and one mouthlike fireplace on one edge, a cluster of columns on the other edge, and three pumpkin- and gourd-shaped blown lamps hanging over a giant philodendron and palm. On the hearth floor, a woman gazed into the fire. She was loosely draped in the folds of an Indian sari, maroon with a band of gold stitching, leaving her shoulder, arm, and back alluringly bare.

Mr. Tiffany saw me admiring it. "It's Lou," he said.

I knew it already, for the love conveyed in every feature.

George turned in a circle, arms out to his sides, palms up. "This is Xanadu, and you are Kublai Khan."

"Oh-ho! I like that," Mr. Tiffany said.

"Even though from different origins, everything is in harmony," George said. "It's Oriental in effect but not in every detail. It's as if you had gone to the same sources of inspiration that Eastern cultures had, but you've evolved your own conception of their principles."

"You have keen aesthetics, Mr. Waldo. It has always been my creed to use whatever seems fittest in wood or stone or glass, no matter its cultural origin."

"Don't you think that beauty can also originate from within?" I asked. "From a person's joy or sadness, and not just from external cultural sources?"

271

"Of course. Like your butterfly lamp. When a person observes nature, his emotions affect his artistic vision. You were obviously bewitched by those butterflies, and I want you to be enchanted by more things in nature."

"That won't be hard."

"Do you actually work here?" George asked.

"I play here. Every day."

He led us through a forest of easels with partially finished paintings to his banquet-sized drawing table in the depths of the room.

"Lately I'm getting interested in clocks," he said, and showed us some drawings. "People who can't afford a window can afford a clock, and that will bring beauty into more homes. Some day, Clara, design me a clock that will make people value time."

Design me. . . . Design me. . . . It was happening. After only one lamp and a couple of windows, he was thinking of me as a designer. I had contributed something unique and expressive of me. I had distinguished myself, and he would use my talents again and again — just what I longed for.

"Let something else bewitch you, and find a way to use it as a motif, like you did with the butterflies. Desire takes over where knowledge leaves off. So many things are yet to be explored. Enamels, for example. And amber."

He dug his hand into a bowl full of irregular amber beads. "Do it. It feels so nice." We both did, and smiled at the sensation, letting them pour out between our fingers.

"And shells." He put a large polished chambered nautilus into George's hands. "Touch it to your cheek," he said. George did, and then he put it alongside mine. Its cool smoothness felt like the deep sea. "Cover your ear with it." The sound of distant surf transported me. "Hold it up to the light." Its iridescent surface revealed striations of pale pink and lime green and aqua. "With a light source inside, the colors are even more pronounced and you can see the veining. I've designed a bronze stand, and it will be wired as a small electrolier."

He held out a large Chinese bowl full of pieces of mother-of-pearl. "Put your hand in here. Play with them."

"They feel like nuggets of satin," I said. Most had smooth surfaces, but some were distressed like baroque pearls. "The smooth ones are elegant, but I think the rough ones are more interesting."

"You're thinking in the right direction." With a flourish he showed us his cuff links. They were irregular mother-of-pearl disks edged in silver. "You'll gain in skill and vision every project you do. Pick out some pieces that appeal to you. Make something with them. Whatever you'd like."

A lamp. It would be a deep sea lamp.

"Do I have to keep costs down?"

"No."

CHAPTER 20
SEA HORSE

A week of pondering passed before I told Alice about the ten mother-of-pearl pieces Mr. Tiffany had let me choose. She picked them up from my worktable one at a time and rubbed her thumb over their whorls and irregularities, each one the size of a quarter.

"They're beautiful."

"Yes, but wanting to use them and then making a design to show them off is something like buying a dress to match a pair of gloves."

"Last time you started with the shade and then designed the base. Now you're doing the opposite."

"I guess it doesn't matter. I might be able to use a tin umbrella pail as a foundation, and on that, I'll build up the shape in modeling clay. Two feet tall."

"Awfully tall for oil."

"I want it dramatic. Maybe there could be a removable inner canister for the oil, like an oatmeal boiler. It would be easier to fill that way."

"Where will the shells go?"

"I think at the shoulder. It's the most prominent part. I'll press some of the shells into the clay and rough out my design to show Mr. Tiffany. If he says it's worth pursuing, I'll have Giuseppe make a plaster cast. I'll draw the design on that."

"Do you have a design in mind?"

"That's where you come in. I need a design for the shade too. Let's go to the aquarium in Battery Park on Sunday."

We were entranced by fish — tiny, rotund, freckled, striped, sleek, bulbous, mean-looking, sweet, spiky, and spooky. For the lampshade, we chose to use some beautiful coral-colored ones, slightly silver-blue on their bellies, with double-pointed tails. We would set them among seaweed leaves in greens and ochers against blue ripple glass.

Looking at the sea horses, I murmured, "What a God, to have conceived of so delicate and calm a creature. Nothing perturbs them. They're at peace no matter what floats by. If only one could live that way."

"They look ancient," Alice said.

"And innocent."

"You've got to use them."

"On the mosaic base, I think."

We sat on a bench in front of the tank and

drew them in various attitudes, some with tails curled forward and their long snouts pointed down, others stretched out with their backs arched. I also drew fans and branches of coral and noted the colors, rose madder dulled with aquamarine, and burnished yellow-orange.

"Don't copy nature," Mr. Tiffany had said. Let nature merely suggest. Express yourself through nature. That made the drawing flow.

On Monday I came to work anxious to see again the clay form I had modeled over an umbrella pail. I removed the dampened muslin. Pieces had cracked and fallen away. The clay had shrunk, and the form was ruined.

"This will *not* destroy me," I said firmly to my penciled sea horses.

I went to see Giuseppe without a form, just with drawings, side view and top view, with dimensions. He said he could work from them to make a plaster model, but I'd have to do some carving to get exactly the shape I had in mind.

I thought it prudent to involve Agnes, so after I made my preliminary drawings of sea horses, coral, and seaweed for the mosaic base, I asked for her advice on positioning the elements naturally.

"There is absolutely nothing like this that I've seen in the decorative arts," Agnes said.

Her eyes shone, giving me a rush of satisfaction.

The Tiffany Week ended Thursdays at five-fifteen, when all the accounts had to be collected for reconciliation — the week's work detailed and recorded, the cost of time and materials figured, and the payroll determined as well, for submission first thing on Fridays. On Thursday afternoons, three o'clock arrived to throw cold water on whatever project I was working on. With dampened spirit, I had to break away, armed with my clipboard, to gather the week's charges from other departments.

In the metal room I was stopped by Alex, the foreman, with a pencil behind his ear and some papers covered with labored figures.

"I thought I'd have to hunt you down. Got anything against me this week?" he said in the slang of the metal room, a way of asking if his department owed my department any money.

"Yes, three dollars and a half for lamp design."

He recorded it mournfully, and I said, "Got anything against me?"

"Only fifty cents."

"What for?"

"Aciding on window 7378."

"But my department is doing all the aciding on that number."

"Well, my man mixes the acid."

"Oh, all right." I borrowed his pencil to make a note of it, and hurried on to the elevator.

As I rang the bell, he called after me, "You forgot to give me back my pencil."

Pencil returned, we each went our separate ways to make out our puny bills against each other.

After dinner, with my accounting sheets spread out on the dining table, I recounted this trifling routine to Bernard while I laboriously entered the amounts and figured the receipts and expenditures.

"What an exorbitant amount of time this accounting takes," I said.

"There are certainly more expedient ways for the departments to tally the charges," he said.

"I'm sure there are, but this one is entrenched, and as a result, I'm forced to do double duty. I refuse to let go of the designing, but I almost regret that I'm good at managing production. If I weren't, I wouldn't have to fiddle around with numbers every week."

"Regret it enough to hide it?" Bernard asked.

"No. It's just that it's a mixed blessing. What I want to do and what I have to do are always fighting each other like alley cats."

"But you love it all the same, don't you?"

He gave me a penetrating look that nearly unnerved me.

"Yes. I love it all the same."

Mr. Tiffany had said he wanted a clock, so I took the risk to design one, determined that he would get a simple one before the month was out. I thought how smooth and lustrous the smaller mother-of-pearl pieces were, so I went to the purchasing agent and asked him to get five hundred flat-backed mother-of-pearl beads, each about a quarter of an inch in diameter.

The next morning I spent a couple of hours way downtown on Maiden Lane, a narrow street south of the Brooklyn Bridge near the docks where the silversmiths and clockmakers had their dark little workshops. One German fellow with curly gray muttonchops had several clock mechanisms, some with short pendulums, ready to be mounted into cases, and one already in a wooden case with a beveled glass door about eight inches high.

"How much for one of these?" I asked, pointing to the mechanisms.

"Come back three days. I put it in."

"No. I don't want it in."

"No case?" His thick eyebrows came together in a hedge of puzzlement.

"That's right. No case."

He scowled. "No. I don't sell. Only finished clocks in boxes."

Pride in his workmanship. I understood that.

"How about if I buy that one in the case now, and two more without the cases?"

He squinted at me as though trying to figure me out, but need overcame his suspicions, and he said eagerly, "Yes. Now I sell."

He called his wife, who came out from the back room in her carpet slippers, chewing. In loud, fast German, he directed her to start wrapping the pieces in newspaper, and he hastened to add up the price, all the time scurrying about as if he wanted to be done with this irrational woman.

Back in the studio I found some rectangular pieces of opalescent glass in swirls of green and blue for panels to be bordered by rows of mother-of-pearl beads. I was on my way to please Mr. Tiffany with clocks.

"Q, R, S, T, U. What comes next?" George asked at dinner.

"W," I said, just to be contrary.

"Nooo. Who started the Staten Island Ferry?" George asked.

"Mr. Staten," Alice answered, picking up my cue.

"Wrong again."

"Who lives in Hyde Park?"

"Edward Hyde," Francie replied. "Dr. Jekyll's evil side."

"Very wrong."

"Then Queen Victoria," Bernard said. "Actually, it's a bit of a jaunt away."

"Such as she is to the Irish, refusing us home rule," Merry muttered.

"Wrong Hyde Park," George said. "What ought to be the most comfortable room in a house?"

"The loo," Bernard said.

Mrs. Hackley hiccuped her disapproval of saying that vile word at the dinner table.

"The bedroom," I suggested quickly to stop her from chastising him.

"Clara's right. So don't you get it?"

"No. We don't get it because we're all bloomin' eejits," Merry said. "I have a house full of 'em. Enough to send a decent landlady like me to an early grave. Ignore 'im and maybe he'll go away."

"I think you'd better tell them, George," Hank said.

"Have you figured it out?"

"Simple," Hank said. "*V* comes after *U* and stands for Vanderbilt, 'the Commodore' Cornelius Vanderbilt, who started ferrying people from Staten Island to Manhattan in a second-hand sailboat when he was a boy, built up a shipping line, then a rail line, and became the richest man on the continent. His grandson Frederick recently purchased an estate on the Hudson called Hyde Park only to tear it down and rebuild it, and hired our own George Waldo to decorate the most comfortable room in the mansion, Vanderbilt's bed-room."

"You're right, comrade!" cried George. "Bravo!"

"How did you make it happen?" asked Dudley.

"When I went to the settlement house to get Edwin's things, I stopped in at Justus Schwab's saloon, a place he frequented. Seedy and very Lower East Side. A bohemian enclave transported from the cafés of Eastern Europe. I talked to immigrant Jewish intellectuals, artists, labor sympathizers, socialists, journalists, and asked them all if they knew or had seen Edwin. Several people knew him, but no one had seen him. One man said that Edwin had made their lives his lifework."

Scorched dry I was, instantly, by emptiness and irony. His passion for helping others made him a rare human being, and I loved him for it enough to think I could give up the work I love, but as it happened, he was the one who forfeited his lifework, allowing me to keep mine. Was that fair? Was that right? Oh, to be at peace, whatever floated by.

"Mostly I listened," George went on. "I didn't understand a lot of it. Quarrels flared up in Yiddish, Russian, German, all at once. Emma Goldman was haranguing. I went back several times to hear arguments about radical reform movements, anarchists, Yiddish theater, Gorky, Zola, Tolstoy, even Whitman. I began to understand why Edwin liked living there."

"If he could stand the smells," Mrs. Hackley said.

In defense of Edwin, I was annoyed at her for having to say that.

"I noticed uptown gentlemen out for adventure in the slums," George continued. "Social tourists, you might call them, at odds with their class. There are even self-styled guides, protectors, and interpreters to squire these fellows around to the cafés where things are happening. I made connections at Schwab's with a few of the uptown interlopers. One of them invited me to the Century Club, where I happened to be introduced to a Monsieur Glaenzer, one of the decorators on the Vanderbilt estate operating out of a warehouse near here. He offered me a post, and I accepted it on the spot."

"Nimble, my boy," Hank said, holding up his glass. "What a scoop! A new chapter in the tale of bohemia turning outsiders into insiders. It's worth an article. 'Products of a culture of bland material comforts seek intense experience with the nation's fiery newcomers.' "

"What was it called? Schwab's? I want to go there," I said. "I can take my wheel."

"Be reasonable, Clara. If George couldn't

find Edwin, you certainly can't," Bernard said.

"That's not why I want to go. I meant that I want to hear Emma Goldman."

"That anarchist?" Bernard scoffed. "Not without a protector."

Calm as a sea horse, I said, "Don't be an old stick-in-the-mud, Bernard. She's a woman acting on her opinions. That's why I want to hear her."

CHAPTER 21
DRAGONFLY

It had seemed no great matter that Edwin hadn't seen the dragonfly at Lake Geneva dazzle me with its gorgeous rainbow wings, but now I wished he had. He'd been tutoring me in concern for the less fortunate, and I had wanted to tutor him in matters of beauty. A person ought to have a counterbalance to downward thought. Allowing beauty a place in the soul was a powerful antidote to the stress and strain of mortal life. It would have done him some good.

I set my clock aside and began to draw the dragonfly as I remembered it. The wings were long and narrow, two on a side. Mr. Nash's iridescent glass would be perfect, glistening in emerald green, turquoise, cobalt, and purple.

Like sea horses, dragonflies were remnants of an ancient epoch when pigs were dinosaurs without brains enough to step around tar pits. What a fecund, swampy world dragonflies saw below them, flashing their brief warnings at dinosaurs too dull to notice their call to escape while they could.

In my drawing, I exaggerated the size of the eyes. I wanted them to glow red-orange like the sun descending on the lake that last happy evening we had together. Molten glass could be dripped into half-spherical molds, or the eyes could be beads. If I used beads, I could have the hole in the bead facing out so a pinpoint of light would shine through. Gracious, what a lark this was!

Then I was stumped. I didn't know what the body was like. I rushed downstairs to the library and bumped into Mr. Belknap coming through the doorway carrying ecclesiastical textile designs.

"Why such a hurry?" he asked.

"Ideas make me hurry."

He was too curious to go on his way. I found a book on insects, which had precise entomological drawings of different sorts of dragonflies. *Libellula lydia.* What a lovely name. *Belle,* French for beautiful. *Lydia.* Feminine. A good omen. Behind the roundish head, the body and tail consisted of seven tapered sections. Each one would have to be a separate piece of glass, with the end one no bigger than a pencil eraser.

"The tails would be lovely in emerald, wouldn't they? For a lamp."

"Ah. Indeed," Mr. Belknap said.

"Do you find them strange-looking, with a

north-south axis and an east-west axis?" I asked.

"No. They're beautifully exotic. Dragonflies are often used as a motif in the Aesthetic Movement."

"I wish you hadn't told me that."

"Why?"

"I would rather it be seen as my own devising."

"Oh, you'll do something original with them. I'm sure of that."

"How can I get the veins in the wings? I want the look of black lace."

"You wouldn't want it painted on?"

"Too time-consuming. Mr. Mitchell would have a mortal fit. He's already complained about the labor cost on the butterfly lamp. I'm afraid if this one is that expensive again, he'll kill it. Or Mr. Platt will, since he's the moneybags. And if they kill this idea, what does that do to the next idea and the next? Until I get the lamps established as a vital part of the business, it's important that each one is approved and goes into production."

"These lamps mean that much to you?"

"They mean the world to me. I conceived them. They're my own expression. I can go anywhere with them. Insects, flowers, fruit, vines, birds. Maybe even landscapes. The possibilities are endless."

"And too expensive. That's not my opinion. It's Mr. Platt's."

"You mean Mr. Scrooge's," I whispered. "Miss Stoney told me his first name is Ebenezer. Is that true?"

"Unfortunately, yes."

"Anyone whose real name is Ebenezer would do well not to aspire to financial occupations."

"Out of kindness, we don't use his first name."

"It still leaves me on edge. I have to make this dragonfly lamp more exquisite and more individual than any blown shade, more art than craft. It's got to have a place in Mr. Tiffany's heart so he'll circumvent the tight fists of Platt, Mitchell, and Company."

Mr. Belknap fidgeted with his thumbnail. "I hate to be the one to tell you. At Mr. Mitchell's suggestion, the men's department has begun to develop leaded-glass shades in simpler geometric designs."

A cannonball landed on my chest.

"No! The idea was mine! The process is mine! Mine even more than Mr. Tiffany's."

My intention to be as unperturbed as a sea horse vanished.

"There's a danger in claiming sole ownership of an idea, Clara. Ideas can originate in more than one place and time. For example, Mr. Tiffany produced leaded-glass wall sconces with Thomas Edison for the Lyceum Theatre."

"Like my department does? With copper

289

foil on small pieces?"

"No. They just dribbled melted lead over a tray of chipped glass. It was all experimental in those days."

"Then it wasn't like mine, but the men doing geometrics with flat glass is a clear usurpation of my process."

"You can't restrict usage of a process, Clara." Mr. Belknap raised his shoulders. "In any case, geometrics will be simpler and faster to produce, and that means they'll be less expensive. Mr. Platt sees it as a money-maker. That should at least give you some assurance of his belief in leaded-glass shades."

"At the same time as it robs me of my specialty."

"Not entirely. Since Mr. Tiffany believes that women have the more acute color sense, you may have to supervise their selectors closely."

"Won't that be a feat of diplomacy!" A bit of Emma Goldman's anarchy sparked in me. "What if I refuse?"

"I wouldn't recommend that. Don't worry. Theirs will be craft. Yours, art."

He gave me an understanding look and turned to the dragonflies. "Maybe the veins could be made in the glass."

"Threads of opaque black glass dripped over the iridescent? It's too intricate to be left to chance. I'd have to be right there directing each trickle of glass."

"Mr. Nash wouldn't allow a woman to work in the hot shop."

"Do you think the metal shop could make filigree overlays in these wing shapes if I designed them?"

"They could. They could do it with acid etching. Do you want me to ask them?"

In a surge of yearning, I said, "I do," and it felt and sounded like a marriage vow.

"I want this to work for you, Clara."

"And I want to matter here."

I walked around the studio to advise on Mr. Tiffany's *Four Seasons* windows. *Spring* had orange and purple tulips in the early morning when the sky was silvery, using clear glass drizzled with angular black threads to represent still-leafless twigs against sky. *Summer* showed lush Oriental poppies with a lake reflecting a cobalt-blue sky at midday. *Autumn* depicted the harvest of apples, Concord grapes, and golden corn, each kernel a separate piece of glass, with an early moon several layers behind the diaphanous sky. *Winter* presented an evening campfire burning below a pine bough covered in melting snow with sparkling drips of water.

The panels were to be positioned two by two in an eight-by-ten-foot rectangle intended for the 1900 Paris Exposition Universelle. The girls took to this project enthusiastically, identifying themselves as "summer girls" or "spring girls," depending on their assignments, learning the French names for the seasons, and greeting one another with lilting *bonjour*s. All this I encouraged because the project presented a challenge. Each panel had areas several layers thick, so progress was slow and I had to keep them from getting discouraged.

The intricate decorative areas framing the four scenes had round, protruding, press-molded cabochons, and hammer-chipped chunks we liked to call jewels, of the type I had given to Wilhelmina. Miss Byrne was the best jewel chipper, so I assigned her to work on all the panels.

"I like the sharp-edged chunks better than rounded cabochons, so may I use more of them?" she asked.

A timid, older woman, she rarely gave her opinion, so I was curious to know what lay behind her request. "In order to give off more intense sparks of light?" I asked.

"Well, they do, but it's because they suggest that someone enjoyed creating them by hand." She smiled at me sheepishly, revealing her delight in spite of herself.

"Ah. Go ahead, then."

I came back to my drawing table and made cutouts of six open-winged dragonflies and placed them nose down around the bottom edge of a wide conical shape I'd made of stiff paper. It looked too regimented. Alice suggested to soften them by putting marsh flowers between them at the upper portion of the cone, but I thought that would compete with the dragonflies. Agnes thought the wings could overlap. I liked that idea, even though it would make it impossible to use the same filigree metal overlay patterns on each wing. Each one would have to be designed and made individually, which would be more expensive.

I went ahead with that plan anyway, and took it to Giuseppe to have the plaster mold made. When he delivered it, I didn't like it. It was too conical, too sharply geometric, especially now that I knew the men's department was making geometric leaded shades. I went to work shaving off the bottom edge to curve it inward. Just that little adjustment made it more graceful. I gave my cartoon to Alice for her to trace it onto the mold and watercolor it according to my color scheme.

When I worked out the cost, using the estimate from the metal shop for the wing overlays; the iridescent glass, which was more expensive; and the fittings and a simple squat vase for an oil canister, I worried. The base was a compromise. I really wanted to make a mosaic one suggesting a pond, but I needed to get the lamp approved, so I settled on the less-expensive blown form. I didn't want to send Mr. Mitchell into a state of apoplexy.

■ ■ ■

By week's end, I was pleased with it and took the painted plaster and some glass samples to the Divinities of the nether floors for approval.

Mr. Mitchell's voice rumbled in his throat before he said, "Original," as if he felt called upon to praise it against his will. "How much, time and materials?"

"Ninety-seven dollars if I use iridescent glass, eighty-seven dollars if I don't."

"Ouff."

"That's without a base, but it includes my design time, which wouldn't be factored in on subsequent models."

He left and came back with the other Crowned Heads: Mr. William Thomas, assistant business manager; Mr. Henry Belknap, artistic director; and Mr. Ebenezer Scrooge Platt, treasurer.

"Mr. Tiffany is feeling poorly, so we'll decide," Mr. Platt said.

"I can wait," I hastened to say. I needed Mr. Tiffany's vote.

Mr. Belknap turned the plaster model to show it off from all directions. "It's exquisite," he declared.

Mr. Platt squinted at it with beady countinghouse eyes. "Impractical on account of the cost." His prominent Adam's apple bounced above his paper collar.

"I agree," said Mr. Thomas.

I figured he was a mouse by his plain, Midwestern farmer looks, his mousy little mouth working as though nibbling on a hay seed, and his thinning, mouse-colored hair. At least Ebenezer Platt was distinguished-looking, with a high swoop of silver-gray hair.

"But it would generate talk," said Mr. Belknap. "It ought to be shown at the Paris Exposition. We have to speculate on extraordinary pieces once in a while despite their cost, for the sake of our reputation and to keep ahead of the competition. I think it's a good investment. It's a bravura piece, and its debut in Paris is bound to be greeted with enthusiasm."

Bless him.

Mr. Tiffany came into the room looking pale except for dark circles under his eyes. His eyebrows popped up when he saw the painted mold. He sat in front of it and gestured for Mr. Belknap to turn it around. I held my breath.

"It's the most interesting lamp in the building. Try some simple foliage at the top. Long, narrow leaves to set off the detail of the dragonflies."

Alice's idea exactly.

"What kind of a base?"

"I thought about a squat, blown form in the green-to-blue range to suggest water."

295

"Too subtle. We need a more obvious element to unify both parts. Model a socle, like a wreath of lily pads, around the bottom of the base, to be made of bronze. It'll be a Japanese touch."

"That will raise the cost even more," said Mr. Mitchell.

Mr. Tiffany ignored him.

The splotch on Mr. Mitchell's cheek reddened. Tiffany's word was law. I lifted the plaster cast and sailed out of the office feeling as mighty as the woman in the harbor with upraised arm.

Mr. Farmer-John Thomas followed behind me.

"You're a dangerous influence here. Don't overreach yourself, Mrs. Driscoll," he said in a threatening voice.

I'm sure he could not detect any unevenness in my stride as I walked between the gilt doors and into the elevator, thinking, *I lift my lamp beside the golden door!* With only the elevator boy to hear, I said, "I am an *influence. I* am an influence."

The prototype dragonfly lamp went into the showroom a month later, prominently placed on a table by itself. The next day, the Tiffany tap came down the hall at breakneck speed. Mr. Tiffany sat down close to my worktable and said, "A rich woman just purchased your dragonfly lamp."

"Wonderful!"

"I told her she couldn't have it."

"Why not?"

"I want the first one to go to London for a show at the Grafton Galleries. I told her you would make her another. And I want three more on the condition that one will be done in a week for that customer."

"I can do it," I blurted, though I wasn't at all sure.

Using my most urgent persuasion, I would have to build a fire under the men who had a part in it — the solderer, the metalworker who would make the burner base, and the bronze caster who would make the filigree on the wings according to my drawings and the socle of lily pads according to my wax model. I knew I could count on Mary McVickar to cut, and to come in an hour early until we finished. I wanted to do the selecting myself.

"The second one will replace the prototype in the showroom," Mr. Tiffany said, "and a third one will go to the Paris Exposition Universelle next year. That one has to be a stunning showpiece that will make La Farge wilt into his boots."

My chance!

"For Paris, how about a squat mosaic base with low belly, no shoulder, and rectangular tesserae placed concentrically in colors of blue and green to represent a pond? It will show off your iridescent glass. And" — I grabbed a breath — "bronze overlays of dragonflies set diagonally as though they're flying over the pond, and water plants growing from the bottom."

"Complicated, but possible. Very possible." His artist's eyes had a shimmery, far-off expression, as though they were seeing parallel to mine, exactly what I had described. He turned his gaze to me, and his minute, slow nod was contemplative, collegial, and — dare I think it? — loving.

"Don't go to them for approval. Bring it to me."

Chapter 22
Wisteria

Bernard was attaching our new improved bicycle lamps when I got home from work that day. They used carbolic acid in the igniting mechanism. That wasn't something I wanted to think about when my mind was swirling with the prospect of making a dragonfly lamp for Paris.

"Care for a little spin tonight?" he asked.

"Oh, no, thanks. I'm too weary."

"Just a wee one before dinner?"

"All I want to do is to lie down awhile and close my eyes. I'm sorry. Let's do it tomorrow evening."

"In that case, would you like me to read more of *A Woman of No Importance* to you?"

It was Francie's choice for this month's play reading.

"No, thanks. I detest that title!"

"I believe Oscar Wilde meant it ironically."

I touched his arm lightly as a way of showing appreciation.

Upstairs in my room I drew down the shade

and fell into sweet oblivion as soon as I hit my pillow, and was awakened by Hank and George in animated conversation coming up the stairs. Oh, Lord, they were heading for my room. I buried myself more deeply at the knock.

"We know you're in there," George said.

"I'm resting."

He opened the door. "That's all right. You don't have to open your eyes. I'll only have to repeat everything if you don't listen now."

"Just don't pace. Sit, and don't talk loud."

He landed with a bounce at the foot of my bed, and Hank took the only comfortable chair. George had been at the Vanderbilt mansion in Hyde Park all week, and launched into a description.

"French classical . . . half-round portico . . . massive columns."

I was aware of his voice in the same way I was aware of birds chirping outside, but I didn't follow what he said any more than what the birds said.

"Gilded moldings . . . herringbone parquet floors . . . Isfahan carpets . . . Brussels tapestries . . ."

Bernard ducked his head in the doorway. "Give the poor woman a little peace. Tell us at dinner."

"She wants to hear now," George protested.

"No, she doesn't. Out. Out."

"Who are you to say what she wants? Her

protector?"

"Everyone, please," I begged.

I felt George leap off the bed, and got twenty minutes' quiet before the dinner bell rang.

"Don't you want to hear what Monsieur and I are going to do for Freddie's bedroom?" George asked, passing a platter of boiled pork sausage.

"Freddie?" Dudley said archly.

"We can't live another minute without knowing," Francie cried. "Save us before we expire."

And off he went again. "Freddie wants his and Louise's bedrooms to be unrestrained fantasy chambers. Since she's such a Francophile, hers will be Louis the Fourteenth, and his will be Italian Renaissance. She can imagine herself as queen to a Louis, and he can imagine himself as a Medici."

"Quiet down, George," Merry said. "Not everyone wants to know."

"Oh, yes, we do," said Miss Lefevre at the other table. "Just so madame doesn't make the mistake of imagining herself queen to Louis the Sixteenth," she said, drawing her finger across her throat and catching the ribbon of her pince-nez, which sent them flying.

"His bedroom will have carved wooden panels containing whimsical characters. Guess who gets to design them!"

"Michelangelo," Francie replied.

"Me!" He grinned a silly grin.

Oh, he was rolling now, back to his old self. I didn't want to diminish his triumph by sharing one of my own. It would keep for another day.

Thursday, Accounting Day, the day I liked least, came all too soon. I hoped to get the design for the mosaic dragonfly base finished by noon so that I wouldn't have to dash around madly from three to five to make the rounds gathering accounts, but I could do it from one to three instead and have the two hours remaining to work out the bills in the studio instead of taking them home.

No chance for that. Mr. Tiffany had gone home sick after the meeting about the dragonfly lamp and stayed home for three days, but apparently he had improved enough to worry about *Winter,* a panel of the *Four Seasons* window. Yesterday he had telephoned Mr. Belknap saying he wanted to see me about it today.

To mark the occasion of a visit to his home, I dressed in my good black skirt, my newest white waist, and a narrow tie of emerald green, which he proclaimed was his favorite color, along with peacock blue, turquoise, and ruby. I put on my black felt hat that I thought he would like because of the iridescent feathers. In the studio, I found a good-sized piece of drizzle glass representing pine needles, wrapped it carefully in flannel, and took the open-air electric car up Madison to Seventy-second Street. I arrived at eleven, which I thought was an appropriate hour.

What a monster of a house it appeared in the daytime. Whoever heard of a medieval spiked portcullis in Manhattan? I was working for an eccentric! I passed under it quickly, walked through the courtyard garden, and took the elevator to the fourth floor. A housekeeper ushered me into the library, where I had never been before.

A large bay window of magnolia panels spread wide before me. The opalescent petals in milky white and pearly cream with blushes of pink reminded me of the glorious magnolia tree in Madison Square Park. The lead cames of various thicknesses had been textured with irregular grooves and ridges and patinated in a dark brown to simulate twigs and branches. Above the vertical panels were square transoms of abundant wisteria entwined on a trellis with blossoms of deep purple, blue, and pink cascading down in various lengths over clear glass.

"Papa fell asleep," said a prim little pixie who had snuck up on me in her pink stockinged feet. She blinked her big blue eyes like her father's. "He tried to stay awake till you came. I don't think he'll wake up until the afternoon."

I felt like a lout to have kept the poor man waiting. The self-possessed elf child tipped her head, expecting a response, and when she righted it, her expertly cut Dutch-girl bob fell back exactly in place.

"I see. And what might your name be?"

"Dorothy."

"Well, Miss Dorothy of, how many, seven years?"

"I'm eight, however small."

"I beg your pardon. Miss Dorothy of eight years, you must tell him when he awakes that I would be happy to come back."

I had been at my desk only fifteen minutes, just long enough to spread out my accounting sheets, when Frank rushed in to summon me by urgent gestures. He always appeared urgent about everything. If I could understand his finger spelling, I would have known it was for the telephone call and I wouldn't have had to go back up three flights of stairs from the office floor to get my hat and coat. As it was, the sweet voice on the line chirped, "Papa woke up and wants to see you now."

Upstairs, downstairs, on with my hat and coat, out the door, and onto the electric car again. It took off with a lurch, and off flew my hat in the wind. I tried to extricate myself and leap off the car to get it while we were rolling along, but two men restrained me as if I were suicidal. At the next stop I got off, calm as a sea horse to show I was in my right mind, then hurried back two blocks, looking for it. I lingered about miserably. It was George's favorite. Fuming that someone had snatched it up in just those few minutes, and anxious not to be late for Mr. Tiffany and get there only to find that he'd fallen asleep again, I boarded the next car and arrived in time.

Little Miss Tiffany took me into a large room with a fire crackling, flowers on every flat surface, and other lovely things that I didn't have the presence of mind to enjoy because Mr. Tiffany lay abed, eyes open, hardly making a mound in the fluffy coverlet. Seeing him so pale and fragile made losing my hat seem less important.

He reached out his hand for me to take. "I apologize for not being awake when you came this morning," he said in a weak voice.

"You've been working too hard."

"I can't seem to help it." He gestured for me to pull a wicker chair cushioned in emerald green toward the bed. "Closer," he said, and with effort he raised himself to a sitting position. He had a rose pinned to his Indian silk dressing gown.

"Do you think that rose will help you breathe better?"

He patted it lightly. "It's my companion. Now, since I missed my Monday rounds, I want to know how all the projects are coming along."

I reported that the last of the three mosaic panels depicting scenes from Homer that we had been working on for Princeton was more than half completed. Since the three panels together were eighty feet wide and we were that far along, he was pleased. I described our progress on the butterfly lamp with Alice's prototype enamel base duplicating the mosaic primroses, and Agnes's magnolia window for the Paris Exposition.

"It's the worst time for me to be away, with windows needing to be installed in four churches by Easter, and the Grafton Galleries show in London, and the things that need to be sent to Paris."

"Don't worry. It will all get done."

At that moment, I thought of my Thursday accounting and wondered just how *that* would get done.

"I'll have to strip the store bare to have enough to make a good showing. What about the *Winter* window?"

"We're doing a lot of triple and quadruple plating to get lovely nuances of depth."

"Don't be afraid to use five or six layers if you have to. You're not the one who has to lift it."

"I'm doing the selecting for the pine boughs, the snow, and the moonlight. It's going well." I unwrapped the glass from my handbag and held it up to the light. Thin green threads against blended blue and white

306

represented pine needles against sky.

"Yes, yes. Good. No paint. Make sure the snow has shadows to suggest that it's melting."

"We found that the drip of melting snow on the upper pine bough catches the light better in clear rather than white glass."

"All right."

"Lillian Palmié is doing the fire in the foreground. She has plated several layers of yellows, golds, and oranges under ripple glass. It really does look like flickering flames. And when the bundled cames are soldered together and get patinated black, they'll look like charred logs."

"Good, but you're foil-wrapping the delicate parts, aren't you?"

"Yes, and the jewel chunks as well. Miss Byrne and I have hammered out some gorgeous jewels. She is our primary cutter for this window. We don't give her any critical piece until we've all agreed on it."

"All pieces are critical." He turned his head to see if that registered. I nodded that it had.

"When I take this to Paris, the French will see Impressionism in glass instead of paint. Instead of the Impressionists using colors and stippling to *show* light, we're painting *with* light. It will be a great comeback after '89 and La Farge's bogus honors."

I doubted that they were entirely bogus. That was just his harbored disappointment

307

surfacing.

"The dragonfly shade for that customer won't be finished in a week because of the metalwork still to be done. I'm sorry, but it was impossible."

"She'll just have to wait. When you finish all three, cut the patterns in brass so they'll last. You'll make a series of them, I'm sure. Do you have a design for the mosaic base for Paris?"

"Not yet. It's only been three days."

"Just wondering. I want to see *Winter* before it's sent to the metal shop."

"You can't stand not to be in the center seeing all these things take shape. Don't you think Rubens or della Robbia was ever sick and had to relinquish their ateliers to others once in a while?"

He choked at that. I brought a glass of water to his lips, and the intimacy in the liberty I took made me tremble. I lingered a few moments in that fleeting closeness before I took the empty glass to the kitchen to refill.

In the breakfast area I noticed maxims burned into the wooden beams of the low ceiling. 'Plain living and high thinking' made me murmur, "Absurd." When I came back to his bedside, I said, "Plain living and high thinking, indeed."

"That was for my father's sake. He thought I was running with a fast crowd after May died, meaning Stanford White and my pals from the Lyceum Theatre project. I thought if I had a house big enough for all three generations, he would feel he was keeping an eye on me. So I designed the two lower floors for him, the third for my sister's family, the fourth floor for us, and the fifth for my studio. Even though I restrained myself in decorating his living space, he called it 'a magpie's nest of incongruous design elements.' He never lived here."

"You have to admit that a man whose taste runs to diamonds, not Hindustani deities, might not be comfortable here."

He raised his shoulders. "You don't have to go just yet, do you?"

I thought of my Thursday accounting. Our business was finished, but this was a rare private hour, and in truth, I wanted as much of him as I could get.

"Not just yet."

"I'm sorry Lou isn't here to greet you. She's at the women's infirmary most weekdays. Some Sunday you'll have to come to the Briars, our house on Long Island. In June our gardens are at their peak. You two can get acquainted then."

"That would be lovely. I'm sure I would find motifs for more lamps there. You know, don't you, how much I want to establish a permanent line of lamps?"

He patted my wrist. "Yes. I know."

"I love the Japonisme of the wisteria transoms in the library here. Can't you just imagine those blossoms hanging vertically around a light source?"

His eyebrows lifted as the idea formed. "Let's make it an electrolier."

"Really?"

"I've been consulting with Thomas Edison. He says that in a couple of years, more people who can afford our lamps will have electricity. And he agrees that the harshness of electric bulbs ought to be softened with colored glass."

"That's wonderful!"

"Now the wisteria base can be a slim bronze standard instead of a bulky oil canister."

"It can be the trunk of the vine!" The air seemed to crackle around us. I scooted to the edge of my chair. "And the leads in the shade can be roughened to look like branches, like those in your magnolia window."

"We'll design it together. You do the shade. I'll do the base. I want it in the Paris Exposition too."

"It's already May. Can we finish it by the entry deadline?"

"We'll make sure of that. Finish *Winter* and the mosaic base for your dragonfly lamp, but then do everything you can to make a prototype wisteria. I'll have Siegfried Bing put it in his Salon de l'Art Nouveau afterward. He's my representative throughout Europe."

Reality set in, and the battle between aesthetics and commercial concerns loomed. "With all those small petals," I said, "there will probably be a thousand pieces of glass to cut."

"Two thousand, I'll wager."

"It will be labor-intensive."

"It will be beautiful," he said in a dreamy voice.

"It will be expensive," I warned.

"Who cares?"

We looked at each other knowing exactly who would care. Then we burst out laughing.

CHAPTER 23
THE HAT, THE FERN,
AND THE GIRLS

Manhattan gleamed. The streets and sidewalks were slick with lacquer from the afternoon rain, and now, on Friday evening, Bernard and I rode slowly and carefully. If we had ridden Thursday evening like he'd wanted to, we would have had dry pavement, but I'd had to tell him that because of the time I spent at Mr. Tiffany's house, I needed to do my weekly accounting that evening at home. Bernard had given me a long scrutinizing look. What was he looking for? Truth? I wasn't the one hiding anything. Disappointed but gentlemanly, he offered to help with the books.

Now our plan was to take a turn around the four small parks in the vicinity, heading south to Union Square, around the large pagoda-like birdcage, up Broadway to Madison Square Park, around the magnolia tree, across to Gramercy Park and around its iron-gated perimeter. I made Bernard stop to appreciate the flower beds of bearded iris, so exotic and sensuous. Then we turned south to Stuyvesant Square on the East Side. He rode right through a puddle, hands on his head, holding out his legs and sending a fan-tail of water on both sides, as free and unencumbered as a boy — hardly consistent with his duplicity of being engaged to one woman and cycling with another.

How long was he going to let it go on without telling me? If I wanted the secret of him, of his privacy, why didn't I just ask him directly: Are you engaged or not? Are you secretly married? Where's your wife? Rigid codes of conduct ingrained in me forbade it, and Alistair was long gone back to merry ole England so I couldn't ask him. Maybe I had misheard Alistair. Maybe he'd said that Bernard was with his financier, not fiancée. Then wouldn't I feel foolish?

It wasn't just my mother's etiquette book that constrained me. Bernard's mystery was convenient. If he ever revealed that he was engaged, it would be blatantly wrong for me to go on outings with him. It was better not to know, so I could continue as we had been, as occasional pleasant companions. His importance, like his presence at the boarding-house, came and went. When he wasn't there, my life was full without him. At the end of our ride, I felt freshened from my week indoors but not enlightened. For the time being, that was just fine.

In the parlor Merry gave me a letter. "This was just brought in by a neighbor. Wrong delivery."

I read the return address.

"Youmans! The milliner who re-blocked and trimmed the hat I lost." In my excitement, I read it to her.

Mrs. Driscoll,

A lady called saying that she found a hat on the street. Seeing our label, she notified us. From her description, I thought it might be yours. If so, please call at number 24, West Thirty-fourth Street, a Mrs. G. Lee.

Yours truly,
Harvey Youmans

"Jammy for you," Merry said. "New Yorkers are a fine lot after all."

After a half day of work on Saturday I went to the address, prepared to pay a reward, but the house seemed far too elegant for the pittance I could offer.

Standing on the stoop, I heard piano music, a slow, measured waltz, vaguely familiar. No, it wasn't "Sidewalks of New York," but something similar in gentleness. Oh, Edwin. My heart heaved. Such a distance I'd come from the night I thrilled to his playing, when he transcended Edwin the Social Worker to become Edwin the Artist. Now what was he?

Edwin the Wanderer? Wherever he was, if he was alive, would he ever play that waltz again and think of me and the magic of that night, the purity of our love like new fallen snow on the sidewalk stretching before us? More important than thinking of me, which might confuse him, was his playing of music, any music. That would do him good.

Holding on to the railing for my equilibrium, I waited until the end of the piece, wringing unutterable sorrow from every note, before I composed myself and sounded the door knocker. A white-haired lady dressed in black opened the door. I explained why I had come, and she quickly invited me in and presented me with the hat.

"Things that have been lost and then found are doubly precious, don't you think?" she said cheerfully. "People too."

Shaken and reeling, I wondered: Would Edwin be doubly precious to me? Would I hold him in my arms and croon over him as if he were a lost lamb I had just found? Would he even want me to? If he had come back that morning at the lake, would I have had to be a watchful guardian, constantly wary of him straying again? The answer eluded me. I looked away, out her bay window, and at the ferns lined up in pots. Orderly. Contained. Cared for.

"They're lovely, aren't they?" she said. "The bay window makes it humid there." She went

315

through the litany of their names and mentioned that the arrowhead was not a true fern. I managed to remark that I had never seen one. Where the leaf was attached to a thin black stem, it was shaped like the tall shoulders of a heart, and the point was stretched long and narrow.

"Starts with a heart and ends with a dagger," she quipped, bright-eyed and pleased with herself.

I felt its puncture.

"That sounds like an opera plot."

"Here, let me cut you some." She clipped the arrowhead and its tiny white blossoms and some maidenhair with a small pair of silver scissors. "They'll last for a week in water."

I accepted them, thanked her, remarked that New York was a city of small graces, and put on my hat, securing it with the hat pin that was still in it. Since it was George's favorite hat, I went straight to his studio. We shared a few minutes of crazy jubilation, with him waving a peacock feather, touching my hat with it, and saying, "Precious, simply precious." His Quirkiness George Waldo. Without knowing it, he lifted me from the grief I had just felt.

Mrs. Hackley had said once that George was in love with himself, but I disagreed. It wasn't overweening pride that was responsible for George's nature. It was merely joy in life and in his own being, a joy so full that it spilled over into his attitude that everyone he encountered would naturally share in that joy. There was a kind of innocence in that.

He had been drawing the figures and animals that would be carved as wall panels in Vanderbilt's bedroom. I let him go back to work, and sat across from him. On the wall behind him hung the famous Aubrey Beardsley ink drawing *The Peacock Skirt*. How assured and daring, those thin dramatic lines flowing through space, black against stark white. One chance to get each line right, or the whole thing would be ruined.

George was daring in his drawing too. He drew like he lived and moved — swiftly, almost recklessly. Although he used a book of animal anatomy to give him basic structure, he ignored some features and exaggerated others for humorous effect. An elephant had his trunk tied into a knot, and was looking cross-eyed at it, with one flap of an ear curled forward. If it could have a caption, it should have been "Now, how did that happen?"

I took up a drawing pencil to render the arrowhead ferns in various orientations, elongating them. It would mean something to me if I used them on the mosaic pond base for the dragonfly lamp. The fern leaves and their small shy blossoms and bead-shaped buds would do well as bronze overlays against blue and green tesserae, the colors of Lake Geneva, with bronze dragonflies darting among the foliage. This lamp would be my farewell to Edwin just as George's egret painting was his — each of them a prayer in beauty that Edwin would fare well.

It was comfortable, both of us quietly working, absorbed in our drawings but aware of each other's easy presence. After a while George's pencil fell out of his hand. His head had sunk down and his eyes were closed. Poor fellow. I got him to stand up and walked him over to his bed. I took off his shoes, he curled onto his side, and I drew up the blanket and tucked it under him.

I realized that I had never in my life tucked in anybody. Wasn't the natural thing to kiss a person good night after you did the tucking? I gazed at him until I was sure he was sleeping peacefully. His fringe of black lashes, just like Edwin's, lay without a flutter. I bent down slowly and found his cheek flushed, warmer than normal against my lingering lips. In some unexplainable healing way, I felt no disloyalty to Edwin in kissing George.

Ever since the contract system started, the work had accelerated, and I had to design quickly to stay ahead of the girls. The selectors chose glass without dawdling over each piece, in order to make more money. It was a dangerous practice if nuanced choices were sacrificed, so it demanded more overseeing

318

on my part. Meanwhile, the cutters wanted to be rated highly by the selectors. Bertie Hodgins could cut three hundred thirty in a day, and Miss Byrne three hundred fifty, astonishing speed. I loved all this activity, but I didn't like being cast in the role of a sporting coach cheering them on: Rah! Rah! Whenever I passed Mr. Mitchell in the corridor, I looked the other way, pretending absorption in thought.

The Princeton University mosaic wasn't quite finished when Mr. Tiffany gave us a new mosaic commission. It was for a memorial chapel honoring Jeptha Wade, founder of the Western Union Telegraph company. The chief window designer under Mr. Tiffany, Frederick Wilson, made preliminary sketches showing a long procession of figures depicting the Old Law and the New Law, Jewish and Christian, in two twenty-five-foot panels. The academic nature of these mosaics didn't appeal to me, but I liked the size of the project: three hundred square feet of small glass tesserae to be selected, cut, and affixed. Such a large project could tide us over for the rest of the year if there would be a slack period of window commissions.

My department had shrunk. Cornelia quit, lamenting that the work was too hard for her, and I'd lost Louise Minnick when she married a printer. Recently two of the original six girls had left, Grace de Luze to become a

319

ceramicist, and Ella Egbert with an engagement ring on her finger, each a severe loss. I was on the lookout for replacements, and the cutting for the new mosaic would be perfect for starting new girls, just one rectangular tessera after another.

At dinner, I asked Hank if he had any promising young girls in the classes he taught at the East Side Artist and Educational Alliance.

"Young? Yes. Olga Zofia Lipska, a Polish girl about fourteen. No formal schooling but extraordinarily talented. I'd like to hold on to her a little longer to see if her originality matures to match her drawing skill. If I turn her over to you, she'll become a Tiffany imitator."

"That's not so bad a thing, Hank."

"Still, I'd like to keep her as long as her family can get by without sending her to work."

"You're going to make me wait, when I need someone now."

"It's very satisfying to encourage and train artists from immigrant families so they'll create from their own experiences. Eventually, the art of Lower East Side immigrants may become more American than that of artists trained in the conservatism at the Met and other art academies."

"You mean pictures of tenements and ash cans?" Mrs. Hackley charged.

"Not exclusively. Beauty comes in many guises. It's a matter of sensibility more than subject matter. I can't help but think what this Polish girl might be capable of, given guidance. No, I can't give her up yet."

"Is it really possible to detect talent in fourteen-year-old children?" Bernard asked.

"Yes, but it's rarely possible to predict whether the divine spark will keep burning with enough steadiness to survive the world," Hank said.

"What kind of a human being becomes an artist?" he asked.

"For visual art, it takes a person who delights in looking long and deeply at something until he sees how its shape can be rendered in changes of hue, and who can recreate that on a flat surface," Hank said.

Bernard finished a mouthful and said, "Then it's only a question of knowing technical tricks?"

"Not so fast, there," Dudley said. "It takes a person who wants to share his pleasure in seeing the world as an aesthetic phenomenon, sorta like a show of color and line going on all the time. He reckons that what he recreates from the world has the power to raise up a person's thoughts or feelings."

"You mean seeing art can make a person moral?" Mrs. Hackley asked, peering at Dudley over her forkful of potatoes. A loaded question.

"If he's open to it, because it makes his soul better. More appreciative and sensitive and compassionate," said Dudley.

"A tall order," Bernard said, "though I may know of someone who might fit the technical requirements. My office boy's sister. Their father is a lithographer, and she draws quite well. She makes Christmas cards, and her father prints them. I'll show you the one I received this year."

"How old is she?"

"Younger than her brother, and he's nineteen."

"If she's already eighteen, that's a problem. That old, and I only have them for a few years and then they leave to get married. Sometimes their joys are so paltry that if a man gives them half a look, it turns them into complete noodles. One kiss and they're gone, and I have to train someone new."

Bernard pulled in his chin. "They can't stay on?"

"Tiffany policy. No married women in the studios."

His expression darkened to a scowl.

"Well, send her on. I'll try her out."

Theresa Baur arrived at the studio wearing a long cobalt-blue feather boa draped over her shirtwaist. Dark-haired, small of stature with furtive eyes, proud of the Christmas cards she brought to show me, she reeked of self-

322

confidence cheaply bought at Woolworth's five-and-dime.

"I'm a quick study, and I aim to get ahead. I have ways to do it, and I'm not afraid to use them." She gave a little flip of the feather boa.

"How old are you?"

"Fifteen."

Men of the old school would call her a brazen wench, but I found her to be ambitious and zestful. At least she didn't lie. Unless those cards weren't her work.

"Can you draw from life?"

"Yes."

I placed paper and a drawing pencil in front of her and pointed to Carrie McNicholl working at the closest table. "Show me."

She produced a remarkable likeness in a short time.

"Have you had any art training?"

"My father is teaching me."

"Do you have a job now?"

"I do typewriting at my father's print shop in Brooklyn."

"Does he pay you?"

"No" issued from her mouth as a shamed murmur.

"Drop the boa into the dustbin on your way out. Wear a tie like women wage earners on Monday. I'll try you out for a week."

"With a week's certain pay?"

"Yes. Six-fifty, probationary. Seven as an

apprentice."

Word must have gotten around that I was hiring, because the next day a girl escorted by a young man I recognized from the Men's Window Department stepped into the studio. He gave the girl a soft push in my direction and left. She came toward me slowly, hands clasped together under her breasts, shoulders hunched forward and wrapped in a shawl in the humble manner of poor women that I'd seen in Dutch and French paintings.

"Yes?"

"My name is Nellie Warner, Miss, and I'm hoping as you might have some work for me. I know how to cut glass."

She was a wholesome-looking girl, with a scattering of cinnamon-colored freckles across her milky cheeks.

"How is it that you know?"

She blushed. "A friend taught me. I can show you if you'd like."

What a melodic voice she had, with a tinge of the Irish in it. I traced a curved pattern onto a piece of glass with grease pencil and handed her my diamond wheel. She grasped it correctly, scored the glass with a steady hand, and snapped it clean.

"I need nippers to finish it off. To groze it, I mean."

She had the vocabulary too.

I handed her a pair. With a minimum of

snips, it was the exact replica of the pattern piece, which I laid over it.

"Can you give it a convex curve?"

"To be sure."

She showed me. It was a tricky task, but she managed admirably. She had certainly been well coached. I hated to put such a talent to work on cutting rectangles until the moon sprouted horns.

"What's his name, Nellie?" I asked in a whisper. She raised her head quickly, surprised and embarrassed, a bud of womanhood. I gestured to the doorway. "Your friend who taught you?"

"Patrick Doyle, Miss."

"You're not engaged, are you?"

"Oh, no, Miss. I'm too young for that. I want to work on me own."

"Well, you can tell Mr. Doyle that he taught you very well, and that you will be starting on Monday at nine o'clock."

"Oh, thank you, Miss. Thank you."

She began to back out the door, hunched forward facing me, but with one more thank you, she turned to the doorway, threw her shoulders back, lifted her chin, and entered New York's paid labor force.

On Monday, Nellie Warner arrived wearing a plain shirtwaist, crisply laundered. Her light red hair shone, done up tidily with a narrow white ribbon. Theresa Baur arrived in a party dress with puffy pink silk sleeves and a ruffled pink dickey with a wide bow.

"Pink to make the boys wink," Minnie whispered on the sly, sizing her up. "An English saying."

"An English sarcasm, in this case," I murmured back.

At least there was no boa to fling about. I'd have to see how long it would take for Theresa's audacity to be based on high-quality work instead of on the accoutrements of frippery imitating uptown women.

I started by showing them two cartoons for the Wade mosaic, each one four feet wide, explaining that cartoons were enlargements from the original painting and would be transferred by stylus onto large sheets of paper that would be mounted on boards inclined at a slight angle.

I introduced them to the selectors, Marion Palmié and Mary McVickar.

"Mary was born in Ireland, so I'm sure you'll get on well with her, Nellie."

"Where in Ireland?" Nellie instantly asked.

"Dunmore, County Waterford, where they make the glass."

Nellie pointed to herself. "Cobh, County Cork, where the immigrant ships leave from."

Their voices rang with love for the old country. I realized that I was creating a community. In this regard, I could matter here. It wasn't just satisfying Mr. Tiffany or creating beauty that would make a person sensitive and compassionate. As Edwin had said, there were other kinds of beauty. I liked to think he would have been pleased with me.

CHAPTER 24
PINS

Four of us wheeled uptown past the French Renaissance château of Cornelius Vanderbilt II, crossed through Grand Army Plaza, and entered Central Park. We dismounted by the pond to rest and enjoy the calm after the noisy streets.

"How far do you think we've come?" Alice asked.

Mr. York looked at his cyclometer. "About two and a half miles."

"Only that? I feel like I've pedaled to Boston."

After watching the ducks awhile, she stood and said, "All right. Up and at 'em. Next stop, the Hanging Gardens of Babylon. For Clara's sake." She raised herself onto the seat and chirped out, "Just think of what has happened to you, Clara. To us. Because you could ride a wheel, Alistair invited you to go on that ride in the country. Because of that, you had the idea of butterflies on a lampshade. And because of that, we're here today!"

And off she went.

We took the East Drive, passing the statue of Shakespeare, and went up Literary Walk to the wisteria pergola. The blooms were at their most glorious, spilling over themselves in profusion. With our necks craned back under an overhead lattice, we breathed in their fragrance. Dense clusters of two-lipped blossoms hung pendulous, lilac-blue and violet-blue and purple, depending on their position on the stems.

"They're darker where they hang lowest," I observed.

"They must open at the highest part of each cluster first, so those blossoms are the first to lose their color," Alice said.

"Eight inches long, those clusters," I marveled.

"Some longer," she noted.

"With blossoms only half an inch long."

"Some shorter."

"Some prettier," Bernard chimed in.

"Some uglier," Mr. York countered.

"Some smellier." Bernard pinched his nose, looking at me playfully.

"Some more pendulous," Mr. York intoned in a deeper-than-usual voice, and the two men snickered.

"All right, you two, just keep on riding as far as you want," I said. "We'll still be here when you come back."

Looking smug and perky, Alice pulled out

our small sketchbooks from the satchel that I'd strapped on my bicycle. "Take your time," she sang out as they rode off.

I sat down on a bench and prepared to draw. "Leaves pinnate."

"Like a feather, with one leaflet at the end," Alice added.

"Foliage only above the blossoms."

"Trunks twisted and gnarled."

"Two entwining around each other," I said. "Like a wizened old married couple."

We became absorbed in drawing until Alice slapped her forehead. "A separate piece of glass for each petal! There'll be a thousand!"

"Two thousand, Mr. Tiffany estimated."

"That will take forever!"

A small, gray-haired woman was making her way slowly down the length of the pergola, picking up fallen blossoms, examining them closely, putting some in a little bakery box, and throwing some away. Petals littered the ground around her like a lavender Persian carpet. She stopped to watch us work.

"Nice pictures, but you only have the drawings. I have the color and the scent. They last a couple of days in a saucer of water."

"Then you can come back and get some fresh ones," Alice told her.

"I live by the el train, and it soots up the air frightfully. Flowers help."

She toddled on, bending her stiff little body precariously, plucking each treasure off the ground, her sweet pinkie finger raised.

Once she was out of earshot, Alice murmured, "Lady Pillager. That'll be us one day."

"Our legs twisted and gnarled with veins like the trunks of wisteria."

"Our noses straining to remember this scent."

It left us both thoughtful for a time, our drawing pencils still.

"She knows what life is for," I mused.

We cocked our heads at each other, hoping that we did too, and that our work to make beautiful things might help others live richer lives. This was the other Tiffany Imperative.

"We can't use the wide cone mold we used for dragonfly," I said. "It has to be more perpendicular to give the illusion of the clusters hanging down."

"Like a pail upside down?"

"No. Straight down. More like a cloche hat with a rounded shoulder between the crown and sides." I drew a rough sketch of the shape of the shade and vine base I had in mind and showed her. "Mr. Tiffany told me this lamp would be electric."

"Electroliers can get really hot," Alice said.

"Then the opening at the top has to be larger than normal. That's fine. There could be a tangled net of leads without glass in the center of the crown, thick leads textured to look like branches."

"There's one problem." Her ominous tone

set me on edge.

"I think I know what you're going to say, and it's going to break my heart."

"The bottom," she wailed.

"Yes. It would be criminal to cut off the blossoms at a bottom ring. They've simply *got* to hang down unevenly, like they do in nature."

"Then the mold has to be taller than the lowest hanging blossom," she said. "But then we can't build up the glass from a bottom ring resting against the mold."

"Start at the top?" I asked.

"What are you? A magician? How are these tiny pieces going to stay without anything to rest on?"

"Wax?"

"And pins," she said. "We'll have to put two pins in the wood for each small bottom piece to rest on."

"A fringe of pins."

When Bernard and Mr. York came back, we packed up and mounted our wheels, our imaginations blossoming but our exuberance darkened, our legs not yet twisted and stiff.

Mr. Mitchell came into the studio one drizzly afternoon and pulled up a stool by my desk, too close for comfort.

"Hello," I said. "I haven't seen you for a while. How are you?"

"What's going on here?"

He never started any conversation with "Good morning" or "How are you?" or "Might I interrupt you for a moment?" Mr. I. M. Business.

The girls were all standing with their hands over their eyes.

"I called a five-minute break for them to stretch their shoulders and rest their eyes. Those rain clouds outside make it dark in here. We've had to work with electric lights all day."

"You do this all the time?"

"Every day we have to work under electric lights. It causes eyestrain."

He blew a puff of air out of his mouth. "Never heard of such a thing. The men don't do it."

"Then the men have superior eyeballs. Or inferior brains."

Theresa dared to snicker.

"You're getting pretty high-and-mighty lately."

"Why, thank you, Mr. Mitchell. Good of you to notice."

Carrie gasped.

He pointed to my drawing. "What's that?"

"I'm designing a wisteria lamp. It will have a new shape, like a tall cloche hat, and a cascade of small petals in shades of violet-blue. I'm sure it will be a popular model."

"He knows you're doing this?" Mr. Mitchell asked.

"We thought of it together. He loves wisteria. Haven't you noticed the transoms in his library?"

"No."

"How unfortunate for you. He's designing the base to look like a wisteria trunk. It's for an electrolier."

"There's no guarantee that electroliers will sell. Besides, we can't have such elaborate lamps. The time involved makes them too expensive. If you make only these expensive one-of-a-kind or eight-of-a-kind lamps, you'll have to be constantly designing new items."

"Which is what I like doing, and what I'm beginning to be good at."

He sat in deep thought for a few minutes while I added a few more blossoms to a wisteria colonnade. The clusters shouldn't hang next to one another like a line of soldiers at roll call. Some should be in front of others, some behind, some branches bursting into blossoms higher than others. The difficulty on a flat plane was to convey in pencil the separation between clusters that one sees with the eye.

"Since the pattern will be repeated five times around the barrel, that reduces my time expenditure," I said.

His scrutiny fell on my plaster model of a new clock.

"Do you honestly suppose anybody is going to buy that clock?"

"I most certainly do. It's more original than any clock in the showroom."

"Indeed. Odd little clock, *for a museum,* but the public wants common white and gold French clocks that sell for a quarter of the price this would be. I tell you, your clock is *too* original. It will never sell."

"Don't be so quick to assume that, Mr. Mitchell. Save yourself from feeling foolish when it does sell."

He pulled his stool even closer.

"If you could content yourself with utilizing your *originality* on a few simple things, you would be doing something useful instead of going off on these crazy tangents."

I gritted my teeth at the sarcastic way he said "originality" and flung out his arm over everything in my studio as if it were trash.

"But Mr. Tiffany, whom I believe is your employer as well as mine, has encouraged me to design more lamps."

He planted his elbow right in the middle of my wisteria study, wrinkling it, a deliberate move. I pushed on his arm enough to free my drawing, and glared at him none too pleasantly.

In a conspiratorial whisper, he said, "Mr. Tiffany will be taking a vacation soon. What I want you to do while he's away, on the sly, so to speak, is to design some simple, cheaper things that can be made more quickly, without so many little pieces." He wiggled his fingers at my one-fifth wisteria drawing.

"Like what?"

"Oh, candlesticks, ink bottles, pin trays, desk sets. Those things will fly off the shelves. If you design some uncomplicated bronze items to suit me, without mosaics, I'll have them made while Mr. Tiffany is away, and I guarantee that they will sell. It will prove to him that there's money in cheaper things."

What a rotten predicament this was turning out to be. He wasn't my boss.

"Cheaper things won't win him awards. Let's see at the end of the Paris Exposition if you still feel that way."

My clipped cadence would indicate to any sensitive person that the conversation was over, and I resumed my work on the wisteria. Someday I would have my say. In a moment I looked up to see his bald dome of a wooden head with a fringe of hair exit the doorway, self-deceptive in its illusion of victory. I imagined it to be stuck with a fringe of pins instead.

■ ■ ■ ■

BOOK FOUR
1900–1903

■ ■ ■ ■

CHAPTER 25
RUBY

Out with the old and in with the new was on everyone's lips that millennial New Year's Eve. Something spectacular was afoot. The denizens of Miss Owens's boardinghouse spilled out onto Irving Place, even the Hackleys and frail Francie. Wrapped in mufflers, we spouted the day's sentiments, fog clouds issuing from our mouths.

"The new century demands new ideas," Merry said.

"Right! Looking ahead to better bread," George shouted, and Merry playfully cuffed him on the jaw.

We laughed. We sang. We joined the mass migration downtown, and greeted strangers familiarly. Francie spoke to a newsboy about the headlines, Dr. Griggs joked with shopgirls, and Alice linked arms with a woman in a babushka. In the sea of people jamming City Hall Park, we strained to hear the messages from monarchs of Europe about a new age of peace, diplomacy, and prosperity, a dawning of hope for the masses.

Mayor Van Wyck gave a speech reminding us of the optimism of early Dutch settlers, and the explosion of commerce with the opening of the Erie Canal, culminating in the burst of entrepreneurial energy in the century just closing. "New York is destined to become the cultural capital of the world," he declared. There it was — the colliding bedfellows of commerce and art both awakening on this rock between two rivers.

Combined choral societies of the city sang a new song, "America the Beautiful," and at the stroke of midnight, City Hall was illuminated with thousands of electric lights. The sudden splendor dazzled us. Speechless, we had never seen anything like it. Tin horns blasted shrilly, kazoos whined, and a deafening cheer went up.

Mr. York gave Alice a shy little peck on the cheek, and Mr. Bainbridge elbowed his way to her, bent her backward, and gave her a melodramatic stage kiss. Mrs. Hackley raised her chin and tugged at Mr. Hackley's coat sleeve, reminding him of his marital duty. Dr. Griggs kissed Merry Owens, who responded with an Irish jig. Dudley and Hank tossed public decorum aside and gave each other a brief manly hug, slapping each other on the back. No one noticed in the mad, happy frenzy of the moment.

When George and I heard, "Should auld

acquaintance be forgot and never brought to mind?" we held tight to each other. Certainly if he were here, if he were living, Edwin with his beautiful patriot dream would have done his bit to "crown thy good with brotherhood from sea to shining sea."

There was no sign of Bernard that night, or New Year's Day, nor for that matter ever since Christmas. That had to mean something, but what? He was certainly an irresistibly charming man — vibrant, caring, witty in that subtle British way — but his unexplained here-today-gone-tomorrow-here-again manner of living was disconcerting. I couldn't afford another mystery man in my life, so I resolved that in this first year of the new century I would fill my mind with work and beauty instead.

To that end, Alice and I arrived early at the studio the first workday of the new year, and what did I find on my desk but a notice from Mr. Mitchell: "Beginning immediately, a new policy requires that the Women's Glass Cutting Department pay the overhead cost of fifty dollars a month for rent of your studio space. Make sure you factor that into your weekly expenditures."

Fury boiled up in me. I slapped the message down on Alice's worktable for her to read.

"That's absurd," Alice said. "We're part of

the company. What a boor. Throwing his weight around."

"He's a skinflint."

"He's a curmudgeon." She raised her voice.

"A finagler." I raised mine.

"A crook." She raised her fist.

"A madman!" I raised mine, holding aloft an imaginary lamp of liberty from oppression.

Passing in the corridor, Frank saw us and raised his fist in the air too. How desperately he wanted to be part of our studio, and how instinctively I wanted to explain our fists in the air, but it was too complicated for pantomime. Alice blew out a breath and said in a flat voice, "New century, new ideas."

On his usual Monday visit that afternoon, Mr. Tiffany said, "Your designs for the metalwork are more inventive than anyone else's in the building."

"With the exception of yours," I replied with a wink. "Thank you! That'll keep me going for a while."

"I'm leaving for Paris in two weeks to arrange for the Exposition Universelle and to meet with Siegfried Bing to select pieces for his Salon de l'Art Nouveau. Be assured that your dragonfly lamp will have a prominent place in my display at the exposition."

"That's wonderful."

"While I'm gone, don't let Mr. Mitchell bully you."

"He's already put the thumbscrews on me by charging rent against my department's profits. For studio space, he says. That's unjust."

"Pay it for now. It'll blow over. What I meant was not to let him squash any of your design ideas. Take them to Mr. Belknap. If he approves, go ahead with them."

"Thank you. I will. I can hardly wait for spring. I want to do some flower shades."

"Good. I'll send up some garden books."

With the dragonfly and wisteria lamps shipped to Paris, I had a break and took out my old drawings for a tree-of-life clock. I wanted to get it critiqued by Hank before he left on a trip to Europe, so I took them home. That evening, George, Dudley, Hank, and Mr. York gathered in the parlor. As I launched into a glowing description with the aid of my drawings, the clock grew into something gargantuan, a complex monster of a grandfather clock instead of a mantel clock. It was too late. In the deathly hush, my toes cramping, I waited none too bravely for their verdict.

Hank, critic-in-training, sporty in his white tennis togs with his legs crossed, was the first to break the silence.

"Do you know what I think is the matter with your clock?"

"No. How can I guess?"

"You don't mind if I tell you?"

"Stop pussyfooting around. I wouldn't have laid my head on the chopping block if I didn't want your criticism."

"There are too many ideas in it. Eight feet of ideas in a two-foot clock and not a quiet spot to rest your eye. You've squeezed in all the symbolism known to art."

"And some that hasn't been invented yet," Mr. York added.

Another silence descended.

Dudley cleared his throat. "I would like to say that it's finer than a she-cat's belly hair, but I can't. You've got this tortured line try-ing to be Art Nouveau but overdoing it in a double whiplash. It's not graceful. It's forced." He traced the line in the air, and it looked like a butterfly's erratic path. "And it doesn't serve as a plant stem, as in the French style. It's just a stray line."

I had thought of my father fly-fishing when I drew that line. As a little girl excited by the line arcing high in the air and whipping back on itself, I used to say, "Make it last, Papa," and when he couldn't, I said, "Do it again, Papa. Just like that one," but they never were exactly the same, and they didn't last longer than the blink of an eye. I had thought to honor him on the tree-of-life clock by mak-ing something of him last through time.

Now I saw the drawing as a pitiful mish-mash driven by sentiment rather than artful principles, as crowded as the overdecoration of Mr. Tiffany's home. Like a fish caught on a line, I had swallowed his aesthetic whole.

"I'm afraid you're right, but isn't it sad? I've grown so fond of each motif that I don't know what to discard."

"You have to be ruthless," Mr. York said. "Cover one element at a time with a piece of paper and ask yourself, would a person miss something there if he didn't know what you had planned for that spot?"

"But don't be like Hercules trying to slay the serpent Hydra, cutting off a head just to have two others grow in its place," Hank warned.

"Maybe you should let it simmer awhile," said George.

Hank raised his index finger. "It's good that you weren't successful at the first go. It's better this way, because it forces you to think more."

A sigh escaped me. "Sad but true. I appreciate you setting me straight."

I put it aside at work and turned my thoughts to what I had done that was successful in order to build on that. The lovely orange fish Alice and I had seen swimming among the undulating strips of seaweed at the aquarium came to mind. I took out Alice's fish drawings and saw that I could design a mosaic wall plaque of two fish swimming among blades of seaweed. Nobody told me I couldn't design plaques.

Creativity happens, I thought, when you look at one thing and see another — like Mr. Tiffany seeing a lamp in a nautilus shell. No one would think of a woven basket in connection with an underwater scene, but I did. Fish swimming among tall seaweed made me think of a current threading its way in front of and behind the warp of reeds. Water made of ripple glass could give the illusion that strips of glass could be pliable, as they might appear underwater. The fish would be recognizable but the rest more abstract, simpler, with fewer "things" in the sea. I sensed a coming breakthrough from Victorian quaintness to a new idiom, and took the drawing to Mr. Belknap. He approved it instantly.

I mustered my courage and said, "I would like to hear your critique of my work as a whole. I'm asking because I value your educated opinion."

"Do you want me to speak as myself or as an employee voicing the Tiffany aesthetics?"

"Both."

"Personally, I think your work is fresh and original. You have an excellent eye for color, unity, and placement of elements. Louis would be in accord with that. However, as the director of style for an art enterprise that must position itself on the leading edge, I would disagree with his taste for so much ornamentation. Everything you do is very ornate, and therefore expensive to translate into glass and metal. The thing you need to work toward is to get good effects in simpler ways."

It was Mr. Pinhead's directive, only founded on principles of art, not commerce, and delivered with more grace. My breath leaked out of me in a long, troubled gush.

"Because of the expense?"

"Not necessarily, although we both work —"

"For a company that needs to get out of the red and into the black. Isn't that true?" I asked.

"Yes."

"Without those considerations, though, is my work too florid?"

"In terms of the coming style, so that we can be ahead of fashion rather than behind, yes. But Louis would disagree."

My shoulders seemed too heavy for me to support, and disappointment toppled me like a wave. What Hank and Dudley had told me was right. I respected them all the more now. After an exaggerated sigh, I said, "I'll just have to claw my way out of Victorian fussiness, if I can. It's the dawning of a new, sleeker century, I suppose."

"Yes again. One which your fish plaque anticipates beautifully."

■ ■ ■ ■

I had begun a free finger-spelling class at Cooper Union, and after the second class I spelled out, awkwardly and laboriously, G-O-O-D M-O-R-N-I-N-G F-R-A-N-K.

His face lit up, and he appeared to grow inches taller. He flashed back his excitement at me with fingers moving at lightning speed. I spelled back, S-L-O-W D-O-W-N. We laughed together. That is, he uttered a mono-syllable of happiness and gave a little tug at my second sleeve. A warm sensation spread in my chest, and I knew it to be mother love.

After that, not a day went by without Frank coming to finger-spell his weather observations slow enough for me to understand. S-N-O-W B-L-A-N-K-E-T, or S-I-L-V-E-R T-H-R-E-A-D R-A-I-N, or S-H-Y M-O-O-N S-L-I-V-E-R.

The morning after the critique of my clock, he laid a jewel of chipped red glass by my hand as I was drawing, and spelled R-U-B-Y F-O-R Y-O-U. With gestures of hammering, he indicated that he had chipped it himself.

For once, I was the one mute.

We weren't so different. His yearning for human connection was as strong as mine. I imagined him observing the world keenly each day and distilling it at night to its quintessence, simple enough that I could grasp it from his fingers the next morning.

At that moment it dawned on me. Frank's restrained simplicity was what would make my clock elegant.

T-H-A-N-K Y-O-U.

CHAPTER 26
JASMINE

"What that boy needs is cod-liver oil," Mrs. Hackley declared with self-appointed authority, standing wide-legged on the porch, knuckles pressed into her pillowy hips. "A teaspoonful every three hours."

"It can't hurt," Dr. Griggs said diplomatically as he and I hurried next door.

George lay on his narrow bed in a fit of coughing with Dudley bent over him holding a glass of water. George managed to drink a little, which helped for a few minutes, and then the coughing started again.

"Get onto your stomach," Dr. Griggs said. "Hang your head over the side. Cough it out."

A horrendous seizure of coughing followed, which left him so weak he couldn't right himself. Dudley helped him onto his back, and George fell asleep immediately. Dr. Griggs said he would bring him some medicine in the morning and then left, but I stayed for a couple of hours, during which another episode happened. Dudley sent me home and said he would stay the night and sleep on some cushions on the model's platform.

After work the next day, I found a note from George waiting for me.

Clara,
I'm at Twenty-second Street and Lexington, southwest corner, apartment two. I'm being taken care of. Come only if you can.
Pax vobiscum.
Your popinjay

It wasn't far, only a block past Gramercy Park, but why the secrecy? Dudley not being home to ask, I went there immediately.

The townhouse had a shiny red door. Inside, a marble floor, a potted palm, a stairway, and two doors on the ground floor, numbers one and two. I knocked at number two. The door opened.

"Mr. Belknap!"

Shock rippled through me.

In his shirtsleeves. No eyebrows. No Brilliantine. He hadn't been at work today.

"I was given this address. Is there a George Waldo here?"

He stepped back from the doorway. "Come in." A solemn voice, and such a look. Worry swam in his eyes. Minute crow's-feet formed, froze in position, and slowly dissolved in resignation. "He's here."

351

In a bedroom of butter-yellow walls and mint-green curtains, George was dozing comfortably against a pile of pillows. Blooming jasmine plants in blue ceramic pots sat on tables on both sides of him.

"His studio is no place for him now," Mr. Belknap explained. "He's too weak to take care of himself, and Dudley has an important portrait sitting to do this week."

"Then you know Dudley too?"

"Yes, Clara. All that you see and all that you imagine is true. I would ask you never to mention it or allude to it in any way."

"Of course," I murmured.

Nothing prepared me for this connection, yet, once grasped, it didn't seem unnatural.

He pulled up the pale yellow quilt that had fallen awry, and brushed George's hair back with a loving gesture. "He asked for you, and I couldn't deny him."

Our voices woke him enough for him to say, "Clara, you came. To give me last rites?"

"Being sick gives you no cause to be ridiculous."

"*Au contraire, madame.* It gives me every right."

Mr. Belknap spooned broth into George's mouth, adeptly, comfortably, as a woman would feed a young child, resuming what he had apparently been doing earlier. What a marvel of caring he was. What a shame that he was forced to constrain it. I felt privileged to see the authentic Mr. Belknap.

He was always meticulous about his appearance, but not today. Without his exact center part oiled in place, his silky blond hair falling forward in straight wisps over his forehead had a young boy's innocence. I saw how fine-looking he was in his natural self, what well-suited features he had — narrow, straight nose, small mouth, and almost invisible blond eyebrows. I watched him take tender care of George, and it was beautiful. He was his own man, and there was something brave and noble and wholly mysterious in that.

All this time that I'd known George and Hank and Dudley, I'd never pursued them in my imagination into their rooms, never thought beyond the joy they took in one another's company as comrades, and the happiness they rendered to me. I'd kept myself from imagining them taking joy in touch, but now I wished it for them.

Mr. Belknap insisted that I sit next to the bed. I remarked on the lovely jasmine.

"A scent strong enough to make a prize-fighter swoon," George said.

"I ran out this morning to the flower shop around the corner because my mother used to drink jasmine tea when she had a cough." Mr. Belknap shrugged. "I thought smelling them might have the same effect."

"You're missing your dinner hour, Clara," George said.

"Dudley is coming any minute to relieve me," Mr. Belknap said. "Might I take you to dinner at the National Arts Club after he arrives?"

"You're a member? I'd love to. I've always wanted to see the inside."

When Dudley arrived he was carrying his zither, intending to strum some southern lullabies to help George sleep, and a letter from Hank, mailed in Paris.

"Read it," George said. "It might be entertaining."

April 6, 1900

"Dear Dud,

"How I wish I'd followed your advice and had taken dancing lessons as part of my education. I've become terribly chummy with an English chap, Walter Radcliff, who snagged an invitation to a swellish dinner dance where I fell into conversation with a fascinating woman. My forwardness when one hasn't been introduced was a faux pas in Continental manners, Rad said. Nevertheless, as the orchestra began a Viennese waltz, she asked me boldly, 'Shall we dance?' Quaking inside, I stumbled through, and afterward Rad said, 'You've just danced with Isadora Duncan. Not many a chap can say that.'

"Rad's an architectural scholar, so he's forever reeling off his excitement about pediments and cornices. He's quite a find in my program of self-education. His endless energy reminds me of our George. Try to get George to relax and take some time off after this Vanderbilt thing is finished."

"Very funny, Hank. I am, but not by choice."

"He's always deep into whatever he is about, and he is incessantly 'at' something tooth and nail. He can't live like that forever."

"Look who's talking."

"The French have such a balanced way of life, taking time to enjoy the morning's café and brioche, lingering over a hot lunch, enjoying the parks, just standing on a bridge instead of rushing pell-mell across it. Rad has adopted it, and has it right, I think. He drinks his morning café noir with cognac to celebrate the day, and he carries with him a small flask to have a nip in honor of some building or other.

"We had a swallow to the Eiffel Tower the other evening at sunset, another one

in front of the opera, and a quick, surreptitious one in the Louvre in homage to
the *Venus de Milo,* Rad's choice, though I
prefer any kouros of the Classical Period.
There's an Athenian torso I especially
admire in which the abdominal muscles
are beautifully delineated and the right
buttock is more contracted than the left,
indicating that the model stood with his
weight unevenly balanced — a more
seductive pose than the kouros of Argos. I
asked Rad to pass me the flask to drink
to the right buttock while the guard's
back was turned.

"The Grand Tour has its hardships. It
breaks me up that I have to leave Paris in
four days because I promised Rad I'd accompany him to some villages that Henry
James mentioned in *A Little Tour of France.*
Never fear, though, about Rad. I'll probably never see him again.

"Ever,
your Hank"

George closed his eyes and nestled deeper
into the pillows. "There you have it, Clara.
Our blithe comet trailing streaks of Continental grandeur."

In the days that followed, Dr. Griggs checked
on George every evening, and feared he was
heading toward pneumonia. Henry, Dudley,

and I took shifts and tried to make him comfortable. George wasn't an easy patient. Once when Dudley and I were changing his bed with him in it, George said, "Don't roll me like a log, Dud. You're not a lumberjack."

"Certainly nurses can do this better," I grumbled. "Maybe it's time for you to be in the hospital."

"No! Hospitals smell like chemical plants. I'd rather die. People can't come to see me there."

"What are you thinking, that you'll be on exhibit like one of Barnum's freaks?" Dudley said.

We were all getting worn out. I went home one Friday night after the dinner hour, and Bernard offered to take me to the Oyster House on Fourth Avenue, but I said no and went straight to bed. In the morning, George seemed worse. I waited till nine o'clock for Henry to get up. Fatigue made him oversleep. He said he would get me some breakfast right away, but Dr. Griggs came and insisted on George being in a hospital. After much persuasion and pouting, George was willing to go, and Dr. Griggs left to make arrangements.

I felt weak from hunger, having eaten only crackers and cheese and a glass of wine at George's bedside the night before. Henry's dainty preparations for breakfast made my anticipation sink. He laid out orange slices in a scalloped pattern on the plate, poured coffee from a silver coffeepot, and brought in the rolls that had been heating in the kitchen. Only one for each of us! I bit into mine without waiting for him. He set up a chafing dish at his end of the long dining room table, broke four eggs and scrambled them, and served me the larger half.

His linen was crisp, his china flowery with a gilt edge. The stemware for water was Favrile glass in iridescent pink from one angle, pale gold from another, shaped like tulips.

"The glasses are exquisite."

I knew from the showroom that similar goblets cost twenty-five dollars a dozen. Almost my week's wage. I picked mine up and set it down with concentration.

"Are they goblets or are they tulips?" Henry asked.

"Tulips," I said, knowing he wanted the other answer. I held my glass aloft. "I am drinking the nectar of a flower."

"You're catching on to the scampishness of the new idiom, more than Louis has. I don't believe he's aware that the new sensibility of presenting one thing as another extends beyond Art Nouveau. It's a duplicity more likely appreciated by those living a duplicity. There's not a name for it yet, though I'm sure one will emerge that will suggest its playfulness."

"And you see it?"

"I'm living it, the ambiguity of a double life. Because Louis is innocent of the wit in duplicity, his products are even more enjoyable to those who know that there's more going on than meets the eye."

"In my lamps as well?"

"Especially in your lamps."

I took a sip of water, pleased to be a participant in this new idiom.

"Have you ever seen Loïe Fuller dance?" he asked. "Swinging yards of fabric so it looks like enormous petals or wings that dwarf her?"

"Yes. She's quite astonishing."

"Is she a hibiscus or a dancer? An exotic butterfly or a dancer? Will your wisteria lamp be a vine or an electrolier?"

"This opens up an entirely new way of enjoying things."

"A less serious way. A sportive way."

"You are initiating me into an inner circle."

He raised his glass in acknowledgment that I was understanding.

"These tulip goblets," I said. "Do you know if Tom Manderson made them?"

"He could have. The company line is that Tiffany made them."

"Like the windows and mosaics and wallpaper and vases and furniture and rugs and tapestries and fabric and clocks, even buttons, and now probably my lamps. Don't you find that absurd, that people would think a single human being could design all those things, much less make them?"

He pushed out his lips. "He had something to do with everything. They're all his aesthetic."

"But not necessarily his design."

"Some of the window designs bear signatures other than his. Mr. Wilson and Miss Northrop sometimes get publicly recognized now."

"Why not a lamp designer?"

He hesitated. "I suppose because the public thinks windows are a higher art than lamps."

"They're flat! Lamps are sculptural, infinitely more difficult."

"Windows are more like paintings, and so they're valued more. Using the Tiffany name on them strengthens his position in the marketplace, his bid for a place in the history of art. I'm not defending that, though. It also strengthens the sales of your lamps."

"Maybe true, but my lamps enhance *his* reputation. It's still a masquerade."

"We all have masquerades of one sort or another."

Because of his stillness, with his fork poised in the air as though waiting for something, I realized he wasn't talking about Mr. Tiffany any longer. He meant himself, and that meant that at least at the opera, I was a partner in his forced masquerade. By the troubled look

360

in his eyes, he knew that I knew it.

"Whatever you think," he said softly, "I have enjoyed taking you to the opera. I hope we may continue to enjoy it together."

"We will. Nothing has changed, Mr. Belknap. I have always felt honored by your invitations, and have enjoyed your company. You're a fine, honorable man." We were suddenly stiff and formal. I paused for him to respond, but he was too tense. "I believe we all feel different in some individual way from others. That pain is a natural part of the bereftness of life."

"Do you feel it, Clara? The bereftness of life?"

"Yes, I do. When I'm longing for intimacy with a man and am constrained."

"By what?"

"By Mr. Tiffany's policy against married women. It forces me to keep love at bay, if I want to stay on, and I do."

After a long moment's thought, he said, "Then we understand something mutual about each other."

"Yes, we do."

He patted his mouth with his napkin. "After this, the formality of surnames is stuffy bourgeois. Please call me Henry."

I wanted to lighten the conversation. Henry didn't deserve moroseness. I looked at my empty plate and said, "This is a beautiful plate, Henry, but it would be even more beautiful if it were doing what it was meant to be doing instead of masquerading as a flower garden. Do you have another roll?"

"Certainly. Let me beat another egg for you too."

His ease and economy of motion made me think he would make a good wife.

Getting stubborn George ready for the hospital and into a horsecab and wrapped in blankets was like ushering a mule into a cage. Dr. Griggs accompanied us, and gave George some whiskey and aromatic ammonia and felt his pulse every few minutes on the way. Fortified, George brightened and looked at the shop windows on Ladies' Mile. At the hospital a nurse whisked him down a hallway in a rolling chair.

We followed, carrying the pots of jasmine, and saw him settled in his narrow white bed. He looked around and lifted one side of his lip in a sneer. "I'll die from sterility here."

"What were you expecting? Freddie Vanderbilt's bedroom?" I said.

When we were about to leave, Henry refrained from touching him since the nurse was right there, but I knew by the aborted movement of his arm that he wanted to, so I said, "Remember that many people love you, George."

CHAPTER 27
POINT PLEASANT

"Good morning!"

A month of worry had passed — acute, prolonged, then diminished — and now Henry came into my studio and closed the double doors behind him. "I have some good news." His lowered his voice. "George will be coming home soon."

"That's a relief."

"He's begun to pace in his room to demonstrate to the nurses that he's well, because he wants to show us the Vanderbilt bedroom before it's transported to Hyde Park."

"A good sign. Back to his own impatient self."

"I took him a bouquet of red carnations to urge him on. He demanded a pin to fasten one on his hospital gown, and practically devoured the rest."

I patted his arm, and he went on his way, a spring in his step.

To celebrate the showing of Vanderbilt's

bedroom, George wore his fedora with the red feather. He walked faster as we approached the warehouse.

"Slow down, George. You just got out —"

"Of prison! White, white, nothing but white! I *had* to get better to get out of that colorless cube." Just outside the carved bedroom door, he said, "Be prepared. Vanderbilt's favorite color is red. Like Lorenzo's."

With a flourish, he opened the door onto the fifteenth century. Red and gold blazed in every direction, and not a square inch went unornamented. The monumental bed was flanked by twisted columns, and gilded Corinthian capitals supported a canopy. A carved frieze, a pastoral tapestry, and a red velvet hanging stitched in gold adorned the walls. A sofa, a settee, and six chairs upholstered in red velvet had Florentine gold stitching.

"I see the Gilded Age is still alive and well. Is this robber baron expecting to entertain in his bedroom?"

"Yes. Just like a Renaissance potentate. Isn't it splendiferous?" George darted around the room, pointing out the sconces, porcelains, and male nudes on pedestals that he had selected.

"Fit for a king, George."

But way too ornate for contemporary taste. Henry Belknap would swoon under the overpowering weight of it. After his assessment of my work, I had thought that maybe I belonged to Medici's court instead of Tiffany's, but now I saw that I didn't. There was no place to rest one's eyes in this room, just like the drawing of my poor, tortured clock.

Saving the thing he was most proud of for last, George whisked away the sheet covering the wood panels carved from his fanciful drawings of faces and animals peeking out from dense foliage. It was a game to find each one. A man with rabbit ears was winking as if to say, "Aha, you found me. Aren't I funny?" Two wizened women had their arms around each other, one crying and the other laughing uproariously. A boy was doing a handstand, his mouth shaping a perfect *O* as though surprised by the look of things upside down.

George turned in a circle, hands on his head. I understood the excitement of having one's concepts executed in the final medium.

"The rest of the room is work for a patron. You did what he wanted. But these panels are the true you, George. A marvel of whimsy."

I had never seen him happier.

A noisy parade of five Palmié sisters, Alice, and I pedaled our wheels on the boardwalk of Point Pleasant, New Jersey. It was nothing more than boards laced together and laid temporarily upon the dunes, to be rolled up in winter. It made our insides jiggle. The fresh salt air was a tonic, and the call of seabirds invigorated us. We came back through the woods to their family's summer cottage on the beach, and had a supper of fish their father had caught. We capped off the day with a sail by moonlight.

The next morning we put on our scanty bathing costumes. What an exhilarating feeling to have nothing around our calves but air! How many sensations had we been missing out on since Alice and I had lifted our school jumpers to wade in Ohio's streams? Now we dared each other to take another step into the cold sea — calves, knees, hips, waist. I made a wild, splashy imitation of swimming a short distance. Then we took a walk.

"Look!" I cried.

"It's Queen Anne's lace," Lillian said.

"Or wild carrot, if you're a naturalist type."

"What's the difference? A weed's a weed," Marion said.

Clusters of tiny white flowers grew out from a single point on the stalk like a burst of fireworks.

"They do remind me of lace," Lillian observed.

"Oh, they're just another kind of dandelion," Marion rejoined.

"They'd be simple to draw."

"No!" Marion wailed. "This is supposed to

be a vacation from work."

"We never think about work when we're here," Lillian said.

"But you don't have to keep a department of thirty girls working."

Here could be the answer to Mr. Mitchell's demand for simpler, smaller, cheaper items.

"Lillian, do you think you could use a stalk of this as a motif for a candlestick? The little cup holding a candle could be a mature cluster curling in on itself, and a tall, slim rod could represent the stalk, and over the disk of the base, you could carve the roots spread out like wiggly spokes of a wheel. What do you think?"

She kept looking at the blossoms I was picking, and I thought I had her.

"I'll answer you on Monday."

And on Monday she said yes.

Over the next few weeks she designed two styles of wild-carrot candlesticks, both of them lovely and delicate. I was as proud of her as a mother hen. Meanwhile I used the same motif for a bronze ink pot. I resisted fancifying it with a single mosaic. Now Mr. Mitchell had three quick moneymakers, and I could finish designing my peacock lamps.

The next weekend Point Pleasant was teeming with poppies. Their crepe-paper petals fluttered and beckoned seductively in saturated vermilion, the Vanderbilt red, bright

367

enough to put out your eyes, with enough variation that we could use marbled and mottled glass. We picked them madly, as in a pagan dance, and carried large bunches home.

At my worktable the next day, I vowed to make this shade simple, but the blossoms had intricate black stamens like spokes around a closed yellow pistil. They wouldn't be identifiable as poppies without the ring of stamens. There was no way around it. They had to be made as metal filigree overlays in the same method as the dragonfly wings. My mind couldn't be regimented into plainness. Even though I simplified the petal shapes, they absolutely cried out for an irregular border of leaves at the bottom, which meant painstaking pins. For the sake of harmony, the leaves *had* to have subtle filigree veins attached on the inside of the glass. And there I was with another elaborate design.

I promised myself that the next lamp would be simple. What should it be? Cyclamen, with its petals aloft like wings in flight? Peony, a nest of petals enfolding something precious? The humble geranium? The stately iris? The hanging begonia? One idea propelled me to another. I was intoxicated by summer, on fire with flowers.

At summer's end, two white buck shoes and two short white linen trouser legs came in the doorway below a huge bouquet of voluptuous peonies topped by a white fedora. Mr. Tiffany had slipped into our studio without warning us with his cane. A little flustered, I hurried to lay out all of our work.

"Time enough for that in a few minutes. I have an announcement."

The instant Mr. Tiffany said that, the girls set down their tools and turned to him. Agnes stood by the door to her studio.

"I'm happy to tell you that the *Four Seasons* windows received much admiration at the Paris Exposition Universelle, so you should be very proud. Miss Northrop's magnolia window received a Diploma of Merit."

Congratulations ensued, and enthusiastic clapping of hands.

"And . . ." Mr. Tiffany paused for dramatic effect, milking the moment. Barnum would have done the same. "Mrs. Driscoll's dragonfly lamp received a Bronze Medal."

The room exploded with applause.

"That should make you feel pretty good, eh?"

"I do. I feel I've taken quite a journey."

Delicately, I inquired about any awards for him by asking about other departments.

With a flash of sheepishness that disappeared into sparkling blue eyes, he said, "I was awarded the Grand Prize for my Favrile glass pieces, and was made a Chevalier of the Legion of Honor of France."

More applause, although I knew some of the girls had no idea what that award signified. I clapped louder and longer than anyone.

He didn't say that Arthur Nash got any recognition, which made me wonder whether the Bronze Medal was granted to me or to the Tiffany Glass and Decorating Company or to Louis Comfort Tiffany, artist, but for the moment, he was pleased with me, and euphoria bubbled up in me deliriously.

After he looked at all that we had accomplished during his absence, he beckoned me into my studio and closed the door behind us.

"When the exposition is over, Siegfried Bing is taking all of the Favrile glass vases, the dragonfly lamp, some blown lamps, and some windows from the exhibition for his Salon de l'Art Nouveau to sell throughout Europe."

"Wonderful."

"But I have to keep him supplied. Europe is a big continent. I expect to be inundated with window commissions in our own cities, so I'm increasing the size of the Men's Window Department to two hundred."

Why was he telling me that? Thoughtless braggadocio?

"Make eight more wisteria lamps for Bing's gallery."

"Gladly. The new ones won't be exactly the same. I'll have selectors develop their own color schemes."

"All the better. I don't like to think of myself as running a factory that produces look-alike art, but I've set things in motion and have to proceed."

This was the right moment to show him the poppy design. "I thought you'd like it because of the deep colors."

"Yes, I do. Always intensify the colors. The small bronze items are well executed and just as important, so I want more. They'll reach more middle-class homes. Even small items can express ideal beauty."

Mr. Mitchell had given him an earful. I felt the conversation shift.

"Who did the poppy watercolor?"

"Alice Gouvy."

"She's the one who did the enamel primrose base?"

"Yes. She's very talented."

"Who designed the Queen Anne's lace items?"

"I did the ink pot, and Lillian Palmié did the candlesticks."

"Very good indeed. They fit in to my new direction."

I felt myself stiffen. "With you, there's always a new direction. You're irrepressible. What do you have up your sleeve now?"

"Lalique got a lot of attention in Paris with his enamels. I've been experimenting with enamel too, on copper. Those pieces in which

371

I used gold and silver foil under the enamel were well received. I've installed a larger enameling kiln in the factory than the one in my home studio, so now I'm ready to open a small enameling department. I want Miss Gouvy to be the head of it."

I went cold to the lips. "She'll be working —"

He didn't look at me. "In Corona."

The word shattered the elation in the air as though it were glass.

"Give me ten minutes and then send her down to my office. When she comes back, send the Palmié girl."

"But Lillian has never done enameling."

He turned on me a look one would give to an ignoramus. "She will learn. We are all continuing students of art." His imperious tone cut me to the bone. "I saw some beautiful French ceramics too."

"I'm sure you did." And I'm sure he caught the sarcasm in my voice.

"Soon we'll expand into ceramics. I want Miss Patricia Gay and Miss Lucy Lantrup for that."

"You're impoverishing my department!"

He raised his shoulders. "Hire more."

Alice and I walked home in a maelstrom of resentment.

"He didn't give me a choice," she fumed.

"He's on top of the world now, and nothing is going to get in his way. He's teeming with ideas. He wants to transcend himself with each new medium."

"But he's so authoritarian," Alice said.

"Autocratic."

"Self-important."

"Self-consumed."

"Vainglorious."

"Omnivorous."

"Obsessed."

"Masterful."

"Brilliant."

"But flawed as a human being," I said.

I wanted to scream or tear something to show that I felt ripped in two. Despite the truth of our character assassination, I adored him. He and I had a bridge that no one else traveled that made us artistic lovers, passionate without a touch of the flesh. He made me thrive, and valuing that, I could do nothing that would endanger it.

At dinner, Alice announced my award. I announced her new assignment. She played with her food and didn't eat. In my room, I played with my kaleidoscope and watched the pieces crash.

CHAPTER 28
WISTERIA

Hank came back from Paris early in September sporting a dragoon's mustache.

"How were the reviews?" I asked at dinner, halfheartedly, wilted from the third day of blazing heat and astronomical humidity.

"He was hailed as a genius who could achieve unlimited effects in glass."

"But did he achieve the Tiffany Imperative?" Bernard asked.

"I believe we can say he was a match for his father this time. I have to tell you, though, that he exhibited under his own name, not the company name."

"Oh, you troublemaker!" Dudley said. "Did you have to bring that up?"

"The newspapers reported that the awards were won by Louis Comfort Tiffany, but as a journalist, I got hold of the jurists' report. Your name was listed as designer of the dragonfly lamp."

He handed it to me, and there I was. And Arthur Nash too. And Agnes.

"So he did have to divulge our names after all."

"Not to the press."

"Oh, no, never to the press. What would it have cost him to share one ounce of glory? What's the point of winning an award if he keeps it a secret?"

Alice lowered her head, George pursed his lips, Merry clucked her tongue, and Bernard gave me a look filled with compassion, holding my frustration in his eyes until I looked away.

"A few critics weren't entirely enthusiastic," Hank admitted. "Maybe, Miss Lefevre, you could translate? I've marked the passage."

"All my teaching, and you still —"

"To get it exact."

"D'accord."

"Monsieur Tiffany went awry in one ecclesiastical window in particular. *The Flight of Souls,* intended to inspire, comes across as cold, melancholy, and gloomy despite its use of his justly famous glass. However, the lower part of this window was taken up by flowers, which served as a pretext to introduce elements of color, and this part shows him to much better advantage because he does not try to serve ideas or sentiment but lets the magic of his material speak in its own right."

375

"I don't know this window," I said. "It must have been made in the men's department."

"Here's a mention in *International Studio*," said Hank.

"I have hinted at the commercialism of this big American concern; it is time to define it more closely. Tiffany certainly does not aim to place himself in the center of Morris & Company's Arts and Crafts Movement in educating public taste and eschewing mass production. His aim is to sell, to persuade, not to elevate."

"Oh, he's going to feel the sword behind that pen," I said.

"It continues. 'But no commercial considerations are allowed to stand in the way of the alert curiosity of the highly gifted artist who is the soul as well as the owner of the company.' "

"So long as Boss Mitchell and Boss Platt are gagged and locked in their offices at Tiffany Hall," I said.

Alice grunted. Polite, feminine Alice definitely grunted.

There was no cooling off indoors, so after dinner some of us went up to the roof to catch any errant breeze, taking wet washcloths to dampen our necks as we sat on a long bench surrounded by chimneys and rooftop water tanks with their curious coolie-hat lids.

376

"Too hot to talk," Mr. York said.

"Too hot to think," said Dudley. "I'm sweating like a prostitute in church."

In a stupor we waited until our rooms cooled off enough to sleep. One by one, the others ventured downstairs to try them out until only Bernard and I were left in the twilight.

"So winning the award means nothing to you?" he ventured to ask.

"It means a great deal to me, but exhibiting everything under his own name is wrong."

"Even though your products are collaborative?"

"Granted, they all are, even across departments. The metalworkers, I mean. He can't name all those who did some work on dragonfly, but everything we produce has a designer, and it's not always Tiffany. That lamp was my concept from the beginning through every stage. If he didn't want to name his designers publicly, then he should have used the company name on his pavilion."

"And you're hurt by this."

"He called leaded-glass lampshades our secret from the first glimmer of the idea. At that moment it meant let's just keep it to ourselves until the right time to develop them. Regardless of his intent, the result is that it remains a secret that he didn't design that lamp. A secret that I exist."

Minutes passed without a word, and I appreciated him at my side to absorb my resentment.

Eventually he said, "I grew up in Gloucester in southwest England. As a boy, I was enchanted by the stained-glass windows in our cathedral, never thinking I would ever come to know someone who made them. On rare sunny days, they sparkled like jewels, and spots of color danced over the floor and pews."

"You thought that *then?*"

"I imagined that your lamps shoot out colors too, so I went to the showroom recently to have a look."

"You were there when I was upstairs?"

"I had no right to disturb you."

"What did you see?"

"The butterflies, the fish, and the dragonflies. Stunning, Clara. Your lamps will last through the ages, and will come to be valued as treasures from our time, worth far more than you can imagine now. I know this. I'm an importer."

Hearing that, I felt my spirit soar. I didn't breathe until his velvet voice came through the semidarkness again.

"Someday, when women are considered equal to men, it will become known that a woman of great importance created those lamps. This isn't the Middle Ages, Clara. You will not be lost to history like the makers of those medieval windows in Gloucester are.

Someone will find you."

Could that be? I drank in this comfort hungrily, momentarily released from the prison of resentment. I could not even find words to thank him, but after some moments of relishing what he said, sharp embarrassment descended. My need for recognition was as transparent to him as a pouting child's. My complaints about Mr. Tiffany seemed petty after hearing Bernard paint a larger picture. At once I saw that I was too preoccupied with the present, and with myself. There was no grace in so nakedly reaching after fame. What would I have to do, or give up, in order to outgrow it?

"The wisteria lamp is finished if you want to take a look," the note said the next day. It was from Alex, the foreman of the Metal Department. If. *If.* What did he think I was? A turtle who lays her eggs and immediately abandons them to hatch and fend for themselves? I beat his messenger boy downstairs and arrived just as Alex was attaching the electric socket to the base.

My disheartened feelings melted away at the sight. I, we, had transformed glass and metal into an illusion of a living plant.

"It's spectacular!"

The open crown for release of heat looked fine as a network of thick, textured leads in a patina of black representing the vines. Five of them snaked all the way down to the irregular bottom edge, diminishing in thickness to become the same width as the other lead lines dividing one column of blossoms from another.

"It was mighty troublesome to solder all those tiny pieces," Alex said.

"It's expertly done. With so many lead lines, they could have overpowered the shade if the solder was laid on too thickly."

"You have Harry to thank for that."

"You did a superb job, Harry," I said. "I know it was difficult."

"I hope I don't see another one of those for a while," he grumbled.

Alex set it on the base and lit it. The brilliance took my breath away. The blossoms sparkled as if a magical vine had produced amethysts and sapphires. I needed to linger over it, glory in it, share it.

"Can you send it up to fifth for a couple of days?"

"No. The boss wants it in his office for a client to see. Then it's going to Paris."

"Then just one day. I want the girls to study it."

"Can't do."

Rage rose, swift and violent, even to my teeth. "But it's mine!"

His stunned look made me think how false that was, how puny my claim. A dozen people, counting both of our departments and the bronze foundry, had worked on it.

"I'm sorry. An hour? Can you do without it for an hour?"

"An hour."

"Harry, will you bring it up? I want you to hear what the girls say."

When Harry delivered it on a cart, and I told the girls that he was the man who put it together, their praise came thick and fast and loud. Harry blushed his happiness. He never got any credit for anything.

"Let's light it," he said.

Everyone quieted. The room crackled with the electricity of suspense. When he turned it on, what squeals and cheers ensued. I thought even Frank could hear them.

Nellie marched right up to him, arm extended. "I want to shake your hand, Mister. I can't imagine how happy a body would be to have that in his house and be able to turn it on whenever he wanted some light."

"There will be more," I said to the girls, but Harry heard it on his way out. His shoulders sagged and he looked cross-eyed in exaggerated despair, and the girls giggled.

"Now that you see how electricity illumines every piece, I want to talk about selection. None of the wisteria lamps we produce will be the same as this or as each other, although we'll be using the same lead lines and patterns. The small size of the pieces lends itself to creating variations."

I gave them the range of colors from white through pale cerulean to Prussian blue, and from mauve through the violet range to purple. The foliage could depict a specific time in the blooming season, using yellow-green and emerald for early spring, with olive and ocher for summer.

"There are two types of color schemes, so before you begin, you'll have to make a choice. In one type, the petals are almost uniform in color, but the clusters contrast, light ones alternating with darker ones."

"Do they both grow on the same vine?" Mary McVickar questioned.

"Not usually, but there could be more than one vine tangled together. The other scheme would follow a pattern of maturation, light tints higher on the cluster, descending to darker shades on the newer, lower blossoms."

"What types of glass would you like us to use?" asked Minnie.

"Mottled glass could have darker spots on a lighter petal, which would provide a smooth transition down the column. Knobby glass, with the texture on the inside of the shade, would give the petals luster."

"What about any background?" Miss Stoney asked.

"You are free to choose how much air you want showing between clusters, and the glass for the air might be transparent, or active with striations, ripples, pinpoint mottling, or blue streaks."

Nellie slapped her hands on the sides of her head. "Too much for a mind to hold."

What a darling. She was becoming my pet.

In the basement one morning I was selecting glass panels for the wisteria lamps when Albert unloaded some gorgeous thick glass in pale yellow gold flecked with orange. Imbedded fractures made it alive. Cut round and beveled, what splendid suns they would be.

I took one panel upstairs and went right to work cutting a four-inch circle and chipping irregular bevels into its perimeter. Mr. Tiffany would love this. He would see it as the radiance of the divine, the new sun on the first morning of creation. Let there be light, and there was light. Accomplished as simply as that. Ultimate power. I held the disk up to my window, and it shot out shafts of yellow light in all directions. And it was good.

Wasn't it the fifth day that God said, "Let the waters bring forth abundantly the moving creatures that hath life?" Dragonflies! There had to be dragonflies darting around each sun on a domed shade, the dome of heaven. No filigree this time. The glass for the wings could have streaks of violet, even magenta, against cerulean and turquoise. In the exuberance of their flight, their wings would overlap, making dazzling variations in color. Feeling that I was soaring, I finished a watercolor study of a one-fifth section by the end of the day, surprising myself with my own swiftness.

Mr. Mitchell came in. I steeled myself and showed it to him. No hello. No comment. Not even a glance at it with his brown wooden eyes. Just a wild launch into a diatribe about the cost of my lamps and my unbridled whims, ending with, "We do not need ten varieties of dragonfly shades."

"Yes, we do. In this room, we most certainly do."

"Why?"

"To keep up the momentum of creation. To keep the girls from becoming complacent about color."

"We are not running a hobby house here, Mrs. Driscoll."

"Unlike you, my women are artists, Mr. Mitchell, and artists are more alive when they see new possibilities of color combinations. If we keep making the same thing, putting the same colored glass in the same spot, lamp after lamp, our color keenness becomes dull."

"Inconsequential. Go ahead and put the same color in the same spot. Your girls can work faster that way."

"That's shortsighted of you. When we make the eight wisteria lamps that Mr. Tiffany asked for, their color schemes will reflect each selector's cultivated taste for nuances of hues, which you obviously don't have. Each shade will be individual. To you that only means that you can charge more. To us it means the boundlessness of creation. Let's face it, Mr. Mitchell, you only value our work for its dollarable quality, not its adorable quality. Your soul doesn't have that capacity."

His whole face reddened, even to his ears.

"What's that you're working on?"

"A new dragonfly lamp with gorgeous yellow suns."

He huffed and puffed and blew out the words, "It's the ugliest thing I've ever seen."

CHAPTER 29
ARCADIA

Those were the last words Mr. Mitchell ever said to me. He went home and died.

The news hit me like a flying hammer. That monstrous sense of responsibility overtook me again. That evening I told Alice that I couldn't help but think I had caused it.

"You think you have that power?" she said.

"I upset him. I returned diatribe for diatribe, decorated with some snide remarks, until he was red in the face. I ought to dress in sackcloth and smear my face with ashes."

"It's a false sense of responsibility you have. You put too much importance on yourself. Throw it off, Clara. It's not yours to take on."

"He was a relative of the Tiffanys."

"Immaterial."

"Maybe my sharpness caused his heart to beat too fast until it gave out."

"Your stepfather would not agree. He believed in only one cause, bigger than you, bigger than us all."

That calmed me somewhat, but the next day in the quiet studio when I called for a five-minute closed-eye rest, it was hard not to feel guilty again. Alice was right about one thing, though. Overblown responsibility was part of my preoccupation with myself.

Despite the rush job on a wisteria lamp for an impatient customer who wanted it for some dinner party, I let the eye rest go on longer than usual. Any hurrying on the wisteria lamps was particularly nerve-racking to the girls. With my eyes closed too, I listened to the clop-clop of a horse's hooves get louder and then softer, a newsboy calling out the headlines, and the scrubwoman scrape her bucket against the floor.

"Time's up," I said.

A deafening crash jolted us. The scrub-woman, cleaning under the sawhorse table holding the wisteria shade, jerked up at my command. She took the whole table with her. In an instant the work of three girls for seven days was in an undistinguishable heap.

The sudden silence in the room spoke more loudly than wails. We dropped to the floor to try to fit the two thousand pieces together. Not a word issued from their mouths about the cost of broken glass that would normally be taken from their wages. I vowed I would find a way for that not to happen.

Only Frank, coming in to collect the trash, let out a strange yawp and crawled under nearby tables to pick up scattered pieces. As for the scrubwoman, she looked around in a dazed way for a minute, and then calmly went on scrubbing elsewhere, the only untroubled person in the room. Was I responsible? She probably thought my "Time's up" was meant for her. *Don't take it on yourself,* Alice would say, but could I be that nonchalant?

Nellie and Carrie hurried to cut new pieces when we couldn't find a quick match. Many of them had a tricky concave curve. After three hours of trying to find pieces to salvage and determine where they belonged, we were all discouraged. "It's all arseways," Mary cried in disgust. Miss Judd had tears in her eyes. Everyone's skirts were dirty. Groveling on the floor was more trouble than starting over. Is it a wisteria vine or an electrolier? Neither. It's a pile of trash. T-H-R-O-W I-T A-W-A-Y, I spelled to Frank. I would take the cost of the broken glass out of my own wages.

"Let's all go home," I said. "We'll start a new one in the morning."

"But the customer. He won't get it in time," Miss Judd said.

"No, he won't. I'll tell Mr. Mitchell — I mean Mr. Thomas — tomorrow."

Bleary-eyed, I shooed everyone out, left Frank to clean up, and took the elevator with Nellie.

"Do you ever wonder what kind of family

buys these lamps and puts them in their houses?" she asked.

"Rich ones," I said drily.

"Don't you wonder whether they love them as much as we do? But we'll never know, will we?"

"No, we won't."

"You might think this is blarney, but do you ever have the feeling that what we do is a little like God making the flowers in the first place, hoping someone will notice?"

"Yes."

"But He keeps on making them anyway, year after year," Nellie said. "Isn't that love, Mrs. Driscoll?"

"The highest kind."

Outside the workers' entrance on Twenty-fifth Street, there was her faithful Patrick Doyle waiting to walk her home in the dark. That was love too.

The world — small and great — careened from its axis. To boarders gathering in the parlor before dinner, I announced, "The year of 1901 will come to be known as the year the Victorian Era died, and the Queen with it, though many purists would hold that it was the other way around. I read in a design magazine that she was a sucker for trite little objects placed symmetrically cheek by jowl on every flat surface in Buckingham Palace. I'm declaring the end of fussy Victorianisms on our overcrowded mantel museum."

I removed the snow globe, the little red rocking horse, the daguerreotype of the Siamese twins, the Jack and Jill figurines, the miniature Dutch windmill, the pirouetting ostrich, and the polka-dotted bunny scratching his behind. I moved the two handsome brass candlesticks to the left side and the upright Chinese plate to the right instead of in the middle.

"There. Now the housekeeper will have less to dust, and we can enjoy a post-Victoria simplicity."

English to the bone, Bernard looked askance at my audacity, and sank into an inordinate sadness at dinner, as if his mother, not the distant Queen, had died. Unwittingly I had wounded him, acting from aesthetics rather than considerateness. I felt awful, especially after he had been so kind to comfort me. I went to my room to think of something nice to do for him. I wanted it to be English so I looked through my volume of Shakespeare. I found the passage about England from *Richard II* with the scattered lines,

This royal throne of kings, this scepter'd
  isle . . .
This precious stone set in the silver
  sea . . .
This blessed plot, this earth, this realm, this
  England.

I had always loved it, but it didn't give me any specific image that I could draw for him. I turned to my Wordsworth. The frontispiece was an etching of the Thames and the Houses of Parliament seen from Westminster Bridge. It wouldn't be a masterpiece, but with "infinite, meticulous labor," I could render it passably and write out neatly below it the first few lines of his sonnet, "Composed upon Westminster Bridge."

Earth has not anything to show more fair;
Dull would he be of soul who could pass
   by
A sight so touching in its majesty:
This City now doth, like a garment, wear
The beauty of the morning.

On the stairway a few days later, I said to him, "I apologize for being disrespectful to your Queen. I know how beloved she was."

"No, no. It wasn't that." His thought trailed off. "It was something else."

I held forward my drawing with the verse. "It's for you."

A bashfulness came over me as he admired it.

"I would have drawn Gloucester Cathedral if I'd had something to go by."

"It's the most thoughtful thing you could have done for me."

391

■ ■ ■

Olga Zofia Lipska, the Polish waif whom
Hank finally let me hire when she promised
to take his evening drawing class, hadn't
shown up to work for three days, so I took
the electric car down Bowery, got off near
the waterfront, and looked for Olga's street
in this Polish neighborhood.

I suspected her absence might be related to
the shooting of President McKinley at the
Pan-American Exposition in Buffalo, where
Mr. Tiffany, with Thomas Edison's collaboration, astonished crowds with his Fountain of
Light. The assassin was the son of Polish immigrants, one Leon Czolgosz, who boasted
in court that he'd been heavily influenced by
Emma Goldman and that he killed the president "because he was the enemy of the good
people."

I stepped aside for two women carrying
bundles of firewood on their heads. Eyes
averted to avoid my gaze, they turned in at a
stoop where men lounged on the steps occupied with their pipes without so much as
moving their legs out of the way for the
women to pass. Another woman selling
wreath-shaped bread like giant crullers did
not look up at me, and farther on, two
women haggling in Polish over frowsy salad
weeds in a basket fell silent when I ap-

proached. Olga's building wasn't a tenement but a large old house divided into small apartments. When she answered my knock, her eyes red from crying, she cowered instantly against her drawings tacked to the wall.

"You don't have to be afraid, Olga."

The drawings were excellent. A still life of an intricate wedge of cabbage, a potato, and a carrot arranged on a plate showed that she had really *seen* the objects, as Hank had said artists do. A scene with her ramshackle house and a shoeless toddler holding a cup under a dripping street faucet revealed the sensitivity Dudley had spoken of too. Her work was delicate, expressive, and nuanced with light and shadow, and I told her so. Now I understood what Hank saw in her, and what he meant about the immigrant experience expressed in art. She would design for me someday, but I would insist she continue under Hank's tutelage at night.

"Are you sick, Olga? Why haven't you come to work?"

"The other girls will hate me because I'm Polish," she murmured. "That murderer was Polish."

"No, they don't hate you. There's too much work to do for them to think about that. So much work that I hired another girl, Julia Zevesky."

Julia had come like a thin, wet puppy asking for a job on a rainy day. She must have walked miles without an umbrella, asking at any business that would let her dripping form enter. Dire need shadowed the skin below her dark, pleading eyes. Though she had no art experience, her eyes made me hire her as an errand girl and cutter's assistant at three-fifty a week, half the standard apprentice's wage.

"Her parents came from Warsaw," I told Olga. "Is that where your family came from?"

"No. Kraków."

"She came to work these last three days."

"Too afraid not to." Olga drew in her lips with a conflicted tremor.

"Please, Olga. Come back to work. We need you. Your family needs you to work, don't they?"

"Yes." A flat whisper.

"All right, then. I'll see you tomorrow."

"Yes."

The entry to the yard of Tiffany Furnaces in Corona was an iron door painted with the words POSITIVELY NO ADMITTANCE EXCEPT ON BUSINESS. I gave it a great heave, brushed the soot off my hands, and lifted my skirt over the rail at the bottom, feeling like part of some massive industry.

I'd been concerned that the bronze filigrees for the poppy lamp wouldn't be ready when we needed them, which meant I had to make the trip to Corona by ferry and train when I had better things to do. It irritated me that these progress checks couldn't be done by telephone, but Mr. Gray, the foundry foreman, insisted he couldn't hear the phone ring. If I didn't make my presence felt, work for my little department was shunted to the rear and the men's projects were done right away because some of their departments were housed in the factory compound. Being on-site, they could push their work along.

At the foundry Mr. Gray said the two styles of bases and finials Mr. Tiffany had designed for the poppy lamp, oil and electric, were almost finished, but the filigrees for the leaves and stamens hadn't been started. With my urging he agreed to do them next.

Walking toward the glasshouse, I was overcome with love for the poppy lamp. I had even dreamed I engraved my name on a vermilion petal. The giddy pleasure transformed itself by degrees into a flaming horror of being found out. My audacity leaked to Mr. Tiffany, who angrily reprimanded me, and our pure artist love was burned to ashes. I had awakened in a cold sweat of shame, relieved that it was only a dream.

In the glasshouse I stood a distance away from Tom Manderson's shop, watching him shape a ten-inch vase. Mr. Nash came up alongside me.

"He can do four of the simpler ones in an

hour," he said.

"He's a master."

"They all are. Last year we produced twenty thousand vases and bowls."

"That's remarkable. Congratulations on your Paris awards for Favrile glass."

"The work itself is the reward."

"You aren't upset that Mr. Tiffany didn't name you in the press releases? He takes all the credit when it's you who turns sand into jewels."

"I'd rather have the good opinion of the men here than the judgment of a few jurists on another continent."

"It's not too much to want both," I ventured.

"I love glass. It's a living thing. To see it pour out glowing and to swirl the colors on the marver, there's nothing like it. That's enough for me."

I looked across the factory to Tom Manderson's workshop. He and the other gaffers and decorators made the vases and goblets Tiffany showed in Paris. Mr. Tiffany had probably never blown glass in a hot shop in his life.

"Do you think it's enough for Tom?"

"Never asked him. We just do our work, feel good when it comes out right, go have a pint of ale together if it does, feel glum when it doesn't, and go have a pint then too."

Maybe it was different for women. Maybe we were more complicated creatures.

"There wouldn't be a Tiffany of such fame without you and Tom," I said.

"But there wouldn't be a Tom Manderson without Tiffany."

I had to accede to that. By the same token, there wouldn't be a Clara Driscoll, designer of leaded-glass lampshades, without Mr. Tiffany *and* Mr. Nash.

I asked him to point me to the enamel studio, walked across the yard, and peeked my head in the doorway. "Surprise!"

"Clara! We didn't expect you," Lillian said. "Here, have some tea."

"Tea while you work?"

She giggled at my astonishment. "A local maid-of-all-work brings it every morning. Lunch too."

"It's just the two of us today," Alice said. "Miss Lantrup is visiting a glaze supplier, and Patricia was feeling poorly so she went home."

Milkweed, wildflowers, seed pods, and a bittersweet vine with orange berries lay scattered on a table, and on another, jars of powdered glass enamels stood in a row, making a rainbow of colors. Watercolor studies of fiddlehead ferns, hollyhocks, and grapevines had been pinned to the walls. I thought how Olga would flourish here.

Alice showed me an enameled plaque with the motif of oyster and mussel shells nestled amid ribbons of mottled olive-green seaweed with raised, cinnamon-colored kelp bulbs. The inside of the oysters had the same satiny nacre that real shells do.

"Exquisite," I said.

"It's called repoussé. We work the shapes with a little hammer and punches. Mr. Tiffany hasn't seen it finished." Her eyes gleamed with anticipation.

"He comes here twice a week, always with some new idea," Lillian said.

"Twice a week!" The icy surprise of that shot through me to my toes. Four artisans could not be producing so much that he would need to advise them twice a week.

I happened to see a card with a drawing of milkweed and some writing in Mr. Tiffany's distinctive script. The crossbars of his *t*'s were formed with a squiggle to the right of the upright part of the *t,* not on it.

Styles are merely the copying of what others have done, perhaps done better than we. God has given us our talents so as not to copy the talents of others, but rather to use our own imagination to obtain the revelation of True Beauty.

Although I knew Mr. Tiffany thought that, he had never written it out just for me.

"That's the way he suggests motifs to us," Lillian said. "Sometimes he sketches something right in front of our eyes, but we don't have to use his ideas if we like ours better."

Alice reached up to a shelf. "I designed this milkweed tray with one pod open to show the inside and the other closed to show the bumpy surface. He had the brilliant idea to make the cover on the closed pod swing open."

"He loves things with movable parts," Lillian said.

I felt the sting of a tiny insect in my heart. I hadn't known that about him. A troubling sense of estrangement had been growing ever since he had come back from France last year. That they knew this and I didn't intensified it.

"He wants us to convey the thing as it is in nature," Alice said, "even to give a hint of air or water surrounding it, like a breeze or a ripple."

Another thing I wasn't aware of. Anticipating something else hurtful, I asked her the procedure here.

"One of us does a watercolored cartoon. He says yes, and we make a model in wax. He says yes again, and we take the model to the foundry, and it comes back as copper in the shape we designed," Alice explained. "Then we apply the enamel as powdered glass if the shape is horizontal, or we paint it with wet enamels if it's vertical. That's called limoges. Then it goes to be fired, and usually we repeat the process many times to give depth to the enamel."

"It's like the Dutch Renaissance painters applying layers of glazes," Lillian said. "Sometimes he brings gold or silver leaf to lay under the enamel to make it shimmer."

Under my skin burned the heat of coveting his two visits a week, but I couldn't say a word. They were my friends. The creative collaboration I had let myself believe I alone had with him was intimate and passionate. Now it was cheapened by seeing his more attentive collaboration with them. I was still just one of his minions. He could give out design ideas in mosaics, furniture, wallpaper, textiles, leaded glass, and now enamels and ceramics to half a dozen people all in one day. I was a fool to be so naïve to think I was special to him.

"Did you know that he's been experimenting for several years with making iridescent enamel?" Alice asked.

"No." The word leaked out weakly.

"He's worked on that with a lady named Julia Munson at his studio in his *home.* Very big secret. Now she's making jewelry."

"For Tiffany and Company?"

"No. For our Mr. Tiffany, combining semiprecious stones like lapis lazuli with enamel," Alice said. " 'Beauty before value,' he says."

Lillian scooted her chair forward and leaned toward me. "Once he pulled out of his pocket a velvet bag of colored gemstones from Tiffany and Company. He just spilled them out, right onto this very table, as if they were beach pebbles. From another bag he drew out a necklace that he and Miss Munson had made with enamels of the same colors over gold. And do you know, the enamels in the necklace were just as rich and beautiful as the loose stones."

"Ah. That's the son driven by the Tiffany Imperative to measure up to the father." At least I was able to tell Lillian one thing she didn't know about him.

"He calls his jewelry 'little missionaries of art,' so I called what we do here 'middle-sized missionaries of art,' " Lillian said. "He liked that."

She looked at Alice as though asking permission to reveal something she'd been dying to tell me all along.

"He has arranged with his father that our pieces will be sold at Tiffany and Company." Her voice rose to a high pitch and quivered on the edge of bragging.

"That's wonderful for you. Congratulations."

Awkward silence filled a moment or two, and I had to look away. I loved them both. I had to remind myself of that. Was my heart so puny that I couldn't share?

"So then you like it out here?"

"It's nice, I suppose," Alice said guardedly, not wanting to hurt me. She knew me well enough to guess my feelings. "No contract system. No deadlines."

"No talk of the cost of a thing?"

"No. We just study nature and make things." Lillian's elation was too full for her to notice its effect on me.

"A perfect little Arcadia, this hideaway haven."

The instant I said that I regretted it. My tone was sharp. They hadn't asked to leave me.

Half sorry that I had come, I left to go back to the studio under storm clouds. Wind tossed the ferry in a sickening motion. So this was what lovers' jealousy felt like — the searing sense that you aren't precious and all-consuming to the one you love, the nausea at seeing attentions given to another, the gnawing reminders in the pit of your stomach, and then the waves of shame down to your bowels for succumbing to an ugly emotion shot through with self, possessiveness, and ill will. I felt sick with the knowledge that I was susceptible to all of that. I would have to take care to hide it. They were my dear friends. I had lost them, and Mr. Tiffany had won them over to him. Their little atelier was the private plaything of a wealthy man whose sole passions were nature and art, and now they were the recipients of that passion. To Alice and Lillian, the little jars of powdered glass might be enough, because of what he gave them.

He had been mine alone, I had thought, and now he wasn't. I would have to live with a bottomless craving for his attention. The pit would never be filled.

A letter awaited me at the boardinghouse that evening with the return address of J&R Lamb Studios, Mr. Tiffany's rivals in glass.

February 3, 1902

Dear Mrs. Driscoll,
    Congratulations on winning a Bronze Medal for your exquisite dragonfly lamp which we had the pleasure of seeing at the Paris Exposition Universelle. Kindly forgive us for allowing more than a year to elapse before sending our congratulations. We had no way of knowing how to contact you privately.
    Since then, we've learned of your talents in design and management, and have been given this address by a Mr. Henry McBride. Please accept our invitation to have a look at our studio and allow us to take you to lunch afterward.
                              Yours truly,
                Mr. Frederick Lamb, President
                              J&R Lamb Studios
                                    since 1857

I folded it small and didn't show it to Alice.

CHAPTER 30
TIFFANY GIRLS
AND A BOY

My curiosity held sway over loyalty after realizing that what I had with Mr. Tiffany wasn't as unique as I had led myself to believe, so I took a day off to meet this Frederick Lamb. He and his art director treated me as though I was an honored artist, and were anxious to show me all their types of glass and the windows being produced.

"We're not making leaded-glass lampshades yet. That's why we've invited you here. We recognize you to be the creative force behind this new art form," Mr. Lamb said.

"How do you know that?"

"Your friend. Mr. McBride. I happened to meet him at the Tiffany pavilion in Paris, then fell out of touch with him until recently when we ran into each other at a gallery."

Their intent was what I had expected — to spirit me away from Tiffany so I could set up a leaded-shade department for them, bringing with me everything I knew. It was underhanded of them, but this wasn't sweet Arcadia. It was cold New York business.

They took me to a grand lunch at Dorlin's. Perhaps they intended to make me an offer while filling me with wine and pâté de foie gras. They'd have to make it fifty dollars a week, not a cent less. It would be a while before I got more than the thirty-five dollars I got now.

"We noticed at the Paris Exposition and in Mr. Bing's Salon de l'Art Nouveau that none of the Tiffany products carried the names of individual designers," Mr. Lamb said, leaning forward, chin jutting out. "That is not the policy at Lamb Studios. We are proud of our design staff and recognize them by name in our brochures and on our products."

"We thought you'd like to know," the art director added under hooded eyes.

How canny of them to worm their way into my private grievance and use it for their own purposes. How did they know? Hank?

"Thank you for mentioning that. Yes, it is important to me."

Could I trust that their public promotion of me would actually occur?

By the end of lunch, the conversation took a leap.

"We would be pleased if you would consider our studio as yours," Mr. Lamb said.

"Would I have total design freedom?"

"Total."

"Would I be saddled with administration duties?"

"No."

"Do you manufacture your own glass?"

"No. We buy from several suppliers."

"Do you have women working for you?"

"Not at this time."

Before leaving, I promised to consider their offer, and it came in the mail, properly, two days later. I opened it alone in my room. Forty-five dollars a week. With two weeks of unpaid vacation, that would be $2,250. By saving money and vacation time, I could travel to Europe! I could see the great museums, cathedrals, fountains. I could have a broader life! But, oh, how much more I liked our spacious studio and all my Tiffany Girls than the bleak, cramped workshop at Lamb's, where I would be the only woman. How would the men there take to a woman coming in as their supervisor?

My Women's Department was a living entity I'd built up myself. Only Agnes and Miss Stoney were left from the original six. I had increased it to thirty-five at one time. We were thirty-two until Mr. Tiffany had sucked away four of my best, so we had only twenty-eight now. The department was mine more than anything else in the world was mine. I gazed around my bedroom at Merry's furniture. I owned no home, no furniture, no jewelry, only a meager wardrobe and a bicycle, but I *had* that department. I felt pulled one way by sentiment and allegiances and another way by a salary increase and the promise of recognition.

Temptation lay heavy on my mind. I imagined marching into Mr. Tiffany's office, slapping down the offer, and demanding that he top it. I could say that Mr. Lamb is proud of his designers and acknowledges them publicly, but I had no evidence for that claim. Or I could leave without explanation. It would be the worst kind of betrayal. I didn't think I was capable of that. I decided to wait out February, and then see how I felt.

February 14. Valentine's Day. Passed without a card or a rose. Still undecided after a week. What if the glass available to me at Lamb Studios wasn't as beautiful or unusual or varied as Mr. Nash's glass? They didn't know the secret of iridescence. That would be frustrating, because it would limit what I could produce.

February 15. At the end of the day, as though it were an afterthought, a young woman carrying a satchel of books came to inquire for a job. Beatrix Hawthorne, twenty-five, was born in England to American parents and lived with them on the Upper West Side.

After getting acquainted and enjoying her

chattiness, I asked what books she was carrying.

"A novel, some poetry, art books. I've studied art more as an observer than a practitioner," she said, opening her satchel. "Here's Vasari's *Lives of the Painters.* I'm reading the chapter about Masaccio now, to uncover the goodness in his soul that allowed him to paint *The Expulsion of Adam and Eve from Eden* with such empathy and heartbreak."

"Only the early painters?"

"Oh, no. I'm wild about Winslow Homer. What that man sees! Do you know his work?"

"A little."

"In his paintings of children, I see a certain melancholy about growing up, and in his seascapes, water gushes right off the canvas and onto your lap. But he said one puzzling thing — that if a man wishes to be an artist, he should never look at pictures."

"Do you agree?"

"Not a jot!"

"Maybe he meant you should look at nature instead," I said. She shrugged. "What's the novel?"

She glanced around the room as if looking for any listeners and said in a low, conspiratorial voice, "Theodore Dreiser's *Sister Carrie.* It's banned because of Carrie's moral decline as an actress. That's unconstitutional, you know."

"How did you get it, then?"

"From a friend in publishing. I'll let you read it after I finish it, if you'd like to."

She spoke with a mixture of accents — British and Bostonian — so I hazarded a question.

"Are you, by chance, distantly related to Nathaniel Hawthorne?"

"He was my grandfather."

"Gracious! Do you remember him?"

"Oh, no. He died before I was born."

"Did you ever get to see the scarlet letter?"

"Oh, don't be naïve. He made that up. Every last thread."

To have even this filament of connection to creative genius thrilled me. I hired her on the spot.

February 19. All the papers carried it on the front page: Charles Lewis Tiffany, founder of Tiffany & Company, dead. The bulk of the vast fortune of the merchant prince passes to Louis Comfort Tiffany, founder of newly renamed Tiffany Studios, now vice president and artistic director of his father's Tiffany & Company.

An awkward quiet reigned in the corridors and in our women's studio, as if our foundation had been shaken. Beatrix brought an editorial from the *Times* that commented that his death was reported around the world. Both companies shut down for the day of the funeral. Tiffany & Company was draped in black. Macy's, B. Altman, W. & J. Sloane, Lord & Taylor, Wanamaker's, and fourteen other stores closed their doors during the hours of the funeral.

Alice and I went to the service together. Charles Tiffany was eulogized as an arbiter of taste, a gentleman whose illustrious career had been built by an iron hand within a velvet glove, and by honesty, propriety, high standards applied to products and service, and the appreciation of elegance. The atmosphere in the church was reverent while the organist concluded with Charles Tiffany's favorite hymn, "Lead, Kindly Light." We watched the parade of bejeweled women in black file past the marble casket which was smothered in chrysanthemums, lilies, and roses, all white, just as Wilhelmina's pine coffin had been. The next week, his son made his Monday rounds as usual, and I gave him my condolences, such as I could offer in my open studio.

February 27. Glowering sky, steady sleet, wind rattling the windows, and a studio full of girls bending over summer flowers. There was something magical in that. I looked out from my desk at the heads lowered earnestly to their work — six on two poppy lamps, with Mary and Miss Stoney as selectors; two wisteria lamps going, with Miss Precise and

Particular Judd and Minnie Henderson selecting; two dragonflies, a deep sea, a butterfly, and the new peony, with Carrie McNicholl in charge, assuming the position Alice had left. At the moment, Nellie was singing softly about the wild mountain heather of Ireland, and Beatrix was squinting under her electric light. With her eyeglasses sans bows perched on her high, thin nose and a pencil balanced behind her ear, she had a capable and determined look.

Julia Zevesky, the waif who had been rain-sodden when she asked for a job, arrived today with an umbrella. Lately Theresa sported a new floppy silk rose on her collar. Minnie wore a slim silver bracelet now, and Anna had a new tortoiseshell comb in her pompadour piled high like a pyramid of popovers. I had given these girls a chance at life in the arts, and they had thrived, and lived better lives. Did I really want to work my fingers to the bone to do that for men?

Mr. Lamb had said I would be entirely unconstrained in my designs. With Mr. Mitchell gone, now was the time to test the limits of how sculptural, bold, individual, elaborate, and expensive my designs could be here. I dug out an unfinished design and began to draw.

The shade was a panoply of connected webs made by a very ambitious spider, as overzealous as Mr. Tiffany, each web slightly

411

different. The lead lines would be the filaments of the web. He would like that — the structural ribs of the shade deriving from the webs themselves. If I felt estranged from Mr. Tiffany and diminished by his attentions to Alice and Lillian, what I needed to do was to *invite* his collaboration more. I knew I wanted blossoms beneath the webs, but it would be better to elicit that from him. Still, it was hard to stop.

I wanted it integrated with a tall mosaic base, all of a piece. What small flower grows on a tall stalk, small enough for there to be many crowded together on the base? One I hadn't used already. With chagrin, I hit upon the perfect one: white narcissus, which shared its name with the Greek youth in love with himself who gazes into the pond at his own reflection, preoccupied with self, self, the self-admiring self, the insatiable self, the self yearning for recognition of its beauty.

When did my need for recognition pulse most urgently? It was in the exhilaration of the act of creation, which made me want to shout to the city, *Look! Look! See what I can do with mere glass to make you see wisteria in February. Let the colors touch you. Revel in the emotions they stimulate. Catch a whiff of the real bud in the brittle reproduction. Surrender to the illusion!*

That people would do so was ultimately more important than knowing who the illusionist was.

Filaments of pain insinuated themselves behind my eyes and grew into shards, some sleek missiles determined in their destination, others jagged, wild, and unpredictable. I turned off my light, laid down my pencil, and gazed out at the girls at work. Frank came by and noticed me not working. He emptied all the trash containers in the workroom and washed the glass easels not in use, and all I did was watch him.

Y-O-U S-A-D T-O-D-A-Y.

I nodded.

To unify base and shade, I could lead Mr. Tiffany to see a few narcissus blossoms on the shade too. Elaborate, yes. Expensive to make, yes. But if Mr. Tiffany felt it was his too, he wouldn't resist. I knew *how* to work here, how to make things happen. The thought of starting over with someone else was wearisome. Maybe it didn't matter who paid me. I was and would always be working for myself. What to do? Allow myself to be caught and bought, or stay within the web I knew?

I showed Frank my sketch.

C-O-B-W-E-B L-A-M-P, I spelled.

Frank made frenzied gestures, flailing his arms, wiping off his face as if he had walked into a web. It was funny and dear, and I laughed, which made him grin back at what appeared to him only a gaping silent mouth.

413

I W-A-N-T Y-O-U H-A-P-P-Y, he spelled, and put his hand over his heart.

I did the same. Impulsively, I gave him the Lamb Studios letter to read. His eyes got big with alarm, and his head wagged furiously from side to side. I should have known he would react that way.

Was the need for recognition so vital that I would give up love in order to get it? Had Mr. Tiffany injured me intentionally? No. I would not creep away just because he gave attention to others. I would not leave without a fight, and my weapons were design ideas.

T-E-A-R I-T U-P, I spelled.

He ripped vigorously and hurled the tiny pieces into his collecting trash can. One escaped and fluttered to the floor. He seized it, threw it in, and brushed his palms together as a sign of finishing the job.

I A-M H-A-P-P-Y N-O-W.

CHAPTER 31
A BRONZE
AND A GARDEN

Mr. Farmer-John Thomas, he of the "Dangerous Influence" accusation, came into my studio and greeted me with a hearty "Good morning! I have some great news for you," as though his cow had just calved. He had slid into Mr. Mitchell's place as slick as oiled glass. "You'll be pleased. In fact, I think you'll be *very* pleased. This will be the highlight of your week."

"Enough preamble, Mr. Thomas. Tell me." What a different approach.

He laid down a sheet of paper. "An order for five more wisteria lamps. That makes twenty to date. Selling at three hundred fifty dollars apiece, that's good business. Peacock, iris lantern, and trumpet creeper — two each." He laid down another sheet. "*Twenty* peony shades. They've been a surprise good seller at one hundred seventy-five dollars. And" — he waved the third sheet with a flourish before he laid it down — "*forty* more dragonfly lamps priced at one hundred thirty dollars, two hundred dollars, and two hundred fifty dollars, depending on size and style." His usually mousy voice rang out strongly.

"Goodness! Who would have thought it?" I said with enough edge to my voice that he might catch my wicked innuendo.

He pointed to a list. "You'll see here the models and sizes and some customer requests for certain color schemes, preferred borders, oil or electric. There's a giant one, a hanging electrolier twenty-eight inches wide. Do two of those so we'll have one for our front showroom."

I felt myself breathing faster at the exciting possibilities, not just at the amount but at the variety.

"These don't add up to forty."

"The rest are your choice." Mr. Thomas stepped back and grinned a none-too-mousy grin. "Enough for today?"

"Quite! I'm overjoyed."

I knew now that I had made the right decision.

After he left, I cleared off my desk to make a chart of assignments, and found a neglected piece of mail. It was a request that I give a talk on women's work at Tiffany Studios before the Women's Educational and Industrial Union in Albany and Boston. I was flattered and felt obligated to do my bid for women in the arts. Although I hardly needed one more thing to think about with all these orders, I dashed off an acceptance.

Mr. Tiffany came in with his hands full, sat on the little kitchen chair, and asked how I was feeling.

"Ecstatic."

"Thought so. Here's something else that will make you happy."

From underneath his papers he pulled out a leather presentation folder tooled with the words EXPOSITION UNIVERSELLE, PARIS, FRANCE, 1900.

"The French. They think we're happy to wait two years before they get around to mailing out the awards," he said.

I opened it. The certificate, which was called a *diplôme*, gave my name, the name of the award, and the identification of *Une lampe avec le motif d'un insecte en forme de dragon.*

I chuckled. "There's a world of difference between a dragon and a dragonfly."

In the lower-right corner was an embossed bronze medallion. "It's quite impressive," I said, an octave above my normal voice.

He pulled out of his pocket a hinged box and laid it in front of me to open. It was the bronze medal itself, nameless except for TIFFANY GLASS AND DECORATING COMPANY.

"I wanted you to see it, but I'd like to use it in a display of all the medals in the showroom. Just for a while."

I closed the box to show it was all right with me, and immediately seized the opportunity to tell him my idea for the cobweb shade over a narcissus mosaic base. I showed him the preliminary drawings and spun out a few threads of description leading up to the coup de grâce which I'd learned from Alice at Corona: "They wouldn't be geometrically circular. They'd be distorted to show that they were being blown by a breeze."

"I like it. I like it. The spontaneity and activity of nature."

The web was doing its work.

"If you use the palest yellow ocher crackle glass with slight fissures below the surface, it would simulate the fine sections of the webs between the leading, as well as reflect ambient light."

"Then are you caught?"

"Like the proverbial fly. You know that crackle glass would catch the early-morning light just like the spiderwebs do in my garden at the Briars. There are usually some on the lilacs. I'll let you know when they're in bloom. You must come see them."

He had invited me before, but for some reason, maybe the bronze medal, this time I thought he meant it.

I was turning in a circle in my bedroom late that afternoon with the certificate in my hand, wondering where to put it, when Merry

418

came down the hall carrying curtains. She peeked in.

"Practicing a new waltz step?"

I showed it to her. She looked properly impressed.

"Do you want a nail?"

"What for?"

"Why, to frame the thing and hang it on the wall."

"I wouldn't defile your wall. I'll just keep it in a drawer, and when someone doesn't think much of me, I'll haul it out and brandish it. And when I'm old and need to convince myself that my being here mattered, I'll take it out and wonder what it was for."

"Being here? In my boardinghouse? Of course it matters. I get fifty-five dollars a month from you."

"Being here on earth, Merry."

"Oh, Lordy. Don't you go getting philosophical on me. You'll be just like Francie if you don't watch out. Married to Plato, she is. Be wide o'that, or you'll be an old maid the likes of her."

We eyed each other head to toe and howled. We were all old maids.

Mr. Tiffany was good for his word, and asked me to come to the Briars on Sunday. He didn't ask anyone else. The visit would be with me alone. I put on my sky-blue poplin, which had been my wedding dress, lo, a dozen years ago, and was happy that it still fit my forty-year-old figure. It was spring at last, and I wanted to breathe spring, see and smell spring, and look like spring. Outside my window, the trees between the stoops were jubilant, dressed in the pigment called Permanent Green Light, but the oil-paint color charts had it all wrong. It wasn't permanent. It was all too brief.

It was pleasurable brushing my hair at my window and looking out on those violet morning shadows I loved. The sparrows of Irving Place were preening too, and gossiping pianissimo, and hopping about with an air of importance. Distant medleys of the city blended into a pleasant humming, punctuated at intervals by the Third Avenue elevated rumbling in a crescendo, grinding its brakes shrilly for the Eighteenth Street station, expelling its *pfft* of steam, then starting up again and fading away in a diminuendo.

I parted my hair carefully, wound my chignon, fluffed up the bow on my straw boater, and set off on foot for the el train going across the Brooklyn Bridge, changed to the Long Island Rail Way there, and got off at the Oyster Bay station. Mr. Tiffany had sent his driver to pick me up in his Rambler Runabout. What a thrill to speed along the road on the high red leather seat, holding my hat against the breeze, hearing the motor purr like a tiger, and seeing the countryside whiz by.

The house overlooked Oyster Bay and was surrounded by birches, chestnuts, and oaks, and behind them, hemlocks and pines. A white shingle neo-Colonial, the house itself wasn't palatial or formidable like his Seventy-second Street mansion, though certainly comfortable. Naturally, for him, it had a tall clock tower, evidence of his preoccupation with height and his imperative punctuality. As I approached, it struck the quarter hour with a resounding peal. Woe be to the son or daughter who was not at the breakfast table before seven bells.

A wide wooden porch wrapped around the house, irises edged a lily pond, and wisteria cascaded from a pergola. Mr. Tiffany was sitting on a driftwood chair on the lawn, painting his garden while wearing — unbelievably! — a white silk pongee suit with, yes, a gardenia in his buttonhole. Except for a big floppy-eared dog dozing at his feet, he was alone. He set down his brush as soon as he saw me, and was full of apologies that his wife was feeling poorly and wouldn't be able to come out to welcome me, and the twins were visiting their aunt. Instead, his youngest daughter, Dorothy, "however small," as she had said, came outside to take me on a tour of the garden.

"Fog comes across the water," Mr. Tiffany

said, "so I like to have a palette of cool, dusky colors like those hollyhocks, foxgloves, hydrangeas, and lilacs against the gray air."

"Do you do any of the planting?"

"A couple times a year I get on my hands and knees for an hour with the gardeners. Then I go wash. I never do the pruning. It hurts too much. I like the creepers to meander. They give a sense of unity to everything. Permitted disorder is intriguingly beautiful. In gardens, I mean, not in people." He glanced down at his daughter affectionately.

"Miss Dorothy, help me find a spiderweb in the lilacs," I said.

Before long, she cried out, "Here's one!"

We traced the filaments to see how they connected one bush to another.

"How did he get from here to there if he doesn't have wings?" she asked.

"It's a mystery, like the Brooklyn Bridge," I said. "Maybe she launched herself on a breeze and hoped for the best."

"Maybe he tried and tried and fell to the ground but climbed back up and kept at it until he succeeded," Mr. Tiffany said, delivering a lesson.

I breathed the fragrance of lilac and watched the pendulous yellow blossoms of a laburnum tree move in the breeze. Dorothy skipped ahead to another pergola draped with white clematis. She picked one and came to her father's side, plucking off the petals and saying, "He loves me. He loves me not."

"Dorothy! Never pick a flower. You know better than that. Picking a flower is like poking a hole in a painting."

"I was just playing."

"Never damage any living thing! Don't ever let me see you doing that again."

I'd never known his voice to have that harshness.

"It's not a crime, Papa. It's just a game." She threw the flower to the ground and stomped on it. "You're mean," she cried, and ran away, swerving to topple his easel on her way into the house.

"I apologize for her behavior. She's sensitive and stubborn and rebellious, just like I was at her age. She's not a happy child."

"That's hard to imagine when she has everything."

"Everything but a good feeling about herself. Her nanny and her mother mention the charms of Annie, the child who died, way too much. Lou works so often at the women's infirmary that I'm afraid Dorothy suffers from a lack of attention. She thinks she's unloved."

"That's common among girls of all ages."

He gave that a moment's thought before he said, "We have some sweet times, though."

On our stroll through the garden, he commented on the shape of the trees, the hue of heliotrope blossoms vibrating against the viridian leaves, the brilliance of an iris petal shot through with sunlight, and the darkness of the edge of the same petal where it was in the shade. Lou must have tired easily in his presence. No wonder she wasn't feeling well and had to rest. He was just too much for daily consumption.

He cupped his hand under a peony tenderly, as if it were the chin of his beloved, for the sake of the frailty of one petal about to fall. "Beauty is everything, isn't it?" His gaze moved from the blossom to my face in the most penetrating way.

No, it isn't, but I refrained from contradicting him.

My mouth tensed involuntarily with an awful tightness. I wished I didn't have my glasses on, wished my nose were smaller, my mouth more upturned, my eyelids less droopy, my hair more stylish. Oh, what was the use? I could fill a book with the ill design of my face. All my observations of New York told me that a plain face led a plain life. With that as a truth, there might not be any possibility for intimacy with any man.

In Mr. Tiffany's eyes, though, my claim to beauty was to make beautiful things, one after another, until he noticed that they came from a beauty within.

When you look at me, don't you see more than a design machine? Don't you see a woman with more than one passion? Don't you see my adoration for you? Don't you recognize the longing heart within the glass I've touched? I ached to ask him these things, but I didn't dare. I didn't want him to think I wanted romance. What I wanted would have to be a finer union than any romance I'd ever known. We stood without moving, looking at each other, until a breeze caught a magnificent double dahlia near us and made it bounce. Our intensity dissolved. The moment was lost.

"So alive. See how many petals are nestled in there?"

"How is it that you came to love flowers so intensely?" I asked, recovering myself.

"Oh, that started when I was a boy. We had a country house overlooking the Hudson, and my father bought an old Dutch farm adjacent as my playground. I loved wildflowers, tiger lilies, dandelions, brooks, trees, birds. I drew and painted them all."

"Sounds idyllic."

He scratched his chin through his beard. "It made me dreamy. No Tiffany male child in generations before me had such leisure, so my father was determined to shorten it."

"How?"

"By trying to entice me into his company as his successor. By showing me gems and teaching me to distinguish garnets from rubies. I cared more about pebbles I found

425

along the river. When other boys took tennis rackets to military school, I took paints. He tried to instill in me the value of a dollar, but I was more interested in the value of a color. He considered that a bald-faced revolt. Things turned sour, and ever since, I've been hell-bent on proving to him that following my own way, I could be just as successful as he was."

"I've known that about you for a long time. It must have been a tremendous burden."

"The Paris Exposition helped balance the scale. Before that, he was as hard as granite."

"Always?"

Mr. Tiffany bent down to pick up a few dried leaves that had fallen.

"I remember a letter I wrote to him from military school, telling him that I was trying to be a man but I couldn't learn the school lessons, my teachers scolded me, and my fellows ridiculed me. In despair I pleaded with him to let me come home. I'll never forget his answer. 'A diamond, though of the first water, without hard grinding and polishing, would always remain without luster.' "

He crushed the leaves in his fist.

"I can't imagine him saying something so uncompassionate."

"All the same, I owe my insistence on perfection to him." Looking off to the bay, he murmured, "He was ninety years old."

"I'm sure he was proud of you."

He raised his shoulders noncommittally.

"Now the lock is off the strongbox." Bitter relish spilled out in his tone. "At last I can build my legacy, my complete and unlimited artistic vision of fine and decorative art."

"More than you've done already?"

"There's a resort called Hotel Laurelton overlooking Cold Spring Harbor not too far from here. I'm buying it, razing it to the ground, and taking over the public picnic grounds too, five hundred acres. The estate I'm building there will *dwarf* what you see here. It will be twice the size of Teddy Roosevelt's mansion on Oyster Bay."

He flung his arm out over the garden and said it with such fire and overweening zeal that it was almost frightening. Something pent up had been released with Charles's death, and was dangerous. His daughter Dorothy knew it, and now so did I.

CHAPTER 32
THE LETTER

The sky cracked open in a violent thunder-storm on my way home from work. What a way for April Fool's Day to announce itself. I'd been hoping for spring sun. My umbrella popped inside out at the corner of Fourth and Twenty-third. I fought with it for seven blocks and was soaked to the skin when I arrived home. In my room I dropped my wet coat, dress, shift, corset, shoes, and stockings onto the floor, dried with a towel, put on my nightgown, and climbed under the covers.

In my comfortable semi-doze, I heard an urgent knock.

"I have to talk to you."

"Yes, George. Come in."

He would anyway, but I liked to remind him that permission was needed.

Even with my eyes closed, I knew he saw the heap of clothes by his cluck of dis-approval, tidiness being one of his sacred principles. I heard him hang my dress and shift and coat on hangers on the curtain rod, and imagined him laying my corset and stockings over the back of the chair. The bed gave way as he sat next to me.

"Edwin is alive."

A jolt into consciousness. I shot upright.

"I received a letter. He wrote it on New Year's Day. But he must have had second thoughts about sending it. Look how rumpled it is."

George gave it to me to read. Postmarked San Francisco. I had trouble holding it still. The handwriting was similar, but faltering and uncontrolled.

January 1, 1902

Dear George,
You must be surprised to hear from me. I don't know how much time has gone by, and I don't know where I went or why. A period in my life is missing.

I came to myself down on the Mississippi, far south. I'm not sure where. I can't remember anything between that time and the previous election night in New York.

"What election? McKinley's in '96? That's hard to believe. We saw him often around that time. I didn't notice any change in him after that day. Did you?"

"No."

429

"He was completely lucid. He didn't forget what he was saying. He didn't go off on a tangent."

"I know."

"This suggests that he remembers what came before election day. His extravagant claims that he'd loved me since the day he met me, for God's sake!"

George winced.

"We weren't engaged until the new year, so he's forgotten that? He remembers an election, but he's forgotten that he loved a woman enough to want to marry her? He's forgotten Lake Geneva? Our night of love? Escaping in the morning? He doesn't remember how he got rid of me?"

"Clara, don't say it that way!"

I pulled up the covers and read on.

I felt I was only capable of doing simple manual labor for fear that I would tax my mind with thinking. I wasn't the same as I was before, so I thought it would be better to be dead to my family and friends. I wandered about and got what simple work I could do. I felt like an immigrant and a lost soul. I joined the army. I hoped it would give me some regularity. That was under another name — I've forgotten what. I was transported with my regiment to California, en route to Manila. I didn't want to go there, so I left the barracks

430

one day and wandered in California under another name. Eventually I felt I was gaining back some stability, so I've taken a good job in a new copper mine in the northern part of the state. I'm expecting to go there soon.

I'm sorry for the worry I've caused you and Mother and Father.

Edwin

And that was all. End of letter. No mention of me. No hint that there was, vaguely, in some folded recesses of his dark and troubled brain, a woman in his life.

"He considered me of no consequence to mention." My voice was pinched with the truth. How little I mattered. I was a woman of no importance.

"We don't know if all of this is true," George said. "We'll probably never know."

"Maybe he doesn't know the truth either."

Numbness gripped me. How fragile my victory over self. I had not conquered The Me Obsession by simply tearing up a job offer.

"Do your parents know?"

"Yes. I told them right away, and was going to tell you immediately after. I've had the letter for three weeks, but they asked me not to tell you until we found out more. It's been hard seeing you practically every day and keeping it from you."

"Don't think about that. For their sake I'm

glad he's alive. I can hardly imagine how they've suffered."

"They contacted a psychiatric doctor in San Francisco who has located him and has sent his son to the mining town to observe him for a while. The report just came today, saying that there's no reason why Edwin should not stay working there, so I felt I could tell you now."

I examined Edwin's letter for a clue to his state of mind, but I could deduce nothing. I wondered whether he had money enough to purchase the paper, the pen, and the ink, or whether he had borrowed them. To some degree, he had focused his thoughts. He had folded the paper evenly, not haphazardly. And then he had kept it for a couple of months, unsure. Or had he mislaid it and was content not to write another, and then discovered it unsent? Did he reconsider sending it, or did he post it without much thought?

"He must have had conflicts we didn't know about," I said. "The intensity of his social dreams distorted his rational mind. The poor huddled masses yearning to breathe free proved too much for him."

George sighed. "What a future he might have had."

Well, it was nice to think so. I let George have that, though the reality might have been that he knew he was a lesser man than we had built him up to be. Maybe he left Lake

Geneva before he had a chance to fail in politics. Maybe he knew his reason could not match his zeal. There would always be this mystery. The letter did nothing to resolve that.

One thing that had bothered me all these years rose up again. How awful that Edwin couldn't feel our compassion. I would have to leave it to George to convey that, if he chose to. Along with compassion, I still felt concern for Edwin's safety, especially at a mine. He was entirely capable of forgetting where he was going or not knowing what he was doing.

"Another occurrence could happen again without warning," I said softly, "and yet it would be unjust to put him in a home for such people."

The thought startled him.

"Should I go see him?" he asked.

"Would it make you feel better?"

"It depends on what I'd find."

"It's a little frightening, isn't it, not knowing what you'll see?"

His face was drawn tight. "Do you want me to tell him about you? To see if he'll remember you? I'll go there for that reason alone if you want me to."

"That's good of you, George."

A chance that my being could be reinstated. A temptation to feed my obsession with self. I had yearned too recklessly for love. I didn't want to make the same mistake again.

"I don't wish him ill, but he's been as if dead to me for nearly six years. It's best that I keep it that way. Please don't be hurt when I say I'm grateful for my own escape. No, don't go on my account."

"Then I don't think I'll go at all. I'll write to him, though. That's only right. Do you want me to mention you?"

"No. That might disturb him. I don't want to destroy the calm he has achieved." I reached out to hold his hand. "I need to let him go, George. Like the beautiful, wild goose you painted."

CHAPTER 33
MAYFLOWER

I was mending a stocking when Alice burst into my room with Lillian's news that the twin Queen Anne next to her family's cottage on the beach at Point Pleasant was for rent from May through September for seventy-five dollars.

"If four of us went in on it, say, Bernard and William —"

" 'William'?"

"Mr. York." The hint of a blush came to her cheeks.

"I'm relieved to know that he owns a first name," I said.

"If the four of us agreed, we'd only have to pay eighteen seventy-five each. And if we don't want to cook, we could have our meals at the Palmiés' for two dollars each for a weekend."

"There's only one thing."

"What's that?"

Stretching the stocking, I took two more stitches before I said, "Bernard. If he's engaged, would he want to bring his fiancée? And would we want her there?"

"This would tell you. If he said yes to the plan and didn't mention bringing her, then you'd know."

Three more stitches and a knot. I snipped the thread. "Not necessarily."

Alice's plan would force the issue. It was ridiculous not to know after all this time, and it was hard to deny my curiosity. At lunchtime the next day when I knew Bernard wouldn't be home, I pushed Merry into her niche of an office and closed the door behind us.

"I have a question to ask you, and I don't want you to tell anyone I asked."

"You want to know what's for dinner tonight? That I can tell you, but not much more. I'm not the fountain of all knowledge, you know."

"I want to know if Bernard is engaged."

"Oh, Lordy."

"Well?"

Her puffy face contorted. "As an upright and honest landlady, I can't divulge my tenants' privacies."

"What about as a friend? Alistair said he was engaged."

She turned to her desk and rearranged the inkwell and blotting roller, and whittled a pencil to a point, all without looking at me.

"As a friend, I'd say that what Alistair told

you is or was true."

"Then is he married now? Where's his wife?"

She waved her pocketknife vaguely before she closed it with a snap. "Truth to tell, I haven't got a baldy."

I slumped on her little stool. "A plague on men with secrets."

"He don't appear much married to me. His strange comings and goings is all I know to tell you."

"I don't relish being a worm," I said.

"A worm. What's a worm got to do with anything?"

"Worms like being kept in the dark. I don't."

A throaty cackle, a tsk-tsk, a head wagging from side to side. "He's a Brit through and through, and like as not, he'll always play his hand close to his chest. Walk well behind your heart is my advice, dearie."

"Thank you," I said, and left, a little embarrassed for having asked.

That evening in Alice's room I braided her hair, a silly attempt to go back to our girlhood when dilemmas about men were only happy conjectures. "Maybe I don't want to know," I said. "It would be easier if there were some chance of him being married."

"Easier? Why?"

"No decision to make."

I let her do the inviting. Bernard and Mr.

York — William, that is — agreed eagerly. I said to Alice in her room, "All this tells us is that he isn't spending summer weekends with her. She might be away for the summer."

"So? What do you care? You're a New Woman."

The next Saturday afternoon, Marion, Lillian, Bernard, William, Alice, and I rode our wheels along the oceanfront, cooled by wind coming off a solid line of white surf. In the village of Point Pleasant, I skidded to a stop in front of a dressmaker's shop that had some bolts of colorful fabric in the window. Everyone piled up behind me, and Bernard and William had to wait in the street while we investigated. The cloth was only seven and a half cents a yard instead of the twenty-five it would be in Manhattan. What fun it would be to have colored aprons instead of the standard black like the men used. With much frivolity the four of us picked our colors and agreed to return the next weekend to get them. Mounting our wheels to go home, we found that Bernard and William had bought potatoes and chops and tomatoes and lemon cookies for a beach supper around a fire.

What a lark this was turning out to be. In front of our cottage, we roasted our chops on skewers whittled from pine branches, and ate them right off the stick like primitives. We bit into our tomatoes whole, and used clamshells to scoop out the fluffy potatoes from the roasted skins, everything tasting better than anything cooked indoors. I stole glances at Bernard. Although I ate most of my meals at the boardinghouse with him usually present, this was different. It was an adventure, outside of our workaday lives, freer. Once he caught me looking at him, and I felt my cheeks flush. We finished the cookies in twilight, mesmerized by the flames.

"They look like wind-tossed orange tulips," I said, and between the flames I saw Bernard looking at me too, with what seemed to be deep interest, maybe even something more, but the light was flickering and I couldn't be sure.

When the fire burned down for the night, all of us took a little walk together, and Bernard fell into step beside me. We spoke of the softness of the air, all misty and still, the briny tang of the sea, and the goodness of the day — nothing more significant than that. Then we drifted into quietness with contained feeling, which left me with unbroached questions.

In bed that night, smelling the lingering smoky odor of the beach fire made me wonder whether Edwin had been eating outdoors by a campfire in some California mining camp. If he were here instead of Bernard, would he have enjoyed the day as much as Bernard seemed to? The Edwin that the letter revealed was gravely altered from the Edwin I had known and loved, and my reaction to him now might be compassion and sadness, but it wasn't love. I turned over in bed to let him go. Content for the time being, I listened to friendly taps of light rain on the metal porch roof and fell asleep wondering if Bernard was listening to them too.

The next day the weather cleared, though it was still as indecisive as a restless cat — cloudy, sunny, cloudy again. Alice wanted to nap on the big swing by the river, and William was off sketching, so that left Bernard, who was reading on the porch, to accompany me on another ride. How richly convenient. How deliciously dangerous. Nevertheless, I would exercise extreme caution.

We set off to explore the back road and found a brook coming out of a wood and emptying into Beaver Dam Creek half a mile away. At the top of the hill we took in the panorama of New Jersey spread out like a map, with little rivers running into the sea, and then strolled along the stream into the woods.

Light came through the canopy of leaves and branches, illuminating droplets of rainwater and shining on a rill spilling off some rocks into the stream. Bubbles formed instantly.

"Look. Live cabochons, only infinitely more fragile." They danced gaily on the surface

440

until they were caught up in the current and swept away.

"What's a cabochon?"

"A glass jewel with a rounded rather than cut surface. We use them in windows."

I left my wheel and went looking for wood violets. Instead, I found some nearly wilted pink blossoms close to the ground.

"What are they?" Bernard asked.

"Trailing arbutus. I think it's also called mayflower."

"Why that name?"

"Whittier called it mayflower in a poem because it was the first flower seen on these shores by the Pilgrims."

"It's also called ground laurel and is the state flower of Massachusetts."

"How do you know that?"

"With a brother like Alistair, I've absorbed a few things."

"Then why did you ask me if you already knew?"

"I wanted to hear you tell me."

I feigned exasperation despite feeling flattered.

"It would be a little tragedy, don't you think? These flowers, blooming with every ounce of energy for all the world to see, if no one came to see them."

"Depends."

I put my hands on my hips. "On?"

"On what you want out of life."

441

"I want beauty."

"Don't kid yourself. That's not all you want."

It irritated me that I could be so easily read, and he couldn't be.

"Maybe they bloom because they can't do otherwise, for the sheer joy of blooming."

"Like you," he said, and picked off a stem with a clump of fragile blossoms, held it to my nose so I could catch the fragrance, and then secured it in my chignon. His fingers grazing my ear tickled pleasantly, and I wished he would touch my neck too, but he stood back to look at me.

"There. Now you're a true nymph of the woods. Do you know that your whole face shines and your eyes sparkle beautifully when you see something beautiful in nature?"

"How can I know that?"

"You could look into a still pool. Just like Narcissus, always looking at and thinking about himself."

I didn't like his insinuation.

"No, I'm not *just* like Narcissus."

One word altered the mood of the day. I thrashed back out of the woods, mounted my wheel, and headed downhill, an erratic rhythm in my chest. The mayflower fell out of my hair and I didn't care. I didn't want to hear that I was too preoccupied with thinking about myself, that badgering, dissatisfied self. I didn't want to hear that I was a nymph but, *too bad, so sad, sorry, I'm engaged.* Or *I'm somewhat married. Partially married. Weirdly married. Depending on the season.* Whatever shoddy, sham, feckless explanation he would give.

CHAPTER 34
THE WEEK

Trying to concentrate on the work before me that Monday, I thought that round clear or green cabochons could suggest morning dewdrops or bubbles in a stream over which dragonflies hovered. Long, narrow cabochons in blues with streaks of white, placed vertically, could suggest rain, the weekend at Point Pleasant rendered in glass. I held smooth green glass under blue ripple glass to see how it would convey the depth of a stream. Building backward from the surface to hint at deep currents suggested something else to me — the currents in a woman's soul, my own. I was only half conscious of them, but there they were, those submerged layers of motivation, the substratum more dictatorial than the surface.

My mental meanderings were interrupted by Frank wildly urging me to go to Mr. Tiffany's studio. I went immediately. Spread out on his carpet lay watercolors for six conjoined, vertical landscape windows depicting a stream coming down from distant mountains with pines, birches, daffodils, and iris on the banks, and lilies in the water.

"You certainly pulled out all the stops on this one," I said. "Classic Tiffany."

"I just finished at one o'clock this morning. Do you like them?"

I laughed at his question. "Of course I do. They evoke an idyllic dreamscape. And I love iris."

"Good. The dimensions will be twenty-eight inches wide by six feet *each*. A client needs them installed for a wedding. Can you get them all finished by Saturday afternoon? They would need to go to the glazing department first thing Monday morning."

I expelled a puff of air. Absurd. He never should have accepted such a rushed commission, but his ambition was too strong to turn it down.

"I'm not forcing you. The men refused to take it on, saying it was impossible."

Oh-ho! I knew how to work him, but he also knew how to work me. His exploitation was transparent, and his sheepish grin revealed that he knew I saw it, but I had ambition too, and he knew that as well.

"Can you give me ten minutes to decide."

"Ten and a half."

"It would need a glass piece poured specially for the zigzag of the stream coming down between those mountains."

445

"I'll get Mr. Nash on it today. I've done a study to scale of that area for him to use. It will be ready on Friday."

"May I take the watercolors to show the girls?"

He was already rolling them.

My heel beat madly against the floor of the elevator as it clanked and crept upward. "Come on. Get going!" I said out loud, and the elevator boy looked offended. "Not you. This blasted machine!" I spent the minute praying that the girls would say yes. It would depend on how I presented it. I would have to pull out all the stops too.

I laid out the six watercolors, asked Agnes to step into the large studio, and said, "Tools down, please.

"You know we're not part of the union. The bosses of the Lead Glaziers and Glass Cutters' Union are not advanced enough to include women in their ranks. That means our jobs are not protected. I have to keep designing things that please The Powers That Be with such a speed that you are kept on as employees. The minute the incoming work diminishes, the Lieutenants downstairs will force me to choose which of you to let go. Meanwhile, you have to keep up your present high standards in selecting and cutting, and keep up your speed. In this, you've done admirably, and our department is now attracting attention outside of New York City. I have a chance to sing your praises in the state capital, and will do so again in Boston shortly."

Murmurs rippled through the room.

"However, we have to continue to prove our skills. A splendid opportunity to do that has been presented to me just now. A client wants these six large landscape windows — aren't they beautiful? — by Saturday afternoon."

"Six days!"

"That's ridiculous," sputtered Miss Byrne.

"You mean five and three quarters," said Miss Precise-as-a-Pin Judd. "What time on Saturday?"

"I'm sure he would give us until five."

No one asked why it was needed so quickly, even Miss Judd. They simply trusted that it was so.

"The Men's Window Department scoffed at the notion that it was possible. They refused the commission. You can imagine what injury this would do to Mr. Tiffany's reputation if he had to deny so important a client. He has offered it to us. He is not demanding that we do it, but just think how firmly it would establish us in the company."

"A feather in your cap," Agnes said in a half-enthusiastic, half-begrudging way.

"I would not accept the job without your consent, because I see no way it could be done unless we lay aside everything else, turn our whole force to this challenge, and put in extra hours. Some years ago, it took us a month to do four conjoined windows for a client's conservatory, but we're a bigger department now."

"And mightier," Nellie put in.

"And we've learned a lot since then. You must understand. It would demand that everyone would come in at six forty-five every morning and work until six o'clock every evening. You will be paid for the extra time. I'm sure you agree that one of the greatest pleasures in life is doing what other people say you cannot do. Mr. Tiffany has given me ten minutes to decide. We have three minutes left."

"Yes, by heaven, we'll do it!" Nellie cried in the stentorian voice she had developed since her humble-pie approach asking for work.

"Yes. Yes!" came other voices.

"There'll be wigs on the green, Nellie, when your Patrick finds out," Mary McVickar warned.

"No matter that. To be sure, we're doin' it, and we're doin' it up grand."

"Then Nellie, you take our answer back to Mr. Tiffany. Tell him the Women's Department is eager and proud to take on this challenge."

"I'll tell His Majesty he'll have the thing in a blink and he'll faint dead away at its beauties, and I won't be lyin'."

And she was out the door.

"We'll call these windows number one, two, three, and so forth." I pointed to each one. "We'll start on the cartoons immediately. Mary, panel one; Minnie, two; Carrie, four; and Mamie, five. Agnes, will you do number three and help us mark in the cutting lines on all of them?"

"All right."

"I'll do panel six. Set up your easels in pictorial order so you can harmonize or match your colors with the adjoining ones. As soon as the lead lines are in, two girls on each panel can do the tracing, numbering, and cutting the pattern pieces. Don't sit doing nothing while your partner does the whole job. Pattern cutters, work top down and bottom up.

"Miss Stoney, will you select for the iris and daffodils at the bottom?"

"I can start while someone else is selecting for the top," she said.

I gave out the assignments for the rest of the selecting. Fannie Gober, panel one; Miss Judd, two; Carrie, three; Mary, four; and Marion, five.

"I'll do panel six until the first of you is finished. Then that person will take over mine. Assistants, you can keep on with your current projects until your cartoon is ready for you. Selectors and cutters, if you don't have an imminent deadline, help Miss Judd

449

on the twenty-eight-inch dragonfly shade. It can't wait until next week. Everything else can. Put cloths over the raw glass you've been using for your present projects so you don't get the palettes of colors confused.

"Miss Byrne, Bertie, Olga, Theresa, Nellie, and Anna, you'll do the cutting. Assistants, we'll use copper foil for the flowers and leaves, so get them sliced, acided, and waxed now. Anticipate each other's needs, and step lively."

"Yur tootin' we will, and won't those scaredy-cat men be ashamed!" Mary said.

It wasn't that I wanted to show up the men. It was that I wanted to astonish Mr. Tiffany. This would certainly keep his gratitude and affection strong. Besides that, I was excited by the challenge.

I took Beatrix down to the basement to write out my glass orders. I chose twenty fifteen-by-twenty-eight-inch pieces of opalescent glass in cerulean, Antwerp blue, and light blue-violet with streaks of pale pink, salmon, and white for the upper reaches of the sky, and tints of lavender for hills. That would get them started. I needed to study the watercolors more to determine what else we needed.

"Oh, 'tis a beauty, that," Albert said, and tapped one piece with his blunt finger. "Excellent choice. 'Tis just like the sky o'er the sea of a summer's eve in Ballynahinch,

County Galway."

"That's nice. You must do us a favor and bring up our requested glass as soon as it's asked for this week. We have a tremendous challenge before us."

"Begging your pardon, but I have a challenge too, the solemn responsibility to faithfully measure the dimensions of every piece, large or small, opalescent or single-color cathedral glass, textured or smooth, in order to charge them according to their warranted price and worth and coolers, especially the coolers, against your departmental account so as to tally —"

"Yes, I *know,* Albert."

"You didn't let me finish," he said peevishly. "So as to tally your expenditures of this vitreous substance in panel form. There it be."

Beatrix was polite enough not to snicker.

"May I sign once for everything I order this week to save time doing it for each request? Then I'll just send down sample colors and you can send them right up."

"That would be highly irregular and unprecedented, perhaps even dangerous to my long-standing system of accurate record-keeping."

I signed, and next to my signature, I wrote, "for all orders through September 13, 1902, my only signature, take it or leave it."

"Tedious old man," I muttered to Beatrix in the elevator. "Remind me never to send

Mary or Nellie down here. We'd never get them back."

"He's hungry for conversation," she said. "He's down there alone all day, just shuffling glass in and out. He wants so much to be important."

"Doesn't everyone? That's what this whole effort is about, Beatrix."

Upstairs, I devised a schedule. Prepare cartoons by Tuesday at ten o'clock. Cut patterns and apply to glass easels by Wednesday at ten o'clock. Select and cut one-third of the way down all panels by Thursday at ten o'clock. The sky and three tiers of hills would have the largest pieces, so that would go quickly. Do the middle ground by Friday noon. That would leave the foreground iris, daffodils, floating lilies, moss, rocks in the river, the most complex portion of the panels, for Saturday, the last day.

I dispatched Julia with an order for copper foil, acid, beeswax, and lead cames; studied the cartoons; and made a list of types of glass we would need, then started on panel six.

On Tuesday morning, an hour earlier than usual, Merry prepared a big breakfast with double the rashers of bacon for me. I arrived at the studio first. As a precaution, I posted a note on the door for the scrubwoman, written in large letters: *Elsie, There is no need for you to clean the studio this week.*

Everyone arrived at quarter to seven, and we fell to work immediately. Agnes was the first to finish her cartoon, so she began marking in the cutting lines, which had to be done artfully, with the lines outlining rather than crossing figurative elements. She had to avoid creating difficult-to-cut pieces and areas that would be too busy with lead lines. She also had to avoid creating a multicolored piece that would be impossible to find. Only an experienced hand could do this well. Miss Stoney began putting in lead lines on another panel.

The moment Agnes finished her cutting lines, she shooed me away from my panel and took over the watercoloring so that I could go down to order glass. It was more than I'd asked her to do, since she wasn't officially part of this department. I never knew what to expect from her.

I took Beatrix again, and prayed that there would be twig glass in dark green for long pine needles.

I ignored Albert's windiness and pulled out glass sheets from their wooden slots while Beatrix recorded the code numbers. I was back upstairs in a flash and took up the watercoloring on my cartoon again, which freed Agnes to mark the cutting lines on Mary's panel. When Carrie finished her cartoon, I handed over the watercoloring on my cartoon to Mary so I could draw in the lead lines on

453

Carrie's panel.

Juggling tasks in this way, we were finished with the cartoons by ten o'clock, on schedule, and the assistants began marking the carbon copies, two girls for each window, and the numbering and pattern cutting began. Selectors were already holding the glass up to the light for the sky and hills.

By Wednesday morning, the selecting and cutting had fully begun. Cutters Nellie, Anna, and Miss Byrne were faster than their selectors, so I put Carrie, Mary, and Minnie as second selectors on different portions of those windows, and still, with Olga's help, Nellie, Anna, and Miss Byrne could keep up, leaving the finish grozing to be done by assistants when necessary.

In the afternoon, hurrying too much while cutting a piece, Olga sent a glass shard deep into her finger. Carrie and Mary worked with her quite a while to get it out with tweezers, to no avail.

"The bloody thing's got to be lanced," Mary concluded.

I lit my alcohol flame and passed a razor blade through it. Theresa, she of the feather boa, gave her an apple to bite into. Olga shook her head no.

"I'm sorry," I whispered as I sliced her skin.

She winced but didn't utter a sound. I spread open the cut, and Nellie pulled out

454

the sliver with tweezers, nearly half an inch long.

Tears ran from Olga's eyes, and her bottom lip was bleeding where she had bitten it. "Thank you," she said weakly.

"Now go hold it under cold water. Carrie, make sure it's wrapped well. Take home these extra bandages, Olga. Keep it clean."

At dinner everyone asked how the work was going, and I gave a report.

"Tomorrow is your accounting day," Bernard said. "Have someone else gather the figures, and I'll do everything tomorrow night, wages and materials."

"I was hoping you might."

"Don't give it another thought."

I looked for the same expression I had seen on his face between the flames of the beach fire, but it wasn't there. He was all business.

On Thursday, I had Minnie step in for Carrie while she gathered my accounts from the various departments. Meanwhile, I selected on window number six. No Irish songs wafted through the studio. Everyone was concentrating, rising to the situation nobly. No one complained about the extra hours.

Mr. Tiffany came in at three o'clock to look over our work. For the first time, the girls ignored the Supreme High Commander and kept working. His expression alternated between smiles of approval and knit brows of worry. He stood behind Fannie, who was working on the branches of the birch trees.

"Use crackle glass for the spaces between leaves and branches. It will make the air full of life."

"Oh, yes!" she said.

"And do more of the leafy areas in spring green to show new growth."

"All right."

He pulled off half a dozen pieces around the pine boughs on Marion's window. "Too dark. Let in more light there between the pine branches. Light suggests spirit."

With quick nervous jerks of her head, she repeated, "More light."

He looked up at the mountains and tugged at his beard. "This won't do. Find one piece of glass for each mountain so you don't have to have a lead line cross them."

Miss Judd's face and neck instantly became splotchy. Poor gal. She was older and was inordinately serious about her work, and chastised herself whenever I had to correct a glass selection she had made.

"I'll go back to the basement and have a look," I said.

"Plate with mottles behind to suggest trees on the lower hills but not on the distant mountains."

He stepped back to get the effect of all six panels together. "Press on, ladies. You're doing fine. And remember, infinite, meticulous labor makes the masterpiece."

"But we don't have *infinite* time, Mr. Tiffany," Nellie said, mimicking his favorite maxim. "Mark my words, this will be finished at five o'clock on Saturday. You come then and shake our hands, and on Monday, you can tell the men what a spanking job we did."

He turned to me. "A bit of a Wilhelmina, isn't she?"

I nodded, awash with love for both girls.

After he left, Theresa said, "Makths the matherpieth. He has a lisp, doesn't he?"

"Only when he's excited about something. Or riled up."

By six o'clock Thursday evening, it was clear that the schedule I'd written looked fine on paper but only on paper. There wasn't always space for the full complement of girls to work on a panel at one time. I sent the girls home with a cheery "Good work. Get to bed early."

Walking home alone, carrying my accounting papers and books, doubt and discouragement took over. A shaft of fear streaked like lightning across my mind: it would be infinitely worse for Mr. Tiffany to have promised his client the windows and have us fail to finish them on time than to have declined the commission at the outset. And I would be the cause of his mortification. I went cold at the thought.

When I entered the parlor, Alice, George, and Bernard exchanged worried looks. With a lingering touch on the back of my hand, Bernard took the accounting records. "I'll have them by your breakfast plate in the morning."

On Friday morning at five o'clock, there they were. Merry burst through the swinging doors from the kitchen like a barmaid, holding two big plates.

"Double rashers and boxty. That's potato pancakes to you," she announced, and then sang out, " 'Boxty on the griddle, boxty in the pan. If you can't make boxty, you'll never get a man.' " There was so much good cheer in her voice that one might have the impression she had wanted to be a boardinghouse cook all her life.

"Two plates! Isn't that overdoing it?"

I heard footsteps behind me.

"No, it isn't. I'm coming with you. Lillian will be there too."

"Oh, Alie-girl," the name I had called her when we were school chums. "Thank you!"

Except for Agnes, the girls started arriving at six, weary and red-eyed. After lunch Agnes finally came out of her studio to help. Either she had ambivalent feelings about wanting us to succeed, or she had work of her own to get out, or she thought it was already too crowded in front of the windows. It was impossible to read her motives.

We still had to do the lower birch trunks, the bottom frieze of irises in the right foreground, the clump of daffodils on the left riverbank, the six lilies and lily pads, and the surrounding water. The press of girls in front of each window made working difficult. Some sat on low stools to work the lower portions, while others stood behind them and stretched over their heads. They knocked each other's elbows and stepped on each other's skirts. Noticing this, Julia took on the self-assigned duty of holding hemlines out of the way. Alice, Lillian, Marion, Beatrix, and I stayed until the sun descended behind the building to the west, when lack of light forced us to stop. Alice and I linked arms on the way home to hold each other up.

This time, George, Hank, Dudley, Bernard, William, Merry, Francie, Dr. Griggs, Miss Lefevre, and the Hackleys all dropped their conversations and Mrs. Slater raised her ear horn when Alice and I came in and collapsed at the dinner table.

"Well? Are you going to make it?" Mrs. Hackley asked, the corners of her mouth lifting, apparently hoping for confirmation that we would. She had come a long way since her criticisms of women working when I moved in.

"Too soon to tell."

"Too soon! Today's Friday, girl!" Without

realizing it, she made the funniest face, lips turned down and pinched together, forehead scowling. At that moment, she glimpsed what we were up against.

"It's not just a question of getting it done on time. It has to be perfect. I have to superintend each step to make sure the colors represent those on the original painting, and to give nuances of shade, sunlight, movement of air, and the effect of one color on a neighboring one."

"In many places we have to plate several layers of glass behind the surface glass to create the right color and depth," Alice said. "That slows our progress."

"And the edges of each window have to match up with the window next to it."

Mrs. Hackley reached across the table and touched my wrist. "I'd lend a hand if I could."

On Saturday morning Alice and I went to work at five-thirty, feeling a little wobbly. In the studio, I wrote on the posted schedule:

Rest tomorrow. The following Sunday, we'll all take the ferry to Coney Island and have our victory picture taken on the beach.

"That ought to cheer them on," Alice said. Until Miss Stoney arrived, I selected for the irises using a palette of mottled blue and white to deep purple and magenta. Alice cut, trimmed, wrapped, and stuck each piece on the glass easel until Nellie came to cut for me. That freed Alice to work on the daffodils, picking up where Miss Stoney left off, doing all the steps herself until Lillian came. By six-thirty all the girls were working except Agnes, who didn't arrive until her usual nine o'clock, and she went directly into her studio, flaunting her privileged status. I almost expected it, but we certainly could have used her.

Carrie and Mary had the two central panels where the river widened and spilled over rocks in the foreground. Getting both panels to match up was critical, and necessitated some redoing.

"Work from the center to the banks, and choose from the same sheet of glass," I said. "Where the sun is shining on the water, use fractured glass with gold and yellow confetti to make it shimmer, and begin to integrate ripple glass as you work downward so that the bottom foreground is completely ripple glass around the water lilies.

"Mary, find some opalescent rose madder for the lilies. Marion, find some emerald glass shading into blue-black for the creases in the upright water-lily leaves. If you can't find any, we'll have to plate in the creases from the rear."

We weren't going to take lunch, but at noon, two deliverymen came in with platters

461

of sandwiches and potato salad and pickles and tea. It must have been Mr. Tiffany's doing.

In the afternoon I directed Fannie Gober to find some dark brown glass to cut in curved slivers to double-pane parts of the birch trunks as the horizontal rings in peeling white bark. I saw that I needed to double-pane the second tier of hills to make it a deeper blue-violet compared to the misty lavender of the more distant hills. We still had the empty space on the edge of panel three where the glass for the river zigzagging down from the distant hills was being made specially. Even if it had been made last Monday, it needed to stay in the annealer several days to cool slowly. Mr. Tiffany had promised it would be here on Friday, but it hadn't come.

As each panel grew downward, I asked Miss Stoney, Mary, Alice, and Miss Judd to critique them and look for areas that could be improved with double or triple plating.

"I think the sky is too pale and simple," Miss Stoney said. "There's no movement or excitement to it."

I hated to hear that, but I agreed. It didn't balance with the activity at the base of the windows.

"Let's try another streaky salmon glass behind it," Mary suggested.

She found some and held it up behind the easel. A sunset was on the way. The second pane had to be applied to entire areas within the cut lines so as not to necessitate new lead lines crossing the sky. We searched our bins and didn't find streaky pieces large enough. My spirit wilted.

"I'm going down," Mary announced, and charged out the door.

I thought it would be a waste of time. Albert would surely have locked the basement tight this late on a Saturday afternoon.

An hour later, Mary came back, singing, " 'Down in Bottle Alley lived Timothy McNally.' " Behind her was Albert, with his leather gloves on, carrying the perfect large piece.

"Well, blow me down," exclaimed Nellie.

Mary's face radiated pure triumph. "I spied 'im at O'Flannery's liftin' his pint, and told him he had a beautiful brogue, so rich and sweet."

"A man can't have the full pint that's owed him with a lass like Mary McVickar a-tugging at his sleeve." He belched. "It did make the boys jealous, to be sure, a bonny lass pleading for me to come away with her. 'Isn't that a sight to behold,' said they. 'An Irishman leaving a pub before dark on a Saturday night.' " He held the glass up to the light. "There you be. A streaky vitreous pane of the decline of the sun over Galway Bay."

"You're our hero, sure," said Nellie.

"We'll settle up next Thursday. You can

count on it," he said to me, and swayed out the door.

At five o'clock, Olga held up a small piece of blue-green ripple glass with her bandaged finger. "Who gets to stick on the last piece?" she asked.

"Clara!" came the thunderous answer.

I took it, gave it a little farewell kiss, and stuck it on.

"I'm getting the boss himself," Nellie said, darted toward the door, and ran into him, chest to chest.

"Oh, begging your pardon, sir."

"You didn't think I'd miss your crowning moment, did you?"

Frank came in behind him, twitching to beat the band, his face strained with fright as he carried the zigzag river piece. We all clapped madly, and it was hard to believe that he couldn't hear it. Only four pieces had to be changed, and the new large piece cut to size to create a perfect match. It had to be done without error. There would be no chance for a replacement. I gave that job to Miss Judd. "Everyone, stop talking!" she demanded. Never had I seen her be so authoritarian. I handed her my diamond cutting wheel. A piece that long and narrow with such sharply concave edges could easily break if mishandled. Everyone watched except Olga, who covered her eyes. With her lips puckered in concentration, Miss Judd measured three times before she made each cut. It was a perfect fit.

Mr. Tiffany examined the panels without a word. The younger girls froze, held their breaths, bit their lips, chewed on their fingernails, squeezed each other's hands, nudged each other's ribs. Beatrix shot him a look that said, "Don't you dare find fault." The Misses Byrne, Judd, and Stoney stood in a row at attention, elder soldiers of the studio. Though I dug my fingernails into my palms, it wasn't from nervousness. It was from the conviction that we had created something sublime.

He crossed his arms and rocked on his heels and toes. "It conveys nature in her most seductive aspects," he said, "with nuances that keep the viewer entranced and discovering little treasures. It's a Tiffany window of the first water," he said, using the diamond-cutting term. "I had my doubts Thursday, but —"

"But you shouldn't have." Nellie slapped her chest. "We in the Women's Department keep our promises," she crowed, thrusting out her hand for him to shake.

CHAPTER 35
WATER LILY

Miss Judd, who considered it a personal principle never to arrive one minute before nine, stood looking at the landscape windows one last time when I arrived at quarter to nine on Monday.

Sheepishly, she explained, "I had to see that they were real before the glaziers came to get them."

Soon others arrived and Mary asked Nellie what Patrick had said.

"He was none too happy that we showed them up, but 'neath his mad, he was proud of me."

"What did he say about the other men?" I asked.

"There was a big carryin'-on. Some were fiery mad, I guess, and want to squeeze us dry. Others were just middling."

That could mean trouble down the road. I was surprised Mr. Tiffany hadn't foreseen that this would pit us against one another. In my mind, it put a damper on our victory.

Most of the girls didn't hear what Nellie reported, so I kept my worries to myself.

A parade of glowering men, Patrick Doyle among them, arrived to carry out the windows to be soldered, four to a panel.

With no sense of self-restraint, Theresa blurted, "You said it couldn't be done. Just take a good, hard look." Nellie jabbed her in the ribs.

"Uppity women," one man muttered.

Without the windows, we stood disoriented, momentarily wondering what to do. The twenty-eight-inch dragonfly shade was the first to be uncovered, and Miss Judd started working. Others followed. In a few minutes, it seemed from outward appearances that no monumental event had taken place in this room, but I knew otherwise.

The lobby of the Women's Educational and Industrial Union in Boston was impressive with flags and banners. The walls were filled with large framed photographs of women leaders in the hat-, glove-, button-, and carpet-making industries. Broad-shouldered, big-bosomed women wearing neckties and often spectacles, they looked strong and confident. Alternating with them were framed newspaper articles of women's victories in labor disputes.

I thought of Edwin. Had he stayed in Manhattan, had we not taken that trip to

Lake Geneva, his photograph might be on the walls of Cooper Union by now. He might have been hailed as the leader who turned the tide in the tailors' strike. He might even be in city or state politics, doing good on a larger scale, and my admiration would have deepened into abiding love.

The large main hall, full to capacity and noisy with hundreds of women's voices, brought me back to the here and now. The air was charged with the energy and potential of future women workers.

I was introduced as "the force behind the expanded opportunity for women in leaded-glass work," and began my talk by explaining how opportunities for women in craft workshops had come about through Mrs. Candace Wheeler's Society of Decorative Art for Women in New York.

"The biggest step forward was to convince women that the work of their hands deserved payment and wasn't just a pleasant domestic pastime. Mrs. Wheeler asserted that creative art was more than a matter of instinct, but of study, so she set up classes and included other art forms, such as enameling, china painting, knitting, small mosaics, and ceramics. She founded the Women's Exchange, where women would not lose their social standing by engaging in a commercial craft enterprise."

I explained that when Mr. Louis Tiffany

observed these women working in needle-work, he saw their dexterity and their fine sensitivity to color. I related his experiments to re-create the saturated colors of the stained-glass windows in France's medieval cathedrals as well as the iridescent glass of ancient civilizations, both with an eye toward a new, American aesthetic.

I described our Women's Department and explained that it fluctuated between twenty-five and thirty-five young women, and bragged a bit about our fine camaraderie during the recent rush order of six windows. When I explained our apprenticeship program, a brave, heavily accented voice asked about wages, and I answered that apprentice glass cutters start at seven dollars a week, and increase as they advance to become selectors, and perhaps apprentice designers, who might make twenty a week. That last amount caused a murmur through the hall.

"A girl can get free art training at Cooper Union and the YWCA in New York, or can come to Tiffany Studios with an innate artistic sense and be trained on the job, though she would probably advance more slowly."

When someone asked how the lamps were made, I trotted out the wooden mold I had brought, and the samples of every stage, and explained the process.

"As yet, women are not permitted in the

Lead Glaziers and Glass Cutters' Union, but I have hopes that it will change. The prevailing thought today is that the decorative arts are more important to the nation than the fine arts of painting and sculpting, because more people see them in homes, churches, and public buildings. So if you direct yourself to this or other decorative arts, you have a chance to take your place as a contributor to American artistic culture."

Hearty applause was followed by a storm of young women at the podium asking me questions and examining the things I had brought, and I felt I had won a victory for women in the decorative arts.

The following evening I came home on the train still elated, and found Alice crying in her room.

"It's all ruined. All our ceramics. Five months of work."

"What happened?"

"We don't even know enough to know."

"Just the wheel-thrown pieces?"

"Coiled and modeled too."

"Does Mr. Tiffany know?"

"He's coming in tomorrow to see them."

I put my arm around her and stroked her hair. Coming so soon after our victory in the glass studio, this was doubly grievous for her.

"In a little while, Alie-girl, it won't matter at all."

470

■ ■ ■ ■

With those women labor leaders still on my mind, I went to Corona with Alice the next day to make sure Mr. Tiffany wouldn't vent his anger like a despot. Without a union to support the Arcadia four, if the results were as bad as Alice had described, this might mean that in a fit of temper, he might fire them. It might necessitate the kind of intervention Edwin had provided for immigrant workers who didn't dare speak up for themselves.

Porcelain tulips, lilies, bowls carved with a milkweed motif, and vases decorated with fern fronds had all slumped, sagged, or completely collapsed in unbearable heat. Where they tipped onto neighboring pieces their glazes stuck them together. Only fourteen pieces made of other clay survived, those untouched by the collapsing porcelains.

We mourned the loss of each one. The stem on Alice's water-lily bowl didn't have the strength to hold itself upright, and the cup of the open blossom drooped permanently onto the base of lily pads.

"It was my favorite," Alice said wistfully. "I loved the frogs on the lily pads. I made each one different."

"Keep it for yourself," I said. "I know it isn't what you intended, but it's still a graceful accident. A sculpture rather than a bowl."

The instant we heard the tapping of his cane on the threshold, Lillian poured out profuse apologies. Alice was so ashamed that she didn't even straighten up to greet him. He took one look and saw disaster. One deep breath that raised his chest was the only sound he made. He picked up one after another without a word, as though sympathetic with their fallen postures. He rotated on his palm the water-lily bowl.

"This is an exquisite design. Who did this?"

"I did," Alice whimpered.

"I want you to make it again, only make the pedestal thicker. You were trying for the delicacy of chinaware, but this is pottery. Let the petals rest on the frogs' heads for support."

"I'm so sorry," she said.

"It's the way with all new things. We worked three years trying to make iridescent glass before we got anything good enough to sell, so don't be discouraged. We'll find another clay that's more stable."

Bless the man. He spoke kindly, as though hundreds, if not thousands, of dollars had not gone up in smoke.

He caught Alice's eye, and added, "What the world calls failure, I call learning."

She pulled her mouth to one side. He had tried, but his words were not a comfort to her.

"Come watch the glassblowing," Mr. Tiffany urged. "We have a new gaffer handling large pieces. It's quite a spectacle." To Alice and Lillian, he added, "It might make you feel better."

Nothing could be more incongruous than Mr. Tiffany, with a rose in the buttonhole of his cream-colored suit, surrounded by grimy, sweating men in a factory full of ash and soot. By contrast, the new barrel-chested, big-bellied gaffer, whose thick lips squeezed a cigar, wore only an undershirt beneath his suspenders.

Mr. Tiffany threw a twenty-dollar gold piece into the glory hole.

"What did you do that for?" Lillian asked. "Are you crazy? That's more than my week's wage."

"It takes gold to make the purest red," he said. "It's soft and will melt quickly."

We waited until the gatherer handed off the blowpipe with an enormous gob of incandescent red glass to the gaffer, who shaped and supported it with a paddle in one hand while he spun the blowpipe with the other, all the time smoking his cigar. The vase was to have a teardrop shape at the bottom, narrowing gracefully to a tall throat. Since vases were blown with the aperture attached to the pipe, this would be an extremely difficult piece to manage with all the weight of the wide base at the opposite end.

After half a dozen trips back into the glory hole, the bulb was about twelve inches tall when the gaffer signaled to the blower for more air to stretch the throat. The weight of the glass on the slender throat pulled it down, almost to the floor, but he quickly spun the blowpipe just in time to bring it back into round.

The safest thing to do would be to stop right there, but he signaled for more air again. Alice and Lillian gasped. Men from other shops came to watch as it grew to twenty-five inches. He almost lost it again at thirty.

"If it falls, there'll be ten pounds of molten glass spreading all over the floor," Mr. Nash said.

"And twenty dollars' worth of gold as well," Lillian flashed back.

The gaffer's bulbous cheeks and triple chin were red with heat and concentration, and the well-chewed cigar was dripping annoyingly down his chin.

"You ain't doing nothing, bub. Hold this," he muttered, handing the soggy stub to Mr. Tiffany.

Caught off guard, Mr. Tiffany took the dripping morsel and held it away from his suit, mortal repugnance writhing on his face. Laughter exploded from everyone but the gaffer and the blower.

The vase grew to a dramatic height, and

finally the gaffer signaled to have it transferred to the pontil, a solid rod with a dab of molten glass on its tip to secure it to the bottom of the vase. He scored it at its rim, tapped gently, and it snapped off the blowpipe cleanly. The show was over. The gaffer reached for his precious butt, put it in his mouth, and said between his teeth, "Thanks, bub."

"This is Mr. Tiffany you gave that to," exhorted Mr. Nash.

The gaffer took one expressionless look at him and signaled his gatherer for a new gob of glass.

"That was about three feet," Mr. Tiffany said. "If you can make one five, I'll put it in a lily pool in my new house."

The gaffer chewed a moment and remarked, cigar still between his teeth, "You don't ask much, do you, bub?"

Out in the yard, all of us laughed again.

Mr. Tiffany tapped his cane jauntily on the cement. "See? Success and disaster are only a moment apart."

His effort at consolation had the opposite effect than he intended. Alice stopped laughing.

CHAPTER 36
BEER, WINE,
AND COGNAC

On Sunday morning Alice and I took the El Train over the Brooklyn Bridge and then the Brooklyn, Flatbush, and Coney Island Railroad. She had felt so downhearted that she hadn't wanted to go to Coney Island, but I insisted, just as I had done with Julia, for a different reason.

Julia had protested that she wouldn't like the place, but I saw beneath that to a deeper reason. She had no money of her own. I suspected that she gave all of her three dollars and fifty cents to her parents. I doubled her pay that week for her fine help during the landscape challenge. She still resisted. It wasn't until I said I would be angry with her if she didn't come that she agreed.

Everyone met at Lucy Vanderveer's restaurant on the boardwalk to eat clams at a penny apiece. A Tin Pan Alley band was playing "In the Good Old Summer Time," and Theresa sang the line, " 'When your day's work is over then you are in clover and life is one beautiful rhyme.' " I'm sure we all felt it.

Those who had to rent a bathing costume for twenty-five cents got a free bowl of clam chowder at Vanderveer's. I pretended that I was given two bathing middies by mistake and didn't let on that one was my own. When I offered the other to Julia, she kept her hands to her sides.

"Take it. I won't have you standing on the shore while the rest of us are in the water."

Reluctantly, she lifted her hands for it, and a few moments later in the bathhouse that Miss Stoney and Miss Judd rented for everyone, I heard Olga speaking forcefully to Julia in Polish.

I paid for our group picture to be taken in our bathing middies before we splashed into the water. Picking up cockleshells, Julia hesitated to wade into the sea.

From a distance farther out, I shouted to her, "It's free, so enjoy it."

Olga waded back to shore and took Julia's hand in order to get her in the water. Only Lillian and Marion knew how to swim, and they tried to teach the brave ones, but mostly we enjoyed the waves in an upright position, holding on to a rope with floats. Julia held on with both hands, looking terrified. What would I have to do to get her to loosen up? When a big breaker crashed over her and she came to the surface afterward, realizing that she hadn't drowned, she smiled with a smile

I had never seen on her face before, spontaneous and radiant. Even dear Miss Prim-and-Proper Judd let loose and squealed when our feet were pulled out from under us.

"I didn't think the old gal had it in her," Alice said just to me.

"Had what?"

"Frivolity."

"It's The Week We Dared that did it."

Later we crowded into a peep-show parlor to see the actualities, moving pictures for individual viewing in boxes. While it was nothing of note to see a man's hat blow off on Madison Avenue, seeing the same thing in a peep show sent them into convulsions. Theresa's favorite was the Fifth Avenue Easter Parade, Miss Judd was thrilled by scenes of firemen in action, and Beatrix was moved to tears by immigrants crowding through turnstiles at Ellis Island.

"Oh, the people who come to New York to seek better lives," she said. "What volumes could be written about them!"

At Famous Feltman's Grills, which boasted service to eight thousand hungry diners at a time, we bought frankfurters for five cents. Marion and Lillian loved the Tyrolean chorus singing German folk songs. We all rode the carousel and rose and sank to the music of a drummer and a piccolo player. And Julia smiled again.

It was hard to keep Mary and Nellie from

478

going into Paddy O'Shea's for a pint, especially when touts at the doorway called them bonny damsels.

"Coom in and 'ave a bit o' the craic, won't you?" one of them said, waving a paddle in the shape of a shamrock.

"They're *not* going in," I said in my firmest civil tone.

"Then can you sing us a diddlyie, lasses, right here on the boardwalk?"

"To be sure we can," said Mary, and started in with " 'Down in Bottle Alley lived Timothy McNally.' "

Nellie joined in for the rest:

"A wealthy politician
And a gentleman at that.
The joy of all the ladies,
The gossoons and the babies,
Who occupy the buildings called
McNally's row of flats.
It's Ireland and Italy,
Jerusalem and Germany,
Chinese and Africans,
And a paradise for rats."

The touts gave a cheer and brought out half-pints for both of them and one for me, and there was nothing I could do but drink the beer along with them and think what a picture the song gave of the flats of Edwin's Fourth Ward.

At Steeplechase Roller Coaster we had to climb up a steep wooden stairway to a high point to get in the cars of the Switchback Railway. Theresa and Nellie stepped right up to get in the front car. Olga pulled Julia along to the second car, the others scrambled in, and Alice and I brought up the rear. After that, only a few of us wanted to go on the Flying Boat. Theresa, who had the strongest constitution, dared others to go on the Loop the Loop with her, then dragged us into Streets of Cairo, where imitators of Little Egypt did the hootchy-kootchy.

Fascinated and envious, not having her boa to fling around, Theresa said, "I'm going to go home and practice!"

"Why wait until you go home?" Mary challenged, launching her hips in an exaggerated gyration. Not to be outdone, Theresa did the same, unleashing her whole midsection in a broad orbit and speeding up the rhythm. Nellie was the next to join, her arms above her head, undulating like sea grass, her face coloring like a ripe peach. Admittedly, I did my share of swiveling too, which had the effect of encouraging others. "Revolting," Miss Stoney declared, stifling a cackle at Miss Judd whirling in a hip-swinging tarantella that put Theresa to shame, but Miss Judd couldn't sustain it, and we all collapsed on one another's shoulders in stitches.

■ ■ ■ ■

We stretched summer as long as we could, and on the last Saturday in September, Alice, William, Bernard, and I set out along the coast road to Point Pleasant Beach, although it was longer than the wooded path. It would be our last visit of the season, and we wanted to linger. The floating docks had been taken up, and the boats were gone, which gave us a touch of melancholy.

In the yard of the cottage, William began to chop the remaining firewood rounds into wedges for the next season. Then Bernard rolled up his sleeves and said, "Let me have a go at it."

When he took the ax, I saw that his pale English forearms had fine light brown hair.

"This makes me feel rather like a true American out west," he said, shaking his shoulders to loosen up.

He took one mighty swing and shaved off only the bark. We laughed, which only made him more determined. Was this the same man who performed that powerful, spontaneous leap on the ice last winter?

"Pity," I said. "You swing your arms gracefully, and you're a top-notch cyclist and skater. I thought you would take to this more easily, but you chop like you're made of sticks." That was almost exactly what he had

481

said to me at the ice rink.

He chuckled at himself. "It's because I forgot the spit." He spit in both palms, rubbed his hands together, and attacked the wood again, improving slightly.

I loved watching him, his finely sculpted jaw working as he prepared for a stroke, his full lips pushing out with his breath each time the ax landed, and I loved that he responded with good humor. Eventually he could land the blade close to where it would do the most good.

"You did very well for the first time," I said, laying on the condescension thick as mud. "I'm sure you can learn, if you practice."

In the evening, Bernard and William took blankets and a bottle of wine, and Alice and I took glasses, and we went down to the mouth of the river where it met the sea in a great crashing of waters. I wanted to walk on the boardwalk over the misty, deserted dunes, but it had already been rolled up.

William uncorked the bottle and poured. "Here's to the end of summer."

"A beautiful summer," Bernard added.

"I wish it would last forever," Alice said.

"You wouldn't value it as much," said Bernard. "When joys are sparse, they sink into you more deeply."

Was that a thought coming from a happily married man?

We finished off the bottle just before a wind

blew in at high tide, and we wrapped ourselves in the blankets, daringly one couple to each. The roar of the breakers rushing toward us, moonlight illuminating the white foam, and especially our enclosed closeness — I caught my breath at the exquisite pleasure of it all. We hobbled with baby steps to the water's edge, which required getting closer to each other and coordinating our movements. We laughed at ourselves, and Bernard said, "I'm sure we can learn to do this if we practice." Reeling a bit from the wine, I pressed myself against his side to feel as much of him as I could, yearning to stay wrapped together all night.

The wind changed its mind and came from the west, which blew the spray backward.

"The waves are like galloping horses with their manes flying," I said. "Or maybe they're the white beards of Tritons blowing their conch-shell trumpets to call land dwellers to worship the sea."

"Your imagination is priceless," Bernard murmured.

"Here's a better idea." I cocked my head, looked at him flirtatiously out of the corner of my eyes, and said, "They're mermaids letting loose their silver locks to entice men to dangerous escapades."

From their studio overlooking Madison Square Park, Hank and Dudley had been watching a building grow on the triangle of land cut by Broadway's diagonal path across Fifth Avenue. It was taller each time I took my wheel across the snarl of traffic there, and I was awed by the architects' daring.

When the scaffolding and barricades were removed Hank suggested that we toast the architects from the top floor. We agreed to meet at the point of the triangle right after work the following day. Coming down through Madison Square Park, I saw the building thrusting skyward above the trees. At a certain angle, only one of its long sides was visible, so it looked like a completely flat building, a mere façade without any width at all, like a giant piece of cardboard balanced on end and painted with windows. It was both disconcerting and thrilling. Walking farther west, I could see a slice of the other side, which made it look more stable.

I crossed the street and found Dudley, Hank, and George, all with silly grins on their faces, waiting for me at the point. Instantly my skirt flew up, billowing in the eddy of wind swirling around the point. When I pushed it down in one place it ballooned up in another. I let out a squeal, and Dudley helped me get control of it.

"Men hang around here just to catch a glimpse of leg," Hank said.

"Then you *knew* this would happen!" I cried.

"Now policemen patrol the corner at night and tell them, 'Skidoo. Get moving.' Since this is at Twenty-third Street, they've named the billowing skirt phenomenon 'Twenty-three Skidoo.'"

"You might have warned me, Mr. Know-it-all."

George was chortling, and I conceded that it *was* funny. Exhilarating too, to be at the mercy of wind.

Looking up at the soaring building, Dudley said, "It's defiant and bold."

"It's like the prow of a ship sailing uptown," Hank observed.

George wagged his head. "It's dizzying."

"You've got to see it from the park," I demanded. We waited for a streetcar to pass, and then crossed. "Don't turn around until I tell you." I was turning, though, to find just the right spot for them to stand so nothing of the back wall would be visible and it would look absolutely thin.

"All right. Turn."

"Egad!" George cried. "It makes my hair stand on end." He gazed awhile and then concluded, "A prime viewing spot," and I agreed until he added, "to see the wind topple it."

"Down home in Tennessee we'd call that an undertaker's dream come true," said Dudley.

"It's not going to happen," Hank said

authoritatively. "It's the new way to build. The outer walls are attached to steel girders inside rather than the building's innards being attached to stone exterior walls."

I had a feeling that good big things were going to happen here.

"Wouldn't Walt have loved to see this?" Dudley remarked. "He would have put in another line in 'Mannahatta.' "

"Do it for him," I urged.

"Let's see. 'Numberless crowded streets, high growths of iron, slender, strong, light, splendidly uprising toward clear skies.' That's his line. Now mine. When, lo! upsprang a building like no other, manly, strong-faced, pointed uptown to a bright future."

"Bravo!" Hank said. "Let's see if we can get to the top." He patted his breast pocket. "For a little liquid ceremony."

George tipped his head way back, swayed, and his arm shot out to Dudley.

"Hold on, comrade," Dudley said.

He looked down and shook his head. "I'm all right. Let's go on up."

No one stopped us at the elevator. We went in with a crowd of people and nervous silence descended. After the ninth floor, we had it to ourselves. "Straight to the top," Hank said to the elevator boy.

My ears popped as though I were in a train going through a tunnel. We stopped with a bounce that made me grab my stomach.

"Twenty-two," the operator announced, and pulled aside the iron grille.

From the hallway, we entered an empty office on the east side and looked down at rooftops. Birds flew below us. What an odd sensation.

"Look. There's Tiffany Studios," I said, feeling oriented now.

We traced Fourth Avenue south and found tiny Gramercy Park, like a rectangular green throw rug. And beyond it, to our great delight, Irving Place.

George stepped up close to the window, looked straight down on Broadway, and slumped to the floor in a dead faint, white to the lips. We all dropped to our knees around him.

"Lay him flat." I undid his necktie.

Hank pulled out his flask, poured cognac onto his handkerchief, and held it to his nose. George moved his head but didn't rouse.

"George! Wake up!" I shouted. "Get his legs up."

Hank handed me the sopping handkerchief to hold to his nose, and lifted George's legs. Dudley slapped George's cheek until his mouth dropped open, and we dribbled in the cognac. We worked with him in this way until he came to and could sit up with his head down between his knees. When his disorientation disappeared, Hank made him drink the rest of the cognac.

"Let it go down easy, comrade," Dudley said. "Jes' like a dose of Southern Comfort."

Eventually he could stand. With Dudley and Hank on both sides of him, we walked him home. Dudley put him to bed in his room, and I fed him some Irish stew left from dinner.

As he ate, he grinned roguishly and said, "I'm the only one who got to drink a cognac to the Flatiron Building."

CHAPTER 37
SNOWBALL

Henry shut my studio doors behind him, sat down close to me, and inquired into my well-being, as if to reassure himself before he proceeded.

"I'm sorry to tell you this, but the principals in the Men's Window Department have been harboring resentment against you ever since you did the six landscape windows."

"Against me personally?"

"Against how you've made this department succeed and grow."

"They had their chance to do those windows."

"Regardless, now that Louis has given you the commissions for the big snowball and wisteria windows, they've taken their anger to the union."

"I was afraid of that."

"As part of the management, I wasn't permitted to sit in on the union meeting, but I suspect they talked strike if your department doesn't stop making windows."

"Strike! When might that happen?"

"Depends on whether the union formalizes a grievance and on how Louis and Mr. Thomas respond to their demands. It might not happen, Clara. I just thought you ought to know."

A sense of foreboding took root in me, but a month passed without further event. I didn't tell the girls, and just went on as though nothing was threatening us. We had begun the intricate wisteria window as well as the snowball window, that round white puff of a flower that demanded subtle glass selection using mottles to suggest individual petals in the round masses. With Miss Judd and Mary McVickar as selectors, the panels were about one-third finished. I knew they would be splendid.

One day Julia came in to work red-eyed and sniffling. Discreetly, Beatrix told me she was crying on the far side of the studio behind a mosaic panel. By noon it hadn't subsided. A girl can't foil-wrap a piece smoothly with vision blurred by tears. Olga lingered at lunchtime after the others left and spoke to her softly in Polish, which got her to stop crying. When I approached, Olga's serious expression, eyebrows pinched together, told me it was a problem too big for either of them to handle.

I sat down next to Julia. "Can you tell me

490

what's bothering you?"

A sob ripped out of her at the awareness of my caring. I waited until she could speak.

"My mother's been sick for a long time. She coughs up yellow. She won't go to a hospital. She just wants to die next to Papa, and he's a drunk," she said bitterly.

"Who earns the money in your house?"

"She does piecework as a lacemaker. Six-fifty a week, but she can't work so much now."

"Why doesn't your father work?"

"He's locked up a lot of the time on Blackwell's Island."

"Do you have brothers and sisters?"

"Three. Two younger than me. My older brother is seventeen. He can't keep a job either."

"Why not?"

"Every time he's caught stealing, he has to go to *The Mercury*."

The grimness of her tale overwhelmed her, and she couldn't go on.

"It's a ship in the harbor that holds bad boys doing their time," Olga explained, holding Julia's hand.

As delicately as I could, I asked if she would like me to speak to her mother about going to a charity hospital.

"She's saved a little money, but she won't use it for a hospital. She says people catch diseases there. It's for her burial, she says."

"Would you like me to come?"

491

Looking down at her lap, she cupped her fist in her other hand and squeezed. Olga said a few soft words in Polish. I waited until she finally gave a slight nod.

The errand into the Lower East Side was made worse by deep, dirty slush in the streets. Julia's apartment was in the rear of a once grand house on the riverfront of the Seventh Ward. On the way up to the third floor, I stepped around an old man hunched on the stairs, weeping quietly. His worn shoes had no laces and the soft tongues hung out sideways like the tongues of thirsty dogs. At least Julia's domicile wasn't a hall room. In fact it consisted of three narrow rooms, one leading into another, bare of any comfortable furniture. Towels hung on nails above a bucket on a stool, and a small mirror and a hairbrush hung from another nail. An oil lamp with a soot-coated glass chimney was perched on a steamer trunk alongside a delicate, half-finished lace collar pinned to a piece of cardboard.

Julia's mother was a pretty little woman still bearing Julia's dimples, but lost in her clothes. Her eyes, pale blue irises set into moonstone, looked past me — rather, through me — through this world to the next. She was tired and glad to die at age thirty-seven. How much pain would it take to turn a person away from life, from wanting another day, and another? How much of it was physical pain and how much was despair? The root cause of her sickness might well have been the hopelessness of her bleak life.

I left sorrowfully, with the mother's half-hearted promise that she would go to the free Nurses' Settlement House hospital on Henry Street, but that, I knew, couldn't cure her despair.

When I least expected it, on Valentine's Day, of all days, the ax fell. Ten of the artisans from the Men's Window Department paraded into the studio in a bluster, elbowed Miss Judd and Mary out of the way, and rolled up the big cartoons for the wisteria and snowball windows.

I darted out of my studio. "Stop! What do you think you're doing?"

They took down the two glass easels from their upright position with glass pieces attached.

"You can't do that!" Mary shouted. "Those are our windows."

"You have no right —" Miss Judd said evenly, forcefully.

"Those windows have been assigned to us, and we intend to finish them," I declared.

"Not anymore you won't." He and another man dumped the pattern pieces onto the glass easels.

Nellie and Theresa grabbed as many as they

493

could, but two men pried them out of their fists.

"I'll report this to Mr. Thomas as a flagrant violation of our rights."

"Uppity woman. Watch your step, or we'll come for the shades next."

I hurried to block the doorway, but one man shoved me out of the way, and they left with the two windows, patterns, cartoons, the original watercolors, and smirks on their faces. Hot rage tore through me, and I lifted my skirt and raced downstairs to the second floor.

I strode into Mr. Thomas's office. "Did you send ten men to get the wisteria and snowball windows?"

"No."

"They've just come and carried them off, patterns, cartoons, and all."

"They shouldn't have."

"Then do something about it!"

"Calm down, Mrs. Driscoll. Have a seat."

"I will not calm down." I pounded my fist on his desk, and he jerked back. "Don't try to pacify me. Don't expect that I'll take it lying down when my department's work is taken from us wrongfully."

"Go back to your studio. I'll see what I can do."

"Wisteria is too small and intricate for men to do. Their fingers are too big for the tiny pieces." I pointed at his, as fat and stiff as cigars. "And snowball blooms are too subtle for them. They don't have the selecting skill. Mr. Tiffany will tell you so himself."

"I said I'll see what I can do."

Mouse!

"I expect those windows back by the end of the day. You can deliver them yourself."

I waited. Six girls sat idle, bewildered, looking to me for information. I asked Joe Briggs what he knew. Nothing. He wasn't involved with windows. Mr. Tiffany was scarce these days, he said, because Mrs. Tiffany was ill.

Joe said, "He's getting involved in photography, so he works a lot in his darkroom at home."

I felt my posture sag. When a new passion ignited him he left the old ones to function more on their own. I could only go to Mr. Thomas again and Mr. Platt, the treasurer, who had always kept aloof from my department. There would be no loyalty there. And Henry didn't have the managerial power.

They were meeting behind closed doors in Mr. Platt's office, so I waited in the corridor. When Mr. Thomas came out and saw me, he muttered, "Later," and escaped, hunch-shouldered, into the men's room. Mr. Platt closed his door in my face but not fast enough, because I saw Henry inside with his head in his hands. The sight of him bent forward like that left me numb.

■ ■ ■ ■

Late that afternoon, Henry came into my studio and closed the doors again.

"I'm sorry, Clara, but this has to be quick. I just wanted you to know that the action of taking the windows by force was sanctioned by the Glaziers and Glass Cutters' Union."

That news went through me like a cold wind. The men were afraid of us! In a perverse way, that puffed me up at the same time that it enraged me.

"Have you been in touch with Mr. Tiffany? Where does he stand?"

"Uncertain, at this point. The men have threatened strike."

"Unless what happens? What concession does he have to make?"

Henry hesitated. His pain to speak further contracted his precise eyebrows.

"Unless the twenty-seven women of your department be 'removed,' their word."

I tapped out an agitated rhythm with the end of a watercolor brush against my worktable, and it resounded in my head after I stopped.

"So they actually mean to get rid of us."

"Certainly Louis can't afford to have a work stoppage in the Men's Window Department," Henry said. "It would shut down their studio here and in Corona."

"So he might agree to their demand? I can't believe that."

"Other departments might strike to support them."

"What does it matter to the metalworkers and foundrymen? I send them work."

"Their union might pressure them for solidarity. I'm sorry. I have to go. Mr. Thomas and Mr. Platt don't even want me talking to you."

That last sliced me to the bone.

Over the next couple of weeks, the recognition that trouble had been snowballing right under my nose descended like wet fog. One afternoon when worry pulsed so fiercely I couldn't work, I went to Agnes's studio, knocked, and didn't wait to enter. I caught a glimpse of her quickly slipping into her apron pocket what looked like a small silver flask. How incongruous, in light of her primness. After all these years, I knew her very little.

I told her what Henry had said. She shook her head slowly. Since she was part of the firm's design staff, any strike would not affect her.

"If the foundrymen sided with the men glass workers, they could effectively shut down my lamp production just by not fulfilling my orders. The same if Albert didn't release any glass to us."

"This has turned serious."

497

"Ever since those men confiscated the two windows, we've had no new window commissions. That has to be Mr. Tiffany's decision, maybe to cool the heat."

"Maybe it was a union demand," she said.

It hurt to imagine him buckling under to them so easily, stooping to shut us out by letting us dry up. He loved our department. I was sure of it.

"Whether he *chose* to stop giving us commissions or he was forced to, it amounts to the same thing — a penalty for talent, punishment for being women. We can't let the girls become idle, Agnes, or one by one they'll be picked off and fired."

"They can do this project when I have it ready." The window depicted a River of Life coming out of distant hills with an apple tree in the foreground. "It's a memorial panel for my father for our church in Flushing. He died last year."

"I didn't know. I'm sorry."

"He had an orchard, and there are many garden wholesalers in Flushing, so I'm hoping the motif will appeal to the congregation."

"I'm sure it will."

"I expect that all other church commissions will go to the men until this is resolved," she said.

"That may be a while."

She tapped her front teeth with her fingernail and looked around the room for ideas.

"A New Orleans couple asked for a magnolia window. I'll prepare it next, and give it to the girls."

"Good. That will occupy two cutters because of the drapery glass."

"And I have an idea for a parrot window on speculation. We'll keep them going. I know you don't want to lose any of them."

"Thank you, Agnes."

"I'm sorry it has come to this." She drew out the flask again and poured two small glasses. "You might need some fire in your belly before this is over, so come to me."

I felt it impolite not to take what she offered. The sip scorched my throat even as it burned away some formality that had existed between us.

"Be prepared. Have a plan."

A rare thing it was for her to reach out to me. I nodded an acknowledgment and stepped out.

A plan. I went to the Astor Library on Lafayette Street and read up on the women's labor movement. I was much impressed by Rose Schneiderman, who organized the girls working in the cap-making trade. They weren't allowed in the union either, but that worked to their advantage because it prevented the bosses from using the union label. As a consequence, the bosses encouraged the women to start a women's union. The

organizing spread quickly from Schneiderman's factory with twelve girls to the thirty
cap- and hat-making factories throughout
the city. When the men went on strike for
higher wages, the women's union went on
strike too, one hundred of them for thirteen
weeks. I couldn't imagine what effort it
must have taken to bolster their spirits for
that long, and remembered Edwin working
day and night to maintain the morale of the
striking tailors. In the end, the cap makers
won an increase from five to seven dollars a
week. That situation was different, but the
solidarity Schneiderman developed was
inspiring. The account didn't give me a plan,
though it did prepare me for what I might
have to do.

In the meantime, I knew Agnes's work
wouldn't occupy all of the girls. I was desperate to keep new shade designs coming faster
than ever so that my own bosses would
recognize our contributions to the business.

Something of Puck got into me, and I
wanted to make a lamp that was a landscape
window in the round, to remind The Powers
downstairs of what we did that one magnificent week that the men refused to attempt. I
set irises alongside a stream with cypress trees
in the distance. It was a radical departure,
and I loved it, not just because it was beautiful but because it meant daring and accomplishment. It would remind the girls of

that week too. I needed to keep that spark alive. In Mr. Tiffany's absence, Henry approved it instantly.

At the first sign of spring, I studied the apple blossoms in Central Park for a vanity lamp that would reuse the small wisteria mold and base. That way I could start someone on it without asking for a new wooden mold to be spun. I was overcome with gratitude for the unknown woman who would buy it without knowing the anxiety that had accompanied its making. All she would know was that her dressing table would have apple blossoms all year round.

An apple and grape lamp gave the girls a wide range of color choices. The more artistic freedom I gave them, the more I realized that these weren't *my* lamps. They were *ours*. It wasn't just my department that was threatened. It was ours.

There was nothing like the tulips in the parks to make one cheerful, and when one sees cheerful things, I reasoned, fear loosens its grip. On a brisk but calm Sunday with the streets splashed with sunlight, I armed myself with a sketch pad and colored pencils and set out on my wheel alone, working out my frustration with the muscles of my legs. Stuyvesant Square was dressed in yellow tulips as bright as canaries. Gramercy Park was bordered in deep red tulips the color of ripe strawberries, and Madison Square Park wore the delicious blush of a peach — a feast of the palate, and the palette. I wanted to swallow that color, that whole tulip, in fact. The desire was so intense that I saw, as a vision of the mind, the peach color already in me.

The impulse to love a flower and to create a lamp were the same to me. It was in the air. It took my breath away. I would fight tooth and nail, if need be, to continue. I tried to hold on to the glory of tulips as I rode home, but nothing can dampen your spirit like the end of a day of respite from ominous forces.

Julia's mother died at home, having refused to go to a hospital. She left a handwritten will in Polish giving the husband ten dollars to prevent his suing the "estate," Julia translated. One hundred fifteen was to be spent on her funeral and burial, the remaining seventy for her children. I just couldn't stomach the Old World notion that paying for one's burial is more important than paying to save one's life.

At the funeral the older brother put on a big act, wailing on his knees. His posturing nauseated me. He'd left Julia the tasks of removal from the morgue, the death certificate, the funeral arrangements, the selection of a plot in Potter's Field, the borrowing of black clothes for the funeral, and the daily responsibility of cooking for the family. Hardest of all, she had to keep the money out of her father's hands. She was only fifteen but looked about twelve. Through it all, she had that sickening, set-jaw look of sticking to her menfolk to the end.

More closed doors! Now even Nellie came into my studio and closed them. There was nothing like a strike brewing to keep the hinges working.

She drew the little chair alongside me. "I have something to tell you." Leaning forward so no one would hear, she asked, "Do you know how Patrick waits for me outside the workers' door?"

"Please don't tell me you're going to get married."

"Oh, no, Mrs. Driscoll. I'm too young for marryin'. You don't have to be worryin' none. My papa won't let me for six more years."

I let out an exaggerated breath of relief, which made her freckled cheeks turn pink.

"It's this. I was about to go through the workers' doorway on Twenty-fifth when I heard some angry voices. Well, not angry." Nellie searched for a word.

"Agitated?"

She looked blank.

"Stirred up?" I shook my hands to give her the idea.

"Something like that. They were arguing. I

503

couldn't hear everything, because I was hiding behind the door, ye see, but I did hear the words *strike, Friday,* and *both doors.* And I heard someone say, mean like, that it was only a matter of time till they take over our lamps too and shut us down for good and all."

A shard of glass thrust beneath my skin would have been easier to take than that.

"I suspected as much. Does Patrick know you heard this?"

"I don't think so. When I heard footsteps coming down the stairs, I had to go out like on every other day."

"You did the right thing. Thank you for telling me. Don't mention it to anyone."

I marched right into Mr. Thomas's office and told him I knew the men's long-range plans, not just to win the exclusive right to make windows but eventually to obliterate our lamp operation as well, which was tantamount to firing us all.

"I will not have my girls ousted by the petty jealousy and fears of the men. We ought to be colleagues, not enemies."

"Granted. I can't speak about windows, but as for shades, the firm will put up a fight." He shuffled papers impatiently. "I would rather see every man in the place out of work for a year than see your department disbanded."

"That's an extravagant statement, but you

are only one. The two hundred men seem like an army to me, and they have the strength of a union behind them. You did nothing to get the two windows returned to us, and you haven't given us any window commissions since. How can I count on you to block the move against our lamps?"

He hesitated. "I'll do what I can."

Equivocator.

"You cannot allow what I have built up for this company to be so disrespected."

"I said I'll do what I can."

"For the good of the company, you had better do better than you did with those stolen windows."

I paced in my bedroom that evening. "Weasel!" I said out loud. Even though I liked Mr. Thomas tolerably better than Mr. Mitchell, I couldn't trust him to support us. He would crumple at the first challenge. "Mouse!" All I'd worked for might be ripped away from us. My girls, what would they do? Go their separate ways to find new jobs? Our beautiful community. Did all that I had built up amount to nothing? "Rat!"

Alice poked her head in the doorway. "Did you see a rat?"

"Yes, a two-legged one. In fact, two hundred of them. The men are going on strike against us. They'll picket on Friday."

"Oh, no!" She flumped down on the bed.

"This is the reward we get for beautiful work. Extinction."

"The reward for being women. What does Mr. Tiffany say?"

"He's been suspiciously scarce lately."

"He could at least send you word of what he intends to do."

"Maybe he doesn't know what he'll do. He's probably feeling tremendous pressure from the union. I can just imagine Mr. Platt telling him to give in and fire us all, pointing out how much money that would save."

"No. That wouldn't happen. Your lamps are moneymakers."

"They'd be given to the men." I took off my shoes and threw them at the corner of the room. "It hurts because I think so much of him, and thought he felt the same about me."

"A man might say, 'Don't take it personally,' and shrug it off, but I know that's impossible for you."

She sat biting her thumbnail, then leapt off the bed and dashed out the door. After a short while, she came back with George, Dudley, and Bernard.

"This stinks awfuller than a she-skunk in heat," Dudley said, and waited expectantly for at least a smile from me.

"What are you going to do?" Bernard asked.

"Stage a march, like the suffragettes. Arms linked."

"Bully! Right up Fourth Avenue. Bust right through their picket line." George swung his fist into the air.

"I meant that sardonically, George."

"Mean it seriously, Clara," Bernard said evenly.

The idea did have merit as a show of force. Rose Schneiderman would certainly think so.

"It's not like we'd be scabs. We aren't strikebreakers hired to do the men's work. We would just be going to our own jobs, together."

"Fifth Avenue might be better," Bernard said. "More visibility. More embarrassment to Tiffany if he closed the department."

"But it's wider. We'll look less effective strung out across it."

"Not if I get the women in Corona to join," Alice said.

"I know Lillian would. You work on them tomorrow, but it's got to be a secret."

"I changed my mind," Bernard said. "Fourth is better. Ripping, in fact. That way, they'll see you coming blocks away and hear the horns on the motorcars. Build up more tension."

"You need a banner," George said.

Dudley was quick to offer to make one. "What do you want it to say?"

"Sissy Tiffany men want women's work. Unfair," said George brightly.

"No, George." I thought a moment. "Tiffany Studios Women's Department declares women's right to work in the arts."

"We need a slogan," Alice said. She darted out to her room and came back brandishing a copy of *Revolution,* Susan B. Anthony's periodical. "We can use her motto. 'The true republic — men, their rights and nothing more; women, their rights and nothing less.'"

"Good."

"Edwin would be proud of you, Clara," George said.

I felt stronger just remembering his rallying speech at Cooper Union.

"Don't tell Henry Belknap. That would destroy the element of surprise."

They all clamored down to dinner.

"Aren't you coming?" Alice asked.

"Not just yet. I have to get my thoughts in order."

I wrote a note for the next day.

Women of Tiffany Studios:

Read this and send it around the room. Make sure it gets back to me.

I've been informed that the Men's Window Department aims to shut us down completely. We must take immediate counteraction, all of us together. Meet at the southwest corner of Madison Square Park right after work. On the way, take a good look at *your* lamps in the

showroom windows.
   Secrecy is important.

Clara

509

CHAPTER 38
MADISON SQUARE PARK

After lunch the next day, I handed the note to Carrie. She read it, gave me a serious glance, and passed it to Nellie. Nellie's hand clamped over her mouth. She looked at me in agony and passed it to Mary. After Mary read it, she gave Nellie a steady, understanding look. When Minnie passed it to Julia Zevesky, Julia stared at it a long time. She took it to Olga, who read it in Polish, and they had a long, heated conversation. I saw that I might have a rugged time ahead of me. Olga passed it to Beatrix, who didn't seem surprised in the least. Note in hand, she knocked on Agnes's door. I hadn't intended to involve Agnes, and I didn't expect her participation, but I would certainly welcome it.

When the note had made the rounds, Miss Stoney handed it to me. "I hope you know what you're doing," she said.

I put it in my pocketbook, the safest place.

At the end of the day, I made Nellie leave

with me through the main entrance on Fourth Avenue to avoid the workers' door on Twenty-fifth Street. I insisted that she walk around the showroom to see the lamps lit.

"You've had something to do with many of these."

Her eyes sparkled as she looked. "Ain't nothing in life so sweet as seeing those flowers all lit up in glass. You can see them bloom summer or winter."

"Just remember that."

She scowled at the laburnum lamp. "Mighty hard, that one. All those tiny yellow pieces with hardly a difference between 'em, and all those ins and outs of the shade." She stepped over to another table. "Trumpet vine was my favorite for a while, but now I like the iris lantern better. Sort of Japanese, I'm guessing."

She lingered longest at the landscape lamp.

"Does that one mean something to you?" I asked.

"The landscape week. Patrick all akilter, proud and pissed."

Outside, Nellie said, "Whatever you have in mind, I can't do it. Patrick would be fightin' mad. This time, it would last. He might even throw me over."

"So mad that he would hit you?"

She tipped her head to one side, squinting with her whole face. "I don't know if he has that in him. Maybe. Irishmen are quick with the fist."

"If he does, he's not worth your love." I shook her arm. "Tell me you agree."

"I can't." It came out as a high squeak.

"Are you sorry you told me about the strike?"

"Nay."

At Madison Square Park I positioned myself facing the magnolia tree, so the girls in front of me would see the Flatiron Building behind me as a mere façade without stability. Julia and Olga had never seen it. Their astonishment unleashed a salvo of high-speed Polish. The building provided the right atmosphere that something monumental was about to take place.

I picked up a fallen magnolia petal and felt its cushiony surface. We had no cushion to fall back on if we weren't unanimous. It was crucial to time the vote exactly at the peak of commitment.

Carrie counted heads. "Twenty-seven, including you."

"This building started as an idea before it took form in steel and stone," I said, loud enough so all could hear. "An idea of beauty and service and stability. There were some who said it couldn't be built. Others said it would topple in a strong wind. It only looks frail from one perspective, which is deceiving. This building grew just as our department has grown and built its strength, and you as individuals have grown, building your skills and your characters. A strong wind is gathering to blow down our little department, but it cannot, since our department was founded on beauty and service too. We have only to prove its stability.

"I'll start with a question. Since the men came into our studio and took our windows, how many new window commissions have we had from the management, not counting Miss Northrop's?"

They looked around at one another, trying to think of any.

"Nary a one," said Mary.

"Right. Not a single one. How many new window commissions do you think we'll get from Mr. Thomas next month?"

"Nary a one," said Mary.

"Or the month after?"

"None," Anna said.

Good. By their serious looks, the hard truth was dawning, at least on some.

"I'm sure we're all grateful to Miss Northrop for supplying us with noncommissioned window designs. How long can we expect that The Powers will let us keep making windows that may or may not sell in the showroom? If there is any lag in sales, one by one you will be let go. Would any of you like to be the one to choose who will be the first to go? The second? The third?"

More sideways glances.

"Today I'm asking you to make a decision, and in order to do that, you need to know one thing. It was at the direction of the Glaziers and Glass Cutters' Union that those ten men came into our studio and took the windows that were rightfully ours. Don't be mistaken. We don't just have those ten men against us. Nor do we only have Tiffany's two hundred male glass artisans against us. We have two hundred plus a strong union of more than a thousand members throughout the city, if it comes to that."

Murmurs all around. Scowls. Eyes narrowed. Mouths agape.

"Why did they start this?" I asked. "Jealousy and fear, but it's a false fear, because there's enough work to go around. So it must be something else too."

"It's because we're women," Theresa said, scowling.

"I've been informed that while their immediate objective was to gain back all window work because they feel threatened by us, they have a long-range plan — to take our lampshades from us too."

Now the murmurs turned to shock and angry protests.

"If that happens, what would we do?" asked Theresa. "Just mosaics?"

"A few of you might be held on to do mosaics. Only two teams do mosaics at the moment. But this is not a case of mosaicists

514

against leaded-glass workers within our department. It's a case of —"

"Men against women," Theresa blurted.

Her audacity was just what I needed.

I raised my voice again. "The union that directed that action does not recognize our existence as capable artisans of the craft. They refuse us membership. If the union won't let us in, we'll have to act with the strength of a union of our own. We have to have a unity of spirits, and we have to have it overnight. A unified front, strong enough not to buckle under the intimidation of men. We are not frail creatures easily toppled any more than this building is." I gave it a backhanded wave. "We only have to prove our worth. You have proved yourselves in the studio by doing six beautiful landscape windows in one week, an astonishing feat. The men hated our competence then, and that hate has festered. Now you have to prove your worth on the street, for all of New York to see."

"They'll call us scabs," Nellie wailed.

"Then they'll be making a mistake. Scabs are hired to break a strike by taking the strikers' jobs so the company can keep functioning. We're just walking to our *own* jobs like every other morning, only we're doing it together. What we have here is the possibility of our whole department being shut down, and all of us on the streets anyway, looking for work.

"I have it on good authority that tomorrow there will be a picket line on Fourth Avenue and on Twenty-fifth Street. In order for you to get to work, you will have to cross that line, wedging your way between them. Don't deceive yourselves. They will not be polite. You will be jeered. You may even be touched. Think of how they treated Miss Judd and Mary in the studio."

"And Nellie and me," Theresa added.

A new wave of shock ripped through the group in whispers and worried looks.

"Their intention is to frighten you so you'll turn back when you see them and not come to work at all. Ever. They think they can usurp our positions by bullying us, the male action of last resort, but nothing except our own fear of action can remove us from our rightful position."

I gave them a few moments to talk among themselves.

"How many of you have fathers who are in a union?"

Half a dozen hands went up, unfortunately not Nellie's.

"Talk to them tonight. They'll tell you about the power of group action. I propose that we meet at the south side of Gramercy Park at nine o'clock."

"We'll be late for work," wailed Miss Precise-and-Punctual Judd.

"That's intentional. We want everyone else

there before us. We want the men on the picket line and The Powers That Be to notice that we're not there, and wonder. We want Mr. Thomas and Mr. Platt and Mr. Tiffany to get nervous. Then we will walk there together, not strolling along the sidewalk as if we're going on a shopping trip. We'll walk abreast up Fourth Avenue, the street of art and commerce. We'll walk out in the street and through the picket line, to our *legitimate* jobs. Walk together to preserve what you've established here, what skills you have developed."

I felt my breath come fast and strong. "What do you say?"

Mary raised the cry. "Yes. We'll walk together."

"Above all, I want there to be no division in the department. We need all of you in order to make a big showing and to stretch across Fourth Avenue." I gave Nellie a hard look. She shrank into the hunch-shouldered posture she had when she came to ask for a job. "We must be unified, whatever the cost to our emotions."

"You have me," said Theresa, lifting her chin high above her lace collar threaded through with pink ribbon.

"Me too," said Carrie.

"What about you, Marion?"

"I'm with you."

"Anna?"

Anna answered in Yiddish.

"Mind telling us what you just said, missy?" Mary asked.

"It's an oath my papa says at his garment workers' union. 'If I turn traitor to the cause I now pledge, may this hand wither from the arm I now raise.' I just felt like saying it."

"That's a fine pledge, Anna. Thank you."

"Miss Byrne?"

The wrinkles in her face tightened and deepened. "It's not dignified."

"How dignified is it to be out of work and turned away because we happen to wear skirts?"

"When you take off that skirt tonight, look for the union label," Anna said. "There's nothing undignified in that."

"I'll come back to you, Miss Byrne. Miss Judd?"

"How many days will we have to do this?"

"As long as there is a picket line. Do you want to go through it alone?"

"It's just walking to work together, isn't it?"

"Yes."

"Then all right. I will."

Miss Stoney gaped at her with eyes as big as pigeon's eggs. "Mildred!"

I'd never known anyone to use Miss Judd's first name.

"Miss Stoney?"

"I can't. I can't embarrass Mr. Tiffany that way, parading in the street like suffragettes."

"How else are you going to get to work?" I asked.

"Couldn't we stay home just one day?"

"It won't be just one day. If you stay home tomorrow it will be harder to come the next day. That's just what they want, to break us out of timidity. I realize some of you think it's inappropriate to associate art with labor unions."

"Or women with labor unions," said Miss Byrne.

"Think of the word *union* in its pure sense, and think of the raw feelings afterward if our department were divided."

I waited, giving her plenty of opportunity to come around.

"I'll come back to you too. Bertie, you raised your hand. What union is your father in?"

"The Gas Stokers' Union."

"He works hard. Shoveling coal?" She nodded. "Do you think of him when you turn up your gas radiator? Are you proud of him? Do you want him to be proud of you?"

"I'm in. He'd strap my backside if I didn't side with you."

Nellie's face contorted into a thousand tight shapes as I went through the list.

"Minnie?"

Her thin English lips were pursed with the effort of deciding. "Indeed."

"Olga?"

A raised hand.

"Beatrix, I recognize that your family history does not include union members. Do you stand with us?"

"Most certainly I do."

"Thank you. Julia, you've had and still have a difficult time at home, but you are an amazingly strong and capable young woman. As strong as another woman from Poland, Miss Rose Schneiderman, who like you, cared for her younger brothers and cooked for the family when she was only a child so her mother could work in a fur coat factory in this city. Eventually Rose worked in a cap-making factory, organized the women there into a union, and raised their wages by two dollars a week. So you see, everyone, Polish women aren't afraid to take on mighty responsibilities. We have built up this department by hard work so there would be a place for you, Julia. Are you with us?"

"I guess so."

I kept looking at her.

"Yes, I am."

"Now, Nellie?" I asked in a firm voice.

No answer.

"Some of you may know that Nellie's sweetheart works in the Men's Window Department. She has something immeasurable at stake."

Sympathetic words surrounded her. Nellie's hand curled around a small gold locket at her throat.

"You don't want to be the only one not with us," Theresa said.

Nellie looked around sheepishly at everyone waiting for her answer. Mary squeezed her arm roughly, and Nellie let go of the locket, raised her hand to her shoulder, and uttered a faltering yes.

"Thank you. Now it's back to you, Miss Byrne."

Her arms were folded across her chest and her shoulders were up to her ears as though she wanted to hide inside herself.

In the back I saw Agnes for the first time. She moved next to Miss Byrne, shoulder to shoulder, and I think it was her mere presence as another senior staff member that made Miss Byrne give her assent.

At that, Miss Stoney's mouth dropped in an expression on the razor edge of outrage. She was well provided for and didn't need the job.

"You love the work, don't you? The glass, the colors."

Her eyes brimmed over.

"Don't think that other leaded-glass companies would be in any hurry to have women in their studio if they see us turned out. There isn't another leaded-glass company in the city that has hired women. I know. I've asked them all. Mr. Tiffany is unique."

All eyes were on Miss Stoney. The younger

girls looked up to her for her talent and respected her as a venerable aunt. She was the last one to commit, and she knew it.

"Miss Stoney, are you walking with us, or are you staying home thinking about us?" I demanded.

"Except for Agnes, I've worked for Mr. Tiffany longer than any of you. Seventeen years. He's been good to me. I can't go against him."

"You won't be." I softened my voice. "Staying home would be going against him, since he depends upon our department."

Everyone waited in silence, giving her time. Some had the grace to look away.

Miss Stoney took a long, nasal breath and stood up straighter. "All right. I'll go with you, only because I don't want your bad opinion of me."

"I appreciate the difficulty. Thank you.

"Bring your lunch, everyone, so we won't have to do this a second time in order to get back in the building in the afternoon. Put it in a drawstring bag and tie it to your waists. You'll need both hands."

I raised my voice as I had seen Edwin do to conclude. "We have a motto for tomorrow, and it's the same motto as Susan B. Anthony's motto. 'The true republic — men, their rights and nothing more; women, their rights and nothing less.' "

"Our rights and nothing less," Mary said,

squeezing Nellie's waist.

"Nothing less," Theresa echoed. "Nothing less."

CHAPTER 39
RED, WHITE, AND BLUE

A light morning fog gave Gramercy Park an ominous air suitable for clandestine affairs, not of the heart but of politics. Alice and I found Theresa waiting for us, wearing her feather boa. I had thought her flighty, but maybe I was wrong. Yesterday she showed some mettle. Miss Judd stepped around the corner precisely at the stroke of nine. Had she been this punctual at birth, arriving at nine months to the minute, and every day since? Lillian, Patricia, and Miss Lantrup from Corona came, which attested to Alice's persuasiveness. I hadn't been sure about Agnes, but there she stood, serious and serene, next to Miss Stoney. Anna outdid herself, swinging around the corner at a trot that bounced the highest pompadour of blond popovers I had ever seen.

"I thought I was late," she said, out of breath.

In a few minutes, Carrie took a count. "We're all here," she announced.

"Thank you for coming, all of you." I looked at Miss Stoney, Nellie, and Agnes in particular.

"We'll wait a bit until the fog lifts, and then we're going to walk together to preserve our jobs and to declare our talents. But we are also walking through that line of men and placards to show that no mean-spirited jealousy can keep us from our rightful work. Be proud to be suffragettes for women in the arts."

Alice and Lillian unrolled the banner. There it was for all eyes peering out of Gramercy Park windows to see: TIFFANY STUDIOS WOMEN'S DEPARTMENT DECLARES WOMEN'S RIGHT TO WORK IN THE ARTS. Theresa, Mary, and Carrie clapped. Judging by the wincing expressions of the Misses Judd, Byrne, and Stoney, for them the banner increased the gravity of our action.

"Remember that Mr. Tiffany needs you. He thinks women have keener sensitivity to color nuances than men do. Never forget that. Walk proud in that knowledge. Shoulders back. Eyes forward. Not down. You are not scabs. You are just going to your legitimate jobs. If we walk abreast down the middle of the street —"

"Why in the street?" Miss Byrne asked. "Why abreast?"

"Because it signals a wrong to be redressed. It shows we're capable of organizing and taking action. It shows we're committed to our cause."

"It shows we ain't afeard," Mary said.

"Mary, you walk next to me on the left. Nellie, you walk on the other side of me. Carrie on the other side of her. Link arms. Alice, you walk on one end. Agnes on the other end. Keep the line tight. When we get to the picket line, fold back behind me into two lines, like the wings of a dragonfly closing. I'll go first. Ignore taunts. Help your partner through. That will mean that you, Agnes, will be the last to enter the building. Good. When Mr. Tiffany sees you, any doubt of our solidarity will vanish. I suspect that he will be on the other side of the showroom door. Everyone, shake his hand. Even if you've never shaken a man's hand in your whole life, start now. Those of you from Corona, drop out of line in front of the building. You don't need to go through the picket line. Thank you for your support.

"When the traffic is clear, I'll lead you across until we take up the whole width of the street. Then I'll come back to the middle of our line."

"When is it ever clear?" muttered Miss Byrne.

"The motorcars will mow us down," Nellie said.

"Not if we hold tight on to each other's waists. Walk firmly in the knowledge that

526

Liberty out there in the harbor is a *lady*."

I gave Nellie a squeeze around her waist. "You're going to the job Patrick trained you for. Right is more powerful than bullying. Walk to the rhythm of 'Women's rights and nothing less.' "

The fog dissipated enough for us to be seen. It actually lent a portentous atmosphere. Theresa flung her feather boa across her shoulders and bellowed out our slogan, and we set off, with Anna's pompadour as our bouncing beacon.

When we reached Fourth Avenue, I saw Bernard standing on the opposite corner, hands behind his back, as though at attention watching the Queen's Foot Guards pass. That he approved of me, that he cared enough to support me with his presence, tightened my throat in a spasm of affection.

He looked down the street for a space between an oncoming streetcar, motorcars, and wagons. In a few moments, he touched his forehead deftly as if in salute and gave an Englishman's restrained nod of encouragement, and I started across, my ducklings following, my footsteps firm on the pavement, feeling at the center of my universe. Once across, I stepped back to the middle of the line. Walking abreast thirty-one strong, we filled the street, and the vehicles waited behind us, none too quietly. Their horns

527

heralded our approach. Nobody could miss us.

In the next block, Dudley stood waiting to see us pass. It was a generous act considering his connection with Henry Belknap. The next, William York looked with concern at Alice at the end of our rank, passing him closely. On the corner of Fourth Avenue and Twenty-fourth, George stood with his small sketchbook held to his chest, and the other arm upraised like Lady Liberty holding a fistful of brushes aloft as if it were a lit torch.

On the corner of Fourth and Twenty-fifth, Mrs. Hackley had planted herself firmly, legs apart. Wearing a navy blue skirt, a white waist, and a slim red tie, she waved a little American flag on a stick in front of her great bosoms. She knew some change for women was afoot, and though her own life might remain unchanged, in years to come she would have the satisfaction of knowing that she had cheered us on, this important day in 1903. Bless her flip-flopping heart.

The men filled the sidewalk, walking in a double line in opposite directions, the loop wrapping around the corner. It seemed as though all two hundred had turned out, each one carrying a homemade placard on a stick. Up to this point, the walk had been easy, but as we approached, with the traffic piled up behind us, the men shook their signs and shouted.

"Women don't need jobs."

"An honest wage for an honest *man*."

"Girlies — stay home where you belong."

I held Nellie tight at my side. "Look Patrick dead in the eye, like the strong woman you are. The issue is bigger than your fear."

We started the dragonfly fold, which put me in the lead of one platoon in the grand army of women who I felt sure would ultimately, someday, win power in the workplace for all women. What a privilege that was!

Nellie took her place behind me next to Mary and in front of Carrie. I held my hand out behind me for her to grab.

One man shouted, "No girlie is going to take my job," right in Mary's face.

"Interloper," another man shouted.

"Job stealer."

"Same to you," I said, calm as a sea horse.

The men tightened their double ranks in front of the door, shouting, "Virago!" and "Upstart bitch!" but I kept moving ahead steadily.

"Nellie, you ought to be ashamed!" I heard.

I felt an arm behind me trying to yank her out of line. I held her tight, and so did Mary and Carrie.

"You have a lot to learn, Patrick," she said quietly.

The two men directly ahead held their position inches away from me though they didn't dare touch me with their hands. With a firm step and an erect posture, I wedged my shoulder between their shoulders, and they let me through. I did the same for the second rank. Our line split theirs, and I opened the showroom door and heard Theresa somewhere behind me saying loudly, "The true republic — women's rights in the arts and nothing less," and then the shrill ripping of our banner.

Just inside, Mr. Tiffany heard it all and motioned for us to enter the building quickly. He looked beyond me to the line of women.

Look at *me!* Don't ignore me, Louis. I did this for you, because I know you need us.

"Good morning. I'm glad to see you, Mrs. Driscoll," he said so stiffly that his nervousness was transparent. "I'm glad to see the others too."

"We're happy to be here, and eager to get to work."

"Top o' the morning to you, sir," Nellie said behind me. I had never heard her say that before.

He couldn't suppress a one-note laugh. "And to you," he said, a bit flustered.

Next to Mr. Tiffany, just like a receiving line at the Tiffany Ball, were Mr. Platt, Mr. Thomas, and Mr. Belknap, who pumped my hand and said, "Good show, Clara." Peeking around the corner, Frank was bouncing his happiness and relief. Never let it be said that because he was deaf he didn't know what was going on around him. He had ways.

We marched up the stairs so that people in other departments would see our banner pass, torn but readable. In our studio, we cheered for ourselves, hugged one another, tacked the banner to two wooden easel frames, and set to work with new resolve.

Around ten-thirty, Mr. Belknap sent me a scribbled note delivered by Frank, saying that Mr. Thomas would be meeting with union leaders at eleven. At noon, Frank brought me another that simply said, *Louis fears bad press.*

All afternoon there was nothing. The girls worked in solemn quietness. Julia spilled a pot of liquid wax. A twelve-inch rectangle of glass slipped out of Miss Stoney's hands and fell to the floor.

Fretful and embarrassed, she said, "That's the first time in seventeen years that I've ever dropped a piece so large."

Sensing an opening to speak, Nellie asked, "Will we have to do that walk again tomorrow?"

"I can't say yet."

The girls worked an hour longer to make up the time lost in the morning, and to find out whether we would have to do it again. At six o'clock, Frank brought another note. I read it aloud.

"Mr. Tiffany refused the demand to fire all

531

women, although he has promised the union that he would make concessions. The union agreed to suspend picketing but continue the work stoppage."

"What concessions?" Carrie asked in a guarded tone.

"It ain't over till we know," said Mary.

"I'm ready to do it again," Theresa declared.

"No. Come to work as you normally do tomorrow," I told them, much to Miss Stoney's and Miss Byrne's relief. "But there might be some men still left at both entrances now, so go down in three groups, with either Miss Judd, Miss Byrne, or Miss Stoney. Nellie, you walk with me."

Mary fell into step with us. "If Patrick gives you any trouble, he'll get a bad dose of hurts from me."

Mr. Belknap was at the showroom door, as if to see us out safely. Henry, a bodyguard! God love him for his intention.

Apparently, Patrick was waiting for Nellie at the workers' entrance, so we had guessed right to use the showroom entrance. I walked her home.

"I'm proud of you, dear."

"It was mighty scary, but I'm glad I did it. Being the only one out would have been terrible hard on me."

"Until this is resolved, you might have a

rough time with Patrick."

"To be sure, there'll be big ructions, all right. I'll have to avoid him till then."

"It might be a long time."

It was a long time. Summer crept upon us with no news. We perspired out our worries about the concessions in front of electric fans, but the men held fast. I remembered one strike placard in particular. WOMEN DON'T NEED EQUAL PAY. There was some consolation in that. It implied that we had been getting it although I still couldn't be sure.

Julia was absent from work awhile to find a home for her younger brothers. I suggested that she go to the University Settlement, where Edwin had worked. Through that agency the younger boys were placed at a farm in Delaware where they could earn their board and go to school, and that would keep them away from the ne'er-do-well brother and father. I was impressed with how she handled everything, and raised her wage permanently to that of a full apprentice.

Still waiting for a settlement to the strike, we made our first weekend trip of the season to Point Pleasant. Alice and I waded up to our waists in the sea under a cerulean sky with wisps of white. Dashed by a few strokes of distant ships, the horizon invited lavish dreams of our lamps and windows finding homes on foreign shores. Even on our own shores, lamps carried the touch of the Tiffany Girls into homes that they could never enter in person. The natural world rolled on untouched by our little dreams and our little dramas, and the buoyancy of being lifted off my feet in the great wide universe lifted my spirit as well.

" 'Roll on, thou deep and dark blue ocean, roll,' " I said.

In the privacy of the broad ocean with the breakers swallowing Lord Byron's words, Alice said, "I have a secret to tell you."

"Is it about William?"

She blushed.

"It is, isn't it?" I took her hands and swung her around in the water.

"It's about Mr. Tiffany."

I let go and stood still.

"You mustn't tell Lillian. I asked him if I could return to work for you."

"And not have that privacy and freedom you have now? You want to come back to deadlines and rush orders and angry men?"

"I love glass better than enamels. And I'm not adept on the potter's wheel. It's not a joy for me. Neither is Miss Lantrup."

"Oh, how I'd love to have you back. What did he say?"

"That I would have to wait until someone quits in your department. Apparently, one concession that he's made is that your department can't grow."

I let out a howl and cut the water with a broad stroke, sending up spray that wet us both. My puny act of emotionalism made no effect on the great bosom of the sea.

The next week, Mr. Thomas came up to the studio looking unbearably smug.

"The war with the union is over at last," he announced.

I was determined to remain calm, whatever the verdict.

"On what terms?"

"The union has agreed to let you make windows, lampshades, and mosaics just as you've been doing, so long as you don't increase your present number of employees."

Just as Alice had warned. I held tight to my resolve.

"I'm glad it's over, and I appreciate you and Mr. Tiffany holding out for our rights, but I'm disappointed about that limitation. The department should be allowed to grow when needs increase. What will happen if we get more orders than the twenty-seven of us can fill?"

"You'll have to give them to the men in Corona."

"What! So inferior specimens will go out to the showroom and be sold at the same price as ours?"

"Mr. Tiffany was forced to make that concession."

535

"I want Tiffany Studios to produce the very best quality of work. Sending floral orders to the men's department won't do that. It would be detrimental to the reputation of Tiffany Studios."

Mouse that he was, he raised his shoulders in a noncommittal, it-can't-be-helped gesture.

"It was also decided that the men won't be making their own designs for their geometric shades."

"Why not?"

"You'll be making them."

"So to keep *them* working *I* have to design shades simple enough for them to produce at the cost of my time designing for my own department? Was that sour irony your recommendation?"

After a sheepish, inappropriate smile, he mumbled, "It was decided."

"May I hire a design assistant?"

"Only when one of your girls leaves. It's the new policy."

"That's squeezing the fruit that feeds you."

"You have to understand how staunchly Mr. Tiffany argued on your behalf. He did not concede to the demand that the men's wages be raised to be above the women's, or that the women's wages be lowered. In light of that, the limitation on the size of your department is a concession you'll have to accept."

"I just foresee trouble down the road."

"We'll cross that bridge when we come to it."

He stood up to go.

"One more thing while I'm here. You step out of line every time you go to Mr. Tiffany for approval of a new design. That's got to stop. Mr. Platt and I don't want him involved with your operations at all. He's too self-indulgent. Come to me."

"You're not an artist."

"I'm the manager."

■ ■ ■ ■

BOOK FIVE
1904–1908

■ ■ ■ ■

CHAPTER 40
LAURELTON HALL

Mrs. Tiffany died in the spring. We were notified where the funeral would be by a bulletin
that circulated through the departments.
Some of the girls thought it better not to go
because they didn't have black waists to go
with their black skirts and they didn't want
to be disrespectful.

Nellie came, wearing a borrowed shirtwaist
much too large but black. So did Julia, wearing the same borrowed black she had worn at
her mother's funeral. Olga covered her white
waist and black skirt with her father's black
coat buttoned up. She must have sweltered in
the church. Agnes, unable to control her sniffling, sat straight-backed in the pew in front
of me next to the three Misses — Stoney,
Byrne, and Judd — all properly attired. The
church was packed with Mrs. Tiffany's uptown society friends, as well as nurses from
the women's infirmary.

I had preserved Mr. Tiffany's mono-
grammed handkerchief wrapped in tissue

paper in my dresser drawer all the years since I cried for Wilhelmina in his office, a keepsake never used again. Now it was a damp lump. I took surreptitious peeks at his still, downcast profile, newly lined by suffering, between the weeping twins, and ached for him.

After the service, the press of people funneled down the aisles to pass in front of the casket. Mr. Tiffany made brave efforts at being gracious to everyone, but his responses were vague, his voice thin and scratchy, and his eyes unfocused. It would be a long time before the spark of light would animate them once again.

Off to the side stood little Dorothy, momentarily alone, in black, with black stockings sagging on her thin legs. I approached her.

"I don't expect you to remember me. I work for your father."

"I know. You came out to the Briars. We found a spider's web."

"I'm sorry about your mama. I'm sure you and your papa are very sad."

"She wanted to stay at the Briars and never live in Laurelton Hall. He didn't love her. He doesn't love us."

"Oh, I'm sure he does."

"He does not! He kept us on the top floor all winter so we wouldn't hear her groaning. We couldn't get near her."

I crouched down to comfort her, but she fled in tears, slipping through the crowd.

How easily a parent's motive could be mis-construed by an injured child.

Henry and I stood at the dress-circle rail at the Metropolitan Opera and looked down on the orchestra section as we always did, and there was Mr. Tiffany — with a woman.

"Who's that with him?" I asked.

"Miss Julia Munson. She used to work in enamels, but now she designs jewelry in his private studio."

"Right there in his house?"

"They've been working together there for several years."

"While Lou was busy dying one floor below? Isn't six months kind of soon to be seen in high society with another woman?" The insinuation escaped sotto voce.

"He has to have women around him, just like he has to have flowers. Rumors about a liaison with the wife of his chemist have circulated for a long time, and he's had a courtesan in Paris for years."

I refused to be shocked, at least outwardly.

At our late-night dinner afterward, Henry volunteered that Mr. Tiffany was out of con-trol.

"He has horrific regrets. Battles with his older daughters. Bouts of solitary drinking. I suspect nearly every night."

"You've seen this?"

"Unfortunately, yes." Henry took a sip of

543

wine. "It's disgusting."

"The daughters know it?"

"How could they not?"

We ate for a while in concerned silence.

"What can we do?" I asked.

"I wish I knew. It seems more sinister than normal bereavement."

"No one thinks his own bereavement is normal, Henry."

He made a gesture of acquiescence with his fork.

"He's spending a king's ransom on Laurelton Hall. It's turning out to be a live-in mausoleum to Lou's memory. Extravagance is his only relief from grief, and without Lou to temper it, he's going wild. I wouldn't be surprised if some visiting journalist would dub it the American Taj Mahal with water closets. The ironic thing is that she never wanted to live there."

"His youngest daughter said as much to me at the funeral."

"I know I can trust you not to repeat this. In my opinion, the reckless spending of his father's fortune assiduously earned over half a century is the most irresponsible, self-indulgent thing Louis could have done. I would even call it insolent, considering that his father covered the losses of Tiffany Studios ever since its inception."

That was a sickening and unexpected earful, not that Henry said it, but that he had cause to say it.

"Have you been there, to Laurelton Hall?" I asked.

"Yes. It's a vast showplace of artistic profligacy. The place and the man are one. If there ever was a time to design extravagances, Clara, it would be now."

"I'll certainly keep that in mind. Tell me about the house."

"It's as wide as a long city block, with a clock tower to keep his staff and children punctual."

"Naturally."

"And an Islamic minaret. Most of it is spectacular, but to my sensibility, the whole of it is excessive."

"It's not the sleeker, modern idiom you espouse?"

He guffawed into his plate. "Hardly, but the central fountain court is exquisite. Pure Tiffany at his most exotic. Moorish, Persian, Turkish, you name it, light and airy. The octagonal space soars three stories to a ceiling of shimmery glass scallops laid like fish scales. The upper and lower balconies are supported by colonnades, which surround an octagonal stone pool, somewhat like an Islamic bath, with calla lilies and floating lotus plants."

"Good information for a lamp design."

"In the center of the pool is a graceful blown vase, as tall as he is. Water is propelled

545

upward inside, and slides down the outside while rotating color wheels beneath make it change hues."

"Then he did make one five feet. The new gaffer, I mean. I saw him make a three-foot one. Afterward, Mr. Tiffany didn't even compliment him. He just wanted a taller one."

"That's the way he is lately, demanding and autocratic. A dark side is emerging, and the new estate gives him an arena to give it unrestrained expression."

"How dark?"

"You judge for yourself. A mural he painted for the smoking room called *The Opium Fiend's Dream* depicts a decadent pasha lounging on silk cushions with his opium pipe. Nightmarish visions float around him." Henry's hand flicked the air as though he were painting. "Serpents, winged beasts, monsters eating humans, men sadistically hacking at victims, human heads impaled on spears and dripping blood."

"How horrible! What could he be thinking?"

"These might be excused as fantasy, but I can't excuse the portrayal of the life cycle of naked Oriental prostitutes from girlhood to lewd womanhood to ravaged old age. It's too vulgar for words. Imagine painting that as a warning for his girls."

A cold shudder streaked through me.

On Monday I went to the company library and studied lotus blossoms in a book of flowers. Such an elegant, simple shape. Each outer petal of a bud was like a heart turned upside down. If Mr. Tiffany loved the lotus, maybe a lotus lamp might give him a moment's reprieve from grief.

The book gave bits of cultural history. In Buddhist tradition, the lotus represented purity floating above the muddy waters of unbridled desire, and a Confucian scholar wrote, "Although growing from the mud, the lotus is unstained." It was the perfect flower to invoke at this time.

I remembered that in the pond in Central Park, lotus buds were plump and round and stood upright on tall stalks, all head on one delicate leg, although some heads were so heavy that the stalks arched over and the buds nearly touched the water. I drew some buds pulling their stems down into an arc. There wasn't anything unique about buds in flat leaded glass. Instead, their roundness made me want them to be three-dimensional. Blown forms! Why not?

I hurried down to the showrooms, where I found pond lily, one of the classic and popular blown lamps. Up from a bronze socle of lily pads, twelve bronze tubes rose close together and then arched out and down in all directions so that the blown bud on the end of each tube hung upside down. The shapes were more like narrow trumpet vine blossoms than water lilies. All the better. My bud shape would be new. It was only the concept that I had wanted to verify.

But how should I position the buds in relation to a leaded-glass shade? Was I designing myself into a conundrum? Whatever I would create, I wouldn't go to Mr. Thomas. I wanted no limits. Mr. Tiffany's profligacy gave me permission to be extravagant. I would go to him.

CHAPTER 41
FIRE

An enormous Christmas tree decorated with blown-glass ornaments was the centerpiece of the reception room of Mr. Tiffany's Seventy-second Street mansion. After attending half a dozen Tiffany Balls there, I was perfectly comfortable. Only Alice, Agnes, the three Misses, Minnie, Beatrix, and Mary seemed equally at ease. Olga walked around the Persian carpets, not daring to step on them. It seemed painful to her to be in a place of such ostentatious wealth and alien style. Her troubled expression revealed some anguish tumbling in her mind. She looked around the room in near panic until she saw the magical butterfly and Japanese lantern window. Then, comfortable with something she could relate to, she was rapt, as still as stone.

Olga was proof that Tiffany Studios was more than an art industry. It was a great social laboratory where a waif formerly curling feathers at a dollar and a half a week could speak to the son of the King of Diamonds. The poorest of my Tiffany Girls had the same delight in color that I had, the same yearning for recognition in the small world of our studio, the same hope for love that shone in their eyes this gala evening.

Alice came toward me with a tea plate of petits fours.

"No sign of the pasha," I said.

"You'd think he would at least make an appearance for five minutes."

Nellie, Theresa, and Mary were especially disappointed not to be greeted by him. They wanted him to see them in their best frocks, and I wanted them to have the experience of interacting with him in this social setting. I waited twenty more minutes.

"I think I know where he is," I said to Alice. "I'm going up."

I went through the doorway into the small vestibule; climbed the narrow, crooked stairs; and pushed open the carved double doors. A fire in one of the cave-like openings in the cedar-trunk chimney cast an apron of light over the floor. The rest was eerie darkness. Mr. Tiffany was slumped in a low chair that was draped with an animal skin, watching the huge logs burn. He raised his glass, took a long draft, and noticed me approaching, apparently without surprise.

"Excuse me. I thought you might like a report of how everyone is enjoying the

550

evening."

"I don't give a sailor's damn whether they are or not."

His intended crassness lost its effect because he couldn't get out the s's in *sailor's* without lisping.

"Don't stand there like a servant girl wringing your hands. Yes, I'm plowed, and I'm going to get more plowed, so don't act shocked. Sit down and have a drink with me. I need some company."

"There's plenty of company downstairs."

"Puh! I'm in mourning. I don't go to parties."

He held up a cut crystal decanter to look through it to the light of the fire before he poured. "Is your friend Alice downstairs?"

"Yes. We came together. We live in the same boardinghouse."

"How cozy." Sarcasm colored his tone. "She's a pretty kitten. She's doing some fine work in Corona."

"Your daughters aren't downstairs. I thought they might serve as hostesses."

"I asked them to. They don't mind me anymore. They hate me now."

"I'm sure they don't."

"Don't placate me, Clara," he said without turning to look at me. "You don't know a thing about what goes on here."

"Perhaps I do. I know you, and I can imagine them."

551

"Has Belknap been giving you an earful? The two of you are getting pretty chummy. He's queer, you know."

"You see what you look for. That doesn't mean anything to me."

"No, it wouldn't. You're prissy in your own way too."

"Louis, pull yourself together. Just because you're miserable and drunk doesn't give you the right to slash everyone who's loyal to you and who cares that you're suffering. I know what it is to lose a spouse. You survive by remembering the good times. You don't wallow in regrets."

"I'll wallow in them if I damn well please. God knows I have enough of them."

He still wouldn't look at me. He just pounded his fist against his chin and watched the flames.

"Take a look on that table," he said.

On it was a check for three hundred thousand dollars, made out to the New York Infirmary for Women and Children.

"That's generous of you."

"Remorse money. She was on the board there."

"Does it make you feel any better?"

He stared at the flames until a log shifted and sent out sparks. "Not a damn bit."

Slowly he lifted his chin, and tears threatened to spill.

"I was too absorbed. I didn't pay enough

attention to her health, or her wishes."

"Berating yourself won't help you."

"It was the same with May, my first wife. I was dead set on going to Algeria to paint exotica in the colors of Delacroix. Nothing was going to stop me, even when the baby died. So we went, but it was too soon after the birth. That was the beginning of the end for her."

What comfort could I offer? Syrupy sympathy laid on an open wound like dollops of honey would be counterproductive. He had dug himself a pit of misery so deep that easy clichés couldn't pull him out.

"You're an extraordinary man, Louis. I know that out of the hell-fires of regret, you can kindle something worthy of your best nature."

"I am. Laurelton Hall."

"I didn't mean something material."

"You know what they call a fellow like me? An egoist."

He took a drink that dribbled out of the corner of his mouth and wiped it with the back of his hand.

"It's one of those academic psychology words that my daughter Julia called me. Different than an egotist, though I may be that too. It's a person who can't *see* beyond his own interests. A fellow who isn't even aware of anything but himself. The opposite of egoism is altruism. I exemplified one. Lou the other. Egoism killed altruism."

"Therefore the check," I said.

"Therefore the bloody check."

"It's still material." And it wasn't earned by him.

He emptied his glass in two gulps.

"The twins are coming in here any minute. We have an appointment at ten o'clock. If they miss it by so much as the first chime, they have to wait until the next night at ten o'clock. I'm training them in punctuality."

"Sometimes that's hard for young girls. How old are they?"

"Almost seventeen."

"How many nights have they had to wait?"

"Three. I know what it's about. We've been through it a dozen times."

"And they've seen you in this state for three nights running?"

"I usually wait until after they've gone to bed, but they know."

He glanced at the enormous grandfather clock standing like a sentinel under the loggia. In the quietness between crackles of the fire, it ticked like a solemn, inexorable metronome.

"Only two more minutes."

"Then I'll leave now."

"Stay!" he ordered, as though I were a pet dog. "This won't take long." A low snort issued from his throat. "I might be more polite with someone else here."

554

He had sharp perceptions of his faults, but he seemed woefully content with them.

We heard steps on the stairs. He hardly turned from the fire when he introduced the twins as Julia and Comfort. They were beautiful, younger renditions of their elegant mother, impeccably groomed, one in peacock blue, the other in emerald green. Canny choices.

"Why aren't you downstairs with the guests?" he asked, indifference flattening his voice.

"It's dreadful and awkward. They ogle everything, even us."

"All they can say is how grateful they are for being invited and how great Mr. Tiffany is."

"Maybe you ought to listen."

"We brought you our applications to Bryn Mawr. They're all filled out," Julia said evenly.

"We need your signature," Comfort said, as though it were something small.

"And a check for each of us."

"Who told you that you could apply?"

"Our teachers."

"I'm the head of this household. Not your teachers."

An angry lisp on the last word.

"Please, Papa."

"Monday at five o'clock is the deadline," Julia wailed.

It seemed a continuation of earlier battles.

Since he didn't hold out his hand for the applications, Comfort put hers on his lap. Julia quickly followed. He looked down at the papers without touching them.

"You still have microbiology listed as your field of study?"

"Yes, Papa. I'm committed to it," Julia said.

"Foolishness! No daughter of mine will become a doctor, wiggling her fingers up people's asses," he said savagely and brushed the applications onto the floor.

Shock crackled right through me.

"Please, Papa. Mama thought girls should have educations as well as boys."

"I am not your mama."

Comfort picked them up, straightened the pages with trembling hands, and set them on the table next to him, right on top of the check to the infirmary.

"Yours says what?"

"Literature and art," Comfort said.

"You don't need a college degree to become an artist. I never had a college degree. You can do your watercolors and write your little stories like you've always done right here under this roof."

"And they all turn out the same because I don't know any more. I've reached the limit of what I can do on my own."

"I don't believe in limits. Mrs. Driscoll here will tell you that."

"Then don't limit us!" Julia shot back.

What could he possibly be thinking? That with university educations, they would surpass him intellectually? What a reversal of the Tiffany Imperative. He hadn't achieved that goal of outdoing his father, and now he was ensuring that his girls wouldn't outdo him. What sickening perversity. But they were strong girls. *Although growing from the mud, the lotus is unstained.* I could only hope.

"We don't understand you," Comfort said.

"There's nothing to understand. I give you everything you could want. You want a beach. I build a beach. Tennis court. Bowling alley. You want a sailboat. I give you a yacht. You want a Thoroughbred. I give you a stable full of them. I give you a beautiful house where you can have gala parties."

"We don't want your house," Julia said. "We never did. It's cold. We wanted to stay at the Briars."

"Mama wanted to stay at the Briars. Who wants to live in a museum? You never listened. You didn't care," Comfort wailed.

"You still don't care about anybody but yourself."

"Don't you dare say that in front of a guest. Or to my face!"

He grabbed the papers and flung them into the fire.

CHAPTER 42
CHESTNUTS, LOTUS,
AND DRAWING PENCILS

On Sunday after the Tiffany Ball, Alice wanted to take our first subway ride. I didn't have the inclination, but the first line had been open two months already, so I agreed for her sake. Expecting it to be cold underground, we put on our wool coats, hats, gloves, and overshoes, and headed through brown slush to the Union Square station three blocks south. A woman smoking a cigarette at the entrance was arrested by a policeman right before our eyes. It irritated me. She wasn't hurting anyone. He wouldn't have arrested a man smoking.

"That's enough to make me take up smoking just to support her right, if it weren't that I detested the idea of breathing dirty smoke."

We paid our nickels and descended.

"Don't you feel like a miner burrowing into the earth?" Alice asked.

The underground station was lit with electricity and lined with green and white tiles. "It's so bright and clean down here," she said. "It's like an expensive bathroom."

The platform fell off into a dark, scary trench of parallel rails, and we could hear the clank and screech of the arriving train. As the mechanical Cyclops with its single headlight roared toward us, it pushed a strong wind ahead of it and we had to hold on to our hats. Everything was engineered so well that the train came within inches of the platform and at the same height. We didn't have to step up as we had to on other trains.

It followed Fourth Avenue uptown. Joe Briggs had told me that Mr. Tiffany was angry that Twenty-third Street wasn't one of the express stations, which he thought would bring more people to his showrooms.

"We're passing Tiffany Studios now," Alice said in a voice like a bird chirping.

"How do you know?"

"I just feel it calling to me. Can't you? It's a happy feeling."

"Even though you can't come back yet?"

"I will someday. He promised."

"Don't depend on it."

There was a seed of truth in what his daughter Julia had said — that he didn't care about anybody but himself. Or he cared for them out of guilt after they were gone. It was clear to me that he was afraid his daughters would leave him. They would leave him eventually, college or not. His tyranny would only bring it on earlier. I wished I had the courage to tell him — it might save him from making an irreparable mistake — but it wasn't my place.

At Grand Central on Forty-second Street the train turned west with a screech until Broadway, where it turned again and sped uptown.

"Don't you feel that we're careening into a modern world?" Alice asked.

"I hadn't thought about it."

"I read in the *Times* that Mayor McClellan started the subway with a silver controller handle made by Tiffany and Company," she said.

"Free publicity. Mr. Tiffany learned that from his father, who learned it from P. T. Barnum."

"Isn't it exciting to think that we have some connection with the big doings in the city?"

"I suppose. Not that it gives us any notoriety."

"Just think. Horsecars and subways exist side by side, just like oil lamps and electroliers. We're in the middle of great changes."

We lost track of where we were until we saw the sign for Grand Circle station at the southwest corner of Central Park.

"What a romp." She patted her cheek and her face lit up with a new idea. "We could come here at lunchtime and eat on green grass next summer."

I tried to acknowledge all of her excited

discoveries, but an inexorable heaviness bore down on me. I couldn't shake off my revulsion at Mr. Tiffany's behavior last night, nor could I tell her why he was on my mind.

Way uptown we emerged onto a viaduct crossing a valley of paved streets of a city that hadn't quite arrived yet. Scattered shacks, poultry farms, and quarries holding out against the uptown march of progress filled the spaces between new smallish mansions.

"How quaint," I said. "Some nouveau-riche matron serving chicken salad at her afternoon tea in her shiny new dining room might have the mood tarnished by the squawk of a chicken being slaughtered next door."

Beatrix lived in one of those grand new houses with her family until she would marry. She had confessed an engagement to a literary man, one Clifford Smythe, who was keen on starting a book review section in *The New York Times,* and she wanted to help. When I had told her she was talented with glass, she replied, "That may be, but I don't want to make it my life." My face must have shown offense, because she hastened to add, "I don't mean it wouldn't be a good life. It just wouldn't be the right life for me."

I had to concede, which was another reason I was moody today, pondering the difference between a good life and a right life. Despite that, I did feel the tingling restlessness of the city growing north. We dove back into the earth and rode to the end of the line at 145th Street.

"It took us only forty-five minutes," Alice said. "We probably went eight miles. Isn't that a marvel?"

"I prefer my wheel. Now what do we do?" I asked.

"We get out and take a look around." Unperturbed by my sullen mood, she led the way.

A woman tending a brazier just outside the subway exit was selling roasted chestnuts. I bought a paper cone of them, and their warmth felt good through my gloves. I passed the cone to Alice.

"Better than a cigarette," she said. "And we won't get arrested."

We wrapped our scarves tighter and strolled aimlessly, eating the chestnuts. The first snow, which had been trampled to brown mush in lower Manhattan, still covered the ground here in pristine white smoothness in the fields and vacant lots. It was as though we had gone to another country.

"Doesn't the snow remind you of Ohio?"

I shrugged.

"Clara, make an effort! I thought of doing this to cheer you up, and you've resisted everything I've said. I know something happened upstairs in Mr. Tiffany's house last night."

"It might break your heart to see him."

"You don't have to tell me, but it's weak of you to let it crush you, and it's unfair to let it spoil our one and only first time on a subway. Just think of it — 1904 will go down in history. The *Times* said that New York will be different from this moment on. Don't you want to remember it with a little happiness? Where's some of that spirit that led us up Fourth Avenue? It's beautiful here. Let me hear you say it."

"I'm sorry. Yes, it is beautiful. Look at that snowman."

It had been planted in front of a wooden dwelling with sagging porch steps. Twigs for arms, a carrot for a nose, faceless otherwise, and a rag tied under its chin. Some family took joy in creating something out of nature, freely given to them, freely offered to the neighborhood. Its humility and its long tradition touched me. I wedged two chestnuts where the eyes should be, and a row of them beneath, curved to make a smile. I had just enough.

"Perfect," Alice said. "They'll come home and discover it, a wonder of Christmas."

On Monday I returned to work on the lotus lamp with some misgivings. Either it would be a jumble of unrelated elements or it would be novel and stunning. I had left off with a fountain of three-dimensional blown buds. Now I worked on the part I knew best, the leaded-glass shade.

Mr. Tiffany liked to show more than one stage in the maturity of a flower. I would give him the elements he liked — fully opened blooms in hues of deep pink, magenta, and red, passionate colors. But I was stumped. How could I suspend the shade around the buds? I drew armatures from the base to the band suggesting upright stems coming out of the water, but no matter how I did it, they were distracting, like a skeleton with redundant bones. Agitated, I tossed down my drawing pencil; paced around the studio, stifling with the radiator heat; and swept off my desk all the drawings of my failed attempts. I threw on my coat for some fresh air and walked around the block, seeing in my mind's eye Mr. Tiffany sweeping off the failed vases in the take-out room. I walked to Fifth Avenue, bought a frankfurter from a street vendor, and kept walking all during the lunch hour. No solution came to mind, but that was just as well. Having a design conundrum for Mr. Tiffany to work on might help to solve more than one problem.

As soon as I returned, Joe Briggs came in to plan the new studio for the company move to Forty-fifth and Madison. We agreed to insist on having hanging light fixtures with opalescent white glass shades instead of the bare lightbulbs, which washed out the colors we were selecting. He showed me his design for a sheet-glass rack with places for labels so we didn't have to guess the color from the edge of the glass.

"Will it do?" He always had a keen desire to please.

"It's perfect."

About thirty I would say he was. He had come to work for Tiffany when he was eighteen, an immigrant from England. In the new building, he was to head a Men's Mosaic Department at one end of our women's studio. That way, he could use some of the girls to help on his huge mosaic commissions, and keep them employed if there was a lull in our work, and he would be on hand to turn and cement our own mosaics. It was the first move toward dissolving distinctions between each department, and an important conceptual change by the management.

Toward that end, Joe had been working with Theresa on a mosaic panel of Christ and Saint John. He was teaching her how the manipulation of color, clarity, and surface could create the sense of pictorial illusion in mosaics that leaded windows have. I heard him explain that the use of clear, colored tesserae backed with textured gold foil invites the viewer to look through the glass to the texture.

"That can create a splendid illusion of depth and distance," he told her. "Use it judiciously, because it will attract the eye away from the opalescent and iridescent pieces, and each of them performs a distinct function too."

He was taking special pains to teach her nuances, and I was happy to see her be so attentive.

In the afternoon, Mr. Tiffany came in on his regular Monday rounds. Even grief could not stop this man. I greeted him with more than usual solicitude, acting as though nothing had happened in his studio, which he seemed to appreciate. Sorrow glazed his eyes and called forth a surge of compassion and love.

"I have something special to show you. Something *extravagant*." I whispered the word mysteriously.

He raised his eyebrows in only a modicum of interest.

Undaunted, I continued to speak softly. "You know about hybrids because of your gardening. This is a hybrid in glass. A hybrid of two styles."

"Oh?"

"Blown *and* leaded glass. A lotus lamp."

He squinted at me playfully, a totally different man than the one I had seen two nights earlier. "You must have some inside information to know I love lotus plants."

"Oh, no. Just a wild guess," I said in mock innocence.

I laid out my two watercolors and explained that I would like the blown buds to dip downward within and slightly above the leaded-glass band, but I stopped there. He didn't respond. Had I overstepped by involving the glassblowing factory?

"Come with me."

He walked out of the women's studio with his quick, short strides, and turned back to make sure I was following him. On the elevator, he said, "It's high time we had another elaborate."

In his office, he thumbed through some French design journals until he found the photograph he was looking for, a slender Art Nouveau water lily lamp by Louis Majorelle. The sinuous stemlike vertical standard supported two upright buds and a fully opened flower. All three were exquisite blown forms.

"The buds are similar to what I had in mind. Only mine, ours, would be upside down."

The caption explained that the inner petals were pale amber and the five outer sepals were coral.

"How's it done, with two colors?"

"It's called cameo work. The inner bulb is blown first in one glass, and then it's sent back to the glory hole of another color. The shape is finalized, and when it's cool, a glass carver grinds away the top layer in some areas to show the coral sepal shapes beneath."

"That's quite involved. Can we do it here?"

"Of course. We don't believe in limits here."

He said it in a soft, sad way that acknowledged it to be the same thing he had said to his daughter. I could use this moment to tell him I thought it was unreasonable of him to deny the twins an education, but his expression was already so dispirited that I let the moment pass.

"How will you hold the leaded-glass band in place?" he asked.

"I need you for that."

He thought for a while, and then said, "Elegance is natural when you follow the principle of repetition. Think about it."

He sat back and gave me time, showing no sign of impatience.

"Repetition. Of course! Attach the band to similar bronze rods used for the buds only arched higher and wider? Yes?"

"Yes. I knew the answer was in you all along."

His pride in me was warm enough to ignite my heart.

"How about the shape of a single round leaf for the base?" he said.

"I was hoping for mosaic —"

"Fine. Give it thin bronze veins splayed out from the vertical standard."

"What are the edges of lotus leaves like?" I asked.

He took up my drawing pencil to show me.

"Some varieties are wavy. Parts of the edge lift off the water, while other parts are slightly submerged."

"Like a girl spinning in a full skirt?"

"Exactly. But remember. Reproducing nature slavishly is not art."

"I know." Inside my chest, wings beat, bells rang, so thrilled I was to be collaborating with him again.

"Ha! This one will top the list." He clapped his hands together and rubbed his palms. "Seven hundred and fifty smackers, I'll wager. Keep this a secret from Mr. Thomas."

Olga lingered after the others left at the end of the day. She looked down at my lotus drawings and pulled in her lips. "I like those fat buds." Her voice was threaded with wistfulness.

"What's on your mind?"

She didn't raise her head to speak to me.

"I have to tell you. I got married on Sunday."

"Olga!" I slammed down my drawing pencil and broke the point. "What could you be thinking?"

She backed away from me with that same taut, pained expression she'd had at the Tiffany Ball.

"You couldn't have asked me first? You couldn't have postponed it?"

"No."

"How old are you?"

"Eighteen."

"And how old is he?"

"Seventeen."

"You make seven-ninety a week. In a month, you would have been getting eight twenty-five. You're one of the best. How much does he make a week?" She wrung her hands in that subservient way I hated. "Tell me!"

"Two dollars."

"Two dollars!" I yelled. "This just makes me sick to think of it. Consider the kind of life you'll have."

It was tempting to ignore her marriage, make her swear to tell no one, just so she would have a decent life and I could keep her.

"You have to think of yourself, Olga, to be watchful for your own concerns."

"If only you knew how little that matters. I'm not like you."

"You could be. You could be in charge of this department someday."

"I could live in a shack with him and call it heaven."

"Easy enough to say that now when there are potatoes on your dinner plate provided by your papa. Did you even consider how much faith Mr. McBride has in you as an artist? How could you have done this?"

She hesitated. "I had to."

"Pregnant? Are you expecting?"

Two tears leapt from her eyes and made a torturous path down her cheeks. I felt like cradling her in my arms. I had lost her. One of the most promising of the young ones, sunk now into the quagmire of the Lower East Side. Hank would be heartsick.

"You've bloomed so beautifully I hate to lose you."

"I hate to go, but nothing is as important as love, Mrs. Driscoll."

Her simple certainty tore through me, a quick, head-to-heart plunge.

"I can go back to curling feathers. I can do it piecework, at home. Or I can roll cigars. A lot of people in the tenements do that. It pays a mite more than curling feathers."

That was what Edwin meant — only the strong come.

"That's a horrible, dirty thing to bring into a house with a baby."

"God gave me this baby for a reason, and I'm going to love him all the way."

"I believe you will. Anything you do, you do heartily." I felt the choking surge just before crying, but all I allowed to come out was a sigh. "All right. Work until the end of the week, and I'll have a little extra for you on Friday."

"Thank you. You're a nice lady."

"Try to take care of yourself."

I hoped she *would* have potatoes to peel.

Potatoes. Even in the Age of Enlighten-
ment, there had been Polish girls or German
or Irish girls whose primary occupation was
peeling potatoes. Maybe they took private
enjoyment in the subtle curves of the lines
their blades left between the dark skin and
the moist whiteness while they dreamed
hopeless dreams. Maybe they experienced
meager pleasure in solitary moments carving
a face or a flower in a potato, and serving it
to their husbands, who, in their exhaustion
from working the soil or the mine or the
docks, bit into the bloom without noticing.
How would Olga's artistry be expressed?
Drawing a baby on the walls of their tenement, then drawing a toddler, then a street
urchin? Only if she could afford a drawing
pencil.

"Here. Take these with you." I handed her
all of mine.

After lunch, along with a note to Mr. Thomas
saying that Olga was leaving, I sent a note to
Mr. Tiffany telling him the same, and added,
"So now we have a place for Alice to return
to what she loves best."

I was offering him a chance to prove that
what Julia had said about his not caring about
anyone else wasn't true. I waited, looking at
my drawing of the flower that grows out of
the muck. Frank brought the answer.

Tell her she can return when she finishes her current enamel, which is coming along beautifully. Have her select for your lotus lamp.

We were reading George Bernard Shaw's *Man and Superman* in Francie's room. Bernard rubbed his hands together as if he were going to wield the ax again, relishing the evening's entertainment. He had the part of Jack Tanner, the confirmed bachelor; Mr. Bainbridge was the devil; and Francie was Ann Whitefield, who was conniving to make Jack marry her.

Well into the second act, Merry came to the door. "Begging your pardon for interrupting, but there's a limey here to see you, Clara. All hot and bothered. Says his name is Joe Briggs."

"From Tiffany's. Send him up."

I left Francie's room to meet him at the top of the stairs. Being protective, Bernard followed me. There was no need for that, but it was caring of him to act the gentleman. We went into my room, and I introduced Joe as Tiffany's most gifted mosaicist and a fine helper in our department. He had that typical ivory English complexion, but tonight his face was even whiter.

"What's the matter?"

"I'm here to say goodbye. I'm going back to England tomorrow."

"Sit down. You'll do no such thing. We need you too much. What could have happened in the *three* hours since I saw you?"

He looked beside me, not at me, as he said, "I've made a mess of my life. Escape is my only solution."

"Nothing is so bad that it can't be remedied. Tell me."

"No one at Tiffany's knows this, and you must never tell anyone. I've been married for eight years."

My mouth fell open. "Why have you kept it a secret?"

Misery was written in his quivering chin. "Because she's a Negro."

I tried not to show my surprise but probably failed.

"I lost my head when I was young, and now I loathe her, and she knows it. You can't hide a thing like that. It's unbearable to go home at night, or even to be in the same room with her."

"Where do you live?"

"The darky quarter. The Tenderloin, close to Hell's Kitchen." He laughed bitterly at the second name. "My life outside the studios has been wretched. The studios have been my haven."

"Eight years. Do you have children?"

A pained tightness formed beneath his eyes. "Two little ones."

"So why this decision now?"

He took a big breath, as if gathering strength to tell me. "It has to do with Theresa. I sometimes meet her at night to do something together. Just for relief."

"Such as?"

"We go to the Haymarket to dance ragtime, or to the Blue Vipers in Brooklyn, or to a gallery. She's a nice girl, and we get along."

I glanced at Bernard, who was scowling.

"A dangerous practice, Joe," I said.

"I know," he mumbled. "Sometimes Marion comes too."

"Have you told them that you're married?"

"No." He screwed up his face at that. "My wife is still in love with me. I had hoped she would get angry and leave me, but she just gets more jealous, to the point of irrationality. She has taken to spying on me."

"How do you know that?"

"Tonight I went to Brooklyn to meet Theresa to go to an art show. Bessie, my wife, confronted us and said, 'Joe is my husband, you little hussy.' She pulled a pistol out of her handbag and backed Theresa against a wall and took a good look at her. She said something like, 'I was going to kill the two of you, but I see you're not a whore, so I'll just warn you to stay away from my man.' She pointed the pistol at Theresa's face and said, 'Remember what this looks like up close so it won't be the last thing you see.' "

What a sordid melodrama. I could hardly believe it.

"You didn't accost her?" Bernard asked. "Knock the gun from her hand like any *man* would do?"

Joe recoiled like a struck dog. "I couldn't move." His voice faltered. "I was too ashamed."

"What happened then?" I asked.

"Marion came out of her house — we were on her street — and Bessie threatened her too. The girls ran off. Bessie vowed to go to Tiffany's tomorrow to tell everyone she's my wife and that I've been fooling around with your girls. I could face death more easily than disgrace, so I'm leaving the country."

Shrunken and mortified, he appealed to me with frightened eyes.

"You're a fine man otherwise, but you have no moral courage."

His hands went up to cover his face. "I know."

"I hope you also know that it threatens my department if Bessie comes."

I could see I had to do something tonight or I'd lose all three. It was nearly nine o'clock. I picked up my shawl.

"Take me to your house," I said.

"I'm going with you," Bernard said.

"I can do it myself, Bernard."

As I headed toward the door, I felt his hand restraining me.

"Don't be headstrong, Clara." His grip on my arm was firm. "What do you think? That I'd let you see this woman with a gun and not go with you? It fairly killed me that I couldn't go with you to the morgue to identify that girl. I had no right, so I yielded like a gentleman. Now I do. It was on my recommendation that you hired Theresa. That gives me a responsibility."

He was so earnest and intense that I agreed.

Joe took us by way of Tin Pan Alley, Twenty-eighth Street between Fifth and Sixth avenues, where the sheet-music publishers were located, to the next block of saloons. A Negro banjo player on a wooden balcony was playing ragtime. Loud Negro voices and piano music spilled out of open tavern doors. At one of them, Joe said with delight, "That's Scott Joplin's 'Maple Leaf Rag.' Bessie's favorite. Theresa's too," he added with chagrin.

What a hodgepodge of emotions he must go through every day.

Joe's block, three blocks farther into the West Side, was unlit, foul-smelling, and frightening. No streetlamps, no sidewalks, and deep ruts in the pavement. It was hard to see sleeping or drunken bodies lying on the ground until we nearly stumbled over them. Out of nowhere two big fellows came toward us in threatening postures.

"Give way," Joe murmured.

I held tight on to Bernard's arm, and he pulled me aside to let them pass.

"The Stovepipe Gang makes their living by mugging visitors to this quarter," Joe said.

"Then how do you get along here?" Bernard asked.

"They know I'm not a visitor. If a chap minds his own business and doesn't butt in or make a ruckus in the Negro dives, he'll be left alone. Nobody bothers us here, whereas they might in a white neighborhood, even half a dozen blocks uptown in the Irish shantytown."

He turned in at a brownstone like all the others we had passed, and we climbed two flights of creaking stairs to his flat. We entered through a bedroom with the mattress on the bare floor and clothes strewn over chair backs in order to get to the living room. On the walls Joe had tacked his unframed watercolors of figures from his mosaic work, street scenes in the darky quarter showing a keen perception of people, and one of a black child bearing a huge bundle of newspapers on his back. Full of pathos, the painting revealed Joe's sensitivity. He watched me looking at it, and his face lifted with hope for my approval.

"You're a gifted artist, Joe. Keep painting,

no matter what."

On one side of the room three wide planks laid across crates served as a drawing table. Joe lit a large oil desk lamp, and I saw two sleeping toddlers nestled against each other under a soiled quilt on the couch.

"I take them in to sleep with Bessie, and I sleep here," he said.

It was almost more than I could absorb. The kitchen was only an alcove, where a colored girl was washing dishes.

"My wife's sister," Joe explained. "Where's Bessie?"

"Out," the sister said.

Bernard and Joe both insisted I sit on the only cushioned chair while they sat on wooden kitchen chairs. Upholstered in corduroy, the armchair wasn't new, but it wasn't shabby either. The chair, the good desk lamp, and some green curtains showed that an effort toward improvement was being made.

We waited until ten o'clock in the airless living room. Every ten minutes Joe begged us to stay ten more. It was a trying ordeal for Bernard to sit still.

"She could be out all night," he said.

Joe lifted his shoulders, not knowing.

"This seems like a task for a minister," Bernard said. "Do you know of one who could come in the morning before you go to work?"

Joe suggested a Negro mission two blocks away, and we went right away. Inside, a program of some sort was in progress. In a room with all dark faces, a portly man was singing about "a better day a-comin'." Bernard inquired about seeing a minister, and while we waited, a tall, striking woman wearing a wine-colored dress rose dramatically, solemnly, and stepped up to the makeshift stage. The room fell silent.

In a sumptuously rich soprano, she sang slowly, her face uplifted.

"There is a balm in Gilead
To make the wounded whole.
There is a balm in Gilead
To heal the sin-sick soul."

I was transfixed. The rich clarity and power and conviction of her voice were worthy of the Met rather than this dingy hall.

"Sometimes I feel discouraged,
And think my work's in vain,
But then the Holy Spirit
Revives my soul again."

"That's for you, Joe," I whispered, but as he nodded miserably, I knew it was for me too.

The graying minister sweating in his clerical vestment took us upstairs to his windowless office. We sat on a bench opposite his desk and under a hanging bulb giving off heat. He put his palms together piously, which struck me as a pretense, and, like King Solomon, asked what the trouble was, regarding us as though he were capable of settling the world's problems in one visit, and furthermore, that we ought to know it.

After explaining the situation, Joe smiled, out of nervousness, I believe, but Bernard took it as a lack of seriousness.

"You're an Englishman, so act like one. Where's your stiff upper lip? Drop your pathetic excuses and your spineless self-pity. You got yourself into this. Running home to England isn't going to make a man of you. Treat her with decency and make the best of it."

He paused only to take a breath before unleashing more of the same. I couldn't believe my eyes and ears. Bernard was the archangel Gabriel, Justice Enthroned. Poor Joe, hunched over, hugging himself and rocking back and forth. The minister held out his hand to get Bernard to stop.

I had to say something. "You can correct your mistake by not seeing the girls anymore. That will be easy, but you'll have to find a way to live with Bessie properly."

After a moment's pause in which we all sat sweating under the heat of the lightbulb, the minister, who hadn't said a word that was helpful so far, intoned in a bass voice, "You are connected to her by God's amazing grace.

Now, do you promise not to deceive her from this day forward?"

Joe nodded in pained contrition.

"Would you like me to see her in the morning to persuade her to forgive you, and to stay away from your workplace?"

"Yes," came his weak answer.

"Son, if the mountain was smooth, you couldn't climb it."

The minister bowed his head a moment — in prayer, I suppose — then stood and slapped his palms and splayed fingers down on the desk as if to say, "Finished, solved."

Bernard had a mind to go home then, but I knew we had to see her. I didn't trust that the minister's visit with Bessie would keep her away from the studios. Out on the street, Joe looked at us as a drowning man might look at a departing lifeboat, so we went to the apartment again and waited. Still agitated, Bernard wrote Bessie a letter, begging her to wait until the following night, when we could see her, before she took any further steps in her revenge. He finished around midnight, and Joe accompanied us down to the street. He saw her coming, so we all went back upstairs.

Bessie wasn't the ill-featured, slovenly woman I had imagined from Joe's description. Except for some blemishes, she was pretty, and still slim after having had two babies. She cried and told how she had followed Joe night after night, how he had lied and had hurt her feelings. My talking to her was of no use to get her to calm down. She had to spill it all out in a torrent. Bernard held up his hand just like the minister had done, as if to say we had heard enough, and miraculously, she stopped.

"Joe has treated you shamefully," he said, "but he made a promise to your minister that he will mend his ways and be faithful to you. He's going to treat you decently and fix up this house for you."

"I don't ask him to fix it up. I'm willing to sit on one soapbox and eat on another. I only want to be *happy*."

Joe looked as though he was bored to death by a play he didn't care for. Bernard couldn't stand it and seized him by his shoulders, shook him, and shouted, "Look me in the eye. You know you've done wrong. Be a man and say so. Don't make me speak for you. Say it yourself."

"I won't lie. I won't see the girls again. But I won't sleep with you."

"Until," Bernard said, shaking him. "Until . . ."

"Until you wash the sheets."

That's all we could get out of him.

The whole depressing situation overwhelmed me so much that I couldn't find any honest way to show my compassion for both of them. Not knowing what else to do, I put my arm around her, which brought on a wild sob. She laid her cheek against mine, slick with sweat and tears, and quieted enough to say, "I don't have a single friend to talk to. I pray to God, but I want a friend."

"Making a scene at Tiffany's won't bring you a friend," I said, "and it certainly won't make Joe love you. Will you promise not to go there?"

"I promise."

At last we got out into the fresh air. Walking home, Bernard kept spitting in the gutters. "I'm sorry. I can't get the taste of that place out of my mouth."

"Didn't you just tell him to stay put the rest of his life?"

"Yes, but he's her husband! And I should think you'd be anxious to get home and wash your face."

"She needed a show of sympathy. It didn't hurt me."

He put his arm around my shoulders. "Well, you're one of a kind. A precious gemstone."

CHAPTER 44
MOON SHELL

Joe came in late the next morning, all humble pie and nervous strain, looking behind him every few minutes.

"It's not over yet, slick as a fiddle. Bessie was still raving this morning until the minister came, saying she was going to lie in wait for Marion to come out the door at the end of the day and pummel her."

"Then Marion and I will leave early. I will walk her to the el train. Go about your business now. It will help."

"Do you want me to stop working with Theresa?"

"No. Go on just as yesterday. There'll be no change."

He walked through the studio to the mosaic easels, his bony shoulders sagging.

At noon I asked Theresa and Marion to join me for lunch. They gave each other nervous glances.

It would have been quicker to go to Peter Cooper's Restaurant near the studio, but the three misses lunched there, and that meant six ears vibrating with curiosity. I had a reason to get Theresa and Marion into Healy's Café on Irving Place and Eighteenth, in addition to their chicken hash, which I loved. On the way, I urged them to try it with chunky applesauce and corn bread.

As we approached the café, a dapper man walking in the opposite direction opened the door for us, and a sheaf of handwritten pages slipped out of his hand.

"Oh, I'm sorry," said Marion.

"It's nothing." The man continued to hold the door for the three of us while his papers were blowing away. Once inside, we watched him chase them, enter the café, and sit at the far table.

"One of the men at my boardinghouse knows him," I said in a near whisper. "He lives alone across the street, and takes his meals here. Rumor has it that he was in prison once. He writes stories here about characters who have lost respectability or integrity and find a way to win it back again. He goes by the name of O. Henry."

Marion's cheeks blanched. Theresa set down her fork.

After we ordered and began to eat, I said, "Joe came to see me last night and told me what happened."

"How come he never admitted he was married?" Accusation sharpened Theresa's voice.

587

"Because he wanted to keep seeing you."

"Oh, Clara, I would never have gone anywhere with him if I'd known he was a married man," Marion said.

"I believe you."

The inadvertent pertinence of her statement gave me a twinge. Her assertion was one I could not make about Bernard.

"It was all innocent enough, I suppose, but obviously that wasn't apparent to Joe's wife," I said. "You both have intruded on a marriage. I know you're hungry for life. I am too. Most people are. We've all seen happy couples on the street and have ached with the question — why not me? But that craving can be properly directed."

I felt the chicken hash pile up in a ball when I heard myself say that, but it tasted so good that I couldn't stop forking it in.

"If your secret meetings continue, even if you try to hide your carrying-on, and the management finds out, one, or two, or all three of you will be fired, and not by me. It's extremely important to Mr. Tiffany personally and to Tiffany Studios that his clients see his staff as beyond reproach."

"We won't tell anyone," Marion said, and nudged Theresa.

"At the moment, both of you are more replaceable than Joe. He's head of the whole Men's Mosaic Department, and there are forty now on the third floor. He has responsibilities far bigger than yours."

"So if anyone has to go —" Theresa said.

"It won't be him. He's on the rise in the company, as well he should be, and I beg you not to utter a word that would dislodge that. He has helped our department immensely."

"But he shouldn't have taken me places if he was married."

"Granted. Understand, the more you say, the greater the chance of being overheard and talked about. Once a girl is talked about, she's done for."

"What's the harm if it's between ourselves?" Theresa asked.

"Because it loosens your tongue. The matter cannot get out. You may think New York is freer than it is. Despite your feather boa, the gay nineties have passed, Theresa. New York is a big city, and you think you can get lost in it. But we aren't anonymous people. Our actions, good or bad, have consequences, and in this case, they could be dire."

Chagrin was written on their faces. As I took a sip of tea, the potential repercussions loomed more threateningly the more I thought about it.

"We still need to be on the alert to prove that women are as capable as men, and that includes working without emotional involvement or disturbances. If it does get out, *all* of the men's departments will have a field day with it, and the management will have second thoughts about any eventual consolidation of our departments. We will have lost what we've gained, and that could affect us in a devastating way.

"Theresa, you're the first of the Tiffany Girls to be working so closely with a man, so the responsibility of proving our capability to do that without entanglements rests on your shoulders. From time immemorial, women have had to be more careful than men in a number of ways. This is one of them. Don't think that The Powers aren't watching. We still operate under the threat of being shut down. All the union needs to fuel their actions again is a morals charge. Do you understand, Theresa?"

"Yes."

"Marion?"

"Yes."

"It remains our privilege to work with the best mosaicist in the country. Keep that in mind."

"Do you want me to continue to cut for him?" Theresa asked.

"Yes. Being under his tutelage puts you in a privileged position. He has taught you a lot. You'll go on just as if nothing has happened. Understand, *nothing* has happened."

They both nodded contritely.

"Now, how about some vanilla ice cream? It's my favorite thing on a hot day."

■ ■ ■ ■

When we finished, I sent them on to the studio and went to my room to lie down with the shade drawn, thinking I would doze for fifteen minutes. Even with my new little fan blowing on me, I lay in nervous perspiration, my eyes wide open. I had done what I had to, but it didn't make me feel good.

How many times had I gone bicycling with Bernard? I couldn't count them. Being with him in a group was one thing, but we had gone bicycling and ice-skating just the two of us. How I had loved it when he performed that spectacular, heart-stopping leap and a full turn in midair, landing in a long-legged arabesque. What a thrill when he scraped to a stop in front of me and grabbed me by the waist, twirling me, my feet flying off the ice.

Confound it all! Was Bernard married or wasn't he? If he was, it was a stranger kind of marriage than Joe's, and he was no better than Joe, nor I than Theresa. We had both let loose with a moral accusation that might just as well be applied to us. If he hadn't put his arm around me, or if I had lifted it off, I might consider our actions honorable, but after all the strain of the evening, I had loved the feel of his arm, loved the caring for me that it showed.

I understood Theresa's hunger for something beautiful and intimate, but she had to have known that Joe was married. She would have picked up on signals: not getting together on weekends and holidays. Valentine's Day passing without a card. Sweet things unsaid. Nervous looking at his watch. Leaving abruptly. Her longing had blinded her to the warnings.

What made Bernard and I different? Every fiber of my being told me he wasn't married, but morally, if there was any sliver of a doubt, I had to give up the luxury of not knowing.

The hash and corn bread topped off with ice cream covered in chocolate syrup lay like a molten gob in my stomach, churning like the earth's innards before a volcano erupts. I got out of bed and tried to vomit into my washbowl, but the hash refused to budge. I lay down again with a wet washcloth over my forehead and eyes. The haunting melody of that woman's hymn came to me — a balm in Gilead. Where was Gilead? Some holy place. Some peaceful place in the mind. How could I get there?

By asking him, no matter how impudent it would be. I wouldn't let Sunday at Point Pleasant pass without finding out. Better to be criticized as insolent than to be thought of as a Jezebel. That wasn't my mother's etiquette handbook speaking. That was me.

During the weekend at the shore, I made it a

point to sit next to Marion at meals at the Palmiés' cottage and to invite her bathing with Alice and me. I tried to make her laugh as I flailed around when a breaker lifted us up. I liked her, and I didn't want any residual ill feelings.

Bernard was quieter than usual even though he entered into the bicycle riding just the same as always; he filled my lamp with fuel, oiled my brakes, adjusted the beach umbrella to shade my eyes, drew out my chair at meals, but he still seemed distant, which hurt me. I was paralyzed to signal to him that I wanted to be alone with him.

I stayed on the porch where he and William were reading in the wicker rockers, and anxiously yanked leaves off the Boston ivy growing against the clapboards of the house. In a few weeks they would be deep, brilliant red. The sound of the vine rustling as I plucked each leaf annoyed them.

"I wish they were red already."

"Patience, Clara."

The one thing I didn't have today.

After our beach supper, I was edgy. Time was running out. Bernard could see that I was restless, and convinced everyone else to go on a bicycle ride to Manasquan Beach for ice-cream cones, leaving the two of us to tend the fire.

Stalling, I picked up a small moon shell that looked like a snail's shell spiraling out from a tiny eye, bleached white on the outside, pearly on the inside. I brushed off the sand, and put it on each of my fingertips. My ring finger happened to be the best fit.

"The life of a shell must be a tremendous struggle," I remarked, looking at it from all directions, perched there on my fingertip.

"In what way?"

"To push that hard protective surface outward in order to grow."

"It has no choice." He lifted the shell off my finger and pocketed it.

"Why did you do that?"

"So I could give it back to you someday to remind you of this evening."

"Is it a special night?"

"I feel it is."

"But you've hardly spoken three words together to me all day."

"I'm a patient man." He gathered the hem of my skirt in his hands. "I saw that you had to mend the rupture with Marion, so I've stayed in the background to let you. Your girls are first to you. Even before yourself."

"Most of the time."

"You've been thinking about Joe and Theresa, haven't you?"

"How can you tell?"

"After living in the same boardinghouse with you for a decade —"

"Off and on," I blurted.

"I know a few things."

I cupped sand in my palm and let it fall between my fingers. "Like what?"

"I know that you love the sea, and poetry, and flowers, and glass, and your work."

"All true."

"And you love the girls in your department, and maybe even Mr. Tiffany." Bernard stirred the fire, and new flames erupted. "And that you hate hypocrisy."

I jerked my head up to his penetrating gaze.

A wistful, maybe even an amused expression passed over his face as he said, "And I know that you flinched when I put my arm around you, but you leaned in to me all the same."

"I just didn't want to be what we had both denounced. That would be the worst hypocrisy. I couldn't stand it if —"

"Clara, stop." He took my hand. "I'm not married, if that's what you're thinking."

Instantly, a flush of heat enveloped me and I backed away.

"Alistair told me you were engaged."

"I was, and I *was* married."

"What happened?"

"You're so obsessively proper that it's kept me from telling you. I waited for you to ask, and when you didn't, I thought it wasn't of interest to you."

"But it was. It is."

Exasperation spilled out of him. "You're a paradox, you know. You're a modern woman in most ways, but you still wrap yourself in the trappings of Victorian etiquette."

I fidgeted at that. "Maybe it takes another generation to emerge fully emancipated. Tell me. Please."

"I became engaged when I saw you falling for Edwin's *character,* and I married a woman named Ann just after you left with him. It was an impulsive reaction that I've regretted, because I hurt someone who was never anything but kind to me. She had character too. She was the head nurse at the children's ward of the Nurses' Settlement House on Henry Street."

"I know of it. The Lower East Side. I told the mother of one of my girls to go there."

"Ann lived in the ward — *settled in* was the euphemism — in order to be available to patients instantly in crises. She was very committed. I tried living there with her in her small room several times. It was unbearable, with children crying constantly and Ann leaping out of bed all hours of the night. I don't have the social worker's zeal like your Edwin had. I wanted us to get a flat like any normal married couple, but she refused to leave the hospital, so I only spent lunch hours with her, and the days she had free. After her exhausting days and nights, there wasn't anything left of her for me."

After a few moments of letting this news settle, I realized our situations were similar.

"We've both been on the neglected end of commitment."

He ran his hand through his hair. Looking into the fire, he nodded agreement, a slow, minute movement.

"Once she went with me on holiday to London, and to Boston and Maine another time, but that was all she allowed herself. So I came back to the boardinghouse to wait for better times."

"Did they come?"

"No. The ward was a den of disease. It wasn't long before she contracted tuberculosis. The end came quickly."

Alarm choked me. "You could have died too, if you had stayed there."

"Yes, I suppose so," he said softly, and we both waited for what would be said next. Etiquette demanded that I say I was sorry he had lost her. Honesty clamped shut my jaw.

"Why didn't you tell me before this?"

"Two reasons. I wanted to get past grief first. I didn't want you to think I was grasping on to you as a quick replacement."

"Are you? Past the grief?"

"I haven't felt a mite of guilt over the enjoyments we have had together. A grieving person would feel guilty for pleasure with any but the memory of the departed. So yes, I'm over it."

He was so sensible. Honorable too.

"I've felt heavy with this secret, with not

telling you, but you didn't ask, and to speak of it unasked would be too awkward in case you didn't care to know."

"I didn't ask for fear of finding out that you were married, at least in some fashion."

He was quiet at that, and reflective. He smoothed a place in the sand and drew a widening spiral, like the side of a moon shell. Riveted, I searched for meaning in it and waited for the second reason.

"Remember a long time ago I went to the Tiffany showroom to see your lamps? It was after you mentioned Tiffany's policy against employing married women. His stodgy conservatism angered me, but I couldn't say anything that would turn you against him. Seeing those lamps made me realize that for the greater good, for generations hence, I shouldn't, couldn't, do or say anything that would put a stop to your important lifework."

I blew out a puff of air, trying to grasp the generosity of his restraint.

"It's hard to believe that you, that anyone, could be so . . ." Unselfish? Loving? I couldn't finish the sentence.

"It hasn't always been easy. When I've wavered, I went back to the showroom to have another look, and that bolstered my decision. I'm ashamed to say that earlier, when you came back without Edwin, I hoped he was dead. That was unconscionable of me,

I realize."

Yes, it was, though it told me how long he had been thinking of me.

"I existed in that suspended state of not knowing what had become of him just like you did, but when the news filtered through the boardinghouse that he was alive, I thought it was hopeless to wish for anything more than our outings."

"He *is* dead, to me, Bernard."

He lifted his face from the fire. "And George?"

"George knows that, and has accepted it."

"That's not what I meant."

I was puzzled. The flickering firelight cast deep shadows in the worry lines of his forehead.

"You can't think I haven't noticed. You love him."

My breath came out slowly, in a revealing sigh. "Not to love that man would be impossible. And he loves me, in the only way he can, like a brother would a sister."

A wave retreated, leaving an expectant quiet before the next one. For the length of that pause stretching before us like an empty road, he waited for me to say something more.

"That doesn't mean I can't love another."

He was slow in reacting, as if he were holding on to the moment, as if it were long-awaited, and therefore one that deserved savoring, deserved a careful, thoughtful response.

He offered his hands, lifted me to my feet, and held me against his chest, warm from the fire. His mouth brushed my ear with words. "The trouble with us is that we've been too polite with each other. We haven't spoken our minds. You've been too Midwestern, and I've been too English, but the dowager queen is dead now. Remember? Fate has offered us a future, if we're brave enough to grasp it."

CHAPTER 45
SQUASH

"They're ready to be turned," Theresa announced proudly.

Working out her contrition on tesserae, she had finished the Christ mosaic alone. Joe was taking some time off, which I agreed would be a good idea for a few weeks, even though we would need him if Theresa finished before he returned. I knew the process of turning and cementing but had never done it myself.

I told Theresa to cut a sheet of oiled paper six inches longer and wider than the dimensions of the panel. I brushed varnish on each tessera, and while they were still sticky, we pressed down the oiled paper until it adhered firmly to every part.

It would be dangerous to go to the Men's Mosaic Department on the third floor to ask their help to turn it upside down. They would think we were unable to handle our big commissions ourselves, and I might have another strike on my hands. I saw no other way. We had to turn it ourselves.

Who could help?

"Mary, you have a way with Albert down in the basement. Say whatever you have to, even listen to him. Just get him up here to help us. Julia, find Frank and tell him to come here."

"*Tell* him. How?"

"Wave at him, take his hand and drag him, say it in Polish. I don't care. Carrie, you get Mr. Belknap. He's none too big, but he'd be willing."

I told Theresa to coat the large marble slab with Venetian turpentine.

Soon I heard, "Look you, Mrs. Driscoll, I have important things to do down in the netherlands. I can't be a-comin' up here to do your bidding at the drop of a hat."

"You're here now, so you can help. We need to turn this upside down on that marble table. There are glass pieces under this paper."

"You expect me to do that me self, do you now? Me with a ruptured spleen that ain't getting any better. You'll send me to the hospital sure, and then who'll pay the bill? Answer me that."

With Albert, the only way was to go at it quickly. Frank and Henry came in, neither of them very strapping. Oh, how I wished Wilhelmina were here.

"Mary, come here on this side and hold the paper in place. Carrie, you do the same on the other side. Ready? One, two three, heave!"

Albert huffed and puffed extravagantly, and Frank grunted, one of the few sounds I'd ever heard him make, but we did it.

When Albert left, I rolled up my sleeves like a man, mixed the cement with a trowel, and cast the first panel. Henry, who had never put on a work apron in his life; and Theresa, who had to tie it for him; and Frank, who was ecstatic about helping us, worked quickly to get it into every crack before it set up. All evening I worried about it congealing correctly and not being horribly messy on the front. The next morning, we had to get it turned right side up again. We found that seven girls and Frank could do it. I held my breath while Theresa and I peeled back the paper on the first one. It wasn't much more messy than usual. I assigned Julia to pick it clean while we set to work to get another panel ready to pour. There were five more to do.

Only one remained to be done when Joe came back looking less pale, even a little ruddy. He closed my studio doors and put a paper sack on my worktable.

"Reach inside."

I pulled out a cucumber, two tomatoes, and three yellow squash with large leaves and floppy blossoms the size of my hand. "What's all this about?"

"Aren't they beautiful colors? I bought a little place in the country this side of White

Plains. Nothing much, just a tumbledown house that I can repair a little at a time, but it has a small orchard and a vegetable garden."

"This doesn't mean that you're leaving the studio to become a farmer, does it?"

"I wouldn't think of it. I can get here on the train in an hour, or I can stay with Bessie's brother in the city a couple of nights a week after she begins to trust me. She was brought up in the country and likes it there. She's proud that she has four hens laying, and she'll can our peaches for winter."

From behind his back, he brought out a jar labeled BESSIE'S SQUASH SOUP. I was deeply touched.

"Then you're happy, or at least happier?"

Waiting for his answer, I twirled a squash blossom, and its petals, textured like crepe paper, fluttered gracefully.

He drew his mouth to one side. "We're finding some satisfaction in what we're doing there. The place is all our own for us to improve together. It's a new beginning."

"I'm glad for you. You did the right thing. And I have something for you to see here."

"Wait. The situation?"

"Theresa and Marion know never to say a word. No one else knows. It's as if it never happened."

I pointed to the mosaic end of the room, where the five finished panels were propped on their easels.

"Who poured?"

"I did! And Frank and Albert and Mr. Belknap helped turn the first one."

"Mr. Belknap! Well, doesn't that beat all."

I shook a squash blossom at him so that it fluttered. "You've just given me an idea, if blown glass could be tooled to look like crepe paper."

Joe grinned the grin of a happier man as he left my studio.

The move to the new Madison Avenue location a month later meant there was much more space in the new studio, more than we needed.

"What were you thinking?" I asked Mr. Tiffany in private in his new, larger office.

"Maybe someday the union will forget my concession to keep the department at twenty-seven."

My private hope burst out of me in one shrill word. "Really?"

Mr. Platt came in and Mr. Tiffany instantly changed the subject to his design for the base of the squash lamp, telling me what I already knew, and he knew that I knew. Mr. Thomas and Henry Belknap arrived, and I offered to leave.

"No. Stay," Mr. Tiffany said. "I want you here."

We sat at the big display table to review the

1906–07 statistics and to go over the price list for the coming year. Never having been invited to these meetings before, I learned that there were two hundred and six workers in the Men's Window and Lampshade Department, forty-two in the Men's Mosaic Department, sixty-four in Corona making and blowing glass, and twenty-seven in my department. Since 1900, lamp production in all departments — the men's geometric leaded shades, the blown shades, and my nature-based shades — had exploded. The price list showed three hundred models of shade and base combinations, with my department producing the most styles. I was thrilled. They had to recognize my strong contribution to the firm.

Geometric shades made by the men's department sold for forty dollars to one hundred and fifty dollars for the twenty-four-inch size. With the larger, straight-edged pieces of glass in their shades, they could make eighty of them in the time it took me to design and make three prototypes with their bases.

In my department, shades *without* bases started at fifty dollars and went to three hundred dollars. The small dragonfly shade was eighty dollars, and then jumped to one hundred thirty dollars and two hundred dollars for the larger or more unusual ones, such as dragonflies flying around and the one with the suns. Small-size florals *with* bases started at ninety dollars, and then leapt to one hundred sixty dollars and one hundred seventy-five dollars for standard sizes. The trumpet creeper lamp was three hundred seventy-five dollars. Then there were the elaborates: wisteria, apple blossom, and pond lily descending at four hundred dollars, and butterfly and cobweb at five hundred dollars. My new Boston ivy would be about the same because of the more expensive red glass poured into specially made molds for leaves. Squash blossom would land between five hundred and seven hundred dollars because of the gaffer's individualized work on each large petal. The cameo work on lotus placed it at seven hundred and fifty dollars, equal to my room and board for a year, now that Merry had raised it again.

The last page contained three lists: the uniques, those we would make one at a time only when the single showroom model was sold: Boston ivy, cobweb, lotus, pond lily descending, laburnum, and iris lantern; those to be discontinued: fruit, cyclamen, pansy, arrowhead, and deep sea, which I loved, as well as a dozen others which cast a pall over my earlier pleasure; and those with reduced prices, which grieved me as well.

"Even a fifty-dollar shade is beyond the range of the average household," Mr. Thomas said. "We have to scale down, weed out the elaborates and uniques, produce for the middle- and lower-range buyers. There's only so many millionaires. It's a limited market."

"Eighteen hundred millionaire families, the *Times* reported," Mr. Tiffany said. "I wouldn't call that limited. One mansion after another is creeping up Fifth Avenue for nearly three miles, and they don't all have a Tiffany lamp yet. New millionaires are arriving from the Midwest every week, and we can expand into stores there as well. Marshall Field has performed well for us. Lamps have done more than any of our products to bring beauty into the American home."

"We're not running a social mission, Louis. We're running an art business. A *commercial* art business."

"Not we. You. You run the business. I run the designing. You do the commerce. I do the art. I don't tell you how to keep your account books, so don't tell me how or what to design. The elaborates have made my reputation. I want them continued, and I want more of them."

His reputation, of course.

"You see the workshops as your playground for trying experiments on a large scale," said Mr. Platt. "We have to stop that, and produce only what we know will sell at a profit. That doesn't include new lamps that take costly hours to design."

"We have to eliminate the expensive low

608

sellers and produce more of the proven high sellers that don't require design time," Mr. Mouse Thomas said.

How my department fit into the company seemed more tenuous as the discussion went on.

"I realize that time means money here," I ventured. "But what about the squash-blossom lamp? It has already been designed. Or is that irrelevant to you?"

"We're going to continue into production," Mr. Tiffany replied.

"I say no, on account of the high price it would have to fetch," Mr. Platt said.

"I say no too," echoed Mr. Thomas, naturally.

That left Henry. Everyone turned to him.

He licked his lips in preparation to speak. "Considering only its sales value is narrow-minded. It's a showpiece. We should have three — one in our showroom, one in Tiffany and Company, and one in Marshall Field."

Mr. Thomas gave a snide glance at Henry for stepping on their marketing toes. I wondered what the repercussions of his incursion from art into commerce would be.

My freedom was beginning to crumble. I appealed to Henry with my eyes but was afraid he wouldn't pick up on my urgent call for help.

"Excuse me, but I think Mr. Belknap has a broader opinion to voice."

"Right," Mr. Tiffany said. "Speak your mind, Henry."

"I contend that it's important to keep creating new designs, from a business standpoint and from an aesthetic one. Repeat customers in our showrooms have to see new models or they won't come again."

"That's right, Henry. Customers. Strike at his Achilles' heel." Mr. Tiffany balled his fist and swung it in front of his chest.

"And the department has to be kept vital with new designs or it atrophies, and that's dangerous. Mrs. Driscoll is not a machine. She's an artist, and an artist has to create according to new vision as it develops, and her department as well."

"We're not running a crafts class, Henry," Mr. Thomas retorted.

My God, the ghost of Mr. Mitchell!

"What Henry says is true," Mr. Tiffany affirmed. "Each artist sees beauty from a different angle, and achieves it only when she's free to explore her own vision."

"How many of the same lamp styles can we make before they become, pardon my saying so, trite?" Henry asked. "Clichéd because they're all too familiar? How will repeat customers take to seeing the lamps they own produced year after year? That will sink us to the level of a factory."

Mr. Tiffany looked smugly at Mr. Platt while Henry won this point for him. "Brilliant, Henry."

The deeper reality hurt. He was depending on someone else to stand up for me. He was handing me off to Henry's guardianship.

"It's cobweb, lotus, pond lily descending, Boston ivy, and now squash blossom that give new life to the medium." Henry was strident now. "Kill those and all those elaborates and one-of-a-kinds of the future swirling in Mrs. Driscoll's imagination and you eventually kill the line of specialty lamps altogether."

"One," snapped Mr. Platt. "Make one squash lamp for our showroom, since you've started."

The balance of power was shifting right before my eyes.

"So we'll go on as we have," Mr. Tiffany asserted, "and Mrs. Driscoll will bring her designs to me, or we'll design together, as we sometimes do. Nothing will change."

"Your father would have seen the reality. He wouldn't have resisted," Mr. Platt said.

"My father is in his grave. What I do is irrelevant to him."

Mr. Platt cleared his throat. "I'm sorry to have to say this in front of Mrs. Driscoll, but you're blind to the realities of the business world, Louis. You always have been, and that's why you're always in the red, which was one thing when your father was here to cover your losses at the end of every year, but it's quite another now, isn't it, when you have to dig into your own pocket to make up the difference?"

I felt like slapping him for shaming Louis so.

"So what if I do? What difference does it make to you, or to the company?"

"How long will you be able to, particularly with your extravagances at Laurelton Hall?"

"Leave Laurelton out of it."

"How long before Laurelton drives you to bankruptcy court? How long, Louis? Do you have any idea?"

All eyes were on him. He squirmed in his oversize chair at the head of the table.

"No. You have no idea. Come next door to my office, and I'll show you."

Tall Ebenezer Platt swept out of the room with long strides, and short Louis Tiffany trotted after, and part of me followed anxiously in his shadow.

Mr. Thomas shuffled a few papers. Henry drummed his perfectly manicured fingernails on the polished table until Mr. Thomas noticed the clicking sound and glared at him. Henry stopped.

After an excruciating quarter-hour of silence, the other two came back.

"Now that *that's* settled," Mr. Platt said, "there will be no more new elaborate shades designed, nor any new unique, one-of-a-kind shades."

"For the time being," Mr. Tiffany said.

"For the time being," Mr. Platt conceded. "Production can be more efficient, and we can get back on track. As for windows, mosaics, and fancy goods, there will be no major change. Adjourned."

Squashed flat. Such a bitter irony. I hurried to the privacy of the elevator, my eyes straight ahead.

On top of all of that, it was a Thursday, and Carrie, who had been doing the accounting lately, was at home ill, so I had to do the payroll myself. The pages of the week's work orders shook as I laid them on my desk. I dumped out the time chits the girls had put in the box. In Mr. Thomas's new system I had to figure each person's time on each project for the week and make the aggregate sum come to the same as the payroll. Forty-five hours on item 29877 — sixteen-inch dragonfly shade. Marion's rate of thirty-six and two-thirds cents per hour equaled sixteen-fifty for the week.

I couldn't concentrate. The numbers blurred. I blinked and stared and blinked again.

I felt awful for Louis, the way Mr. Platt humiliated him. Henry did what he could, but it was Mr. Tiffany who should have spoken up for me. The whole thing was disheartening. And where would it lead? The indispensability I believed I had achieved was

<hr />
613

shriveling.

At home I asked Merry to have my dinner tray sent up to my room, something I rarely did.

She looked at me with a scowl aimed at the world. "A fierce day for you, was it? I'll send up a cuppa right away. The way you like it, with milk and honey. It'll do your brave heart a world of good, dearie."

Fortifying myself with tea, I spread out all the papers and dumped the girls' accounting chits onto the bed and started. I'd done only six when the kitchen girl came back with my dinner tray. I thought eating might soothe me. Baked shad, potato pancakes, and boiled turnips with carrots. Not very exciting. I ate half and went back to work.

A knock on my door startled me.

"Booth Accounting Service. Do you have work for me?"

I opened the door. He took one look at me and the bed, and said, "Oh, dear, you've got the wrong thing on the bed. It should be you, not the papers. Let me do the books. Lie down. Close your eyes."

He put the piles on the floor and opened the bedcovers. I was still in my dress. He gestured for me to take it off.

"I won't look," he said, and turned around.

I took the pins out of my hair and let it fall, and then unbuttoned the dress.

"Need any help?" he asked brightly.

614

"Only with the accounting."

"Just offering."

I put on my nightdress, and he spun around.

"You're too slow. How much can a man stand?"

He laid me down and traced the lace on my gown with his index finger. "*Mmm, pretty.*" He combed my hair between his fingers. "It's very long. I've always wondered."

With one knee on the bed, he placed a whisper of a kiss on each eyelid, and I was left with the lovely, sad feeling of his elbows, arms, and wrists sliding through my hands as he raised himself upright. *Forget the damn accounting. Just lie here with me,* I felt like saying.

Instead I said, "It's a new system. Their pay varies — there's a list — but I have to account for their time on each project each day."

"I'll figure it out by what you've already done." He gathered the papers and sat at my desk with his back to me.

"My assistant usually records the times. I've always thought of her as fussy and uninteresting. Now I appreciate her for taking this burden off my shoulders."

"I know how to take it off your shoulders permanently."

"How? Quit?"

"In a manner of speaking."

He untied his necktie, and the swishing sound it made sliding under his collar as he pulled it through was decisive and intimate. The back of his neck had two thin creases that disappeared when he looked down at the papers. I longed to touch him there with my lips.

"Close your eyes, Clara," he crooned, knowing I was looking at him.

"There was a big argument in Mr. Tiffany's office today. Business management won. Louis and Henry and I lost. For the time being, I'm not to design any new elaborate lamps."

Saying it made it seem less traumatic, of smaller importance in Bernard's presence.

"For the time being, rest."

Maybe that was the answer. For the time being, go slower at work. Don't be so intense.

It surprised me that I could relax with Bernard so close and me in my nightdress. The warm spirit of love enveloped me peacefully, and my eyes closed of their own accord.

I went into Mr. Platt's office the next morning to deliver the account book to him. Opening it to the right page, I found, written on Bernard's page of calculations: *So marry me. Don't you know I love you?*

Stunned, I caught my breath and stared at the words until reason reigned. Marriage had proved a trickster. Ebenezer leaned over to

look with his flinty eyes, and I quickly
crumpled the loose page, slammed the book
shut, and handed it over.

I flattened out the page at my desk. It was no
quip. It was a sincere proposal. Bernard was
too aware that love was sacred to write such
a thing lightly. It deserved an equally sincere
answer.

Mary came in to ask for her next assignment. I folded the paper quickly and put it in
my pocketbook, but a dozen times that day I
took it out to read it again.

I made sure I got home before Bernard did,
and wrote on my good deckle-edged statio-
nery:

Dearest,
Please give me time. It's a big change.
Know that I love you.

Your Clara

I slipped it under his door.

Chapter 46
Ebb Tide

"I'm going with you if it's the last thing I do," George announced to everyone in the parlor.

Dudley and Hank chorused a firm "No!"

George scowled and pouted in one humorous expression. It had been a year of struggle for him. Fainting spells, wrenching coughs, hospital stays, conflicting diagnoses, frenzied painting despite fevers — for unfettered joy, or to leave something behind, I wasn't sure. Beneath his funny pout he was genuinely disconsolate at the thought of being left alone on New Year's Eve.

"I'll stay here with you, if you'd like," I told him.

"Clara!" Bernard said in alarm, and I saw in his eyes that he wanted me with him.

Tenseness streaked through me. What had I done? All talk, all motion in the room, stopped instantly. All eyes shifted from Bernard to me to George.

Raising his chin imperiously, George pulled

his shoulders back and said, "George Waldo, a cosmos, of Manhattan the son. Give me streets and faces. Give me Broadway. Give me strong voices, pageants, passions. Give me one more year."

"All right, Walt. Just so you bundle up," Hank said.

Bernard and I sent each other our mutual relief in loving looks.

Dudley made George wear two woolen sweaters, a muffler, and a stocking cap. George put on two overcoats — his own, which Dudley buttoned in the back to keep out the wind, and Hank's larger one over it, buttoned in the front. He nearly suffocated in the subway, and I felt the hot, erratic fever of his excitement burning.

Hank chuckled. "You look like a Maine fisherman."

"Maybe Winslow Homer will paint me."

As well as he could, cocooned in multiple sleeves, he struck a pose as if looking out across a stormy sea — prophetically, it seemed to me.

Emerging from the subway at Forty-second Street, Bernard held me by the hand and I held Alice's and she held William's and the others followed as we threaded our way down Broadway, passing brothels, mansions, lobster palaces, and a stable to get into the thick of the crowd singing, shouting, blowing tin horns, beating on drums. At Times Square we craned our necks to see the dome on top of the Times Tower, three stories taller than the Flatiron Building.

"Whoever invented the word *skyscraper* was stupid," George muttered. "It should be *skytoucher* or *skypiercer*. Scrape is the wrong movement."

"My, aren't we cantankerous tonight," Dudley said, and patted George's cheek.

For the last three years the Owens boarders had celebrated New Year's Eve here to see the Times Tower lit from base to dome, and to gape at fireworks sparkling the sky. This year the fireworks had been banned. Instead, a great ball lit with a hundred twenty-five-watt bulbs was to descend on a flagpole on top of the building.

"It should rise into the new year instead of fall," George said.

At one minute to midnight, the ball blazed into light and began to creep downward. We joined in yelling the countdown, and George coughed his way through it.

In the cacophony of voices and trumpets and drumbeats, Bernard pressed me to him and kissed me without stopping until we broke apart to take a breath and laugh ourselves silly. He pulled me toward him again and touched my ear with his tongue and whispered, "Clara, darling, 1908 is going to be our year."

■ ■ ■ ■

George declined rapidly after that. Henry Belknap paid for a private hospital room again, but after a short time there, George insisted on living out his days in his studio. He painted when he could, Merry prepared special meals for him, and Henry brought George's favorite delicacies from Delmonico's.

"Do you think there'll be paint in heaven, Dud?" George asked one day as I came in with a tray of Irish stew and corn bread, hoping he would eat.

"Watercolor or oil?"

"I'm not fussy."

"Assuming that's where you'll go," Dudley said.

"Either way. If I enter heaven, it will be through the back door. If I enter hell, it will be through the back door, which will be wide open for me."

Dudley snickered.

"The most ridiculous, useless thing is a funeral procession. What good does it do for the celebrity of the day? I want mine now."

"Now?"

"Sunday will do. Hire me a carriage, Hank, big enough for the four of us."

On Sunday, Dudley dressed him in woolens again and tried to put the stocking cap on him.

"No! I insist on my fedora with the red feather." He flung his red silk scarf around his neck. His vanity was alive and well, a good sign. Dudley obliged and found his fedora.

In front of the hackney pulled by a black mare, a happenstance that brought a grunt from George, he said, "I want to sit in front with the driver."

"Be sensible." Dudley pushed him inside.

"When was I ever?" he muttered. "Do you have a Whitman with you, Hank?"

Hank went inside to get one.

George opened the trapdoor in the roof and said to the driver, "To the Brooklyn Bridge. Up onto the bridge."

Nothing less grandiose could serve him.

George kept his eyes glued to the window as we went down Irving Place and onto Broadway, all the way down to City Hall Park and then up onto the bridge. At the midway point he ordered the driver to stop.

"I can't do that, sir."

"Accommodate him, if you can," Hank said through the roof opening. "I'll make it worth your effort."

The driver drew in the reins, and traffic went around us.

"I want to feel it up here," George said, and elbowed his way out of the carriage with struggling breaths. He seized the cables to feel them vibrate with the mighty force of Brooklyn and Manhattan. There was bravery and passion and beloved eccentricity in him yet.

"Being so high above the river, I'm halfway to heaven already. Now read me some of 'Crossing Brooklyn Ferry.'"

We all stood close around him to block the wind while Hank read.

"Flood-tide below me! I watch you face to
    face! . . .
I too many and many a time cross'd the
    river . . .
Saw the white sails of schooners and
    sloops — saw the ships at anchor,
The sailors at work in the rigging, or out
    astride the spars . . .
I too walk'd the streets of Manhattan
    Island, and bathed in the waters around
    it;
I too felt the curious abrupt questionings
    stir within me,
In the day, among crowds of people,
    sometimes they came upon me,
In my walks home late at night, or as I lay
    in my bed, they came upon me . . .
but . . . I was Manhattanese, friendly and
    proud!"

Hank turned the page, looking for something else. George gazed eastward over the tidewater flowing back into Upper New York Bay as if to fix it in his mind for eternity.

"Flow on, river! flow with the flood-tide, and
    ebb with the ebb-tide!
Frolic on, crested and scallop-edged
    waves!
Gorgeous clouds of the sunset! drench with
    your splendor me."

George looked up to the sky and repeated,
"Drench with your splendor me."

A passenger steamer's sustained and melancholy whistle blew long and longing, carrying
the tone of departure and loss.

"To Central Park," George told the driver.
"Take Fifth Avenue."

He wanted the spectacle of New York one
more time, and I was an earnest acolyte in
his procession.

As we went up Ladies' Mile, he peered
between window shoppers into the department store windows, and said to Dudley,
"Buy Clara a scrumptious dress. She looks
divine in emerald green."

I knew enough not to counter that love.
"You're generous, George."

"So have you been." He reached for my
hand. "I'm sorry I put you through that with
Edwin." His voice cracked. "I wanted you in
my life so badly."

"No need to say it."

In the park, he looked hungrily at skeletal
trees not yet budding out with new leaves,
the grass barely beginning its renewal of life,

still sparse and scruffy.

"Sublime," he murmured. "It has never looked better."

Beauty isn't just in the eye, after all.

"I want them back again — those days I worked too hard and played too little."

In the gloaming on the way home, we circled quiet Gramercy Park. "Clop, clop, clop," he said, matching the horse's rhythm. "Like a timepiece counting out my seconds."

He fixed his gaze at the Players Club as though seeing right through the wall to his portrait of Modjeska.

"That at least will last," he said.

I understood that, felt it keenly beneath my ribs, an ever-present pressure to declare the self for future ages.

After that, he never touched a brush.

The next week was another deadly meeting among The Powers. Henry said I had better attend. I was on edge, hoping to hear that "for the time being" was over, and that I could resume my previous freedom of design.

There were no cheerful greetings, no pleasantries. That alone prepared me for the worst. Mr. Tiffany's tie stud today was an ominous-looking black pearl. Before we got under way with figures, I leapt into the moment's void.

"I know you've prepared some numbers for us to see, but I just want to say that you can't treat art as statistics only, or its makers as soulless mechanics. It's the feeling I have for nature and color and glass, and the delight I take in designing new shapes and arranging the elements of the motif, that have made leaded-glass shades a significant addition to the income of the company. They will continue to be if you give me back the prerogative of designing more elaborates. They are in complete accord with Mr. Tiffany's wish to continue building his reputation."

Willingly, desperately, I acquiesced my reputation for his. Anything to save the vitality of my department.

"Thank you," Mr. Tiffany said. "We appreciate your statement and your position." Pain slicked his eyes. He must have known what was coming.

Mr. Thomas passed around copies of the prospectus and the future recommendations. I saw that only six lamps of my new designs had gone into production since the last meeting, all of them low-priced — nasturtium, small begonia, poinsettia, black-eyed Susan, and two versions of tulip. In prior years that would have been the work of four months, not a year.

Cheaper lamps meant reusing the shade shapes and previously designed bases. I hated to admit it, but some days the repetition of shapes held no excitement for me. Without the possibility of complex invention, the delight in deciding where lead lines would go and in choosing glass had faded.

The list of new discontinued lamps reduced me to dust and ashes — a death knell for peacock, grape, apple and grape, pansy, snowball, geranium, daffodil, and all three tulips — tulip tree, scattered tulip, and tulip clusters. What did the Lieutenants have against tulips? I half expected butterfly, lotus, cobweb, and squash blossom, the expensive elaborates, to be discontinued, and they were, making the life of the squash blossom ebb the quickest of all. Could my heart ever beat as wildly as it had when I was designing them?

The small apple blossom was on the list to be discontinued, with a notation that there was only one left in stock. Whoever would buy it would never know that it was the swan song of this motif, and maybe of its maker. Trumpet creeper was there too, with the price of the five left in stock slashed from three hundred seventy-five dollars to two hundred dollars. Bargain-basement price. Liquidate them. No longer desirable. Recoup our losses.

I faced Mr. Thomas and Mr. Platt across the table with eyes that surely sent shards of glass into theirs. Mr. Tiffany at the head of the table was somber, his shoulders drooping. I wanted to send him a signal to take courage, but he had turned away from me. I leveled at him a look that anyone there could see cried out, "Speak for me!"

Impotent and staring, he said nothing, and

my heart cracked.

If there had been an argument like last time, I would have felt that there was hope. The funereal silence was a hundred times worse. The pages themselves declared the message: commerce had triumphed over art. It had eroded love and spit back numbers, not feelings.

"The moratorium on elaborates will continue," Mr. Thomas said.

I knew that the days when Louis's word was law had ebbed, but I never expected him to sacrifice me without a fight. A profound disappointment in him, that he would let it come to this, welled up, and I fought back tears.

Clasping my hands that had created those elaborates, I said, "I'm convinced that such a short-sighted prohibition is a grave mistake for the future of the company. How long before the originality and enthusiasm of the Women's Glass Cutting Department will dry up?"

I rose to leave.

Mr. Thomas cleared his throat. "One more thing, Mrs. Driscoll. With anticipated lower production, we can't keep your full complement of artisans. Who is your slowest worker?"

"I don't like to say." The exacting care Miss Judd took in every task naturally required more time. I would quit before I ever gave them her name! "Slowest sometimes means finest."

"Well, whoever it is, she and one more of your choosing will have to go."

Rebellion boiled. "Then I'll design a mosaic to keep all twenty-seven of us."

"They're only made to order now," Mr. Thomas said. "You have two weeks to reduce your department by two."

Feeling a curdling in my stomach, I strode quickly to the door and heard Henry murmur, "I'm sorry."

I walked home alone, bewildered, knowing my creativity had been strangled along with my department. No one was getting married soon, so I couldn't use that to decrease our number. For the first time, I wished someone was. I refused to choose. There was a reason for keeping each one.

In former days, I would have wailed in self-pity to Alice. Now I slipped a note under Bernard's door.

Come to me.

I laid out the pages on my bed and waited, feeling the approach of change. The minutes crawled. I picked up the kaleidoscope and watched the glass shards slip into a new pattern.

It wasn't long before he knocked and

peeked in.

"Is it George?" he said softly.

"It's Tiffany's. There was a meeting."

I pointed to the pages and he stood by the bed, stately and serious, picking up each page, studying it, putting it down, picking up another, while I chewed on my thumbnail.

"Look at all the discontinued ones. It felt like murder." My voice was petulant. I couldn't help it.

"Are the sales slipping?"

"I'm not privy to any sales figures. I only see the orders. The moratorium on designing new elaborates is still in effect, I suspect forever. As an artist, I can't expand any more. I'm like a blown vessel that has reached its capacity for thinness, and the glassblower has to stop or it will lose its shape and individuality."

He stacked the pages and set them on my desk, sat on the bed, and pulled me over to sit next to him.

"Your individuality is greater than as an artist, Clara. Do you think that's all there is to the woman? Do you think I'm in love only with the artist? Do you think I haven't seen the beauty of your character? Your strength in leading the girls, your compassion in responding to the issues of their lives? That I haven't fed off your joy in cycling, in parks, woods, the sea, the crush of New York? That I haven't recognized a lovely, vibrant woman of intelligence and humor and passion and keen sensitivity and a thousand intense and beautiful feelings? A woman with a bigger capacity to love than she admits. A woman I've loved for years."

A swirling exhilaration exploded in me. Breathless and half frightened at the prospects, I glimpsed my larger self shining in his eyes, and I loved him for showing it to me.

"Why didn't you tell me before this?"

"How could I force the issue when I saw every day how much you love your work and the girls? Besides, do you think I wanted to risk another love affair with a woman more committed to work than to life?"

Edging toward accusation, the words resounded with hard truth.

"Over time, I recognized that I'd rather go along as we have been rather than to force you to sacrifice what you love and maybe make a mistake and come to resent me," he said. "But now, with this moratorium, maybe you see things differently. Maybe you can see possibilities for yourself outside Tiffany Studios. On your own, or with me."

"It's a big change." Though not one I hadn't contemplated.

"An enormous change. I realize that. I've read your note a hundred times. I can barely imagine what it would mean to you to give up what you love, but it would kill me to see you stay there out of loyalty to a policy that does not value you because you are a woman."

"Policy! It's not loyalty to a policy, Bernard. I hate the policy. It has ruined lives."

Olga. Wilhelmina. If only they could have kept working. It was bigger than just Tiffany policy. All across the city that policy held women in its unholy grip.

"Think what you just said, Clara. 'Ruined lives.' Think of the import of what you said."

Although the policy constrained me too, there was an ironic safety in it. I could finally admit to myself why I had let the years slip by without asking Bernard if he was married. I was just as afraid of learning that he *wasn't* as learning that he *was.* Now, without the security of the slim possibility that he was a married man, the protection from having to make a decision that would force me to leave Tiffany's was gone. I hugged my pillow against my ribs, knowing that I stood on the edge of a precipice. Olga and Wilhelmina and Ella and Cornelia and Edith and Beatrix had all left to get married under their own individual circumstances. Had they all sensed a similar precipice, even for a moment? No. Not Olga. Her certainty that nothing was as important as love was a case of wisdom out of the mouths of babes.

Gently, Bernard took the pillow away, turned me toward him, and cradled my wrists in his open palms. "When I was a little boy living in Gloucester, I watched workers make a clearing for a street of row houses. They chopped down all the trees. A bird sat on a stump. A worker tossed it in the air to fly away, but it came back to the stump. The next week, I found only feathers and part of a wing. It had perished out of fear to go beyond what it knew. Do you understand?"

I felt my soul moving closer to his.

"Yes."

George hung on under the care of Dudley, Hank, and Henry for another week. At his bedside the next Sunday, I dribbled water into his mouth from a straw, and Dudley tried to make him comfortable. Weaker and struggling more for breath, he turned his head to him.

"Don't cry over me, Dud. It's better to die young than . . ." We waited. "To be an aging, feeble nellie."

Dudley's face distorted.

"Tell me again my favorite lines."

"I float in the regions of your love, O man, O sharer of my roving life," Dudley managed to say.

Hank opened the book and read softly,

"And as to you Death, and you bitter hug of
    mortality, it is idle to try to alarm me . . .
The smallest sprout shows there is really
    no death."

Light passed from the window, and none of us wanted to leave the bed for so much as half a minute to draw the shade, so it became a big black eye looking in at us. Hank lit the oil lamp. George's breath coming irregularly now sounded like the retreat of a wave over pebbles.

"Read, 'All goes onward.' "

Dudley found the page and tried to read, but no sound came. He handed the book to me.

"All goes onward and outward — nothing
  collapses,
And to die is different from what any one
  supposed, and luckier."

With Dudley holding his right hand and Hank his left, and I on my knees warming his cold feet against my breasts, we waited to receive the last precious ounce of him. Minute by inexorable minute, the skin of his face lost its fever flush and became bluish gray.

He took a jagged breath, struggled to say, "Look. The geese are flying," and relaxed at last.

Dudley's head dropped to George's chest in a muffled sob.

After some minutes, Hank said in a pinched voice, "Frolic on, comrade."

He stepped out onto the stoop to give Dud-

634

ley time with him alone. I followed him, we touched hands, and I went back to the boardinghouse alone.

Bernard leapt to his feet in the dimly lit parlor and enfolded me. His arms, hands, eyes, breath, all spoke comfort.

"It wasn't brutal," I murmured against his chest. "They loved him so. Such extraordinary, generous love."

Seeing Bernard's folded white handkerchief, and the tenderness with which he offered it, I wept.

CHAPTER 47
LIFEWORK

Bernard knocked at my door in the morning as I was getting ready to go to the studio.

"Don't go today," he said. "There's nothing there that can't wait. We'll go to Central Park, or to Point Pleasant. Wherever you want."

"No. You have to go to work."

"You are more important. Love is more important than work, Clara. Be reasonable. Let me help you."

"I have to go." I laced up my shoes.

"You've been married to Tiffany Studios for at least a dozen years. You've proven your loyalty and your talent. You don't have to go to the grave still proving it. And to whom? Nobody cares, Clara, as much as you do. Now won't you take a day with me? You've just had two big blows. Take time to put yourself together again."

"I have to tell someone there, George's friend."

"You can't send a message?"

"No. I have to tell him myself. And I have to see Mr. Tiffany."

I could see the hurt in his eyes. He was holding my arms, but not so tightly that I couldn't free myself.

"Just remember that I know you and love you better than anyone," he said.

I nodded, assured that he loved me in the way I had always longed for, but this had to be done this morning, while the resolve was hot. I walked quickly out the door and turned off Irving Place to Fourth Avenue to catch the subway. It would get me there before I changed my mind.

Going into Tiffany Studios, I said to myself, Hold fast the fort, dear women. I went to Henry's office first, and closed the door behind me.

"I already know. Hank came to tell me last night." We both stood numb in each other's arms. "Hank and Dudley and I may have been his lovers," he said softly, "but you were his finest friend."

"We said some lines from Whitman right at the end."

"Hank told me."

I wiped away tears.

"Take care of yourself, Clara. You don't have to stay at the studio."

I looked at him curiously.

"I meant today, but take it as you wish."

With utter delicacy, he added, "Onward and outward."

"Thank you for everything you did for him, and for me."

I went across the corridor into the ladies' room, blew my nose, tidied my hair, pulled back my shoulders, and looked in the mirror. What I saw was the face of a survivor — one who would find her own surprises, design her own adventures. In the next five minutes, I would have to tear myself away from him, the loved one who, like Edwin, like Francis, came close but did not measure up. Too many disappointments tumbled one after another. I breathed in resolve. Then I entered Mr. Tiffany's office.

"I'm glad I found you before you started your rounds. I was afraid I'd be too late." I sat down at the side of his desk. Three gardenias floated in an enamel bowl. Maybe it had been made by Alice.

"There's no other way to say this. I have to leave." My voice did not quaver.

His face contorted. He turned the opal ring on his pinkie finger back and forth, a small, agitated movement. "May I ask why?"

"I can't grow any more here."

"I feared as much at the meeting." He hunched over the gardenias for a long moment, and suddenly straightened himself. "I could move you to enamels."

"No. It's more than that."

He inclined his head toward me. "Is it a man in your life?" His eyebrows went up in avuncular curiosity.

"I lost a dear friend yesterday. You met him once at a Christmas ball and took us up to your studio. He's the brother of the man I left the company for a long time ago. Our friendship wasn't a romance, but it made me see how vital love is in a fully lived life. Art alone can't suffice."

He stared at the bowl of gardenias, his fist pressing against his mouth. "I've come to suspect that myself," he said.

"There is another man who gives me the loving regard I've always wanted."

"What if I bent the rule in your case? Our little secret."

"If I marry him? No. I'm done with secrets. Thank you, though."

"Then an open breaking of policy under mitigating circumstances? No one else is capable to lead the department."

I could have fainted dead away at the hugeness of his offer. This I was unprepared for. It was staggering, and wonderful — solid evidence of his recognition of me, that I mattered that much to him — a solution. My much simplified tree-of-life clock sitting on his mantel ticked out the moments when my chance for both, Louis and Bernard, existed side by side.

"That's kind of you to offer."

It seemed a precursor, and I wanted to be there when it happened. But if my leaving made him consider loosening the strings, maybe it was my last act of love for the Tiffany Girls. Maybe someday Olga could come back to work here.

"There was a time when I wanted that. Under the current business situation, though, it wouldn't make a difference."

"I see."

"It's been a once-in-a-lifetime partnership, Louis, and I've grown tremendously under your guidance. The joy of our collaboration has been central to my life. Mr. Platt and Mr. Thomas have destroyed any further opportunity for that."

The corners of his mouth tightened downward. "That's going to hurt me too."

"What I leave undone here will be taken up by someone behind me in the great parade of creativity."

"I can't imagine who."

"Make Alice head designer, but don't saddle her with administrative responsibility. It divides a person to have to focus on art and commerce."

"That's been my Achilles' heel. Commercial concerns have smothered the breath of life of art for the time being, but I can't expect you to wait around until it revives."

"Carrie McNicholl would be a good department head. She's very organized, she knows the skills of each girl, and she knows the bookkeeping. Anna Ring can assist her with it."

He wrote down their names.

"Another thing. My salary is more than that of two of the newer girls together. Now you don't have to fire any of them."

"I'll tell that to Mr. Thomas." He let out a long, loud breath, a sigh. "I don't know how I'll get along without you. Your devotion and contributions have been inestimable, and your inventiveness has been brilliant."

"And I don't know how I'll get along without you, your genius on fire, and Mr. Belknap, and my girls, and Frank."

It was my life's cup spilling over, and a lump of love formed in my throat.

I opened my pocketbook. We had been so formal and careful, but I wanted something lighter today too.

"I love the poetry of Emily Dickinson. This morning I copied out a verse for you." I handed it to him, and he read it to himself slowly.

We never know how high we are
Till we are called to rise;
And then, if we are true to plan,
Our statures touch the skies —

"I know you've always wanted to be taller. I understand that. I've always wanted to be prettier."

A mix of feelings creased the skin under his eyes. "The verse means more than that, and you know it." He took out his billfold and slipped it in.

"One thing I've been meaning to tell you." I grinned to prepare him for something quibbling. "Shorten those two pedestals. That will make you appear taller."

He scowled at them, and his mouth opened slowly. "You're right. All these years." He shook his head as though he were amused, but when he turned to me, his amusement dissolved. "Then we're through? Isn't there anything else?"

"Yes. There is one thing. If I might say so, your daughters have as much right to an education as your son."

"I have conceded to some night classes."

"That's a start. You'll do more in winning back their love by supporting their goals than by refusing."

He pondered that a few moments, and then said, "I want you to know that what you saw that night in my studio doesn't happen anymore. I was at my lowest when you saw me."

"I knew you could pull yourself out of it."

After an awkward moment, I told him I would finish out the week so as to leave everything in order.

He asked if he could take me to lunch. I

felt a tremor of panic. Time exclusively with Louis — how I had yearned for that. Out of recognition for the policy concession he had offered, I thought I should accept, yet the urgency of getting to Bernard beat strongly in me.

"Any other time, I would love that, but I have someone waiting for me, I hope."

We stood. The cord connecting us unraveled, though not so fast that we did not feel the prolonged, inevitable tearing away, as though we were cupping each other's chins like peonies, holding for one more moment the eyes of the once beloved before stepping away.

I hurried from the subway back to Irving Place, and was out of breath. Or maybe I was short of breath because of the momentous decision I had made. Exhilaration made me sweep through the parlor and run up the stairs. Bernard didn't answer my urgent knock on the door to his room. Of course not. He was at work, but where was that? I went through the corridor calling, "Bernard? Merry?" and found her in the pantry.

"Did Bernard go to work today? Do you know where his office is?"

"Why, dearie, he left here this morning with a bag packed."

"Good God! Not another disappearing man!"

643

"He looked fearful sad."

"If he comes back, tell him I went looking for him. Keep him here."

On a slim hunch I hurried to the station and got there in time for the eleven-fifteen to Point Pleasant. The train crept along at a snail's pace. I could have *run* there faster.

He must have thought I chose Tiffany over him. I bit my lip until it bled. I should have told him, but I hadn't been sure that I'd go through with it.

At the station, I felt like lifting my skirt and racing down the wooded path toward the cottage like a madwoman, but that wouldn't change anything. He was either there or he wasn't. I forced myself to walk along the coast in a measured pace, all senses alert to remember this momentous act.

Waves licked at the sand deliciously, sensually, like a blue-gray silk scarf undulating, calming me. A soft-breasted sandpiper chased each retreating wavelet seaward, poked her long arched beak into bubbling sand to get some morsel, and raced back up the beach on slender, elegant legs before the next wave would catch her — inward and outward, rhythmically, tirelessly doing her lifework. I was awash with love for her.

I stopped in front of the house, presenting myself simply, without a tremor. He'd been sitting on the porch steps, but he stood up the instant he saw me, honoring me with elegant posture. I didn't move, stretching the moment, both of us gathering what each other's presence meant.

"What are you doing here?" I finally asked.

"Thinking."

"About what?"

"About you. Trying to make myself not love you. Trying to let you go."

"Have you had any success?"

"Not a smidgen."

I moved onto the porch close to him and saw the adoration in his eyes flower into a beautiful future, a new life that would begin from this moment.

"Don't try anymore."

He held out his arms for me, and I stepped in, telling him with my eyes that I felt the love in him embrace the love in me. He reached into his pocket and put the moon shell on the end of my ring finger.

"Will you?"

"Yes."

AFTERWORD

Clara married Edward Booth, known in this novel as Bernard Booth, from Gloucester, England, on September 1, 1909, in Montclair, New Jersey. She was forty-seven, and he was her junior by six years. He had immigrated to New York within a year of Clara's move to Manhattan, and was married to an unknown woman sometime between 1893 and 1907 for an indeterminate amount of time. The particulars of that marriage were, perforce, my invention.

Clara and Edward Booth continued living at Miss Owens's boardinghouse as a married couple while she developed a modest career painting silk scarves with flowers and sunset skyscapes. None have survived. The couple also owned a house in Point Pleasant. Booth retired in 1930, and they moved to Ormond Beach, Florida, while still spending the summers at Point Pleasant. Clara died November 6, 1944, at the age of eighty-two, and her ashes were interred in the cemetery in Tallmadge, Ohio, her family home. Booth died in 1953 at the age of eighty-five.

The intimate circumstances of Clara's marriage to Francis Driscoll are unknown.

As to whether Clara independently conceived of leaded-glass lampshades, there is still question. According to the New-York Historical Society exhibition catalog *A New Light on Tiffany: Clara Driscoll and the Tiffany Girls,* "Although not specifically stated in her letters, it was possibly Clara who hit upon the idea of making leaded shades with nature-based themes." Given that the first leaded shades appearing in 1898 were coincident with Clara's return to Tiffany Studios, it is highly likely.

Alice Gouvy left Tiffany Studios in 1907, before Clara left, and returned to Ohio to teach school. Agnes Northrop continued to work for Tiffany Studios until it closed, and then for its offshoot, Westminster Studios. She remained active as a designer of leaded windows until age ninety-four. Her memorial window for her father is in the Bowne Street Community Church in Flushing, Queens, New York. Carrie McNicholl stayed on at Tiffany Studios until 1930 working as a secretary. Nothing is known of the subsequent lives of Nellie Warner, Mary McVickar, Anna Ring, Theresa Baur, and the three misses.

George Waldo exhibited at the Salon of the

Société Nationale des Beaux-Arts in 1894. He died in 1904 at the age of thirty-seven. Nothing more was heard from his brother after the one letter.

Dudley Carpenter, originally of Nashville, Tennessee, kept a residence in Paris, where he studied at Académie Julian. He eventually went west, sculpting and painting as a California Impressionist in Santa Barbara. His studio became a gathering place for artists, students, and patrons. There he shaped a generation of Southern California painters. He died in 1946.

Henry McBride became the art critic for *The New York Sun* and worked in that capacity for thirty-seven years, as well as being a contributing editor of *ArtNews* and a writer for *L'Âge Nouveau* and *Cahiers d'Art* in Paris. His keen recognition of artistic talent was prophetic. He was the first to discover Thomas Eakins, and he became an early champion of modernism. His article "The Lost Children of New York," about the Lower East Side, was published in *Harper's Weekly* in January 1894. His correspondence revealed that he prodded and cajoled Mrs. Hackley into being more progressive. He retreated annually to a rustic cabin in rural Pennsylvania, where he enjoyed chopping wood, carrying water, and reading biographies of people he wished to emulate.

Louis Comfort Tiffany continued to receive

awards and remained active in the arts the rest of his life. The modern styles introduced at the Armory Show in New York in 1913 and the effects of the First World War, as well as changing artistic tastes, resulted in diminished production at Tiffany Studios. Louis Tiffany resigned as art director of his father's Tiffany & Company in 1918. Arthur Nash retired in 1919, and Tiffany withdrew his financial support of the studios and furnaces in 1928, leaving the management of the studios to Joe Briggs as president, and leaving the furnaces to Douglas Nash, a relative of Arthur Nash. Tiffany Studios filed for bankruptcy in 1932, although Briggs kept it functioning until the time of his own death. Louis Comfort Tiffany died in 1933 in the Seventy-second Street house. By 1937, it was razed and a seventeen-story apartment building was completed on the premises.

The Louis Comfort Tiffany Foundation, which he created in 1919 to aid gifted young artists, provided studio space at Laurelton Hall. A fire destroyed most of Laurelton Hall in 1957, including most of the records of work production, a factor that made Clara's letters so valuable. Surviving architectural features of Laurelton Hall — notably the fountain court and the loggia — were rescued and donated to the Metropolitan Museum of Art, while windows and lamps collected by Mr. and Mrs. Hugh F. McKean became the basis for the Charles Hosmer Morse Museum of American Art in Winter Park, Florida.

The New-York Historical Society also has a substantial collection of lamps, one hundred and thirty-two from one donor, Dr. Egon Neustadt, which made it an appropriate venue for the exhibit *A New Light on Tiffany: Clara Driscoll and the Tiffany Girls,* in 2007, curated by Martin Eidelberg, Nina Gray, and Margaret K. Hofer, just two years after Clara Driscoll's revealing correspondence became known. Her letters and the resulting exhibit and catalog served as the impetus and inspiration for this novel.

ACKNOWLEDGMENTS

Were it not for the zest of Victorians for regular and detailed letter writing, the world would not have known of Clara Driscoll, and this book would not have been possible. I am grateful for the care with which Clara's correspondence has been handled by archivists and conservators, and their enthusiasm in providing me full access to the letters. I refer to the Queens Historical Society board of trustees and staff, including Marisa Berman, executive director, and Richard Hourahan, collections manager; the Kelso House Museum Archives under the stewardship of Judi Allen, curator, housed at the Kent State University Library, Department of Special Collections; and Craig Simpson, special collections librarian, KSU. I thank both the Queens Historical Society and the Kelso House Museum for allowing me to use a handful of brief passages verbatim.

Deserving special recognition are the three curators who mounted the exhibit at the

New-York Historical Society that brought Clara Driscoll and the work of the Tiffany Girls to the public eye: Martin Eidelberg, Nina Gray, and Margaret K. Hofer, whose jointly written and fascinating catalog, *A New Light on Tiffany: Clara Driscoll and the Tiffany Girls,* was of inestimable value. I thank them for their willingness to share their knowledge, and for their goodwill.

Several other individuals were generous with their time, and I appreciate their expertise as well: Alice Cooney Frelinghuysen, curator of American decorative arts at the Metropolitan Museum of Art, New York; and Arlie Sulka, owner and managing director, and Eric Silver, director of the Lillian Nassau Gallery, New York. The late Mrs. Nassau was the first gallery owner to have realized the significance and value of Tiffany lamps, saving many from being destroyed for their bronze.

The Charles Hosmer Morse Museum of American Art in Winter Park, Florida, is primarily dedicated to decorative art produced by Tiffany Studios. Jennifer Thalheimer, curator and collection manager, was a continual and cheerful source of information during the research and writing phases of this book, and I thank her for her understanding responses to my string of questions. Donna Climenhage, curator, and Catherine Hinman, public relations director, were also on hand with their help.

For introducing me to Tiffany glass and to the process of making a leaded-glass lampshade in a hands-on way, I wish to thank Lindsy Parrott, director and curator, and Susan Greenbaum, conservator, of the Neustadt Collection of Tiffany Glass, at Queens Museum of Art.

Particular books of scholarship on Tiffany provided wonderful source material: *The Lamps of Louis Comfort Tiffany* by Martin Eidelberg, *Louis Comfort Tiffany and Laurelton Hall: An Artist's Country Estate* by Alice Cooney Frelinghuysen, *Tiffany by Design: An In-Depth Look at Tiffany Lamps* by Nina Gray, *The Lost Treasures of Louis Comfort Tiffany* by Hugh F. McKean, and *The Lamps of Tiffany* by Dr. Egon Neustadt, as well as a related biography, *The Last Tiffany* by Michael John Burlingham. For the rest of my sources, please see www.svreeland.com/tif-biblio.html.

Thank you to Marna Hostetler, my interlibrary loan angel at the Thomas Cooper Library of the University of South Carolina, for going the extra page and never giving up in our search for obscure material, and to Ginny Hall of the Lake Geneva, Wisconsin, Public Library for her descriptive answers to my questions.

I have had many insightful critical readers of the manuscript in its various stages. For this, my gratitude goes to John Baker, Barbara Braun, Terry Cantor, Mark Doten, Kip Gray, John H. Ritter, Ron Schmidt, and especially Julie Brickman, who helped me to develop Clara's relationship with Tiffany more deeply.

I count myself fortunate to have Jane von Mehren as my editor at Random House. Trusting her artful judgment, and grateful for her explanations, I have learned volumes, and am happy to be under her wing again. I am also grateful to assistant editor Rebecca Shapiro and senior editor Caitlin Alexander, both of whom provided valuable criticism.

Always, for book after book, I have had my agent, Barbara Braun, at my side to give wise counsel, astute literary guidance, and knowledgeable comradeship in art museums. It was she who took me to the Metropolitan Museum of Art in 2007 to see the exhibit *Louis Comfort Tiffany and Laurelton Hall*, and it was her husband, John Baker, who found a newspaper article about the New-York Historical Society exhibit *A New Light on Tiffany: Clara Driscoll and the Tiffany Girls*, and urged us to go. Heartfelt gratitude to them both.

ABOUT THE AUTHOR

Susan Vreeland is the *New York Times* bestselling author of five books, including *Luncheon of the Boating Party, Life Studies, The Passion of Artemisia, The Forest Lover,* and *Girl in Hyacinth Blue.* She lives in San Diego.

The employees of Thorndike Press hope you have enjoyed this Large Print book. All our Thorndike, Wheeler, and Kennebec Large Print titles are designed for easy reading, and all our books are made to last. Other Thorndike Press Large Print books are available at your library, through selected bookstores, or directly from us.

For information about titles, please call:

(800) 223-1244

or visit our Web site at:

http://galc.ccngage.com/thorndike

To share your comments, please write:

Publisher
Thorndike Press
295 Kennedy Memorial Drive
Waterville, ME 04901